I0550102

Mardi, and A Voyage Thither by Herman Melville

Volume I (of II)

Dedicated to My Brother, ALLAN MELVILLE

Herman Melville was born in New York City on August 1st, 1819, the third of eight children.

At the age of 7 Melville contracted scarlet fever which was to permanently diminish his eyesight. At this time Melville was described as being "very backwards in speech and somewhat slow in comprehension."

His father died when he was 12 leaving the family in very straitened times. Just 14 Melville took a job in a bank paying $150 a year that he obtained via his uncle, Peter Gansevoort, who was one of the directors of the New York State Bank.

After a failed stint as a surveyor he signed on to go to sea and travelled across the Atlantic to Liverpool and then on further voyages to the Pacific on adventures which would soon become the architecture of his novels. Whilst travelling he joined a mutiny, was jailed, fell in love with a South Pacific beauty and became known as a figure of opposition to the coercion of native Hawaiians to the Christian religion.

He drew from these experiences in his books Typee, Omoo, and White-Jacket. These were published as novels, the first initially in London in 1846.

By 1851 his masterpiece, Moby Dick, was ready to be published. It is perhaps, and certainly at the time, one of the most ambitious novels ever written. However, it never sold out its initial print run of 3,000 and Melville's earnings on this masterpiece were a mere $556.37.

In succeeding years his reputation waned and he found life increasingly difficult. His family was growing, now four children, and a stable income was essential.

With his finances in a disappointing state Melville took the advice of friends that a change in career was called for. For many others public lecturing had proved very rewarding. From late 1857 to 1860, Melville embarked upon three lecture tours, where he spoke mainly on Roman statuary and sightseeing in Rome.

In 1876 he was at last able to publish privately his 16,000 line epic poem Clarel. It was to no avail. The book had an initial printing of 350 copies, but sales failed miserably.

On December 31st, 1885 Melville was at last able to retire. His wife had inherited several small legacies and provide them with a reasonable income.

Herman Melville, novelist, poet, short story writer and essayist, died at his home on September 28rh 1891 from cardiovascular disease.

Index of Contents

Preface

Not long ago, having published two narratives of voyages in the Pacific, which, in many quarters, were received with incredulity, the thought occurred to me, of indeed writing a romance of Polynesian adventure, and publishing it as such; to see whether, the fiction might not, possibly, be received for a verity: in some degree the reverse of my previous experience.

This thought was the germ of others, which have resulted in Mardi. New York, January, 1849.

Chapter I

Foot In Stirrup

We are off! The courses and topsails are set: the coral-hung anchor swings from the bow: and together, the three royals are given to the breeze, that follows us out to sea like the baying of a hound. Out spreads the canvas—alow, aloft-boom-stretched, on both sides, with many a stun' sail; till like a hawk, with pinions poised, we shadow the sea with our sails, and reelingly cleave the brine.

But whence, and whither wend ye, mariners?

We sail from Ravavai, an isle in the sea, not very far northward from the tropic of Capricorn, nor very far westward from Pitcairn's island, where the mutineers of the Bounty settled. At Ravavai I had stepped ashore some few months previous; and now was embarked on a cruise for the whale, whose brain enlightens the world.

And from Ravavai we sail for the Gallipagos, otherwise called the Enchanted Islands, by reason of the many wild currents and eddies there met.

Now, round about those isles, which Dampier once trod, where the Spanish bucaniers once hived their gold moidores, the Cachalot, or sperm whale, at certain seasons abounds.

But thither, from Ravavai, your craft may not fly, as flies the sea-gull, straight to her nest. For, owing to the prevalence of the trade winds, ships bound to the northeast from the vicinity of Ravavai are fain to take something of a circuit; a few thousand miles or so. First, in pursuit of the variable winds, they make all haste to the south; and there, at length picking up a stray breeze, they stand for the main: then, making their easting, up helm, and away down the coast, toward the Line.

This round-about way did the Arcturion take; and in all conscience a weary one it was. Never before had the ocean appeared so monotonous; thank fate, never since.

But bravo! in two weeks' time, an event. Out of the gray of the morning, and right ahead, as we sailed along, a dark object rose out of the sea; standing dimly before us, mists wreathing and curling aloft, and creamy breakers frothing round its base.—We turned aside, and, at length, when day dawned, passed Massafuero. With a glass, we spied two or three hermit goats winding down to the sea, in a ravine; and presently, a signal: a tattered flag upon a summit beyond. Well knowing, however, that there was nobody on the island but two or three noose-fulls of runaway convicts from Chili, our captain had no mind to comply with their invitation to land. Though, haply, he may have erred in not sending a boat off with his card.

A few days more and we "took the trades." Like favors snappishly conferred, they came to us, as is often the case, in a very sharp squall; the shock of which carried away one of our spars; also our fat old cook off his legs; depositing him plump in the scuppers to leeward.

In good time making the desired longitude upon the equator, a few leagues west of the Gallipagos, we spent several weeks chassezing across the Line, to and fro, in unavailing search for our prey. For some of their hunters believe, that whales, like the silver ore in Peru, run in veins through the ocean. So, day after day, daily; and week after week, weekly, we traversed the self-same longitudinal intersection of the self-same Line; till we were almost ready to swear that we felt the ship strike every time her keel crossed that imaginary locality.

At length, dead before the equatorial breeze, we threaded our way straight along the very Line itself. Westward sailing; peering right, and peering left, but seeing naught.

It was during this weary time, that I experienced the first symptoms of that bitter impatience of our monotonous craft, which ultimately led to the adventures herein recounted.

But hold you! Not a word against that rare old ship, nor its crew. The sailors were good fellows all, the half, score of pagans we had shipped at the islands included. Nevertheless, they were not precisely to my mind. There was no soul a magnet to mine; none with whom to mingle sympathies; save in deploring the calms with which we were now and then overtaken; or in hailing the breeze when it came. Under other and livelier auspices the tarry knaves might have developed qualities more attractive. Had we sprung a leak, been "stove" by a whale, or been blessed with some despot of a captain against whom to stir up some spirited revolt, these shipmates of mine might have proved limber lads, and men of mettle. But as it was, there was naught to strike fire from their steel.

There were other things, also, tending to make my lot on ship-board very hard to be borne. True, the skipper himself was a trump; stood upon no quarter-deck dignity; and had a tongue for a sailor. Let me do him justice, furthermore: he took a sort of fancy for me in particular; was sociable, nay, loquacious, when I happened to stand at the helm. But what of that? Could he talk sentiment or philosophy? Not a bit. His library was eight inches by four: Bowditch, and Hamilton Moore.

And what to me, thus pining for some one who could page me a quotation from Burton on Blue Devils; what to me, indeed, were flat repetitions of long-drawn yarns, and the everlasting stanzas of Black-eyed Susan sung by our full forecastle choir? Staler than stale ale.

Ay, ay, Arcturion! I say it in no malice, but thou wast exceedingly dull. Not only at sailing: hard though it was, that I could have borne; but in every other respect. The days went slowly round and round, endless and uneventful as cycles in space. Time, and time- pieces; How many centuries did my hammock tell, as pendulum-like it swung to the ship's dull roll, and ticked the hours and ages. Sacred forever be the Areturion's fore-hatch—alas! sea-moss is over it now—and rusty forever the bolts that held together that old sea hearth-stone, about which we so often lounged. Nevertheless, ye lost and leaden hours, I will rail at ye while life lasts.

Well: weeks, chronologically speaking, went by. Bill Marvel's stories were told over and over again, till the beginning and end dovetailed into each other, and were united for aye. Ned Ballad's songs were sung till the echoes lurked in the very tops, and nested in the bunts of the sails. My poor patience was clean gone.

But, at last after some time sailing due westward we quitted the Line in high disgust; having seen there, no sign of a whale.

But whither now? To the broiling coast of Papua? That region of sun- strokes, typhoons, and bitter pulls after whales unattainable. Far worse. We were going, it seemed, to illustrate the Whistonian theory concerning the damned and the comets;—hurried from equinoctial heats to arctic frosts. To be short, with the true fickleness of his tribe, our skipper had abandoned all thought of the Cachalot. In desperation, he was bent upon bobbing for the Right whale on the Nor'-West Coast and in the Bay of Kamschatska.

To the uninitiated in the business of whaling, my feelings at this juncture may perhaps be hard to understand. But this much let me say: that Right whaling on the Nor'-West Coast, in chill and dismal fogs, the sullen inert monsters rafting the sea all round like Hartz forest logs on the Rhine, and submitting to the harpoon like half-stunned bullocks to the knife; this horrid and indecent Right whaling, I say, compared to a spirited hunt for the gentlemanly Cachalot in southern and more genial seas, is as the butchery of white bears upon blank Greenland icebergs to zebra hunting in Caffraria, where the lively quarry bounds before you through leafy glades.

Now, this most unforeseen determination on the part of my captain to measure the arctic circle was nothing more nor less than a tacit contravention of the agreement between us. That agreement needs not to be detailed. And having shipped but for a single cruise, I had embarked aboard his craft as one might put foot in stirrup for a day's following of the hounds. And here, Heaven help me, he was going to carry me off to the Pole! And on such a vile errand too! For there was something degrading in it. Your true whaleman glories in keeping his harpoon unspotted by blood of aught but Cachalot. By my halidome, it touched the knighthood of a tar. Sperm and spermaceti! It was unendurable.

"Captain," said I, touching my sombrero to him as I stood at the wheel one day, "It's very hard to carry me off this way to purgatory. I shipped to go elsewhere."

"Yes, and so did I," was his reply. "But it can't be helped. Sperm whales are not to be had. We've been out now three years, and something or other must be got; for the ship is hungry for oil, and her hold a gulf to look into. But cheer up my boy; once in the Bay of Kamschatka, and we'll be all afloat with what we want, though it be none of the best."

Worse and worse! The oleaginous prospect extended into an immensity of Macassar. "Sir," said I, "I did not ship for it; put me ashore somewhere, I beseech." He stared, but no answer vouchsafed; and for a moment I thought I had roused the domineering spirit of the sea-captain, to the prejudice of the more kindly nature of the man.

But not so. Taking three turns on the deck, he placed his hand on the wheel, and said, "Right or wrong, my lad, go with us you must. Putting you ashore is now out of the question. I make no port till this ship is full to the combings of her hatchways. However, you may leave her if you can." And so saying he entered his cabin, like Julius Caesar into his tent.

He may have meant little by it, but that last sentence rung in my ear like a bravado. It savored of the turnkey's compliments to the prisoner in Newgate, when he shoots to the bolt on him.

"Leave the ship if I can!" Leave the ship when neither sail nor shore was in sight! Ay, my fine captain, stranger things have been done. For on board that very craft, the old Arcturion, were four tall fellows, whom two years previous our skipper himself had picked up in an open boat, far from the farthest shoal. To be sure, they spun a long yarn about being the only survivors of an Indiaman burnt down to the water's edge. But who credited their tale? Like many others, they were keepers of a secret: had doubtless contracted a disgust for some ugly craft still afloat and hearty, and stolen away from her, off soundings. Among seamen in the Pacific such adventures not seldom occur. Nor are they accounted great wonders. They are but incidents, not events, in the career of the brethren of the order of South Sea rovers. For what matters it, though hundreds of miles from land, if a good whale-boat be under foot, the Trades behind, and mild, warm seas before? And herein lies the difference between the Atlantic and Pacific:—that once within the Tropics, the bold sailor who has a mind to quit his ship round Cape Horn, waits not for port. He regards that ocean as one mighty harbor.

Nevertheless, the enterprise hinted at was no light one; and I resolved to weigh well the chances. It's worth noticing, this way we all have of pondering for ourselves the enterprise, which, for others, we hold a bagatelle.

My first thoughts were of the boat to be obtained, and the right or wrong of abstracting it, under the circumstances. But to split no hairs on this point, let me say, that were I placed in the same situation again, I would repeat the thing I did then. The captain well knew that he was going to detain me unlawfully: against our agreement; and it was he himself who threw out the very hint, which I merely adopted, with many thanks to him.

In some such willful mood as this, I went aloft one day, to stand my allotted two hours at the mast-head. It was toward the close of a day, serene and beautiful. There I stood, high upon the mast, and away, away, illimitably rolled the ocean beneath. Where we then were was perhaps the most unfrequented and least known portion of these seas. Westward, however, lay numerous groups of islands, loosely laid down upon the charts, and invested with all the charms of dream-land. But soon these regions would be past; the mild equatorial breeze exchanged for cold, fierce squalls, and all the horrors of northern voyaging.

I cast my eyes downward to the brown planks of the dull, plodding ship, silent from stem to stern; then abroad.

In the distance what visions were spread! The entire western horizon high piled with gold and crimson clouds; airy arches, domes, and minarets; as if the yellow, Moorish sun were setting behind some vast Alhambra. Vistas seemed leading to worlds beyond. To and fro, and all over the towers of this Nineveh in the sky, flew troops of birds. Watching them long, one crossed my sight, flew through a low arch, and was lost to view. My spirit must have sailed in with it; for directly, as in a trance, came upon me the cadence of mild billows laving a beach of shells, the waving of boughs, and the voices of maidens, and the lulled beatings of my own dissolved heart, all blended together.

Now, all this, to be plain, was but one of the many visions one has up aloft. But coming upon me at this time, it wrought upon me so, that thenceforth my desire to quit the Arcturion became little short of a frenzy.

Chapter II

A Calm

Next day there was a calm, which added not a little to my impatience of the ship. And, furthermore, by certain nameless associations revived in me my old impressions upon first witnessing as a landsman this phenomenon of the sea. Those impressions may merit a page.

To a landsman a calm is no joke. It not only revolutionizes his abdomen, but unsettles his mind; tempts him to recant his belief in the eternal fitness of things; in short, almost makes an infidel of him.

At first he is taken by surprise, never having dreamt of a state of existence where existence itself seems suspended. He shakes himself in his coat, to see whether it be empty or no. He closes his eyes, to test the reality of the glassy expanse. He fetches a deep breath, by way of experiment, and for the sake of witnessing the effect. If a reader of books, Priestley on Necessity occurs to him; and he believes in that old Sir Anthony Absolute to the very last chapter. His faith in Malte Brun, however, begins to fail; for the geography, which from boyhood he had implicitly confided in, always assured him, that though expatiating all over the globe, the sea was at least margined by land. That over against America, for example, was Asia. But it is a calm, and he grows madly skeptical.

To his alarmed fancy, parallels and meridians become emphatically what they are merely designated as being: imaginary lines drawn round the earth's surface.

The log assures him that he is in such a place; but the log is a liar; for no place, nor any thing possessed of a local angularity, is to be lighted upon in the watery waste.

At length horrible doubts overtake him as to the captain's competency to navigate his ship. The ignoramus must have lost his way, and drifted into the outer confines of creation, the region of the everlasting lull, introductory to a positive vacuity.

Thoughts of eternity thicken. He begins to feel anxious concerning his soul.

The stillness of the calm is awful. His voice begins to grow strange and portentous. He feels it in him like something swallowed too big for the esophagus. It keeps up a sort of involuntary interior humming in him, like a live beetle. His cranium is a dome full of reverberations. The hollows of his very bones are as whispering galleries. He is afraid to speak loud, lest he be stunned; like the man in the bass drum.

But more than all else is the consciousness of his utter helplessness. Succor or sympathy there is none. Penitence for embarking avails not. The final satisfaction of despairing may not be his with a relish. Vain the idea of idling out the calm. He may sleep if he can, or purposely delude himself into a crazy fancy, that he is merely at leisure. All this he may compass; but he may not lounge; for to lounge is to be idle; to be idle implies an absence of any thing to do; whereas there is a calm to be endured: enough to attend to, Heaven knows.

His physical organization, obviously intended for locomotion, becomes a fixture; for where the calm leaves him, there he remains. Even his undoubted vested rights, comprised in his glorious liberty of volition, become as naught. For of what use? He wills to go: to get away from the calm: as ashore he would avoid the plague. But he can not; and how foolish to revolve expedients. It is more hopeless than a bad marriage in a land where there is no Doctors' Commons. He has taken the ship to wife, for better or for worse, for calm or for gale; and she is not to be shuffled off. With yards akimbo, she says unto him scornfully, as the old beldam said to the little dwarf:—"Help yourself"

And all this, and more than this, is a calm.

Chapter III

A King For A Comrade

At the time I now write of, we must have been something more than sixty degrees to the west of the Gallipagos. And having attained a desirable longitude, we were standing northward for our arctic destination: around us one wide sea.

But due west, though distant a thousand miles, stretched north and south an almost endless Archipelago, here and there inhabited, but little known; and mostly unfrequented, even by whalemen, who go almost every where. Beginning at the southerly termination of this great chain, it comprises the islands loosely known as Ellice's group; then, the Kingsmill isles; then, the Radack and Mulgrave clusters. These islands had been represented to me as mostly of coral formation, low and fertile, and abounding in a variety of fruits. The language of the people was said to be very similar to that or the Navigator's islands, from which, their ancestors are supposed to have emigrated.

And thus much being said, all has been related that I then knew of the islands in question. Enough, however, that they existed at all; and that our path thereto lay over a pleasant sea, and before a reliable

Trade-wind. The distance, though great, was merely an extension of water; so much blankness to be sailed over; and in a craft, too, that properly managed has been known to outlive great ships in a gale. For this much is true of a whale-boat, the cunningest thing in its way ever fabricated by man.

Upon one of the Kingsmill islands, then, I determined to plant my foot, come what come would. And I was equally determined that one of the ship's boats should float me thither. But I had no idea of being without a companion. It would be a weary watch to keep all by myself, with naught but the horizon in sight.

Now, among the crew was a fine old seaman, one Jarl; how old, no one could tell, not even himself. Forecastle chronology is ever vague and defective. "Man and boy," said honest Jarl, "I have lived ever since I can remember." And truly, who may call to mind when he was not? To ourselves, we all seem coeval with creation. Whence it comes, that it is so hard to die, ere the world itself is departed.

Jarl hailed from the isle of Skye, one of the constellated Hebrides. Hence, they often called him the Skyeman. And though he was far from being piratical of soul, he was yet an old Norseman to behold. His hands were brawny as the paws of a bear; his voice hoarse as a storm roaring round the old peak of Mull; and his long yellow hair waved round his head like a sunset. My life for it, Jarl, thy ancestors were Vikings, who many a time sailed over the salt German sea and the Baltic; who wedded their Brynhildas in Jutland; and are now quaffing mead in the halls of Valhalla, and beating time with their cans to the hymns of the Scalds. Ah! how the old Sagas run through me!

Yet Jarl, the descendant of heroes and kings, was a lone, friendless mariner on the main, only true to his origin in the sea-life that he led. But so it has been, and forever will be. What yeoman shall swear that he is not descended from Alfred? what dunce, that he is not sprung of old Homer? King Noah, God bless him! fathered us all. Then hold up your heads, oh ye Helots, blood potential flows through your veins. All of us have monarchs and sages for kinsmen; nay, angels and archangels for cousins; since in antediluvian days, the sons of God did verily wed with our mothers, the irresistible daughters of Eve. Thus all generations are blended: and heaven and earth of one kin: the hierarchies of seraphs in the uttermost skies; the thrones and principalities in the zodiac; the shades that roam throughout space; the nations and families, flocks and folds of the earth; one and all, brothers in essence—oh, be we then brothers indeed! All things form but one whole; the universe a Judea, and God Jehovah its head. Then no more let us start with affright. In a theocracy, what is to fear? Let us compose ourselves to death as fagged horsemen sleep in the saddle. Let us welcome even ghosts when they rise. Away with our stares and grimaces. The New Zealander's tattooing is not a prodigy; nor the Chinaman's ways an enigma. No custom is strange; no creed is absurd; no foe, but who will in the end prove a friend. In heaven, at last, our good, old, white-haired father Adam will greet all alike, and sociality forever prevail. Christian shall join hands between Gentile and Jew; grim Dante forget his Infernos, and shake sides with fat Rabelais; and monk Luther, over a flagon of old nectar, talk over old times with Pope Leo. Then, shall we sit by the sages, who of yore gave laws to the Medes and Persians in the sun; by the cavalry captains in Perseus, who cried, "To horse!" when waked by their Last Trump sounding to the charge; by the old hunters, who eternities ago, hunted the moose in Orion; by the minstrels, who sang in the Milky Way when Jesus our Saviour was born. Then shall we list to no shallow gossip of Magellans and Drakes; but give ear to the voyagers who have circumnavigated the Ecliptic; who rounded the Polar Star as Cape Horn. Then shall the Stagirite and Kant be forgotten, and another folio than theirs be turned over for wisdom; even the folio now spread with horoscopes as yet undeciphered, the heaven of heavens on high.

Now, in old Jarl's lingo there was never an idiom. Your aboriginal tar is too much of a cosmopolitan for that. Long companionship with seamen of all tribes: Manilla-men, Anglo-Saxons, Cholos, Lascars, and Danes, wear away in good time all mother-tongue stammerings. You sink your clan; down goes your nation; you speak a world's language, jovially jabbering in the Lingua-Franca of the forecastle.

True to his calling, the Skyeman was very illiterate; witless of Salamanca, Heidelberg, or Brazen-Nose; in Delhi, had never turned over the books of the Brahmins. For geography, in which sailors should be adepts, since they are forever turning over and over the great globe of globes, poor Jarl was deplorably lacking. According to his view of the matter, this terraqueous world had been formed in the manner of a tart; the land being a mere marginal crust, within which rolled the watery world proper. Such seemed my good Viking's theory of cosmography. As for other worlds, he weened not of them; yet full as much as Chrysostom.

Ah, Jarl! an honest, earnest Wight; so true and simple, that the secret operations of thy soul were more inscrutable than the subtle workings of Spinoza's.

Thus much be said of the Skyeman; for he was exceedingly taciturn, and but seldom will speak for himself.

Now, higher sympathies apart, for Jarl I had a wonderful liking; for he loved me; from the first had cleaved to me.

It is sometimes the case, that an old mariner like him will conceive a very strong attachment for some young sailor, his shipmate; an attachment so devoted, as to be wholly inexplicable, unless originating in that heart-loneliness which overtakes most seamen as they grow aged; impelling them to fasten upon some chance object of regard. But however it was, my Viking, thy unbidden affection was the noblest homage ever paid me. And frankly, I am more inclined to think well of myself, as in some way deserving thy devotion, than from the rounded compliments of more cultivated minds.

Now, at sea, and in the fellowship of sailors, all men appear as they are. No school like a ship for studying human nature. The contact of one man with another is too near and constant to favor deceit. You wear your character as loosely as your flowing trowsers. Vain all endeavors to assume qualities not yours; or to conceal those you possess. Incognitos, however desirable, are out of the question. And thus aboard of all ships in which I have sailed, I have invariably been known by a sort of thawing-room title. Not,—let me hurry to say,—that I put hand in tar bucket with a squeamish air, or ascended the rigging with a Chesterfieldian mince. No, no, I was never better than my vocation; and mine have been many. I showed as brown a chest, and as hard a hand, as the tarriest tar of them all. And never did shipmate of mine upbraid me with a genteel disinclination to duty, though it carried me to truck of main-mast, or jib-boom-end, in the most wolfish blast that ever howled.

Whence then, this annoying appellation? for annoying it most assuredly was. It was because of something in me that could not be hidden; stealing out in an occasional polysyllable; an otherwise incomprehensible deliberation in dining; remote, unguarded allusions to Belles-Lettres affairs; and other trifles superfluous to mention.

But suffice it to say, that it had gone abroad among the Areturion's crew, that at some indefinite period of my career, I had been a "nob." But Jarl seemed to go further. He must have taken me for one of the House of Hanover in disguise; or, haply, for bonneted Charles Edward the Pretender, who, like the

Wandering Jew, may yet be a vagrant. At any rate, his loyalty was extreme. Unsolicited, he was my laundress and tailor; a most expert one, too; and when at meal-times my turn came round to look out at the mast-head, or stand at the wheel, he catered for me among the "kids" in the forecastle with unwearied assiduity. Many's the good lump of "duff" for which I was indebted to my good Viking's good care of me. And like Sesostris I was served by a monarch. Yet in some degree the obligation was mutual. For be it known that, in sea-parlance, we were chummies.

Now this chummying among sailors is like the brotherhood subsisting between a brace of collegians (chums) rooming together. It is a Fidus-Achates-ship, a league of offense and defense, a copartnership of chests and toilets, a bond of love and good feeling, and a mutual championship of the absent one. True, my nautical reminiscenses remind me of sundry lazy, ne'er-do-well, unprofitable, and abominable chummies; chummies, who at meal times were last at the "kids," when their unfortunate partners were high upon the spars; chummies, who affected awkwardness at the needle, and conscientious scruples about dabbling in the suds; so that chummy the simple was made to do all the work of the firm, while chummy the cunning played the sleeping partner in his hammock. Out upon such chummies!

But I appeal to thee, honest Jarl, if I was ever chummy the cunning. Never mind if thou didst fabricate my tarpaulins; and with Samaritan charity bind up the rents, and pour needle and thread into the frightful gashes that agonized my hapless nether integuments, which thou calledst "ducks;"—Didst thou not expressly declare, that all these things, and more, thou wouldst do for me, despite my own quaint thimble, fashioned from the ivory tusk of a whale? Nay; could I even wrest from thy willful hands my very shirt, when once thou hadst it steaming in an unsavory pickle in thy capacious vat, a decapitated cask? Full well thou knowest, Jarl, that these things are true; and I am bound to say it, to disclaim any lurking desire to reap advantage from thy great good nature.

Now my Viking for me, thought I, when I cast about for a comrade; and my Viking alone.

Chapter IV

A Chat In The Clouds

The Skyeman seemed so earnest and upright a seaman, that to tell the plain truth, in spite of his love for me, I had many misgivings as to his readiness to unite in an undertaking which apparently savored of a moral dereliction. But all things considered, I deemed my own resolution quite venial; and as for inducing another to join me, it seemed a precaution so indispensable, as to outweigh all other considerations.

Therefore I resolved freely to open my heart to him; for that special purpose paying him a visit, when, like some old albatross in the air, he happened to be perched at the foremast-head, all by himself, on the lookout for whales never seen.

Now this standing upon a bit of stick 100 feet aloft for hours at a time, swiftly sailing over the sea, is very much like crossing the Channel in a balloon. Manfred-like, you talk to the clouds: you have a fellow feeling for the sun. And when Jarl and I got conversing up there, smoking our dwarfish "dudeens," any sea-gull passing by might have taken us for Messrs. Blanchard and Jeffries, socially puffing their after-dinner Bagdads, bound to Calais, via Heaven, from Dover. Honest Jarl, I acquainted with all: my conversation with the captain, the hint implied in his last words, my firm resolve to quit the ship in one of her boats, and the facility with which I thought the thing could be done. Then I threw out many inducements, in the shape of pleasant anticipations of bearing right down before the wind upon the sunny isles under our lee.

He listened attentively; but so long remained silent that I almost fancied there was something in Jarl which would prove too much for me and my eloquence.

At last he very bluntly declared that the scheme was a crazy one; he had never known of such a thing but thrice before; and in every case the runaways had never afterwards been heard of. He entreated me to renounce my determination, not be a boy, pause and reflect, stick to the ship, and go home in her like a man. Verily, my Viking talked to me like my uncle.

But to all this I turned a deaf ear; affirming that my mind was made up; and that as he refused to accompany me, and I fancied no one else for a comrade, I would go stark alone rather than not at all. Upon this, seeing my resolution immovable, he bluntly swore that he would follow me through thick and thin.

Thanks, Jarl! thou wert one of those devoted fellows who will wrestle hard to convince one loved of error; but failing, forthwith change their wrestling to a sympathetic hug.

But now his elderly prudence came into play. Casting his eye over the boundless expanse below, he inquired how far off were the islands in question.

"A thousand miles and no less."

"With a fair trade breeze, then, and a boat sail, that is a good twelve days' passage, but calms and currents may make it a month, perhaps more." So saying, he shook his old head, and his yellow hair streamed.

But trying my best to chase away these misgivings, he at last gave them over. He assured me I might count upon him to his uttermost keel.

My Viking secured, I felt more at ease; and thoughtfully considered how the enterprise might best be accomplished.

There was no time to be lost. Every hour was carrying us farther and farther from the parallel most desirable for us to follow in our route to the westward. So, with all possible dispatch, I matured my plans, and communicated them to Jarl, who gave several old hints—having ulterior probabilities in view—which were not neglected.

Strange to relate, it was not till my Viking, with a rueful face, reminded me of the fact, that I bethought me of a circumstance somewhat alarming at the first blush. We must push off without chart or quadrant; though, as will shortly be seen, a compass was by no means out of the question. The chart, to be sure, I did not so much lay to heart; but a quadrant was more than desirable. Still, it was by no means indispensable. For this reason. When we started, our latitude would be exactly known; and whether, on our voyage westward, we drifted north or south therefrom, we could not, by any possibility, get so far out of our reckoning, as to fail in striking some one of a long chain of islands, which, for many degrees, on both sides of the equator, stretched right across our track.

For much the same reason, it mattered little, whether on our passage we daily knew our longitude; for no known land lay between us and the place we desired to reach. So what could be plainer than this: that if westward we patiently held on our way, we must eventually achieve our destination?

As for intervening shoals or reefs, if any there were, they intimidated us not. In a boat that drew but a few inches of water, but an indifferent look-out would preclude all danger on that score. At all events, the thing seemed feasible enough, notwithstanding old Jarl's superstitious reverence for nautical instruments, and the philosophical objections which might have been urged by a pedantic disciple of Mercator.

Very often, as the old maxim goes, the simplest things are the most startling, and that, too, from their very simplicity. So cherish no alarms, if thus we addressed the setting sun—"Be thou, old pilot, our guide!"

Chapter V

Seats Secured And Portmanteaus Packed

But thoughts of sextants and quadrants were the least of our cares.

Right from under the very arches of the eyebrows of thirty men— captain, mates, and crew—a boat was to be abstracted; they knowing nothing of the event, until all knowledge would prove unavailing.

Hark ye:

At sea, the boats of a South Sea-man (generally four in number, spare ones omitted,) are suspended by tackles, hooked above, to curved timbers called "davits," vertically fixed to the ship's sides.

Now, no fair one with golden locks is more assiduously waited upon, or more delicately handled by her tire-women, than the slender whale- boat by her crew. And out of its element, it seems fragile enough to justify the utmost solicitude. For truly, like a fine lady, the fine whale-boat is most delicate when idle, though little coy at a pinch.

Besides the "davits," the following supports are provided Two small cranes are swung under the keel, on which the latter rests, preventing the settling of the boat's middle, while hanging suspended by the bow and stern. A broad, braided, hempen band, usually worked in a tasteful pattern, is also passed round both gunwales; and secured to the ship's bulwarks, firmly lashes the craft to its place. Being elevated above the ship's rail, the boats are in plain sight from all parts of the deck.

Now, one of these boats was to be made way with. No facile matter, truly. Harder than for any dashing young Janizary to run off with a sultana from the Grand Turk's seraglio. Still, the thing could be done, for, by Jove, it had been.

What say you to slyly loosing every thing by day; and when night comes, cast off the band and swing in the cranes? But how lower the tackles, even in the darkest night, without a creaking more fearful than the death rattle? Easily avoided. Anoint the ropes, and they will travel deftly through the subtle windings of the blocks.

But though I had heard of this plan being pursued, there was a degree of risk in it, after all, which I was far from fancying. Another plan was hit upon; still bolder; and hence more safe. What it was, in the right place will be seen.

In selecting my craft for this good voyage, I would fain have traversed the deck, and eyed the boats like a cornet choosing his steed from out a goodly stud. But this was denied me. And the "bow boat" was, perforce, singled out, as the most remote from the quarter-deck, that region of sharp eyes and relentless purposes.

Then, our larder was to be thought of; also, an abundant supply of water; concerning which last I determined to take good heed. There were but two to be taken care of; but I resolved to lay in sufficient store of both meat and drink for four; at the same time that the supplemental twain thus provided for were but imaginary. And if it came to the last dead pinch, of which we had no fear, however, I was food for no man but Jarl.

Little time was lost in catering for our mess. Biscuit and salt beef were our sole resource; and, thanks to the generosity of the Areturion's owners, our ship's company had a plentiful supply. Casks of both, with heads knocked out, were at the service of all. In bags which we made for the purpose, a sufficiency of the biscuit was readily stored away, and secreted in a corner of easy access. The salt beef was more difficult to obtain; but, little by little, we managed to smuggle out of the cask enough to answer our purpose.

As for water, most luckily a day or two previous several "breakers" of it had been hoisted from below for the present use of the ship's company.

These "breakers" are casks, long and slender, but very strong. Of various diameters, they are made on purpose to stow into spaces intervening between the immense butts in a ship's hold.

The largest we could find was selected, first carefully examining it to detect any leak. On some pretense or other, we then rolled them all over to that side of the vessel where our boat was suspended, the selected breaker being placed in their middle.

Our compendious wardrobes were snugly packed into bundles and laid aside for the present. And at last, by due caution, we had every thing arranged preliminary to the final start. Let me say, though, perhaps to the credit of Jarl, that whenever the most strategy was necessary, he seemed ill at ease, and for the most part left the matter to me. It was well that he did; for as it was, by his untimely straight-forwardness, he once or twice came near spoiling every thing. Indeed, on one occasion he was so unseasonably blunt, that curiously enough, I had almost suspected him of taking that odd sort of interest in one's welfare, which leads a philanthropist, all other methods failing, to frustrate a project deemed bad; by pretending clumsily to favor it. But no inuendoes; Jarl was a Viking, frank as his fathers; though not so much of a bucanier.

Chapter VI

Eight Bells

The moon must be monstrous coy, or some things fall out opportunely, or else almanacs are consulted by nocturnal adventurers; but so it is, that when Cynthia shows a round and chubby disk, few daring deeds are done. Though true it may be, that of moonlight nights, jewelers' caskets and maidens' hearts have been burglariously broken into—and rifled, for aught Copernicus can tell.

The gentle planet was in her final quarter, and upon her slender horn I hung my hopes of withdrawing from the ship undetected.

Now, making a tranquil passage across the ocean, we kept at this time what are called among whalemen "boatscrew-watches." That is, instead of the sailors being divided at night into two bands, alternately on deck every four hours, there were four watches, each composed of a boat's crew, the "headsman" (always one of the mates) excepted. To the officers, this plan gives uninterrupted repose—"all-night-in," as they call it, and of course greatly lightens the duties of the crew.

The harpooneers head the boats' crews, and are responsible for the ship during the continuance of their watches.

Now, my Viking being a stalwart seaman, pulled the midship oar of the boat of which I was bowsman. Hence, we were in the same watch; to which, also, three others belonged, including Mark, the harpooner. One of these seamen, however, being an invalid, there were only two left for us to manage.

Voyaging in these seas, you may glide along for weeks without starting tack or sheet, hardly moving the helm a spoke, so mild and constant are the Trades. At night, the watch seldom trouble themselves with keeping much of a look-out; especially, as a strange sail is almost a prodigy in these lonely waters. In some ships, for weeks in and weeks out, you are puzzled to tell when your nightly turn on deck really comes round; so little heed is given to the standing of watches, where in the license of presumed safety, nearly every one nods without fear.

But remiss as you may be in the boats-crew-watch of a heedless whaleman, the man who heads it is bound to maintain his post on the quarter-deck until regularly relieved. Yet drowsiness being incidental to all natures, even to Napoleon, beside his own sentry napping in the snowy bivouac; so, often, in snowy moonlight, or ebon eclipse, dozed Mark, our harpooneer. Lethe be his portion this blessed night, thought I, as during the morning which preceded our enterprise, I eyed the man who might possibly cross my plans.

But let me come closer to this part of my story. During what are called at sea the "dog-watches" (between four o'clock and eight in the evening), sailors are quite lively and frolicsome; their spirits even flow far into the first of the long "night-watches;" but upon its expiration at "eight bells" (midnight), silence begins to reign; if you hear a voice it is no cherub's: all exclamations are oaths.

At eight bells, the mariners on deck, now relieved from their cares, crawl out from their sleepy retreats in old monkey jackets, or coils of rigging, and hie to their hammocks, almost without interrupting their dreams: while the sluggards below lazily drag themselves up the ladder to resume their slumbers in the open air.

For these reasons then, the moonless sea midnight was just the time to escape. Hence, we suffered a whole day to pass unemployed; waiting for the night, when the star board-quarter-boats'-watch, to which we belonged, would be summoned on deck at the eventful eight of the bell.

But twenty-four hours soon glide away; and "Starboleens ahoy; eight bells there below;" at last started me from a troubled doze.

I sprang from my hammock, and would have lighted my pipe. But the forecastle lamp had gone out. An old sea-dog was talking about sharks in his sleep. Jarl and our solitary watch-mate were groping their way into their trowsers. And little was heard but the humming of the still sails aloft; the dash of the waves against the bow; and the deep breathing of the dreaming sailors around.

Chapter VII

A Pause

Good old Arcturion! Maternal craft; that rocked me so often in thy heart of oak, I grieve to tell how I deserted thee on the broad deep. So far from home, with such a motley crew, so many islanders, whose heathen babble echoing through thy Christian hull, must have grated harshly on every carline.

Old ship! where sails thy lone ghost now? For of the stout Arcturion no word was ever heard, from the dark hour we pushed from her fated planks. In what time of tempest, to what seagull's scream, the drowning eddies did their work, knows no mortal man. Sunk she silently, helplessly, into the calm depths of that summer sea, assassinated by the ruthless blade of the swordfish? Such things have been. Or was hers a better fate? Stricken down while gallantly battling with the blast; her storm-sails set; helm manned; and every sailor at his post; as sunk the Hornet, her men at quarters, in some distant gale.

But surmises are idle. A very old craft, she may have foundered; or laid her bones upon some treacherous reef; but as with many a far rover, her fate is a mystery.

Pray Heaven, the spirit of that lost vessel roaming abroad through the troubled mists of midnight gales—as old mariners believe of missing ships—may never haunt my future path upon the waves. Peacefully may she rest at the bottom of the sea; and sweetly sleep my shipmates in the lowest watery zone, where prowling sharks come not, nor billows roll.

By quitting the Arcturion when we did, Jarl and I unconsciously eluded a sailor's grave. We hear of providential deliverances. Was this one? But life is sweet to all, death comes as hard. And for myself I am almost tempted to hang my head, that I escaped the fate of my shipmates; something like him who blushed to have escaped the fell carnage at Thermopylae.

Though I can not repress a shudder when I think of that old ship's end, it is impossible for me so much as to imagine, that our deserting her could have been in any way instrumental in her loss. Nevertheless, I would to heaven the Arcturion still floated; that it was given me once more to tread her familiar decks.

Chapter VIII

They Push Off, Velis Et Remis

And now to tell how, tempted by devil or good angel, and a thousand miles from land, we embarked upon this western voyage.

It was midnight, mark you, when our watch began; and my turn at the helm now coming on was of course to be avoided. On some plausible pretense, I induced our solitary watchmate to assume it; thus leaving myself untrammeled, and at the same time satisfactorily disposing of him. For being a rather fat fellow, an enormous consumer of "duff," and with good reason supposed to be the son of a farmer, I made no doubt, he would pursue his old course and fall to nodding over the wheel. As for the leader of the watch—our harpooner—he fell heir to the nest of old jackets, under the lee of the mizzen-mast, left nice and warm by his predecessor.

The night was even blacker than we had anticipated; there was no trace of a moon; and the dark purple haze, sometimes encountered at night near the Line, half shrouded the stars from view.

Waiting about twenty minutes after the last man of the previous watch had gone below, I motioned to Jarl, and we slipped our shoes from our feet. He then descended into the forecastle, and I sauntered aft toward the quarter-deck. All was still. Thrice did I pass my hand full before the face of the slumbering lubber at the helm, and right between him and the light of the binnacle.

Mark, the harpooneer, was not so easily sounded. I feared to approach him. He lay quietly, though; but asleep or awake, no more delay. Risks must be run, when time presses. And our ears were a pointer's to catch a sound.

To work we went, without hurry, but swiftly and silently. Our various stores were dragged from their lurking-places, and placed in the boat, which hung from the ship's lee side, the side depressed in the water, an indispensable requisite to an attempt at escape. And though at sundown the boat was to windward, yet, as we had foreseen, the vessel having been tacked during the first watch, brought it to leeward.

Endeavoring to manhandle our clumsy breaker, and lift it into the boat, we found, that by reason of the intervention of the shrouds, it could not be done without, risking a jar; besides straining the craft in lowering. An expedient, however, though at the eleventh hour, was hit upon. Fastening a long rope to the breaker, which was perfectly tight, we cautiously dropped it overboard; paying out enough line, to insure its towing astern of the ship, so as not to strike against the copper. The other end of the line we then secured to the boat's stern.

Fortunately, this was the last thing to be done; for the breaker, acting as a clog to the vessel's way in the water, so affected her steering as to fling her perceptibly into the wind. And by causing the helm to work, this must soon rouse the lubber there stationed, if not already awake. But our dropping overboard the breaker greatly aided us in this respect: it diminished the ship's headway; which owing to the light breeze had not been very great at any time during the night. Had it been so, all hope of escaping without first arresting the vessel's progress, would have been little short of madness. As it was, the sole daring of the deed that night achieved, consisted in our lowering away while the ship yet clove the brine, though but moderately.

All was now ready: the cranes swung in, the lashings adrift, and the boat fairly suspended; when, seizing the ends of the tackle ropes, we silently stepped into it, one at each end. The dead weight of the breaker astern now dragged the craft horizontally through the air, so that her tackle ropes strained hard. She quivered like a dolphin. Nevertheless, had we not feared her loud splash upon striking the wave, we might have quitted the ship almost as silently as the breath the body. But this was out of the question, and our plans were laid accordingly.

"All ready, Jarl?"

"Ready."

"A man overboard!" I shouted at the top of my compass; and like lightning the cords slid through our blistering hands, and with a tremendous shock the boat bounded on the sea's back. One mad sheer and plunge, one terrible strain on the tackles as we sunk in the trough of the waves, tugged upon by the towing breaker, and our knives severed the tackle ropes—we hazarded not unhooking the blocks—our oars were out, and the good boat headed round, with prow to leeward.

"Man overboard!" was now shouted from stem to stern. And directly we heard the confused tramping and shouting of the sailors, as they rushed from their dreams into the almost inscrutable darkness.

"Man overboard! Man overboard!" My heart smote me as the human cry of horror came out of the black vaulted night.

"Down helm!" was soon heard from the chief mate. "Back the main-yard! Quick to the boats! How's this? One down already? Well done! Hold on, then, those other boats!"

Meanwhile several seamen were shouting as they strained at the braces.

"Cut! cut all! Lower away! lower away!" impatiently cried the sailors, who already had leaped into the boats.

"Heave the ship to, and hold fast every thing," cried the captain, apparently just springing to the deck. "One boat's enough. Steward; show a light there from the mizzen-top. Boat ahoy!—Have you got that man?"

No reply. The voice came out of a cloud; the ship dimly showing like a ghost. We had desisted from rowing, and hand over hand were now hauling in upon the rope attached to the breaker, which we soon lifted into the boat, instantly resuming our oars.

"Pull! pull, men! and save him!" again shouted the captain.

"Ay, ay, sir," answered Jarl instinctively, "pulling as hard as ever we can, sir."

And pull we did, till nothing could be heard from the ship but a confused tumult; and, ever and anon, the hoarse shout of the captain, too distant to be understood.

We now set our sail to a light air; and right into the darkness, and dead to leeward, we rowed and sailed till morning dawned.

Chapter IX

The Watery World Is All Before Them

At sea in an open boat, and a thousand miles from land!

Shortly after the break of day, in the gray transparent light, a speck to windward broke the even line of the horizon. It was the ship wending her way north-eastward.

Had I not known the final indifference of sailors to such disasters as that which the Arcturion's crew must have imputed to the night past (did not the skipper suspect the truth) I would have regarded that little speck with many compunctions of conscience. Nor, as it was, did I feel in any very serene humor. For the consciousness of being deemed dead, is next to the presumable unpleasantness of being so in reality. One feels like his own ghost unlawfully tenanting a defunct carcass. Even Jarl's glance seemed so queer, that I begged him to look another way.

Secure now from all efforts of the captain to recover those whom he most probably supposed lost; and equally cut off from all hope of returning to the ship even had we felt so inclined; the resolution that had thus far nerved me, began to succumb in a measure to the awful loneliness of the scene. Ere this, I had regarded the ocean as a slave, the steed that bore me whither I listed, and whose vicious propensities, mighty though they were, often proved harmless, when opposed to the genius of man. But now, how changed! In our frail boat, I would fain have built an altar to Neptune.

What a mere toy we were to the billows, that jeeringly shouldered us from crest to crest, as from hand to hand lost souls may be tossed along by the chain of shades which enfilade the route to Tartarus.

But drown or swim, here's overboard with care! Cheer up, Jarl! Ha! Ha! how merrily, yet terribly, we sail! Up, up—slowly up—toiling up the long, calm wave; then balanced on its summit a while, like a plank on a rail; and down, we plunge headlong into the seething abyss, till arrested, we glide upward again. And thus did we go. Now buried in watery hollows—our sail idly flapping; then lifted aloft— canvas bellying; and beholding the furthest horizon.

Had not our familiarity with the business of whaling divested our craft's wild motions of its first novel horrors, we had been but a rueful pair. But day-long pulls after whales, the ship left miles astern; and entire dark nights passed moored to the monsters, killed too late to be towed to the ship far to leeward:—all this, and much more, accustoms one to strange things. Death, to be sure, has a mouth as black as a wolf's, and to be thrust into his jaws is a serious thing. But true it most certainly is—and I speak from no hearsay— that to sailors, as a class, the grisly king seems not half so hideous as he appears to those who have only regarded him on shore, and at a deferential distance. Like many ugly mortals, his features grow less frightful upon acquaintance; and met over often and sociably, the old adage holds true, about familiarity breeding contempt. Thus too with soldiers. Of the quaking recruit, three pitched battles make a grim grenadier; and he who shrank from the muzzle of a cannon, is now ready to yield his mustache for a sponge.

And truly, since death is the last enemy of all, valiant souls will taunt him while they may. Yet rather, should the wise regard him as the inflexible friend, who, even against our own wills, from life's evils triumphantly relieves us.

And there is but little difference in the manner of dying. To die, is all. And death has been gallantly encountered by those who never beheld blood that was red, only its light azure seen through the veins. And to yield the ghost proudly, and march out of your fortress with all the honors of war, is not a thing of sinew and bone. Though in prison, Geoffry Hudson, the dwarf, died more bravely than Goliah, the giant; and the last end of a butterfly shames us all. Some women have lived nobler lives, and died nobler deaths, than men. Threatened with the stake, mitred Cranmer recanted; but through her fortitude, the lorn widow of Edessa stayed the tide of Valens' persecutions. 'Tis no great valor to perish sword in hand, and bravado on lip; cased all in panoply complete. For even the alligator dies in his mail, and the swordfish never surrenders. To expire, mild-eyed, in one's bed, transcends the death of Epaminondas.

Chapter X

They Arrange Their Canopies And Lounges, And Try To Make Things Comfortable

Our little craft was soon in good order. From the spare rigging brought along, we made shrouds to the mast, and converted the boat- hook into a handy boom for the jib. Going large before the wind, we set this sail wing-and-wing with the main-sail. The latter, in accordance with the customary rig of whale-boats, was worked with a sprit and sheet. It could be furled or set in an instant. The bags of bread we stowed away in the covered space about the loggerhead, a useless appurtenance now, and therefore removed. At night, Jarl used it for a pillow; saying, that when the boat rolled it gave easy play to his head. The precious breaker we lashed firmly amidships; thereby much improving our sailing.

Now, previous to leaving the ship, we had seen to it well, that our craft was supplied with all those equipments, with which, by the regulations of the fishery, a whale-boat is constantly provided: night and day, afloat or suspended. Hanging along our gunwales inside, were six harpoons, three lances, and a blubber-spade; all keen as razors, and sheathed with leather. Besides these, we had three waifs, a couple of two-gallon water-kegs, several bailers, the boat-hatchet for cutting the whale-line, two auxiliary knives for the like purpose, and several minor articles, also employed in hunting the leviathan. The line and line-tub, however, were on ship-board.

And here it may be mentioned, that to prevent the strain upon the boat when suspended to the ship's side, the heavy whale-line, over two hundred fathoms in length, and something more than an inch in diameter, when not in use is kept on ship-board, coiled away like an endless snake in its tub. But this tub is always in readiness to be launched into the boat. Now, having no use for the line belonging to our craft, we had purposely left it behind.

But well had we marked that by far the most important item of a whale-boat's furniture was snugly secured in its place. This was the water-tight keg, at both ends firmly headed, containing a small compass, tinder-box and flint, candles, and a score or two of biscuit. This keg is an invariable precaution against what so frequently occurs in pursuing the sperm whale—prolonged absence from the ship, losing sight of her, or never seeing her more, till years after you reach home again. In this same keg of ours seemed coopered up life and death, at least so seemed it to honest Jarl. No sooner had we got clear from the Arcturion, than dropping his oar for an instant, he clutched at it in the dark.

And when day at last came, we knocked out the head of the keg with the little hammer and chisel, always attached to it for that purpose, and removed the compass, that glistened to us like a human eye. Then filling up the vacancy with biscuit, we again made all tight, driving down the hoops till they would budge no more.

At first we were puzzled to fix our compass. But at last the Skyeman out knife, and cutting a round hole in the after-most thwart, or seat of the boat, there inserted the little brass case containing the needle.

Over the stern of the boat, with some old canvas which my Viking's forethought had provided, we spread a rude sort of awning, or rather counterpane. This, however, proved but little or no protection from the glare of the sun; for the management of the main-sail forbade any considerable elevation of the shelter. And when the breeze was fresh, we were fain to strike it altogether; for the wind being from aft, and getting underneath the canvas, almost lifted the light boat's stem into the air, vexing the counterpane as if it were a petticoat turning a gusty corner. But when a mere breath rippled the sea, and the sun was fiery hot, it was most pleasant to lounge in this shady asylum. It was like being transferred from the roast to cool in the cupboard. And Jarl, much the toughest fowl of the two, out of an abundant kindness for his comrade, during the day voluntarily remained exposed at the helm, almost two hours to my one. No lady-like scruples had he, the old Viking, about marring his complexion, which already was more than bronzed. Over the ordinary tanning of the sailor, he seemed masked by a visor of japanning, dotted all over with freckles, so intensely yellow, and symmetrically circular, that they seemed scorched there by a burning glass.

In the tragico-comico moods which at times overtook me, I used to look upon the brown Skyeman with humorous complacency. If we fall in with cannibals, thought I, then, ready-roasted Norseman that thou art, shall I survive to mourn thee; at least, during the period I revolve upon the spit.

But of such a fate, it needs hardly be said, we had no apprehension.

Chapter XI

Jarl Afflicted With The Lockjaw

If ever again I launch whale-boat from sheer-plank of ship at sea, I shall take good heed, that my comrade be a sprightly fellow, with a rattle-box head. Be he never so silly, his very silliness, so long as he be lively at it, shall be its own excuse.

Upon occasion, who likes not a lively loon, one of your giggling, gamesome oafs, whose mouth is a grin? Are not such, well-ordered dispensations of Providence? filling up vacuums, in intervals of social stagnation relieving the tedium of existing? besides keeping up, here and there, in very many quarters indeed, sundry people's good opinion of themselves? What, if at times their speech is insipid as water after wine? What, if to ungenial and irascible souls, their very "mug" is an exasperation to behold, their clack an inducement to suicide? Let us not be hard upon them for this; but let them live on for the good they may do.

But Jarl, dear, dumb Jarl, thou wert none of these. Thou didst carry a phiz like an excommunicated deacon's. And no matter what happened, it was ever the same. Quietly, in thyself, thou didst revolve upon thine own sober axis, like a wheel in a machine which forever goes round, whether you look at it or no. Ay, Jarl! wast thou not forever intent upon minding that which so many neglect—thine own especial business? Wast thou not forever at it, too, with no likelihood of ever winding up thy moody affairs, and striking a balance sheet?

But at times how wearisome to me these everlasting reveries in my one solitary companion. I longed for something enlivening; a burst of words; human vivacity of one kind or other. After in vain essaying to get something of this sort out of Jarl, I tried it all by myself; playing upon my body as upon an instrument; singing, halloing, and making empty gestures, till my Viking stared hard; and I myself paused to consider whether I had run crazy or no.

But how account for the Skyeman's gravity? Surely, it was based upon no philosophic taciturnity; he was nothing of an idealist; an aerial architect; a constructor of flying buttresses. It was inconceivable, that his reveries were Manfred-like and exalted, reminiscent of unutterable deeds, too mysterious even to be indicated by the remotest of hints. Suppositions all out of the question.

His ruminations were a riddle. I asked him anxiously, whether, in any part of the world, Savannah, Surat, or Archangel, he had ever a wife to think of; or children, that he carried so lengthy a phiz. Nowhere neither. Therefore, as by his own confession he had nothing to think of but himself, and there was little but honesty in him (having which, by the way, he may be thought full to the brim), what could I fall back upon but my original theory: namely, that in repose, his intellects stepped out, and left his body to itself.

Chapter XII

More About Being In An Open Boat

On the third morning, at break of day, I sat at the steering oar, an hour or two previous having relieved Jarl, now fast asleep. Somehow, and suddenly, a sense of peril so intense, came over me, that it could hardly have been aggravated by the completest solitude.

On a ship's deck, the mere feeling of elevation above the water, and the reach of prospect you command, impart a degree of confidence which disposes you to exult in your fancied security. But in an open boat, brought down to the very plane of the sea, this feeling almost wholly deserts you. Unless the waves, in their gambols, toss you and your chip upon one of their lordly crests, your sphere of vision is little larger than it would be at the bottom of a well. At best, your most extended view in any one direction, at least, is in a high, slow-rolling sea; when you descend into the dark, misty spaces, between long and uniform swells. Then, for the moment, it is like looking up and down in a twilight glade, interminable; where two dawns, one on each hand, seem struggling through the semi-transparent tops of the fluid mountains.

But, lingering not long in those silent vales, from watery cliff to cliff, a sea-chamois, sprang our solitary craft,—a goat among the Alps!

How undulated the horizon; like a vast serpent with ten thousand folds coiled all round the globe; yet so nigh, apparently, that it seemed as if one's hand might touch it.

What loneliness; when the sun rose, and spurred up the heavens, we hailed him as a wayfarer in Sahara the sight of a distant horseman. Save ourselves, the sun and the Chamois seemed all that was left of life in the universe. We yearned toward its jocund disk, as in strange lands the traveler joyfully greets a face from home, which there had passed unheeded. And was not the sun a fellow-voyager? were we not both wending westward? But how soon he daily overtook and passed us; hurrying to his journey's end.

When a week had gone by, sailing steadily on, by day and by night, and nothing in sight but this self-same sea, what wonder if disquieting thoughts at last entered our hearts? If unknowingly we should pass the spot where, according to our reckoning, our islands lay, upon what shoreless sea would we launch? At times, these forebodings bewildered my idea of the positions of the groups beyond. All became vague and confused; so that westward of the Kingsmil isles and the Radack chain, I fancied there could be naught but an endless sea.

Chapter XIII

Of The Chondropterygii, And Other Uncouth Hordes Infesting The South Seas

At intervals in our lonely voyage, there were sights which diversified the scene; especially when the constellation Pisces was in the ascendant.

It's famous botanizing, they say, in Arkansas' boundless prairies; I commend the student of Ichthyology to an open boat, and the ocean moors of the Pacific. As your craft glides along, what strange monsters float by. Elsewhere, was never seen their like. And nowhere are they found in the books of the naturalists.

Though America be discovered, the Cathays of the deep are unknown. And whoso crosses the Pacific might have read lessons to Buffon. The sea-serpent is not a fable; and in the sea, that snake is but a garden worm. There are more wonders than the wonders rejected, and more sights unrevealed than you or I ever ever dreamt of. Moles and bats alone should be skeptics; and the only true infidelity is for a live man to vote himself dead. Be Sir Thomas Brown our ensample; who, while exploding "Vulgar Errors," heartily hugged all the mysteries in the Pentateuch.

But look! fathoms down in the sea; where ever saw you a phantom like that? An enormous crescent with antlers like a reindeer, and a Delta of mouths. Slowly it sinks, and is seen no more.

Doctor Faust saw the devil; but you have seen the "Devil Fish."

Look again! Here comes another. Jarl calls it a Bone Shark. Full as large as a whale, it is spotted like a leopard; and tusk-like teeth overlap its jaws like those of the walrus. To seamen, nothing strikes more terror than the near vicinity of a creature like this. Great ships steer out of its path. And well they may;

since the good craft Essex, and others, have been sunk by sea-monsters, as the alligator thrusts his horny snout through a Carribean canoe.

Ever present to us, was the apprehension of some sudden disaster from the extraordinary zoological specimens we almost hourly passed.

For the sharks, we saw them, not by units, nor by tens, nor by hundreds; but by thousands and by myriads. Trust me, there are more sharks in the sea than mortals on land.

And of these prolific fish there are full as many species as of dogs. But by the German naturalists Muller and Henle, who, in christening the sharks, have bestowed upon them the most heathenish names, they are classed under one family; which family, according to Muller, king-at-arms, is an undoubted branch of the ancient and famous tribe of the Chondropterygii.

To begin. There is the ordinary Brown Shark, or sea attorney, so called by sailors; a grasping, rapacious varlet, that in spite of the hard knocks received from it, often snapped viciously at our steering oar. At times, these gentry swim in herds; especially about the remains of a slaughtered whale. They are the vultures of the deep.

Then we often encountered the dandy Blue Shark, a long, taper and mighty genteel looking fellow, with a slender waist, like a Bond- street beau, and the whitest tiers of teeth imaginable. This dainty spark invariably lounged by with a careless fin and an indolent tail. But he looked infernally heartless.

How his cold-blooded, gentlemanly air, contrasted with the rude, savage swagger of the Tiger Shark; a round, portly gourmand; with distended mouth and collapsed conscience, swimming about seeking whom he might devour. These gluttons are the scavengers of navies, following ships in the South Seas, picking up odds and ends of garbage, and sometimes a tit-bit, a stray sailor. No wonder, then, that sailors denounce them. In substance, Jarl once assured me, that under any temporary misfortune, it was one of his sweetest consolations to remember, that in his day, he had murdered, not killed, shoals of Tiger Sharks.

Yet this is all wrong. As well hate a seraph, as a shark. Both were made by the same hand. And that sharks are lovable, witness their domestic endearments. No Fury so ferocious, as not to have some amiable side. In the wild wilderness, a leopard-mother caresses her cub, as Hagar did Ishmael; or a queen of France the dauphin. We know not what we do when we hate. And I have the word of my gentlemanly friend Stanhope, for it; that he who declared he loved a good hater was but a respectable sort of Hottentot, at best. No very genteel epithet this, though coming from the genteelest of men. But when the digger of dictionaries said that saying of his, he was assuredly not much of a Christian. However, it is hard for one given up to constitutional hypos like him; to be filled with the milk and meekness of the gospels. Yet, with deference, I deny that my old uncle Johnson really believed in the sentiment ascribed to him. Love a hater, indeed! Who smacks his lips over gall? Now hate is a thankless thing. So, let us only hate hatred; and once give love play, we will fall in love with a unicorn. Ah! the easiest way is the best; and to hate, a man must work hard. Love is a delight; but hate a torment. And haters are thumbscrews, Scotch boots, and Spanish inquisitions to themselves. In five words—would they were a Siamese diphthong—he who hates is a fool.

For several days our Chamois was followed by two of these aforesaid Tiger Sharks. A brace of confidential inseparables, jogging along in our wake, side by side, like a couple of highwaymen, biding their time till you come to the cross-roads. But giving it up at last, for a bootless errand, they dropped farther and farther astern, until completely out of sight. Much to the Skyeman's chagrin; who long stood in the stern, lance poised for a dart.

But of all sharks, save me from the ghastly White Shark. For though we should hate naught, yet some dislikes are spontaneous; and disliking is not hating. And never yet could I bring myself to be loving, or even sociable, with a White Shark. He is not the sort of creature to enlist young affections.

This ghost of a fish is not often encountered, and shows plainer by night than by day. Timon-like, he always swims by himself; gliding along just under the surface, revealing a long, vague shape, of a milky hue; with glimpses now and then of his bottomless white pit of teeth. No need of a dentist hath he. Seen at night, stealing along like a spirit in the water, with horrific serenity of aspect, the White Shark sent many a thrill to us twain in the Chamois.

By day, and in the profoundest calms, oft were we startled by the ponderous sigh of the grampus, as lazily rising to the surface, he fetched a long breath after napping below.

And time and again we watched the darting albicore, the fish with the chain-plate armor and golden scales; the Nimrod of the seas, to whom so many flying fish fall a prey. Flying from their pursuers, many of them flew into our boat. But invariably they died from the shock. No nursing could restore them. One of their wings I removed, spreading it out to dry under a weight. In two days' time the thin membrane, all over tracings like those of a leaf, was transparent as isinglass, and tinted with brilliant hues, like those of a changing silk.

Almost every day, we spied Black Fish; coal-black and glossy. They seemed to swim by revolving round and round in the water, like a wheel; their dorsal fins, every now and then shooting into view, like spokes.

Of a somewhat similar species, but smaller, and clipper-built about the nose, were the Algerines; so called, probably, from their corsair propensities; waylaying peaceful fish on the high seas, and plundering them of body and soul at a gulp. Atrocious Turks! a crusade should be preached against them.

Besides all these, we encountered Killers and Thrashers, by far the most spirited and "spunky" of the finny tribes. Though little larger than a porpoise, a band of them think nothing of assailing leviathan himself. They bait the monster, as dogs a bull. The Killers seizing the Right whale by his immense, sulky lower lip, and the Thrashers fastening on to his back, and beating him with their sinewy tails. Often they come off conquerors, worrying the enemy to death. Though, sooth to say, if leviathan gets but one sweep al them with his terrible tail, they go flying into the air, as if tossed from Taurus' horn.

This sight we beheld. Had old Wouvermans, who once painted a bull bait, been along with us, a rare chance, that, for his pencil. And Gudin or Isabey might have thrown the blue rolling sea into the picture. Lastly, one of Claude's setting summer suns would have glorified the whole. Oh, believe me, God's creatures fighting, fin for fin, a thousand miles from land, and with the round horizon for an arena; is no ignoble subject for a masterpiece.

Such are a few of the sights of the great South Sea. But there is no telling all. The Pacific is populous as China.

Chapter XIV

Jarl's Misgivings

About this time an event took place. My good Viking opened his mouth, and spoke. The prodigy occurred, as, jacknife in hand, he was bending over the midship oar; on the loom, or handle, of which he kept our almanac; making a notch for every set sun. For some forty-eight hours past, the wind had been light and variable. It was more than suspected that a current was sweeping us northward.

Now, marking these things, Jarl threw out the thought, that the more wind, and the less current, the better; and if a long calm came on, of which there was some prospect, we had better take to our oars.

Take to our oars! as if we were crossing a ferry, and no ocean leagues to traverse. The idea indirectly suggested all possible horrors. To be rid of them forthwith, I proceeded to dole out our morning meal. For to make away with such things, there is nothing better than bolting something down on top of them; albeit, oft repeated, the plan is very apt to beget dyspepsia; and the dyspepsia the blues.

But what of our store of provisions? So far as enough to eat was concerned, we felt not the slightest apprehension; our supplies proving more abundant than we had anticipated. But, curious to tell, we felt but little inclination for food. It was water, bright water, cool, sparkling water, alone, that we craved. And of this, also, our store at first seemed ample. But as our voyage lengthened, and breezes blew faint, and calms fell fast, the idea of being deprived of the precious fluid grew into something little short of a mono- mania; especially with Jarl.

Every hour or two with the hammer and chisel belonging to the tinder box keg, he tinkered away at the invaluable breaker; driving down the hoops, till in his over solicitude, I thought he would burst them outright.

Now the breaker lay on its bilge, in the middle of the boat, where more or less sea-water always collected. And ever and anon, dipping his finger therein, my Viking was troubled with the thought, that this sea-water tasted less brackish than that alongside. Of course the breaker must be leaking. So, he would turn it over, till its wet side came uppermost; when it would quickly become dry as a bone. But now, with his knife, he would gently probe the joints of the staves; shake his head; look up; look down; taste of the water in the bottom of the boat; then that of the sea; then lift one end of the breaker; going through with every test of leakage he could dream of. Nor was he ever fully satisfied, that the breaker was in all respects sound. But in reality it was tight as the drum-heads that beat at Cerro- Gordo. Oh! Jarl, Jarl: to me in the boat's quiet stern, steering and philosophizing at one time and the same, thou and thy breaker were a study.

Besides the breaker, we had, full of water, the two boat-kegs, previously alluded to. These were first used. We drank from them by their leaden spouts; so many swallows three times in the day; having no other means of measuring an allowance. But when we came to the breaker, which had only a bung-hole, though a very large one, dog- like, it was so many laps apiece; jealously counted by the observer. This plan, however, was only good for a single day; the water then getting beyond the reach of the tongue. We therefore daily poured from the breaker into one of the kegs; and drank from its spout. But to obviate the absorption inseparable from decanting, we at last hit upon something better,—my comrade's shoe, which, deprived of its quarters, narrowed at the heel, and diligently rinsed out in the sea, was converted into a handy but rather limber ladle. This we kept suspended in the bung-hole of the breaker, that it might never twice absorb the water.

Now pewter imparts flavor to ale; a Meerschaum bowl, the same to the tobacco of Smyrna; and goggle green glasses are deemed indispensable to the bibbing of Hock. What then shall be said of a leathern goblet for water? Try it, ye mariners who list.

One morning, taking his wonted draught, Jarl fished up in his ladle a deceased insect; something like a Daddy-long-legs, only more corpulent. Its fate? A sea-toss? Believe it not; with all those precious drops clinging to its lengthy legs. It was held over the ladle till the last globule dribbled; and even then, being moist, honest Jarl was but loth to drop it overboard.

For our larder, we could not endure the salt beef; it was raw as a live Abyssinian steak, and salt as Cracow. Besides, the Feegee simile would not have held good with respect to it. It was far from being "tender as a dead man." The biscuit only could we eat; not to be wondered at; for even on shipboard, seamen in the tropics are but sparing feeders.

And here let not, a suggestion be omitted, most valuable to any future castaway or sailaway as the case may be. Eat not your biscuit dry; but dip it in the sea: which makes it more bulky and palatable. During meal times it was soak and sip with Jarl and me: one on each side of the Chamois dipping our biscuit in the brine. This plan obviated finger-glasses at the conclusion of our repast. Upon the whole, dwelling upon the water is not so bad after all. The Chinese are no fools. In the operation of making your toilet, how handy to float in your ewer!

Chapter XV

A Stitch In Time Saves Nine

Like most silent earnest sort of people, my good Viking was a pattern of industry. When in the boats after whales, I have known him carry along a roll of sinnate to stitch into a hat. And the boats lying motionless for half an hour or so, waiting the rising of the chase, his fingers would be plying at their task, like an old lady knitting. Like an experienced old-wife too, his digits had become so expert and conscientious, that his eyes left them alone; deeming optic supervision unnecessary. And on this trip of ours, when not otherwise engaged, he was quite as busy with his fingers as ever: unraveling old Cape Horn hose, for yarn wherewith to darn our woolen frocks; with great patches from the skirts of a condemned reefing jacket, panneling the seats of our "ducks;" in short, veneering our broken garments with all manner of choice old broadcloths.

With the true forethought of an old tar, he had brought along with him nearly the whole contents of his chest. His precious "Ditty Bag," containing his sewing utensils, had been carefully packed away in the bottom of one of his bundles; of which he had as many as an old maid on her travels. In truth, an old salt is very much of an old maid, though, strictly speaking, far from deserving that misdeemed appellative. Better be an old maid, a woman with herself for a husband, than the wife of a fool; and Solomon more than hints that all men are fools; and every wise man knows himself to be one. When playing the sempstress, Jarl's favorite perch was the triangular little platform in the bow; which being the driest and most elevated part of the boat, was best adapted to his purpose. Here for hours and hours together the honest old tailor would sit darning and sewing away, heedless of the wide ocean around; while forever, his slouched Guayaquil hat kept bobbing up and down against the horizon before us.

It was a most solemn avocation with him. Silently he nodded like the still statue in the opera of Don Juan. Indeed he never spoke, unless to give pithy utterance to the wisdom of keeping one's wardrobe in repair. But herein my Viking at times waxed oracular. And many's the hour we glided along, myself deeply pondering in the stem, hand upon helm; while crosslegged at the other end of the boat Jarl laid down patch upon patch, and at long intervals precept upon precept; here several saws, and there innumerable stitches.

Chapter XVI

They Are Becalmed

On the eighth day there was a calm.

It came on by night: so that waking at daybreak, and folding my arms over the gunwale, I looked out upon a scene very hard to describe. The sun was still beneath the horizon; perhaps not yet out of sight from the plains of Paraguay. But the dawn was too strong for the stars; which, one by one, had gone out, like waning lamps after a ball.

Now, as the face of a mirror is a blank, only borrowing character from what it reflects; so in a calm in the Tropics, a colorless sky overhead, the ocean, upon its surface, hardly presents a sign of existence. The deep blue is gone; and the glassy element lies tranced; almost viewless as the air.

But that morning, the two gray firmaments of sky and water seemed collapsed into a vague ellipsis. And alike, the Chamois seemed drifting in the atmosphere as in the sea. Every thing was fused into the calm: sky, air, water, and all. Not a fish was to be seen. The silence was that of a vacuum. No vitality lurked in the air. And this inert blending and brooding of all things seemed gray chaos in conception.

This calm lasted four days and four nights; during which, but a few cat's-paws of wind varied the scene. They were faint as the breath of one dying.

At times the heat was intense. The heavens, at midday, glowing like an ignited coal mine. Our skin curled up like lint; our vision became dim; the brain dizzy.

To our consternation, the water in the breaker became lukewarm, brackish, and slightly putrescent; notwithstanding we kept our spare clothing piled upon the breaker, to shield it from the sun. At last, Jarl enlarged the vent, carefully keeping it exposed. To this precaution, doubtless, we owed more than we then thought. It was now deemed wise to reduce our allowance of water to the smallest modicum consistent with the present preservation of life; strangling all desire for more.

Nor was this all. The upper planking of the boat began to warp; here and there, cracking and splintering. But though we kept it moistened with brine, one of the plank-ends started from its place; and the sharp, sudden sound, breaking the scorching silence, caused us both to spring to our feet. Instantly the sea burst in; but we made shift to secure the rebellious plank with a cord, not having a nail; we then bailed out the boat, nearly half full of water.

On the second day of the calm, we unshipped the mast, to prevent its being pitched out by the occasional rolling of the vast smooth swells now overtaking us. Leagues and leagues away, after its fierce raging, some tempest must have been sending to us its last dying waves. For as a pebble dropped into a pond ruffles it to its marge; so, on all sides, a sea-gale operates as if an asteroid had fallen into the brine; making ringed mountain billows, interminably expanding, instead of ripples.

The great September waves breaking at the base of the Neversink Highlands, far in advance of the swiftest pilot-boat, carry tidings. And full often, they know the last secret of many a stout ship, never heard of from the day she left port. Every wave in my eyes seems a soul.

As there was no steering to be done, Jarl and I sheltered ourselves as well as we could under the awning. And for the first two days, one at a time, and every three or four hours, we dropped overboard for a bath, clinging to the gun-wale; a sharp look-out being kept for prowling sharks. A foot or two below the surface, the water felt cool and refreshing.

On the third day a change came over us. We relinquished bathing, the exertion taxing us too much. Sullenly we laid ourselves down; turned our backs to each other; and were impatient of the slightest casual touch of our persons. What sort of expression my own countenance wore, I know not; but I hated to look at Jarl's. When I did it was a glare, not a glance. I became more taciturn than he. I can not tell what it was that came over me, but I wished I was alone. I felt that so long as the calm lasted, we were without help; that neither could assist the other; and above all, that for one, the water would hold out longer than for two. I felt no remorse, not the slightest, for these thoughts. It was instinct. Like a desperado giving up the ghost, I desired to gasp by myself.

From being cast away with a brother, good God deliver me!

The four days passed. And on the morning of the fifth, thanks be to Heaven, there came a breeze. Dancingly, mincingly it came, just rippling the sea, until it struck our sails, previously set at the very first token of its advance. At length it slightly freshened; and our poor Chamois seemed raised from the dead.

Beyond expression delightful! Once more we heard the low humming of the sea under our bow, as our boat, like a bird, went singing on its way.

How changed the scene! Overhead, a sweet blue haze, distilling sunlight in drops. And flung abroad over the visible creation was the sun-spangled, azure, rustling robe of the ocean, ermined with wave crests; all else, infinitely blue. Such a cadence of musical sounds! Waves chasing each other, and sporting and frothing in frolicsome foam: painted fish rippling past; and anon the noise of wings as sea- fowls flew by.

Oh, Ocean, when thou choosest to smile, more beautiful thou art than flowery mead or plain!

Chapter XVII

In High Spirits, They Push On For The Terra Incognita

There were now fourteen notches on the loom of the Skyeman's oar:—So many days since we had pushed from the fore-chains of the Arcturion. But as yet, no floating bough, no tern, noddy, nor reef-bird, to denote our proximity to land. In that long calm, whither might not the currents have swept us?

Where we were precisely, we knew not; but according to our reckoning, the loose estimation of the knots run every hour, we must have sailed due west but little more than one hundred and fifty leagues; for the most part having encountered but light winds, and frequent intermitting calms, besides that prolonged one described. But spite of past calms and currents, land there must be to the westward. Sun, compass, stout hearts, and steady breezes, pointed our prow thereto. So courage! my Viking, and never say drown!

At this time, our hearts were much lightened by discovering that our water was improving in taste. It seemed to have been undergoing anew that sort of fermentation, or working, occasionally incident to ship water shortly after being taken on board. Sometimes, for a period, it is more or less offensive to taste and smell; again, however, becoming comparatively limpid.

But as our water improved, we grew more and more miserly of so priceless a treasure.

And here it may be well to make mention of another little circumstance, however unsentimental. Thorough-paced tar that he was, my Viking was an inordinate consumer of the Indian weed. From the Arcturion, he had brought along with him a small half-keg, at bottom impacted with a solitary layer of sable Negrohead, fossil- marked, like the primary stratum of the geologists. It was the last tier of his abundant supply for the long whaling voyage upon which he had embarked upwards of three years previous. Now during the calm, and for some days after, poor Jarl's accustomed quid was no longer agreeable company. To pun: he eschewed his chew. I asked him wherefore. He replied that it puckered up his mouth, above all provoked thirst, and had somehow grown every way distasteful. I was sorry; for the absence of his before ever present wad impaired what little fullness there was left in his cheek; though, sooth to say, I no longer called upon him as of yore to shift over the enormous morsel to starboard or larboard, and so trim our craft.

The calm gone by, once again my sea-tailor plied needle and thread; or turning laundress, hung our raiment to dry on oars peaked obliquely in the thole-pins. All of which tattered pennons, the wind being astern, helped us gayly on our way; as jolly poor devils, with rags flying in the breeze, sail blithely through life; and are merry although they are poor!

Chapter XVIII

My Lord Shark And His Pages

There is a fish in the sea that evermore, like a surly lord, only goes abroad attended by his suite. It is the Shovel-nosed Shark. A clumsy lethargic monster, unshapely as his name, and the last species of his kind, one would think, to be so bravely waited upon, as he is. His suite is composed of those dainty little creatures called Pilot fish by sailors. But by night his retinue is frequently increased by the presence of several small luminous fish, running in advance, and flourishing their flambeaux like link-boys lighting the monster's way. Pity there were no ray-fish in rear, page-like, to carry his caudal train.

Now the relation subsisting between the Pilot fish above mentioned and their huge ungainly lord, seems one of the most inscrutable things in nature. At any rate, it poses poor me to comprehend. That a monster so ferocious, should suffer five or six little sparks, hardly fourteen inches long, to gambol about his grim hull with the utmost impunity, is of itself something strange. But when it is considered, that by a reciprocal understanding, the Pilot fish seem to act as scouts to the shark, warning him of danger, and apprising him of the vicinity of prey; and moreover, in case of his being killed, evincing their anguish by certain agitations, otherwise inexplicable; the whole thing becomes a mystery unfathomable. Truly marvels abound. It needs no dead man to be raised, to convince us of some things. Even my Viking marveled full as much at those Pilot fish as he would have marveled at the Pentecost.

But perhaps a little incident, occurring about this period, will best illustrate the matter in hand.

We were gliding along, hardly three knots an hour, when my comrade, who had been dozing over the gunwale, suddenly started to his feet, and pointed out an immense Shovel-nosed Shark, less than a boat's length distant, and about half a fathom beneath the surface. A lance was at once snatched from its place; and true to his calling, Jarl was about to dart it at the fish, when, interested by the sight of its radiant little scouts, I begged him to desist.

One of them was right under the shark, nibbling at his ventral fin; another above, hovering about his dorsal appurtenance; one on each flank; and a frisking fifth pranking about his nose, seemingly having something to say of a confidential nature. They were of a bright, steel-blue color, alternated with jet black stripes; with glistening bellies of a silver-white. Clinging to the back of the shark, were four or five Remoras, or sucking-fish; snaky parasites, impossible to remove from whatever they adhere to, without destroying their lives. The Remora has little power in swimming; hence its sole locomotion is on the backs of larger fish. Leech-like, it sticketh closer than a false brother in prosperity; closer than a beggar to the benevolent; closer than Webster to the Constitution. But it feeds upon what it clings to; its feelers having a direct communication with the esophagus.

The shark swam sluggishly; creating no sign of a ripple, but ever and, anon shaking his Medusa locks, writhing and curling with horrible life. Now and then, the nimble Pilot fish darted from his side—this way and that—mostly toward our boat; but previous to taking a fresh start ever returning to their liege lord to report progress.

A thought struck me. Baiting a rope's end with a morsel of our almost useless salt beef, I suffered it to trail in the sea. Instantly the foremost scout swam toward it; hesitated; paused; but at last advancing, briskly snuffed at the line, and taking one finical little nibble, retreated toward the shark. Another moment, and the great Tamerlane himself turned heavily about; pointing his black, cannon-like nose directly toward our broadside. Meanwhile, the little Pilot fish darted hither and thither; keeping up a mighty fidgeting, like men of small minds in a state of nervous agitation.

Presently, Tamerlane swam nearer and nearer, all the while lazily eyeing the Chamois, as a wild boar a kid. Suddenly making a rush for it, in the foam he made away with the bait. But the next instant, the uplifted lance sped at his skull; and thrashing his requiem with his sinewy tail, he sunk slowly, through his own blood, out of sight. Down with him swam the terrified Pilot fish; but soon after, three of them were observed close to the boat, gliding along at a uniform pace; one an each side, and one in advance; even as they had attended their lord. Doubtless, one was under our keel.

"A good omen," said Jarl; "no harm will befall us so long as they stay."

But however that might be, follow us they did, for many days after: until an event occurred, which necessitated their withdrawal.

Chapter XIX

Who Goes There?

Jarl's oar showed sixteen notches on the loom, when one evening, as the expanded sun touched the horizon's rim, a ship's uppermost spars were observed, traced like a spider's web against its crimson disk. It looked like a far-off craft on fire.

In bright weather at sea, a sail, invisible in the full flood of noon, becomes perceptible toward sunset. It is the reverse in the morning. In sight at gray dawn, the distant vessel, though in reality approaching, recedes from view, as the sun rises higher and higher. This holds true, till its vicinity makes it readily fall within the ordinary scope of vision. And thus, too, here and there, with other distant things: the more light you throw on them, the more you obscure. Some revelations show best in a twilight.

The sight of the stranger not a little surprised us. But brightening up, as if the encounter were welcome, Jarl looked happy and expectant. He quickly changed his demeanor, however, upon perceiving that I was bent upon shunning a meeting.

Instantly our sails were struck; and calling upon Jarl, who was somewhat backward to obey, I shipped the oars; and, both rowing, we stood away obliquely from our former course.

I divined that the vessel was a whaler; and hence, that by help of the glass, with which her look-outs must be momentarily sweeping the horizon, they might possibly have descried us; especially, as we were due east from the ship; a direction, which at sunset is the one most favorable for perceiving a far-off object at sea. Furthermore, our canvas was snow-white and conspicuous. To be sure, we could not be certain what kind of a vessel it was; but whatever it might be, I, for one, had no mind to risk an encounter; for it was quite plain, that if the stranger came within hailing distance, there would be no resource but to link our fortunes with hers; whereas I desired to pursue none but the Chamois'. As for the Skyeman, he kept looking wistfully over his shoulder; doubtless, praying Heaven, that we might not escape what I sought to avoid.

Now, upon a closer scrutiny, being pretty well convinced that the stranger, after all, was steering a nearly westerly course—right away from us—we reset our sail; and as night fell, my Viking's entreaties, seconded by my own curiosity, induced me to resume our original course; and so follow after the vessel, with a view of obtaining a nearer glimpse, without danger of detection. So, boldly we steered for the sail.

But not gaining much upon her, spite of the lightness of the breeze (a circumstance in our favor: the chase being a ship, and we but a boat), at my comrade's instigation, we added oars to sails, readily guiding our way by the former, though the helm was left to itself.

As we came nearer, it was plain that the vessel was no whaler; but a small, two-masted craft; in short, a brigantine. Her sails were in a state of unaccountable disarray, only the foresail, mainsail, and jib being set. The first was much tattered; and the jib was hoisted but half way up the stay, where it idly flapped, the breeze coming from over the taffrail. She continually yawed in her course; now almost presenting her broadside, then showing her stern.

Striking our sails once more, we lay on our oars, and watched her in the starlight. Still she swung from side to side, and still sailed on.

Not a little terrified at the sight, superstitious Jarl more than insinuated that the craft must be a gold-huntress, haunted. But I told him, that if such were the case, we must board her, come gold or goblins. In reality, however, I began to think that she must have been abandoned by her crew; or else, that from sickness, those on board were incapable of managing her.

After a long and anxious reconnoiter, we came still nearer, using our oars, but very reluctantly on Jarl's part; who, while rowing, kept his eyes over his shoulder, as if about to beach the little Chamois on the back of a whale as of yore. Indeed, he seemed full as impatient to quit the vicinity of the vessel, as before he had been anxiously courting it.

Now, as the silent brigantine again swung round her broadside, I hailed her loudly. No return. Again. But all was silent. With a few vigorous strokes, we closed with her, giving yet another unanswered hail; when, laying the Chamois right alongside, I clutched at the main-chains. Instantly we felt her dragging us along. Securing our craft by its painter, I sprang over the rail, followed by Jarl, who had snatched his harpoon, his favorite arms. Long used with that weapon to overcome the monsters of the deep, he doubted not it would prove equally serviceable in any other encounter.

The deck was a complete litter. Tossed about were pearl oyster shells, husks of cocoa-nuts, empty casks, and cases. The deserted tiller was lashed; which accounted for the vessel's yawing. But we could not conceive, how going large before the wind; the craft could, for any considerable time, at least, have guided herself without the help of a hand. Still, the breeze was light and steady.

Now, seeing the helm thus lashed, I could not but distrust the silence that prevailed. It conjured up the idea of miscreants concealed below, and meditating treachery; unscrupulous mutineers— Lascars, or Manilla-men; who, having murdered the Europeans of the crew, might not be willing to let strangers depart unmolested. Or yet worse, the entire ship's company might have been swept away by a fever, its infection still lurking in the poisoned hull. And though the first conceit, as the last, was a mere surmise, it was nevertheless deemed prudent to secure the hatches, which for the present we accordingly barred down with the oars of our boat. This done, we went about the deck in search of water. And finding some in a clumsy cask, drank long and freely, and to our thirsty souls' content.

The wind now freshening, and the rent sails like to blow from the yards, we brought the brigantine to the wind, and brailed up the canvas. This left us at liberty to examine the craft, though, unfortunately, the night was growing hazy.

All this while our boat was still towing alongside; and I was about to drop it astern, when Jarl, ever cautious, declared it safer where it was; since, if there were people on board, they would most likely be down in the cabin, from the dead-lights of which, mischief might be done to the Chamois.

It was then, that my comrade observed, that the brigantine had no boats, a circumstance most unusual in any sort of a vessel at sea. But marking this, I was exceedingly gratified. It seemed to indicate, as I had opined, that from some cause or other, she must have been abandoned of her crew. And in a good measure this dispelled my fears of foul play, and the apprehension of contagion. Encouraged by these reflections, I now resolved to descend, and explore the cabin, though sorely against Jarl's counsel. To be sure, as he earnestly said, this step might have been deferred till daylight; but it seemed too wearisome to wait. So bethinking me of our tinder-box and candles, I sent him into the boat for them. Presently, two candles were lit; one of which the Skyeman tied up and down the barbed end of his harpoon; so that upon going below, the keen steel might not be far off, should the light be blown out by a dastard.

Unfastening the cabin scuttle, we stepped downward into the smallest and murkiest den in the world. The altar-like transom, surmounted by the closed dead-lights in the stem, together with the dim little sky- light overhead, and the somber aspect of every thing around, gave the place the air of some subterranean oratory, say a Prayer Room of Peter the Hermit. But coils of rigging, bolts of canvas, articles of clothing, and disorderly heaps of rubbish, harmonized not with this impression. Two doors, one on each side, led into wee little state- rooms, the berths of which also were littered. Among other things, was a large box, sheathed with iron and stoutly clamped, containing a keg partly filled with powder, the half of an old cutlass, a pouch of bullets, and a case for a sextant—a brass plate on the lid, with the maker's name. London. The broken blade of the cutlass was very rusty and stained; and the iron hilt bent in. It looked so tragical that I thrust it out of sight.

Removing a small trap-door, opening into the space beneath, called the "run," we lighted upon sundry cutlasses and muskets, lying together at sixes and sevens, as if pitched down in a hurry.

Casting round a hasty glance, and satisfying ourselves, that through the bulkhead of the cabin, there was no passage to the forward part of the hold, we caught up the muskets and cutlasses, the powder keg and the pouch of bullets, and bundling them on deck, prepared to visit the other end of the vessel. Previous to so doing, however, I loaded a musket, and belted a cutlass to my side. But my Viking preferred his harpoon.

In the forecastle reigned similar confusion. But there was a snug little lair, cleared away in one corner, and furnished with a grass mat and bolster, like those used among the Islanders of these seas. This little lair looked to us as if some leopard had crouched there. And as it turned out, we were not far from right. Forming one side of this retreat, was a sailor's chest, stoutly secured by a lock, and monstrous heavy withal. Regardless of Jarl's entreaties, I managed to burst the lid; thereby revealing a motley assemblage of millinery, and outlandish knick-knacks of all sorts; together with sundry rude Calico contrivances, which though of unaccountable cut, nevertheless possessed a certain petticoatish air, and latitude of skirt, betokening them the habiliments of some feminine creature; most probably of the human species.

In this strong box, also, was a canvas bag, jingling with rusty old bell-buttons, gangrened copper bolts, and sheathing nails; damp, greenish Carolus dollars (true coin all), besides divers iron screws, and battered, chisels, and belaying-pins. Sounded on the chest lid, the dollars rang clear as convent bells. These were put aside by Jarl the sight of substantial dollars doing away, for the nonce, with his superstitious Misgivings. True to his kingship, he loved true coin; though abroad on the sea, and no land but dollarless dominions ground, all this silver was worthless as charcoal or diamonds. Nearly one and the same thing, say the chemists; but tell that to the marines, say the illiterate Jews and the jewelers. Go, buy a house, or a ship, if you can, with your charcoal! Yea, all the woods in Canada charred down to cinders would not be worth the one famed Brazilian diamond, though no bigger than the egg of a carrier pigeon. Ah! but these chemists are liars, and Sir Humphrey Davy a cheat. Many's the poor devil they've deluded into the charcoal business, who otherwise might have made his fortune with a mattock.

Groping again into the chest, we brought to light a queer little hair trunk, very bald and rickety. At every corner was a mighty clamp, the weight of which had no doubt debilitated the box. It was jealously secured with a padlock, almost as big as itself; so that it was almost a question, which was meant to be security to the other. Prying at it hard, we at length effected an entrance; but saw no golden moidores, no ruddy doubloons; nothing under heaven but three pewter mugs, such as are used in a ship's cabin, several brass screws, and brass plates, which must have belonged to a quadrant; together with a famous lot of glass beads, and brass rings; while, pasted on the inside of the cover, was a little colored print, representing the harlots, the shameless hussies, having a fine time with the Prodigal Son.

It should have been mentioned ere now, that while we were busy in the forecastle, we were several times startled by strange sounds aloft. And just after, crashing into the little hair trunk, down came a great top-block, right through the scuttle, narrowly missing my Viking's crown; a much stronger article, by the way, than your goldsmiths turn out in these days. This startled us much; particularly Jarl, as one might suppose; but accustomed to the strange creakings and wheezings of the masts and yards of old vessels at sea, and having many a time dodged stray blocks accidentally falling from aloft, I thought little more of the matter; though my comrade seemed to think the noises somewhat different from any thing of that kind he had even heard before.

After a little more turning over of the rubbish in the forecastle, and much marveling thereat, we ascended to the deck; where we found every thing so silent, that, as we moved toward the taffrail, the Skyeman unconsciously addressed me in a whisper.

Chapter XX

Noises And Portents

I longed for day. For however now inclined to believe that the brigantine was untenanted, I desired the light of the sun to place that fact beyond a misgiving.

Now, having observed, previous to boarding the vessel, that she lay rather low in the water, I thought proper to sound the well. But there being no line-and-sinker at hand, I sent Jarl to hunt them up in the arm-chest on the quarter-deck, where doubtless they must be kept. Meanwhile I searched for the "breaks," or pump-handles, which, as it turned out, could not have been very recently used; for they were found lashed up and down to the main-mast.

Suddenly Jarl came running toward me, whispering that all doubt was dispelled;—there were spirits on board, to a dead certainty. He had overheard a supernatural sneeze. But by this time I was all but convinced, that we were alone in the brigantine. Since, if otherwise, I could assign no earthly reason for the crew's hiding away from a couple of sailors, whom, were they so minded, they might easily have mastered. And furthermore, this alleged disturbance of the atmosphere aloft by a sneeze, Jarl averred to have taken place in the main-top; directly underneath which I was all this time standing, and had heard nothing. So complimenting my good Viking upon the exceeding delicacy of his auriculars, I bade him trouble himself no more with his piratical ghosts and goblins, which existed nowhere but in his own imagination.

Not finding the line-and-sinker, with the spare end of a bowline we rigged a substitute; and sounding the well, found nothing to excite our alarm. Under certain circumstances, however, this sounding a ship's well is a nervous sort of business enough. 'Tis like feeling your own pulse in the last stage of a fever.

At the Skyeman's suggestion, we now proceeded to throw round the brigantine's head on the other tack. For until daylight we desired to alter the vessel's position as little as possible, fearful of coming unawares upon reefs.

And here be it said, that for all his superstitious misgivings about the brigantine; his imputing to her something equivalent to a purely phantom-like nature, honest Jarl was nevertheless exceedingly downright and practical in all hints and proceedings concerning her. Wherein, he resembled my Right Reverend friend, Bishop Berkeley— truly, one of your lords spiritual—who, metaphysically speaking, holding all objects to be mere optical delusions, was, notwith- standing, extremely matter-of-fact in all matters touching matter itself. Besides being pervious to the points of pins, and possessing a palate capable of appreciating plum-puddings:—which sentence reads off like a pattering of hailstones.

Now, while we were employed bracing round the yards, whispering Jarl must needs pester me again with his confounded suspicions of goblins on board. He swore by the main-mast, that when the fore-yard swung round, he had heard a half-stifled groan from that quarter; as if one of his bugbears had been getting its aerial legs jammed. I laughed:— hinting that goblins were incorporeal. Whereupon he besought me to ascend the fore-rigging and test the matter for myself But here my mature judgment got the better of my first crude opinion. I civilly declined. For assuredly, there was still a possibility, that the fore-top might be tenanted, and that too by living miscreants; and a pretty hap would be mine, if, with hands full of rigging, and legs dangling in air, while surmounting the oblique futtock- shrouds, some unseen arm should all at once tumble me overboard. Therefore I held my peace; while Jarl went on to declare, that with regard to the character of the brigantine, his mind was now pretty fully made up;— she was an arrant impostor, a shade of a ship, full of sailors' ghosts, and before we knew where we were, would dissolve in a supernatural squall, and leave us twain in the water. In short, Jarl, the descendant of the superstitious old Norsemen, was full of old Norse conceits, and all manner of Valhalla marvels concerning the land of goblins and goblets. No wonder then, that with this catastrophe in prospect, he again entreated me to quit the ill-starred craft, carrying off nothing from her ghostly hull. But I refused.

One can not relate every thing at once. While in the cabin, we came across a "barge" of biscuit, and finding its contents of a quality much superior to our own, we had filled our pockets and occasionally regaled ourselves in the intervals of rummaging. Now this sea cake- basket we had brought on deck. And for the first time since bidding adieu to the Arcturion having fully quenched our thirst, our appetite returned with a rush; and having nothing better to do till day dawned, we planted the bread-barge in the middle of the quarter-deck; and crossing our legs before it, laid close seige thereto, like the Grand Turk and his Vizier Mustapha sitting down before Vienna.

Our castle, the Bread-Barge was of the common sort; an oblong oaken box, much battered and bruised, and like the Elgin Marbles, all over inscriptions and carving:—foul anchors, skewered hearts, almanacs, Burton-blocks, love verses, links of cable, Kings of Clubs; and divers mystic diagrams in chalk, drawn by old Finnish mariners; in casting horoscopes and prophecies. Your old tars are all Daniels. There was a round hole in one side, through which, in getting at the bread, invited guests thrust their hands.

And mighty was the thrusting of hands that night; also, many and earnest the glances of Mustapha at every sudden creaking of the spars or rigging. Like Belshazzar, my royal Viking ate with great fear and trembling; ever and anon pausing to watch the wild shadows flitting along the bulwarks.

Chapter XXI

Man Ho!

Slowly, fitfully, broke the morning in the East, showing the desolate brig forging heavily through the water, which sluggishly thumped under her bows. While leaping from sea to sea, our faithful Chamois, like a faithful dog, still gamboled alongside, confined to the main- chains by its painter. At times, it would long lag behind; then, pushed by a wave like lightning dash forward; till bridled by its leash, it again fell in rear.

As the gray light came on, anxiously we scrutinized the features of the craft, as one by one they became more plainly revealed. Every thing seemed stranger now, than when partially visible in the dingy night. The stanchions, or posts of the bulwarks, were of rough stakes, still incased in the bark. The unpainted sides were of a dark-colored, heathenish looking wood. The tiller was a wry-necked, elbowed bough, thrusting itself through the deck, as if the tree itself was fast rooted in the hold. The binnacle, containing the compass, was defended at the sides by yellow matting. The rigging— shrouds, halyards and all—was of "Kaiar," or cocoa-nut fibres; and here and there the sails were patched with plaited rushes.

But this was not all. Whoso will pry, must needs light upon matters for suspicion. Glancing over the side, in the wake of every scupper- hole, we beheld a faded, crimson stain, which Jarl averred to be blood. Though now he betrayed not the slightest trepidation; for what he saw pertained not to ghosts; and all his fears hitherto had been of the super-natural.

Indeed, plucking up a heart, with the dawn of the day my Viking looked bold as a lion; and soon, with the instinct of an old seaman cast his eyes up aloft.

Directly, he touched my arm,—"Look: what stirs in the main-top?"

Sure enough, something alive was there.

Fingering our arms, we watched it; till as the day came on, a crouching stranger was beheld.

Presenting my piece, I hailed him to descend or be shot. There was silence for a space, when the black barrel of a musket was thrust forth, leveled at my head. Instantly, Jarl's harpoon was presented at a dart;—two to one;—and my hail was repeated. But no reply.

"Who are you?"

"Samoa," at length said a clear, firm voice.

"Come down from the rigging. We are friends."

Another pause; when, rising to his feet, the stranger slowly descended, holding on by one hand to the rigging, for but one did he have; his musket partly slung from his back, and partly griped under the stump of his mutilated arm.

He alighted about six paces from where we stood; and balancing his weapon, eyed us bravely as the Cid.

He was a tall, dark Islander, a very devil to behold, theatrically arrayed in kilt and turban; the kilt of a gay calico print, the turban of a red China silk. His neck was jingling with strings of beads.

"Who else is on board?" I asked; while Jarl, thus far covering the stranger with his weapon, now dropped it to the deck.

"Look there:—Annatoo!" was his reply in broken English, pointing aloft to the fore-top. And lo! a woman, also an Islander; and barring her skirts, dressed very much like Samoa, was beheld descending.

"Any more?"

"No more."

"Who are you then; and what craft is this?"

"Ah, ah—you are no ghost;—but are you my friend?" he cried, advancing nearer as he spoke; while the woman having gained the deck, also approached, eagerly glancing.

We said we were friends; that we meant no harm; but desired to know what craft this was; and what disaster had befallen her; for that something untoward had occurred, we were certain.

Whereto, Samoa made answer, that it was true that something dreadful had happened; and that he would gladly tell us all, and tell us the truth. And about it he went.

Now, this story of his was related in the mixed phraseology of a Polynesian sailor. With a few random reflections, in substance, it will be found in the six following chapters.

Chapter XXII

What Befel The Brigantine At The Pearl Shell Islands

The vessel was the Parki, of Lahina, a village and harbor on the coast of Mowee, one of the Hawaian isles, where she had been miserably cobbled together with planks of native wood, and fragments of a wreck, there drifted ashore.

Her appellative had been bestowed in honor of a high chief, the tallest and goodliest looking gentleman in all the Sandwich Islands. With a mixed European and native crew, about thirty in number (but only four whites in all, captain included), the Parki, some four months previous, had sailed from her port on a voyage southward, in quest of pearls, and pearl oyster shells, sea-slugs, and other matters of that sort.

Samoa, a native of the Navigator Islands, had long followed the sea, and was well versed in the business of oyster diving and its submarine mysteries. The native Lahineese on board were immediately subordinate to him; the captain having bargained with Samoa for their services as divers.

The woman, Annatoo, was a native of a far-off, anonymous island to the westward: whence, when quite young, she had been carried by the commander of a ship, touching there on a passage from Macao to Valparaiso. At Valparaiso her protector put her ashore; most probably, as I afterward had reason to think, for a nuisance.

By chance it came to pass that when Annatoo's first virgin bloom had departed, leaving nothing but a lusty frame and a lustier soul, Samoa, the Navigator, had fallen desperately in love with her. And thinking the lady to his mind, being brave like himself, and doubtless well adapted to the vicissitudes of matrimony at sea, he meditated suicide—I would have said, wedlock—and the twain became one. And some time after, in capacity of wife, Annatoo the dame, accompanied in the brigantine, Samoa her lord. Now, as Antony flew to the refuse embraces of Caesar, so Samoa solaced himself in the arms of this discarded fair one. And the sequel was the same. For not harder the life Cleopatra led my fine frank friend, poor Mark, than Queen Annatoo did lead this captive of her bow and her spear. But all in good time.

They left their port; and crossing the Tropic and the Line, fell in with a cluster of islands, where the shells they sought were found in round numbers. And here—not at all strange to tell besides the natives, they encountered a couple of Cholos, or half-breed Spaniards, from the Main; one half Spanish, the other half quartered between the wild Indian and the devil; a race, that from Baldivia to Panama are notorious for their unscrupulous villainy.

Now, the half-breeds having long since deserted a ship at these islands, had risen to high authority among the natives. This hearing, the Parki's captain was much gratified; he, poor ignorant, never before having fallen in with any of their treacherous race. And, no doubt, he imagined that their influence over the Islanders would tend to his advantage. At all events, he made presents to the Cholos; who, in turn, provided him with additional divers from among the natives. Very kindly, also, they pointed out the best places for seeking the oysters. In a word, they were exceedingly friendly; often coming off to the brigantine, and sociably dining with the captain in the cabin; placing the salt between them and him.

All things went on very pleasantly until, one morning, the half- breeds prevailed upon the captain to go with them, in his whale-boat, to a shoal on the thither side of the island, some distance from the spot where lay the brigantine. They so managed it, moreover, that none but the Lahineese under Samoa, in whom the captain much confided, were left in custody of the Parki; the three white men going along to row; for there happened to be little or no wind for a sail.

Now, the fated brig lay anchored within a deep, smooth, circular lagoon, margined on all sides but one by the most beautiful groves. On that side, was the outlet to the sea; perhaps a cable's length or more from where the brigantine had been moored. An hour or two after the party were gone, and when the boat was completely out of sight, the natives in shoals were perceived coming off from the shore; some in canoes, and some swimming. The former brought bread fruit and bananas, ostentatiously piled up in their proas; the latter dragged after them long strings of cocoanuts; for all of which, on nearing the vessel, they clamorously demanded knives and hatchets in barter.

From their actions, suspecting some treachery, Samoa stood in the gangway, and warned them off; saying that no barter could take place until the captain's return. But presently one of the savages stealthily climbed up from the water, and nimbly springing from the bob-stays to the bow-sprit, darted a javelin full at the foremast, where it vibrated. The signal of blood! With terrible outcries, the rest, pulling forth their weapons, hitherto concealed in the canoes, or under the floating cocoanuts, leaped into the low chains of the brigantine; sprang over the bulwarks; and, with clubs and spears, attacked the aghast crew with the utmost ferocity.

After one faint rally, the Lahineese scrambled for the rigging; but to a man were overtaken and slain.

At the first alarm, Annatoo, however, had escaped to the fore-top- gallant-yard, higher than which she could not climb, and whither the savages durst not venture. For though after their nuts these Polynesians will climb palm trees like squirrels; yet, at the first blush, they decline a ship's mast like Kennebec farmers.

Upon the first token of an onslaught, Samoa, having rushed toward the cabin scuttle for arms, was there fallen upon by two young savages. But after a desperate momentary fray, in which his arm was mangled, he made shift to spring below, instantly securing overhead the slide of the scuttle. In the cabin, while yet the uproar of butchery prevailed, he quietly bound up his arm; then laying on the transom the captain's three loaded muskets, undauntedly awaited an assault.

The object of the natives, it seems, was to wreck the brigantine upon the sharp coral beach of the lagoon. And with this intent, one of their number had plunged into the water, and cut the cable, which was of hemp. But the tide ebbing, cast the Parki's head seaward—toward the outlet; and the savages, perceiving this, clumsily boarded the fore-tack, and hauled aft the sheet; thus setting, after a fashion, the fore-sail, previously loosed to dry.

Meanwhile, a gray-headed old chief stood calmly at the tiller, endeavoring to steer the vessel shoreward. But not managing the helm aright, the brigantine, now gliding apace through the water, only made more way toward the outlet. Seeing which, the ringleaders, six or eight in number, ran to help the old graybeard at the helm. But it was a black hour for them. Of a sudden, while they were handling the tiller, three muskets were rapidly discharged upon them from the cabin skylight. Two of the savages dropped dead. The old steersman, clutching wildly at the helm, fell over it, mortally wounded; and in a wild panic at seeing their leaders thus unaccountably slain, the rest of the natives leaped overboard and made for the shore.

Hearing the slashing, Samoa flew on deck; and beholding the foresail set, and the brigantine heading right out to sea, he cried out to Annatoo, still aloft, to descend to the topsail-yard, and loose the canvas there. His command was obeyed. Annatoo deserved a gold medal for what she did that day. Hastening down the rigging, after loosing the topsail, she strained away at the sheets; in which operation she was assisted by Samoa, who snatched an instant from the helm.

The foresail and fore-topsail were now tolerably well set; and as the craft drew seaward, the breeze freshened. And well that it did; for, recovered from their alarm, the savages were now in hot pursuit; some in canoes, and some swimming as before. But soon the main-topsail was given to the breeze, which still freshening, came from over the quarter. And with this brave show of canvas, the Parki made gallantly for the outlet; and loud shouted Samoa as she shot by the reef, and parted the long swells without. Against these, the savages could not swim. And at that turn of the tide, paddling a canoe therein was almost equally difficult. But the fugitives were not yet safe. In full chase now came in sight the whale-boat manned by the Cholos, and four or five Islanders. Whereat, making no doubt, that all the whites who left the vessel that morning had been massacred through the treachery of the half-breeds; and that the capture of the brigantine had been premeditated; Samoa now saw no other resource than to point his craft dead away from the land.

Now on came the devils buckling to their oars. Meantime Annatoo was still busy aloft, loosing the smaller sails—t'gallants and royals, which she managed partially to set.

The strong breeze from astern now filling the ill-set sails, they bellied, and rocked in the air, like balloons, while, from the novel strain upon it, every spar quivered and sprung. And thus, like a frightened gull fleeing from sea-hawks, the little Parki swooped along, and bravely breasted the brine.

His shattered arm in a hempen sling, Samoa stood at the helm, the muskets reloaded, and planted full before him on the binnacle. For a time, so badly did the brigantine steer, by reason of her ill- adjusted sails, made still more unmanageable by the strength of the breeze,—that it was doubtful, after all, notwithstanding her start, whether the fugitives would not yet fall a prey to their hunters. The craft wildly yawed, and the boat drew nearer and nearer. Maddened by the sight, and perhaps thinking more of revenge for the past, than of security for the future, Samoa, yielding the helm to Annatoo, rested his muskets on the bulwarks, and taking long, sure aim, discharged them, one by one at the advancing foe.

The three reports were answered by loud jeers from the savages, who brandished their spears, and made gestures of derision; while with might and main the Cholos tugged at their oars.

The boat still gaining on the brigantine, the muskets were again reloaded. And as the next shot sped, there was a pause; when, like lightning, the headmost Cholo bounded upwards from his seat, and oar in hand, fell into the sea. A fierce yell; and one of the natives springing into the water, caught the sinking body by its long hair; and the dead and the living were dragged into the boat. Taking heart from this fatal shot, Samoa fired yet again; but not with the like sure result; merely grazing the remaining half-breed, who, crouching behind his comrades, besought them to turn the boat round, and make for the shore. Alarmed at the fate of his brother, and seemingly distrustful of the impartiality of Samoa's fire, the pusillanimous villain refused to expose a limb above the gunwale.

Fain now would the pursuers have made good their escape; but an accident forbade. In the careening of the boat, when the stricken Cholo sprung overboard, two of their oars had slid into the water; and together with that death-griped by the half-breed, were now floating off; occasionally lost to view, as they sunk in the trough of the sea. Two of the Islanders swam to recover them; but frightened by the whirring of a shot over their heads, as they unavoidably struck out towards the Parki, they turned quickly about; just in time to see one of their comrades smite his body with his hand, as he received a bullet from Samoa.

Enough: darting past the ill-fated boat, they swam rapidly for land, followed by the rest; who plunged overboard, leaving in the boat the surviving Cholo—who it seems could not swim—the wounded savage, and the dead man.

"Load away now, and take thy revenge, my fine fellow," said Samoa to himself. But not yet. Seeing all at his mercy, and having none, he quickly laid his fore-topsail to the mast; "hove to" the brigantine; and opened fire anew upon the boat; every swell of the sea heaving it nearer and nearer. Vain all efforts to escape. The wounded man paddled wildly with his hands the dead one rolled from side to side; and the Cholo, seizing the solitary oar, in his frenzied heedlessness, spun the boat round and round; while all the while shot followed shot, Samoa firing as fast as Annatoo could load. At length both Cholo and savage fell dead upon their comrades, canting the boat over sideways, till well nigh awash; in which manner she drifted off.

Chapter XXIII

Sailing From The Island They Pillage The Cabin

There was a small carronade on the forecastle, unshipped from its carriage, and lashed down to ringbolts on the deck. This Samoa now loaded; and with an ax knocking off the round knob upon the breech, rammed it home in the tube. When, running the cannon out at one of the ports, and studying well his aim, he let fly, sunk the boat, and buried his dead.

It was now late in the afternoon; and for the present bent upon avoiding land, and gaining the shoreless sea, never mind where, Samoa again forced round his craft before the wind, leaving the island astern. The decks were still cumbered with the bodies of the Lahineese, which heel to point and crosswise, had, log-like, been piled up on the main-hatch. These, one by one, were committed to the sea; after which, the decks were washed down.

At sunrise next morning, finding themselves out of sight of land, with little or no wind, they stopped their headway, and lashed the tiller alee, the better to enable them to overhaul the brigantine; especially the recesses of the cabin. For there, were stores of goods adapted for barter among the Islanders; also several bags of dollars.

Now, nothing can exceed the cupidity of the Polynesian, when, through partial commerce with the whites, his eyes are opened to his nakedness, and he perceives that in some things they are richer than himself.

The poor skipper's wardrobe was first explored; his chests of clothes being capsized, and their contents strown about the cabin floor.

Then took place the costuming. Samoa and Annatoo trying on coats and pantaloons, shirts and drawers, and admiring themselves in the little mirror panneled in the bulk-head. Then, were broken open boxes and bales; rolls of printed cotton were inspected, and vastly admired; insomuch, that the trumpery found in the captain's chests was disdainfully doffed: and donned were loose folds of calico, more congenial to their tastes.

As case after case was opened and overturned, slippery grew the cabin deck with torrents of glass beads; and heavy the necks of Samoa and Annatoo with goodly bunches thereof.

Among other things, came to light brass jewelry,—Rag Fair gewgaws and baubles a plenty, more admired than all; Annatoo, bedecking herself like, a tragedy queen: one blaze of brass. Much mourned the married dame, that thus arrayed, there was none to admire but Samoa her husband; but he was all the while admiring himself, and not her.

And here must needs be related, what has hitherto remained unsaid. Very often this husband and wife were no Darby and Joan. Their married life was one long campaign, whereof the truces were only by night. They billed and they cooed on their arms, rising fresh in the morning to battle, and often Samoa got more than a hen-pecking. To be short, Annatoo was a Tartar, a regular Calmuc, and Samoa—Heaven help him—her husband.

Yet awhile, joined together by a sense of common danger, and long engrossed in turning over their tinsel acquisitions without present thought of proprietorship, the pair refrained from all squabbles. But soon burst the storm. Having given every bale and every case a good shaking, Annatoo, making an estimate of the whole, very coolly proceeded to set apart for herself whatever she fancied. To this, Samoa objected; to which objection Annatoo objected; and then they went at it.

The lady vowed that the things were no more Samoa's than hers; nay, not so much; and that whatever she wanted, that same would she have. And furthermore, by way of codicil, she declared that she was slave to nobody.

Now, Samoa, sad to tell, stood in no little awe of his bellicose spouse. What, though a hero in other respects; what, though he had slain his savages, and gallantly carried his craft from their clutches:—Like the valiant captains Marlborough and Belisarius, he was a poltroon to his wife. And Annatoo was worse than either Sarah or Antonina.

However, like every thing partaking of the nature of a scratch, most conjugal squabbles are quickly healed; for if they healed not, they would never anew break out: which is the beauty of the thing. So at length they made up but the treaty stipulations of Annatoo told much against the interests of Samoa. Nevertheless, ostensibly, it was agreed upon, that they should strictly go halves; the lady, however, laying special claim to certain valuables, more particularly fancied. But as a set-off to this, she generously renounced all claims upon the spare rigging; all claims upon the fore-mast and mainmast; and all claims upon the captain's arms and ammunition. Of the latter, by the way, Dame Antonina stood in no need. Her voice was a park of artillery; her talons a charge of bayonets.

Chapter XXIV

Dedicated To The College Of Physicians And Surgeons

By this time Samoa's wounded arm was in such a state, that amputation became necessary. Among savages, severe personal injuries are, for the most part, accounted but trifles. When a European would be taking to his couch in despair, the savage would disdain to recline.

More yet. In Polynesia, every man is his own barber and surgeon, cutting off his beard or arm, as occasion demands. No unusual thing, for the warriors of Varvoo to saw off their own limbs, desperately wounded in battle. But owing to the clumsiness of the instrument employed—a flinty, serrated shell—the operation has been known to last several days. Nor will they suffer any friend to help them; maintaining, that a matter so nearly concerning a warrior is far better attended to by himself. Hence it may be said, that they amputate themselves at their leisure, and hang up their tools when tired. But, though thus beholden to no one for aught connected with the practice of surgery, they never cut off their own heads, that ever I heard; a species of amputation to which, metaphorically speaking, many would-be independent sort of people in civilized lands are addicted.

Samoa's operation was very summary. A fire was kindled in the little caboose, or cook-house, and so made as to produce much smoke. He then placed his arm upon one of the windlass bitts (a short upright timber, breast-high), and seizing the blunt cook's ax would have struck the blow; but for some reason distrusting the precision of his aim, Annatoo was assigned to the task. Three strokes, and the limb, from just above the elbow, was no longer Samoa's; and he saw his own bones; which many a centenarian can not say. The very clumsiness of the operation was safety to the subject. The weight and bluntness of the instrument both deadened the pain and lessened the hemorrhage. The wound was then scorched, and held over the smoke of the fire, till all signs of blood vanished. From that day forward it healed, and troubled Samoa but little.

But shall the sequel be told? How that, superstitiously averse to burying in the sea the dead limb of a body yet living; since in that case Samoa held, that he must very soon drown and follow it; and how, that equally dreading to keep the thing near him, he at last hung it aloft from the topmast-stay; where yet it was suspended, bandaged over and over in cerements. The hand that must have locked many others in friendly clasp, or smote a foe, was no food, thought Samoa, for fowls of the air nor fishes of the sea.

Now, which was Samoa? The dead arm swinging high as Haman? Or the living trunk below? Was the arm severed from the body, or the body from the arm? The residual part of Samoa was alive, and therefore we say it was he. But which of the writhing sections of a ten times severed worm, is the worm proper?

For myself, I ever regarded Samoa as but a large fragment of a man, not a man complete. For was he not an entire limb out of pocket? And the action at Teneriffe over, great Nelson himself—physiologically speaking—was but three-quarters of a man. And the smoke of Waterloo blown by, what was Anglesea but the like? After Saratoga, what Arnold? To say nothing of Mutius Scaevola minus a hand, General Knox a thumb, and Hannibal an eye; and that old Roman grenadier, Dentatus, nothing more than a bruised and battered trunk, a knotty sort of hemlock of a warrior, hard to hack and hew into chips, though much marred in symmetry by battle-ax blows. Ah! but these warriors, like anvils, will stand a deal of hard hammering. Especially in the old knight-errant times. For at the battle of Brevieux in Flanders, my glorious old gossiping ancestor, Froissart, informs me, that ten good knights, being suddenly unhorsed, fell stiff and powerless to the plain, fatally encumbered by their armor. Whereupon, the rascally burglarious peasants, their foes, fell to picking their visors; as burglars, locks; or oystermen, oysters; to get at their lives. But all to no purpose. And at last they were fain to ask aid of a blacksmith; and not till then, were the inmates of the armor dispatched. Now it was deemed very hard, that the mysterious state- prisoner of France should be riveted in an iron mask; but these knight-errants did voluntarily prison themselves in their own iron Bastiles; and thus helpless were murdered there-in. Days of chivalry these, when gallant chevaliers died chivalric deaths!

And this was the epic age, over whose departure my late eloquent and prophetic friend and correspondent, Edmund Burke, so movingly mourned. Yes, they were glorious times. But no sensible man, given to quiet domestic delights, would exchange his warm fireside and muffins, for a heroic bivouac, in a wild beechen wood, of a raw gusty morning in Normandy; every knight blowing his steel-gloved fingers, and vainly striving to cook his cold coffee in his helmet.

Chapter XXV

Peril A Peace-Maker

A few days passed: the brigantine drifting hither and thither, and nothing in sight but the sea, when forth again on its stillness rung Annatoo's domestic alarum. The truce was up. Most egregiously had the lady infringed it; appropriating to herself various objects previously disclaimed in favor of Samoa. Besides, forever on the prowl, she was perpetually going up and down; with untiring energy, exploring every nook and cranny; carrying off her spoils and diligently secreting them. Having little idea of feminine adaptations, she pilfered whatever came handy:—iron hooks, dollars, bolts, hatchets, and stopping not at balls of marline and sheets of copper. All this, poor Samoa would have borne with what patience he might, rather than again renew the war, were it not, that the audacious dame charged him with peculations upon her own private stores; though of any such thing he was innocent as the bowsprit.

This insulting impeachment got the better of the poor islander's philosophy. He keenly resented it. And the consequence was, that seeing all domineering useless, Annatoo flew off at a tangent; declaring that, for the future, Samoa might stay by himself; she would have nothing more to do with him. Save when unavoidable in managing the brigantine, she would not even speak to him, that she wouldn't, the monster! She then boldly demanded the forecastle—in the brig's case, by far the pleasantest end of the ship—for her own independent suite of apartments. As for hapless Belisarius, he might do what he pleased in his dark little den of a cabin.

Concerning the division of the spoils, the termagant succeeded in carrying the day; also, to her quarters, bale after bale of goods, together with numerous odds and ends, sundry and divers. Moreover, she laid in a fine stock of edibles, so as, in all respects possible, to live independent of her spouse.

Unlovely Annatoo! Unfortunate Samoa! Thus did the pair make a divorce of it; the lady going upon a separate maintenance,—and Belisarius resuming his bachelor loneliness. In the captain's state room, all cold and comfortless, he slept; his lady whilome retiring to her forecastle boudoir; beguiling the hours in saying her pater-nosters, and tossing over and assorting her ill-gotten trinkets and finery; like Madame De Maintenon dedicating her last days and nights to continence and calicoes.

But think you this was the quiet end of their conjugal quarrels? Ah, no! No end to those feuds, till one or t'other gives up the ghost.

Now, exiled from the nuptial couch, Belisarius bore the hardship without a murmur. And hero that he was, who knows that he felt not like a soldier on a furlough? But as for Antonina, she could neither get along with Belisarius, nor without him. She made advances. But of what sort? Why, breaking into the cabin and purloining sundry goods therefrom; in artful hopes of breeding a final reconciliation out of the temporary outburst that might ensue.

Then followed a sad scene of altercation; interrupted at last by a sudden loud roaring of the sea. Rushing to the deck, they beheld themselves sweeping head-foremost toward a shoal making out from a cluster of low islands, hitherto, by banks of clouds, shrouded from view.

The helm was instantly shifted; and the yards braced about. But for several hours, owing to the freshness of the breeze, the set of the currents, and the irregularity and extent of the shoal, it seemed doubtful whether they would escape a catastrophe. But Samoa's seamanship, united to Annatoo's industry, at last prevailed; and the brigantine was saved.

Of the land where they came so near being wrecked, they knew nothing; and for that reason, they at once steered away. For after the fatal events which had overtaken the Parki at the Pearl Shell islands, so fearful were they of encountering any Islanders, that from the first they had resolved to keep open sea, shunning every appearance of land; relying upon being eventually picked up by some passing sail.

Doubtless this resolution proved their salvation. For to the navigator in these seas, no risk so great, as in approaching the isles; which mostly are so guarded by outpost reefs, and far out from their margins environed by perils, that the green flowery field within, lies like a rose among thorns; and hard to be reached as the heart of proud maiden. Though once attained, all three—red rose, bright shore, and soft heart—are full of love, bloom, and all manner of delights. The Pearl Shell islands excepted.

Besides, in those generally tranquil waters, Samoa's little craft, though hundreds of miles from land, was very readily managed by himself and Annatoo. So small was the Parki, that one hand could brace the main-yard; and a very easy thing it was, even to hoist the small top-sails; for after their first clumsy attempt to perform that operation by hand, they invariably led the halyards to the windlass, and so managed it, with the utmost facility.

Chapter XXVI

Containing A Pennyweight Of Philosophy

Still many days passed and the Parki yet floated. The little flying- fish got used to her familiar, loitering hull; and like swallows building their nests in quiet old trees, they spawned in the great green barnacles that clung to her sides.

The calmer the sea, the more the barnacles grow. In the tropical Pacific, but a few weeks suffice thus to encase your craft in shell armor. Vast bunches adhere to the very cutwater, and if not stricken off, much impede the ship's sailing. And, at intervals, this clearing away of barnacles was one of Annatoo's occupations. For be it known, that, like most termagants, the dame was tidy at times, though capriciously; loving cleanliness by fits and starts. Wherefore, these barnacles oftentimes troubled her; and with a long pole she would go about, brushing them aside. It beguiled the weary hours, if nothing more; and then she would return to her beads and her trinkets; telling them all over again; murmuring forth her devotions, and marking whether Samoa had been pilfering from her store.

Now, the escape from the shoal did much once again to heal the differences of the good lady and her spouse. And keeping house, as they did, all alone by themselves, in that lonely craft, a marvel it is, that they should ever have quarreled. And then to divorce, and yet dwell in the same tenement, was only aggravating the evil. So Belisarius and Antonina again came together. But now, grown wise by experience, they neither loved over-keenly, nor hated; but took things as they were; found themselves joined, without hope of a sundering, and did what they could to make a match of the mate. Annatoo concluded that Samoa was not wholly to be enslaved; and Samoa thought best to wink at Annatoo's foibles, and let her purloin when she pleased.

But as in many cases, all this philosophy about wedlock is not proof against the perpetual contact of the parties concerned; and as it is far better to revive the old days of courtship, when men's mouths are honey-combs: and, to make them still sweeter, the ladies the bees which there store their sweets; when fathomless raptures glimmer far down in the lover's fond eye; and best of all, when visits are alternated by absence: so, like my dignified lord duke and his duchess, Samoa and Annatoo, man and wife, dwelling in the same house, still kept up their separate quarters. Marlborough visiting Sarah; and Sarah, Marlborough, whenever the humor suggested.

Chapter XXVII

In Which The Past History Op The Parki Is Concluded

Still days, days, days sped by; and steering now this way, now that, to avoid the green treacherous shores, which frequently rose into view, the Parki went to and fro in the sea; till at last, it seemed hard to tell, in what watery world she floated. Well knowing the risks they ran, Samoa desponded. But blessed be ignorance. For in the day of his despondency, the lively old lass his wife bade him be of stout heart, cheer up, and steer away manfully for the setting sun; following which, they must inevitably arrive at her own dear native island, where all their cares would be over. So squaring their yards, away they glided; far sloping down the liquid sphere.

Upon the afternoon of the day we caught sight of them in our boat, they had sighted a cluster of low islands, which put them in no small panic, because of their resemblance to those where the massacre had taken place. Whereas, they must have been full five hundred leagues from that fearful vicinity. However, they altered their course to avoid it; and a little before sunset, dropping the islands astern, resumed their previous track. But very soon after, they espied our little sea-goat, bounding over the billows from afar.

This they took for a canoe giving chase to them. It renewed and augmented their alarm.

And when at last they perceived that the strange object was a boat, their fears, instead of being allayed, only so much the more increased. For their wild superstitions led them to conclude, that a white man's craft coming upon them so suddenly, upon the open sea, and by night, could be naught but a phantom. Furthermore, marking two of us in the Chamois, they fancied us the ghosts of the Cholos. A conceit which effectually damped Samoa's courage, like my Viking's, only proof against things tangible. So seeing us bent upon boarding the brigantine; after a hurried over-turning of their chattels, with a view of carrying the most valuable aloft for safe keeping, they secreted what they could; and together made for the fore-top; the man with a musket, the woman with a bag of beads. Their endeavoring to secure these treasures against ghostly appropriation originated in no real fear, that otherwise they would be stolen: it was simply incidental to the vacant panic into which they were thrown. No reproach this, to Belisarius' heart of game; for the most intrepid Feegee warrior, he who has slain his hecatombs, will not go ten yards in the dark alone, for fear of ghosts.

Their purpose was to remain in the top until daylight; by which time, they counted upon the withdrawal of their visitants; who, sure enough, at last sprang on board, thus verifying their worst apprehensions.

They watched us long and earnestly. But curious to tell, in that very strait of theirs, perched together in that airy top, their domestic differences again broke forth; most probably, from their being suddenly forced into such very close contact.

However that might be, taking advantage of our descent into the cabin, Samoa, in desperation fled from his wife, and one-armed as he was, sailor-like, shifted himself over by the fore and aft-stays to the main-top, his musket being slung to his back. And thus divided, though but a few yards intervened, the pair were as much asunder as if at the opposite Poles.

During the live-long night they were both in great perplexity as to the extraordinary goblins on board. Such inquisitive, meddlesome spirits, had never before been encountered. So cool and systematic; sagaciously stopping the vessel's headway the better to rummage;—the very plan they themselves had adopted. But what most surprised them, was our striking a light, a thing of which no true ghost would be guilty. Then, our eating and drinking on the quarter- deck including the deliberate investment of Vienna; and many other actions equally strange, almost led Samoa to fancy that we were no shades, after all, but a couple of men from the moon.

Yet they had dimly caught sight of the frocks and trowsers we wore, similar to those which the captain of the Parki had bestowed upon the two Cholos, and in which those villains had been killed. This, with the presence of the whale boat, united to chase away the conceit of our lunar origin. But these considerations renewed their first superstitious impressions of our being the ghosts of the murderous half-breeds.

Nevertheless, while during the latter part of the night we were reclining beneath him, munching our biscuit, Samoa eyeing us intently, was half a mind to open fire upon us by way of testing our corporeality. But most luckily, he concluded to defer so doing till sunlight; if by that time we should not have evaporated.

For dame Annatoo, almost from our first boarding the brigantine, something in our manner had bred in her a lurking doubt as to the genuineness of our atmospheric organization; and abandoned to her speculations when Samoa fled from her side, her incredulity waxed stronger and stronger. Whence we came she knew not; enough, that we seemed bent upon pillaging her own precious purloinings. Alas! thought she, my buttons, my nails, my tappa, my dollars, my beads, and my boxes!

Wrought up to desperation by these dismal forebodings, she at length shook the ropes leading from her own perch to Samoa's; adopting this method of arousing his attention to the heinousness of what was in all probability going on in the cabin, a prelude most probably to the invasion of her own end of the vessel. Had she dared raise her voice, no doubt she would have suggested the expediency of shooting us so soon as we emerged from the cabin. But failing to shake Samoa into an understanding of her views on the subject, her malice proved futile.

When her worst fears were confirmed, however, and we actually descended into the forecastle; there ensued such a reckless shaking of the ropes, that Samoa was fain to hold on hard, for fear of being tossed out of the rigging. And it was this violent rocking that caused the loud creaking of the yards, so often heard by us while below in Annatoo's apartment.

And the fore-top being just over the open forecastle scuttle, the dame could look right down upon us; hence our proceedings were plainly revealed by the lights that we carried. Upon our breaking open her strong-box, her indignation almost completely overmastered her fears. Unhooking a top-block, down it came into the forecastle, charitably commissioned with the demolition of Jarl's cocoa-nut, then more exposed to the view of an aerial observer than my own. But of it turned out, no harm was done to our porcelain.

At last, morning dawned; when ensued Jarl's discovery as the occupant of the main-top; which event, with what followed, has been duly recounted.

And such, in substance, was the first, second, third and fourth acts of the Parki drama. The fifth and last, including several scenes, now follows.

Chapter XXVIII

Suspicions Laid, And Something About The Calmuc

Though abounding in details full of the savor of reality, Samoa's narrative did not at first appear altogether satisfactory. Not that it was so strange; for stranger recitals I had heard.

But one reason, perhaps, was that I had anticipated a narrative quite different; something agreeing with my previous surmises.

Not a little puzzling, also, was his account of having seen islands the day preceding; though, upon reflection, that might have been the case, and yet, from his immediately altering the Parki's course, the Chamois, unknowingly might have sailed by their vicinity. Still, those islands could form no part of the chain we were seeking. They must have been some region hitherto undiscovered.

But seems it likely, thought I, that one, who, according to his own account, has conducted himself so heroically in rescuing the brigantine, should be the victim of such childish terror at the mere glimpse of a couple of sailors in an open boat, so well supplied, too, with arms, as he was, to resist their capturing his craft, if such proved their intention? On the contrary, would it not have been more natural, in his dreary situation, to have hailed our approach with the utmost delight? But then again, we were taken for phantoms, not flesh and blood. Upon the whole, I regarded the narrator of these things somewhat distrustfully. But he met my gaze like a man. While Annatoo, standing by, looked so expressively the Amazonian character imputed to her, that my doubts began to waver. And recalling all the little incidents of their story, so hard to be conjured up on the spur of a presumed necessity to lie; nay, so hard to be conjured up at all; my suspicions at last gave way. And I could no longer harbor any misgivings.

For, to be downright, what object could Samoa have, in fabricating such a narrative of horrors—those of the massacre, I mean—unless to conceal some tragedy, still more atrocious, in which he himself had been criminally concerned? A supposition, which, for obvious reasons, seemed out of the question. True, instances were known to me of half- civilized beings, like Samoa, forming part of the crews of ships in these seas, rising suddenly upon their white ship-mates, and murdering them, for the sake of wrecking the ship on the shore of some island near by, and plundering her hull, when stranded.

But had this been purposed with regard to the Parki, where the rest of the mutineers? There was no end to my conjectures; the more I indulged in them, the more they multiplied. So, unwilling to torment myself, when nothing could be learned, but what Samoa related, and stuck to like a hero; I gave over conjecturing at all; striving hard to repose full faith in the Islander.

Jarl, however, was skeptical to the last; and never could be brought completely to credit the tale. He stoutly maintained that the hobgoblins must have had something or other to do with the Parki.

My own curiosity satisfied with respect to the brigantine, Samoa himself turned inquisitor. He desired to know who we were; and whence we came in our marvelous boat. But on these heads I thought best to withhold from him the truth; among other things, fancying that if disclosed, it would lessen his deference for us, as men superior to himself. I therefore spoke vaguely of our adventures, and assumed the decided air of a master; which I perceived was not lost upon the rude Islander. As for Jarl, and what he might reveal, I embraced the first opportunity to impress upon him the importance of never divulging our flight from the Arcturion; nor in any way to commit himself on that head: injunctions which he faithfully promised to observe.

If not wholly displeased with the fine form of Samoa, despite his savage lineaments, and mutilated member, I was much less conciliated by the person of Annatoo; who, being sinewy of limb, and neither young, comely, nor amiable, was exceedingly distasteful in my eyes. Besides, she was a tigress. Yet how avoid admiring those Penthesilian qualities which so signally had aided Samoa, in wresting the Parki from its treacherous captors. Nevertheless, it was indispensable that she should at once be brought under prudent subjection; and made to know, once for all, that though conjugally a rebel, she must be nautically submissive. For to keep the sea with a Calmuc on board, seemed next to impossible. In most military marines, they are prohibited by law; no officer may take his Pandora and her bandbox off soundings.

By the way, this self-same appellative, Pandora, has been bestowed upon vessels. There was a British ship by that name, dispatched in quest of the mutineers of the Bounty. But any old tar might have prophesied her fate. Bound home she was wrecked on a reef off New South Wales. Pandora, indeed! A pretty name for a ship: fairly smiting Fate in the face. But in this matter of christening ships of war, Christian nations are but too apt to be dare-devils. Witness the following: British names all—The Conqueror, the Defiance, the Revenge, the Spitfire, the Dreadnaught, the Thunderer, and the Tremendous; not omitting the Etna, which, in the Roads of Corfu, was struck by lightning, coming nigh being consumed by fire from above. But almost potent as Moses' rod, Franklin's proved her salvation.

With the above catalogue, compare we the Frenchman's; quite characteristic of the aspirations of Monsieur:—The Destiny, the Glorious, the Magnanimous, the Magnificent, the Conqueror, the Triumphant, the Indomitable, the Intrepid, the Mont-Blanc. Lastly, the Dons; who have ransacked the theology of the religion of peace for fine names for their fighting ships; stopping not at designating one of their three-deckers, The Most Holy Trinity. But though, at Trafalgar, the Santissima Trinidada thundered like Sinai, her thunders were silenced by the victorious cannonade of the Victory.

And without being blown into splinters by artillery, how many of these Redoubtables and Invincibles have succumbed to the waves, and like braggarts gone down before hurricanes, with their bravadoes broad on their bows.

Much better the American names (barring Scorpions, Hornets, and Wasps;) Ohio, Virginia, Carolina, Vermont. And if ever these Yankees fight great sea engagements—which Heaven forefend!—how glorious, poetically speaking, to range up the whole federated fleet, and pour forth a broadside from Florida to Maine. Ay, ay, very glorious indeed! yet in that proud crowing of cannon, how shall the shade of peace-loving Penn be astounded, to see the mightiest murderer of them all, the great Pennsylvania, a very namesake of his. Truly, the Pennsylvania's guns should be the wooden ones, called by men-of-war's-men, Quakers.

But all this is an episode, made up of digressions. Time to tack ship, and return.

Now, in its proper place, I omitted to mention, that shortly after descending from the rigging, and while Samoa was rehearsing his adventures, dame Annatoo had stolen below into the forecastle, intent upon her chattels. And finding them all in mighty disarray, she returned to the deck prodigiously, excited, and glancing angrily toward Jarl and me, showered a whole torrent of objurgations into both ears of Samoa.

This contempt of my presence surprised me at first; but perhaps women are less apt to be impressed by a pretentious demeanor, than men.

Now, to use a fighting phrase, there is nothing like boarding an enemy in the smoke. And therefore, upon this first token of Annatoo's termagant qualities, I gave her to understand—craving her pardon—that neither the vessel nor aught therein was hers; but that every thing belonged to the owners in Lahina. I added, that at all hazards, a stop must be put to her pilferings. Rude language for feminine ears; but how to be avoided? Here was an infatuated woman, who, according to Samoa's account, had been repeatedly detected in the act of essaying to draw out the screw-bolts which held together the planks. Tell me; was she not worse than the Load-Stone Rock, sailing by which a stout ship fell to pieces?

During this scene, Samoa said little. Perhaps he was secretly pleased that his matrimonial authority was reinforced by myself and my Viking, whose views of the proper position of wives at sea, so fully corresponded with his own; however difficult to practice, those purely theoretical ideas of his had hitherto proved.

Once more turning to Annatoo, now looking any thing but amiable, I observed, that all her clamors would be useless; and that if it came to the worst, the Parki had a hull that would hold her.

In the end she went off in a fit of the sulks; sitting down on the windlass and glaring; her arms akimbo, and swaying from side to side; while ever and anon she gave utterance to a dismal chant. It sounded like an invocation to the Cholos to rise and dispatch us.

Chapter XXIX

What They Lighted Upon In Further Searching The Craft, And The Resolution They Came To

Descending into the cabin with Samoa, I bade him hunt up the brigantine's log, the captain's writing-desk, and nautical instruments; in a word, aught that could throw light on the previous history of the craft, or aid in navigating her homeward.

But nearly every thing of the kind had disappeared: log, quadrant, and ship's papers. Nothing was left but the sextant-case, which Jarl and I had lighted upon in the state-room.

Upon this, vague though they were, my suspicions returned; and I closely questioned the Islander concerning the disappearance of these important articles. In reply, he gave me to understand, that the nautical instruments had been clandestinely carried down into the forecastle by Annatoo; and by that indefatigable and inquisitive dame they had been summarily taken apart for scientific inspection. It was impossible to restore them; for many of the fixtures were lost, including the colored glasses, sights, and little mirrors; and many parts still recoverable, were so battered and broken as to be entirely useless. For several days afterward, we now and then came across bits of the quadrant or sextant; but it was only to mourn over their fate.

However, though sextant and quadrant were both unattainable, I did not so quickly renounce all hope of discovering a chronometer, which, if in good order, though at present not ticking, might still be made in some degree serviceable. But no such instrument was to be seen. No: nor to be heard of; Samoa himself professing utter ignorance.

Annatoo, I threatened and coaxed; describing the chronometer—a live, round creature like a toad, that made a strange noise, which I imitated; but she knew nothing about it. Whether she had lighted upon it unbeknown to Samoa, and dissected it as usual, there was now no way to determine. Indeed, upon this one point, she maintained an air of such inflexible stupidity, that if she were really fibbing, her dead-wall countenance superseded the necessity for verbal deceit.

It may be, however, that in this particular she was wronged; for, as with many small vessels, the Parki might never have possessed the instrument in question. All thought, therefore, of feeling our way, as we should penetrate farther and farther into the watery wilderness, was necessarily abandoned.

The log book had also formed a portion of Annatoo's pilferings. It seems she had taken it into her studio to ponder over. But after amusing herself by again and again counting over the leaves, and wondering how so many distinct surfaces could be compacted together in so small a compass, she had very suddenly conceived an aversion to literature, and dropped the book overboard as worthless. Doubtless, it met the fate of many other ponderous tomes; sinking quickly and profoundly. What Camden or Stowe hereafter will dive for it?

One evening Samoa brought me a quarto half-sheet of yellowish, ribbed paper, much soiled and tarry, which he had discovered in a dark hole of the forecastle. It had plainly formed part of the lost log; but all the writing thereon, at present decipherable, conveyed no information upon the subject then nearest my heart.

But one could not but be struck by a tragical occurrence, which the page very briefly recounted; as well, as by a noteworthy pictorial illustration of the event in the margin of the text. Save the cut, there was no further allusion to the matter than the following:— "This day, being calm, Tooboi, one of the Lahina men, went overboard for a bath, and was eaten up by a shark. Immediately sent forward for his bag."

Now, this last sentence was susceptible of two meanings. It is truth, that immediately upon the decease of a friendless sailor at sea, his shipmates oftentimes seize upon his effects, and divide them; though the dead man's clothes are seldom worn till a subsequent voyage. This proceeding seems heartless. But sailors reason thus: Better we, than the captain. For by law, either scribbled or unscribbled, the effects of a mariner, dying on shipboard, should be held in trust by that officer. But as sailors are mostly foundlings and castaways, and carry all their kith and kin in their arms and their legs, there hardly ever appears any heir-at-law to claim their estate; seldom worth inheriting, like Esterhazy's. Wherefore, the withdrawal of a dead man's "kit" from the forecastle to the cabin, is often held tantamount to its virtual appropriation by the captain. At any rate, in small ships on long voyages, such things have been done.

Thus much being said, then, the sentence above quoted from the Parki's log, may be deemed somewhat ambiguous. At the time it struck me as singular; for the poor diver's grass bag could not have contained much of any thing valuable unless, peradventure, he had concealed therein some Cleopatra pearls, feloniously abstracted from the shells brought up from the sea.

Aside of the paragraph, copied above, was a pen-and-ink sketch of the casualty, most cruelly executed; the poor fellow's legs being represented half way in the process of deglutition; his arms firmly grasping the monster's teeth, as if heroically bent upon making as tough a morsel of himself as possible.

But no doubt the honest captain sketched this cenotaph to the departed in all sincerity of heart; perhaps, during the melancholy leisure which followed the catastrophe. Half obliterated were several stains upon the page; seemingly, lingering traces of a salt tear or two.

From this unwonted embellishment of the text, I was led to infer, that the designer, at one time or other, must have been engaged in the vocation of whaling. For, in India ink, the logs of certain whalemen are decorated by somewhat similar illustrations.

When whales are seen, but not captured, the fact is denoted by an outline figure representing the creature's flukes, the broad, curving lobes of his tail. But in those cases where the monster is both chased and killed, this outline is filled up jet black; one for every whale slain; presenting striking objects in turning over the log; and so facilitating reference. Hence, it is quite imposing to behold, all in a row, three or four, sometime five or six, of these drawings; showing that so many monsters that day jetted their last spout. And the chief mate, whose duty it is to keep the ship's record, generally prides himself upon the beauty, and flushy likeness to life, of his flukes; though, sooth to say, many of these artists are no Landseers.

After vainly searching the cabin for those articles we most needed, we proceeded to explore the hold, into which as yet we had not penetrated. Here, we found a considerable quantity of pearl shells; cocoanuts; an abundance of fresh water in casks; spare sails and rigging; and some fifty barrels or more of salt beef and biscuit. Unromantic as these last mentioned objects were, I lingered over them long, and in a revery. Branded upon each barrel head was the name of a place in America, with which I was very familiar. It is from America chiefly, that ship's stores are originally procured for the few vessels sailing out of the Hawaiian Islands.

Having now acquainted myself with all things respecting the Parki, which could in any way be learned, I repaired to the quarter-deck, and summoning round me Samoa, Annatoo, and Jarl, gravely addressed them.

I said, that nothing would give me greater satisfaction than forthwith to return to the scene of the massacre, and chastise its surviving authors. But as there were only four of us in all; and the place of those islands was wholly unknown to me; and even if known, would be altogether out of our reach, since we possessed no instruments of navigation; it was quite plain that all thought of returning thither was entirely useless. The last mentioned reason, also, prevented our voyaging to the Hawaiian group, where the vessel belonged; though that would have been the most advisable step, resulting, as it would, if successful, in restoring the ill-fated craft to her owners.

But all things considered, it seemed best, I added, cautiously to hold on our way to the westward. It was our easiest course; for we would ever have the wind from astern; and though we could not so much as hope to arrive at any one spot previously designated, there was still a positive certainty, if we floated long enough, of falling in with islands whereat to refresh ourselves; and whence, if we thought fit, we might afterward embark for more agreeable climes. I then reminded them of the fact, that so long as we kept the sea, there was always some prospect of encountering a friendly sail; in which event, our solicitude would be over.

All this I said in the mild, firm tone of a superior; being anxious, at once to assume the unquestioned supremacy. For, otherwise, Jarl and I might better quit the vessel forthwith, than remain on board subject to the outlandish caprices of Annatoo, who through Samoa would then have the sway. But I was sure of my Viking; and if Samoa proved docile, had no fear of his dame.

And therefore during my address, I steadfastly eyed him; thereby learning enough to persuade me, that though he deferred to me at present, he was, notwithstanding, a man who, without precisely meditating mischief, could upon occasion act an ugly part. But of his courage, and savage honor, such as it was, I had little doubt. Then, wild buffalo that he was, tamed down in the yoke matrimonial, I could not but fancy, that if upon no other account, our society must please him, as rendering less afflictive the tyranny of his spouse.

For a hen-pecked husband, by the way, Samoa was a most terrible fellow to behold. And though, after all, I liked him; it was as you fancy a fiery steed with mane disheveled, as young Alexander fancied Bucephalus; which wild horse, when he patted, he preferred holding by the bridle. But more of Samoa anon.

Our course determined, and the command of the vessel tacitly yielded up to myself, the next thing done was to put every thing in order. The tattered sails were replaced by others, dragged up from the sail-room below; in several places, new running-rigging was rove; blocks restrapped; and the slackened stays and shrouds set taught. For all of which, we were mostly indebted to my Viking's unwearied and skillful marling-spike, which he swayed like a scepter.

The little Parki's toilet being thus thoroughly made for the first time since the massacre, we gave her new raiment to the breeze, and daintily squaring her yards, she gracefully glided away; honest old Jarl at the helm, watchfully guiding her path, like some devoted old foster-father.

As I stood by his side like a captain, or walked up and down on the quarter-deck, I felt no little importance upon thus assuming for the first time in my life, the command of a vessel at sea. The novel circumstances of the case only augmented this feeling; the wild and remote seas where we were; the character of my crew, and the consideration, that to all purposes, I was owner, as well as commander of the craft I sailed.

Chapter XXX

Hints For A Full Length Of Samoa

My original intention to touch at the Kingsmill Chain, or the countries adjacent, was greatly strengthened by thus encountering Samoa; and the more I had to do with my Belisarius, the more I was pleased with him. Nor could I avoid congratulating myself, upon having fallen in with a hero, who in various ways, could not fail of proving exceedingly useful.

Like any man of mark, Samoa best speaks for himself; but we may as well convey some idea of his person. Though manly enough, nay, an obelisk in stature, the savage was far from being sentimentally prepossessing. Be not alarmed; but he wore his knife in the lobe of his dexter ear, which, by constant elongation almost drooped upon his shoulder. A mode of sheathing it exceedingly handy, and far less brigandish than the Highlander's dagger concealed in his leggins.

But it was the mother of Samoa, who at a still earlier day had punctured him through and through in still another direction. The middle cartilage of his nose was slightly pendent, peaked, and Gothic, and perforated with a hole; in which, like a Newfoundland dog carrying a cane, Samoa sported a trinket: a well polished nail.

In other respects he was equally a coxcomb. In his style of tattooing, for instance, which seemed rather incomplete; his marks embracing but a vertical half of his person, from crown to sole; the other side being free from the slightest stain. Thus clapped together, as it were, he looked like a union of the unmatched moieties of two distinct beings; and your fancy was lost in conjecturing, where roamed the absent ones. When he turned round upon you suddenly, you thought you saw some one else, not him whom you had been regarding before.

But there was one feature in Samoa beyond the reach of the innovations of art:—his eye; which in civilized man or savage, ever shines in the head, just as it shone at birth. Truly, our eyes are miraculous things. But alas, that in so many instances, these divine organs should be mere lenses inserted into the socket, as glasses in spectacle rims.

But my Islander had a soul in his eye; looking out upon you there, like somebody in him. What an eye, to be sure! At times, brilliantly changeful as opal; in anger, glowing like steel at white heat.

Belisarius, be it remembered, had but very recently lost an arm. But you would have thought he had been born without it; so Lord Nelson- like and cavalierly did he sport the honorable stump.

But no more of Samoa; only this: that his name had been given him by a sea-captain; to whom it had been suggested by the native designation of the islands to which he belonged; the Saviian or Samoan group, otherwise known as the Navigator Islands. The island of Upolua, one of that cluster, claiming the special honor of his birth, as Corsica does Napoleon's, we shall occasionally hereafter speak of Samoa as the Upoluan; by which title he most loved to be called.

It is ever ungallant to pass over a lady. But what shall be said of Annatoo? As I live, I can make no pleasing portrait of the dame; for as in most ugly subjects, flattering would but make the matter worse. Furthermore, unalleviated ugliness should ever go unpainted, as something unnecessary to duplicate. But the only ugliness is that of the heart, seen through the face. And though beauty be obvious, the only loveliness is invisible.

Chapter XXXI

Rovings Alow And Aloft

Every one knows what a fascination there is in wandering up and down in a deserted old tenement in some warm, dreamy country; where the vacant halls seem echoing of silence, and the doors creak open like the footsteps of strangers; and into every window the old garden trees thrust their dark boughs, like the arms of night-burglars; and ever and anon the nails start from the wainscot; while behind it the mice rattle like dice. Up and down in such old specter houses one loves to wander; and so much the more, if the place be haunted by some marvelous story.

And during the drowsy stillness of the tropical sea-day, very much such a fancy had I, for prying about our little brigantine, whose tragic hull was haunted by the memory of the massacre, of which it still bore innumerable traces.

And so far as the indulgence of quiet strolling and reverie was concerned, it was well nigh the same as if I were all by myself. For Samoa, for a time, was rather reserved, being occupied with thoughts of his own. And Annatoo seldom troubled me with her presence. She was taken up with her calicoes and jewelry; which I had permitted her to retain, to keep her in good humor if possible. And as for My royal old Viking, he was one of those individuals who seldom speak, unless personally addressed.

Besides, all that by day was necessary to navigating the Parki was, that—somebody should stand at the helm; the craft being so small, and the grating, whereon the steersman stood, so elevated, that he commanded a view far beyond the bowsprit; thus keeping Argus eyes on the sea, as he steered us along. In all other respects we left the brigantine to the guardianship of the gentle winds.

My own turn at the helm—for though commander, I felt constrained to do duty with the rest—came but once in the twenty-four hours. And not only did Jarl and Samoa, officiate as helmsmen, but also Dame Annatoo, who had become quite expert at the business. Though Jarl always maintained that there was a slight drawback upon her usefulness in this vocation. Too much taken up by her lovely image partially reflected in the glass of the binnacle before her, Annatoo now and then neglected her duty, and led us some devious dances. Nor was she, I ween, the first woman that ever led men into zigzags.

For the reasons above stated, I had many spare hours to myself. At times, I mounted aloft, and lounging in the slings of the topsail yard—one of the many snug nooks in a ship's rigging—I gazed broad off upon the blue boundless sea, and wondered what they were doing in that unknown land, toward which we were fated to be borne. Or feeling less meditative, I roved about hither and thither; slipping over, by the stays, from one mast to the other; climbing up to the truck; or lounging out to the ends of the yards; exploring wherever there was a foothold. It was like climbing about in some mighty old oak, and resting in the crotches.

To a sailor, a ship's ropes are a study. And to me, every rope-yarn of the Parki's was invested with interest. The outlandish fashion of her shrouds, the collars of her stays, the stirrups, seizings, Flemish-horses, gaskets,—all the wilderness of her rigging, bore unequivocal traces of her origin.

But, perhaps, my pleasantest hours were those which I spent, stretched out on a pile of old sails, in the fore-top; lazily dozing to the craft's light roll.

Frequently, I descended to the cabin: for the fiftieth time, exploring the lockers and state-rooms for some new object of curiosity. And often, with a glimmering light, I went into the midnight hold, as into old vaults and catacombs; and creeping between damp ranges of casks, penetrated into its farthest recesses.

Sometimes, in these under-ground burrowings, I lighted upon sundry out-of-the-way hiding places of Annatoo's; where were snugly secreted divers articles, with which she had been smitten. In truth, no small portion of the hull seemed a mine of stolen goods, stolen out of its own bowels. I found a jaunty shore-cap of the captain's, hidden away in the hollow heart of a coil of rigging; covered over in a manner most touchingly natural, with a heap of old ropes; and near by, in a breaker, discovered several entire pieces of calico, heroically tied together with cords almost strong enough to sustain the mainmast.

Near the stray light, which, when the hatch was removed, gleamed down into this part of the hold, was a huge ground-tier butt, headless as Charles the First. And herein was a mat nicely spread for repose; a discovery which accounted for what had often proved an enigma. Not seldom Annatoo had been among the missing; and though, from stem to stern, loudly invoked to come forth and relieve the poignant distress of her anxious friends, the dame remained perdu; silent and invisible as a spirit. But in her own good time, she would mysteriously emerge; or be suddenly espied lounging quietly in the forecastle, as if she had been there from all eternity.

Useless to inquire, "Where hast thou been, sweet Annatoo?" For no sweet rejoinder would she give.

But now the problem was solved. Here, in this silent cask in the hold, Annatoo was wont to coil herself away, like a garter-snake under a stone.

Whether-she-thus stood sentry over her goods secreted round about: whether she here performed penance like a nun in her cell; or was moved to this unaccountable freak by the powers of the air; no one could tell. Can you?

Verily, her ways were as the ways of the inscrutable penguins in building their inscrutable nests, which baffle all science, and make a fool of a sage.

Marvelous Annatoo! who shall expound thee?

Chapter XXXII

Xiphius Platypterus

About this time, the loneliness of our voyage was relieved by an event worth relating.

Ever since leaving the Pearl Shell Islands, the Parki had been followed by shoals of small fish, pleasantly enlivening the sea, and socially swimming by her side. But in vain did Jarl and I search among their ranks for the little, steel-blue Pilot fish, so long outriders of the Chamois. But perhaps since the Chamois was now high and dry on the Parki's deck, our bright little avant-couriers were lurking out of sight, far down in the brine; racing along close to the keel.

But it is not with the Pilot fish that we now have to do.

One morning our attention was attracted to a mighty commotion in the water. The shoals of fish were darting hither and thither, and leaping into the air in the utmost affright. Samoa declared, that their deadly foe the Sword fish must be after them.

And here let me say, that, since of all the bullies, and braggarts, and bravoes, and free-booters, and Hectors, and fish-at-arms, and knight-errants, and moss-troopers, and assassins, and foot-pads, and gallant soldiers, and immortal heroes that swim the seas, the Indian Sword fish is by far the most remarkable, I propose to dedicate this chapter to a special description of the warrior. In doing which, I but follow the example of all chroniclers and historians, my Peloponnesian friend Thucydides and others, who are ever mindful of devoting much space to accounts of eminent destroyers; for the purpose, no doubt, of holding them up as ensamples to the world.

Now, the fish here treated of is a very different creature from the Sword fish frequenting the Northern Atlantic; being much larger every way, and a more dashing varlet to boot. Furthermore, he is denominated the Indian Sword fish, in contradistinction from his namesake above mentioned. But by seamen in the Pacific, he is more commonly known as the Bill fish; while for those who love science and hard names, be it known, that among the erudite naturalists he goeth by the outlandish appellation of "Xiphius Platypterus."

But I waive for my hero all these his cognomens, and substitute a much better one of my own: namely, the Chevalier. And a Chevalier he is, by good right and title. A true gentleman of Black Prince Edward's bright day, when all gentlemen were known by their swords; whereas, in times present, the Sword fish excepted, they are mostly known by their high polished boots and rattans.

A right valiant and jaunty Chevalier is our hero; going about with his long Toledo perpetually drawn. Rely upon it, he will fight you to the hilt, for his bony blade has never a scabbard. He himself sprang from it at birth; yea, at the very moment he leaped into the Battle of Life; as we mortals ourselves spring all naked and scabbardless into the world. Yet, rather, are we scabbards to our souls. And the drawn soul of genius is more glittering than the drawn cimeter of Saladin. But how many let their steel sleep, till it eat up the scabbard itself, and both corrode to rust-chips. Saw you ever the hillocks of old Spanish anchors, and anchor-stocks of ancient galleons, at the bottom of Callao Bay? The world is full of old Tower armories, and dilapidated Venetian arsenals, and rusty old rapiers. But true warriors polish their good blades by the bright beams of the morning; and gird them on to their brave sirloins; and watch for rust spots as for foes; and by many stout thrusts and stoccadoes keep their metal lustrous and keen, as the spears of the Northern Lights charging over Greenland.

Fire from the flint is our Chevalier enraged. He takes umbrage at the cut of some ship's keel crossing his road; and straightway runs a tilt at it; with one mad lounge thrusting his Andrea Ferrara clean through and through; not seldom breaking it short off at the haft, like a bravo leaving his poignard in the vitals of his foe.

In the case of the English ship Foxhound, the blade penetrated through the most solid part of her hull, the bow; going completely through the copper plates and timbers, and showing for several inches in the hold. On the return of the ship to London, it was carefully sawn out; and, imbedded in the original wood, like a fossil, is still preserved. But this was a comparatively harmless onslaught of the valiant Chevalier. With the Rousseau, of Nantucket, it fared worse. She was almost mortally stabbed; her assailant withdrawing his blade. And it was only by keeping the pumps clanging, that she managed to swim into a Tahitian harbor, "heave down," and have her wound dressed by a ship-surgeon with tar and oakum. This ship I met with at sea, shortly after the disaster.

At what armory our Chevalier equips himself after one of his spiteful tilting-matches, it would not be easy to say. But very hard for him, if ever after he goes about in the lists, swordless and disarmed, at the mercy of any caitiff shark he may meet.

Now, seeing that our fellow-voyagers, the little fish along-side, were sorely tormented and thinned out by the incursions of a pertinacious Chevalier, bent upon making a hearty breakfast out of them, I determined to interfere in their behalf, and capture the enemy.

With shark-hook and line I succeeded, and brought my brave gentleman to the deck. He made an emphatic landing; lashing the planks with his sinewy tail; while a yard and a half in advance of his eyes, reached forth his terrible blade.

As victor, I was entitled to the arms of the vanquished; so, quickly dispatching him, and sawing off his Toledo, I bore it away for a trophy. It was three-sided, slightly concave on each, like a bayonet; and some three inches through at the base, it tapered from thence to a point.

And though tempered not in Tagus or Guadalquiver, it yet revealed upon its surface that wavy grain and watery fleckiness peculiar to tried blades of Spain. It was an aromatic sword; like the ancient caliph's, giving out a peculiar musky odor by friction. But far different from steel of Tagus or Damascus, it was inflexible as Crocket's rifle tube; no doubt, as deadly.

Long hung that rapier over the head of my hammock. Was it not storied as the good trenchant blade of brave Bayard, that other chevalier? The knight's may have slain its scores, or fifties; but the weapon I preserved had, doubtless, run through and riddled its thousands.

Chapter XXXIII

Otard

And here is another little incident.

One afternoon while all by myself curiously penetrating into the hold, I most unexpectedly obtained proof, that the ill-fated captain of the Parki had been a man of sound judgment and most excellent taste. In brief, I lighted upon an aromatic cask of prime old Otard.

Now, I mean not to speak lightly of any thing immediately connected with the unfortunate captain. Nor, on the other hand, would I resemble the inconsolable mourner, who among other tokens of affliction, bound in funereal crape his deceased friend's copy of Joe Miller. Is there not a fitness in things?

But let that pass. I found the Otard, and drank there-of; finding it, moreover, most pleasant to the palate, and right cheering to the soul. My next impulse was to share my prize with my shipmates. But here a judicious reflection obtruded. From the sea-monarchs, his ancestors, my Viking had inherited one of their cardinal virtues, a detestation and abhorrence of all vinous and spirituous beverages; insomuch, that he never could see any, but he instantly quaffed it out of sight. To be short, like Alexander the Great and other royalties, Jarl was prone to overmuch bibing. And though at sea more sober than a Fifth Monarchy Elder, it was only because he was then removed from temptation. But having thus divulged my Viking's weak; side, I earnestly entreat, that it may not disparage him in any charitable man's estimation. Only think, how many more there are like him to say nothing further of Alexander the Great—especially among his own class; and consider, I beseech, that the most capacious-souled fellows, for that very reason, are the most apt to be too liberal in their libations; since, being so large-hearted, they hold so much more good cheer than others.

For Samoa, from his utter silence hitherto as to aught inebriating on board, I concluded, that, along with his other secrets, the departed captain had very wisely kept his Otard to himself.

Nor did I doubt, but that the Upoluan, like all Polynesians, much loved getting high of head; and in that state, would be more intractable than a Black Forest boar. And concerning Annatoo, I shuddered to think, how that Otard might inflame her into a Fury more fierce than the foremost of those that pursued Orestes.

In good time, then, bethinking me of the peril of publishing my discovery;—bethinking me of the quiet, lazy, ever-present perils of the voyage, of all circumstances, the very worst under which to introduce an intoxicating beverage to my companions, I resolved to withhold it from them altogether.

So impressed was I with all this, that for a moment, I was almost tempted to roll over the cask on its bilge, remove the stopper, and suffer its contents to mix with the foul water at the bottom of the hold.

But no, no: What: dilute the brine with the double distilled soul of the precious grape? Haft himself would have haunted me!

Then again, it might come into play medicinally; and Paracelsus himself stands sponsor for every cup drunk for the good of the abdomen. So at last, I determined to let it remain where it was: visiting it occasionally, by myself, for inspection.

But by way of advice to all ship-masters, let me say, that if your Otard magazine be exposed to view— then, in the evil hour of wreck, stave in your spirit-casks, ere rigging the life-boat.

Chapter XXXIV

How They Steered On Their Way

When we quitted the Chamois for the brigantine, we must have been at least two hundred leagues to the westward of the spot, where we had abandoned the Arcturion. Though how far we might then have been, North or South of the Equator, I could not with any certainty divine.

But that we were not removed any considerable distance from the Line, seemed obvious. For in the starriest night no sign of the extreme Polar constellations was visible; though often we scanned the northern and southern horizon in search of them. So far as regards the aspect of the skies near the ocean's rim, the difference of several degrees in one's latitude at sea, is readily perceived by a person long accustomed to surveying the heavens.

If correct in my supposition, concerning our longitude at the time here alluded to, and allowing for what little progress we had been making in the Parki, there now remained some one hundred leagues to sail, ere the country we sought would be found. But for obvious reasons, how long precisely we might continue to float out of sight of land, it was impossible to say. Calms, light breezes, and currents made every thing uncertain. Nor had we any method of estimating our due westward progress, except by what is called Dead Reckoning,—the computation of the knots run hourly; allowances' being made for the supposed deviations from our course, by reason of the ocean streams; which at times in this quarter of the Pacific run with very great velocity.

Now, in many respects we could not but feel safer aboard the Parki than in the Chamois. The sense of danger is less vivid, the greater the number of lives involved. He who is ready to despair in solitary peril, plucks up a heart in the presence of another. In a plurality of comrades is much countenance and consolation.

Still, in the brigantine there were many sources of uneasiness and anxiety unknown to me in the whale-boat. True, we had now between us and the deep, five hundred good planks to one lath in our buoyant little chip. But the Parki required more care and attention; especially by night, when a vigilant look-out was indispensable. With impunity, in our whale-boat, we might have run close to shoal or reef; whereas, similar carelessness or temerity now, might prove fatal to all concerned.

Though in the joyous sunlight, sailing through the sparkling sea, I was little troubled with serious misgivings; in the hours of darkness it was quite another thing. And the apprehensions, nay terrors I felt, were much augmented by the remissness of both Jarl and Samoa, in keeping their night-watches. Several times I was seized with a deadly panic, and earnestly scanned the murky horizon, when rising from slumber I found the steersman, in whose hands for the time being were life and death, sleeping upright against the tiller, as much of a fixture there, as the open-mouthed dragon rudely carved on our prow.

Were it not, that on board of other vessels, I myself had many a time dozed at the helm, spite of all struggles, I would have been almost at a loss to account for this heedlessness in my comrades. But it seemed as if the mere sense of our situation, should have been sufficient to prevent the like conduct in all on board our craft.

Samoa's aspect, sleeping at the tiller, was almost appalling. His large opal eyes were half open; and turned toward the light of the binnacle, gleamed between the lids like bars of flame. And added to all, was his giant stature and savage lineaments.

It was in vain, that I remonstrated, begged, or threatened: the occasional drowsiness of my fellow-voyagers proved incurable. To no purpose, I reminded my Viking that sleeping in the night-watch in a craft like ours, was far different from similar heedlessness on board the Arcturion. For there, our place upon the ocean was always known, and our distance from land; so that when by night the seamen were permitted to be drowsy, it was mostly, because the captain well knew that strict watchfulness could be dispensed with.

Though in all else, the Skyeman proved a most faithful ally, in this one thing he was either perversely obtuse, or infatuated. Or, perhaps, finding himself once more in a double-decked craft, which rocked him as of yore, he was lulled into a deceitful security.

For Samoa, his drowsiness was the drowsiness of one bent on sleep, come dreams or death. He seemed insensible to the peril we ran. Often I sent the sleepy savage below, sad, steered myself till morning. At last I made a point of slumbering much by day, the better to stand watch by night; though I made Samoa and Jarl regularly go through with their allotted four hours each.

It has been mentioned, that Annatoo took her turn at the helm; but it was only by day. And in justice to the lady, I must affirm, that upon the whole she acquitted herself well. For notwithstanding the syren face in the binnacle, which dimly allured her glances, Annatoo after all was tolerably heedful of her steering. Indeed she took much pride therein; always ready for her turn; with marvelous exactitude calculating the approaching hour, as it came on in regular rotation. Her time-piece was ours, the sun. By night it must have been her guardian star; for frequently she gazed up at a particular section of the heavens, like one regarding the dial in a tower.

By some odd reasoning or other, she had cajoled herself into the notion, that whoever steered the brigantine, for that period was captain. Wherefore, she gave herself mighty airs at the tiller; with extravagant gestures issuing unintelligible orders about trimming the sails, or pitching overboard something to see how fast we were going. All this much diverted my Viking, who several times was delivered of a laugh; a loud and healthy one to boot: a phenomenon worthy the chronicling.

And thus much for Annatoo, preliminary to what is further to be said. Seeing the drowsiness of Jarl and Samoa, which so often kept me from my hammock at night, forcing me to repose by day, when I far preferred being broad awake, I decided to let Annatoo take her turn at the night watches; which several times she had solicited me to do; railing at the sleepiness of her spouse; though abstaining from all reflections upon Jarl, toward whom she had of late grown exceedingly friendly.

Now the Calmuc stood her first night watch to admiration; if any thing, was altogether too wakeful. The mere steering of the craft employed not sufficiently her active mind. Ever and anon she must needs rush from the tiller to take a parenthetical pull at the fore- brace, the end of which led down to the bulwarks near by; then refreshing herself with a draught or two of water and a biscuit, she would continue to steer away, full of the importance of her office. At any unusual flapping of the sails, a violent stamping on deck announced the fact to the startled crew. Finding her thus indefatigable, I readily induced her to stand two watches to Jarl's and Samoa's one; and when she was at the helm, I permitted myself to doze on a pile of old sails, spread every evening on the quarter-deck.

It was the Skyeman, who often admonished me to "heave the ship to" every night, thus stopping her headway till morning; a plan which, under other circumstances, might have perhaps warranted the slumbers of all. But as it was, such a course would have been highly imprudent. For while making no onward progress through the water, the rapid currents we encountered would continually be drifting us eastward; since, contrary to our previous experience, they seemed latterly to have reversed their flow, a phenomenon by no means unusual in the vicinity of the Line in the Pacific. And this it was that so prolonged our passage to the westward. Even in a moderate breeze, I sometimes fancied, that the impulse of the wind little more than counteracted the glide of the currents; so that with much show of sailing, we were in reality almost a fixture on the sea.

The equatorial currents of the South Seas may be regarded as among the most mysterious of the mysteries of the deep. Whence they come, whither go, who knows? Tell us, what hidden law regulates their flow. Regardless of the theory which ascribes to them a nearly uniform course from east to west, induced by the eastwardly winds of the Line, and the collateral action of the Polar streams; these currents are forever shifting. Nor can the period of their revolutions be at all relied upon or predicted.

But however difficult it may be to assign a specific cause for the ocean streams, in any part of the world, one of the wholesome effects thereby produced would seem obvious enough. And though the circumstance here alluded to is perhaps known to every body, it may be questioned, whether it is generally invested with the importance it deserves. Reference is here made to the constant commingling and purification of the sea-water by reason of the currents.

For, that the ocean, according to the popular theory, possesses a special purifying agent in its salts, is somewhat to be doubted. Nor can it be explicitly denied, that those very salts might corrupt it, were it not for the brisk circulation of its particles consequent upon the flow of the streams. It is well known to seamen, that a bucket of sea-water, left standing in a tropical climate, very soon becomes highly offensive; which is not the case with rainwater.

But I build no theories. And by way of obstructing the one, which might possibly be evolved from the statement above, let me add, that the offensiveness of sea-water left standing, may arise in no small degree from the presence of decomposed animal matter.

Chapter XXXV

Ah, Annatoo!

In order to a complete revelation, I must needs once again discourse of Annatoo and her pilferings; and to what those pilferings led. In the simplicity of my soul, I fancied that the dame, so much flattered as she needs must have been, by the confidence I began to repose in her, would now mend her ways, and abstain from her larcenies. But not so. She was possessed by some scores of devils, perpetually her to mischief on their own separate behoof, and not less for many of her pranks were of no earthly advantage to her, present or prospective.

One day the log-reel was missing. Summon Annatoo. She came; but knew nothing about it. Jarl spent a whole morning in contriving a substitute; and a few days after, pop, we came upon the lost: article hidden away in the main-top.

Another time, discovering the little vessel to "gripe" hard in steering, as if some one under water were jerking her backward, we instituted a diligent examination, to see what was the matter. When lo; what should we find but a rope, cunningly attached to one of the chain-plates under the starboard main-channel. It towed heavily in the water. Upon dragging it up—much as you would the cord of a ponderous bucket far down in a well—a stout wooden box was discovered at the end; which opened, disclosed sundry knives, hatchets, and ax-heads.

Called to the stand, the Upoluan deposed, that thrice he had rescued that identical box from Annatoo's all-appropriating clutches.

Now, here were four human beings shut up in this little oaken craft, and, for the time being, their interests the same. What sane mortal, then, would forever be committing thefts, without rhyme or reason. It was like stealing silver from one pocket and decanting it into the other. And what might it not lead to in the end?

Why, ere long, in good sooth, it led to the abstraction of the compass from the binnacle; so that we were fain to substitute for it, the one brought along in the Chamois.

It was Jarl that first published this last and alarming theft. Annatoo being at the helm at dawn, he had gone to relieve her; and looking to see how we headed, was horror-struck at the emptiness of the binnacle.

I started to my feet; sought out the woman, and ferociously demanded the compass. But her face was a blank; every word a denial.

Further lenity was madness. I summoned Samoa, told him what had happened, and affirmed that there was no safety for us except in the nightly incarceration of his spouse. To this he privily assented; and that very evening, when Annatoo descended into the forecastle, we barred over her the scuttle-slide. Long she clamored, but unavailingly. And every night this was repeated; the dame saying her vespers most energetically.

It has somewhere been hinted, that Annatoo occasionally cast sheep's eyes at Jarl. So I was not a little surprised when her manner toward him decidedly changed. Pulling at the ropes with us, she would give him sly pinches, and then look another way, innocent as a lamb. Then again, she would refuse to handle the same piece of rigging with him; with wry faces, rinsed out the wooden can at the water cask, if it so chanced that my Viking had previously been drinking therefrom. At other times, when the honest Skyeman came up from below, she would set up a shout of derision, and loll out her tongue; accompanying all this by certain indecorous and exceedingly unladylike gestures, significant of the profound contempt in which she held him.

Yet, never did Jarl heed her ill-breeding; but patiently overlooked and forgave it. Inquiring the reason of the dame's singular conduct, I learned, that with eye averted, she had very lately crept close to my Viking, and met with no tender reception.

Doubtless, Jarl, who was much of a philosopher, innocently imagined that ere long the lady would forgive and forget him. But what knows a philosopher about women?

Ere long, so outrageous became Annatoo's detestation of him, that the honest old tar could stand it no longer, and like most good-natured men when once fairly roused, he was swept through and through with a terrible typhoon of passion. He proposed, that forthwith the woman should be sacked and committed to the deep; he could stand it no longer.

Murder is catching. At first I almost jumped at the proposition; but as quickly rejected it. Ah! Annatoo: Woman unendurable: deliver me, ye gods, from being shut up in a ship with such a hornet again.

But are we yet through with her? Not yet. Hitherto she had continued to perform the duties of the office assigned her since the commencement of the voyage: namely, those of the culinary department. From this she was now deposed. Her skewer was broken. My Viking solemnly averring, that he would eat nothing more of her concocting, for fear of being poisoned. For myself, I almost believed, that there was malice enough in the minx to give us our henbane broth.

But what said Samoa to all this? Passing over the matter of the cookery, will it be credited, that living right among us as he did, he was yet blind to the premeditated though unachieved peccadilloes of his spouse? Yet so it was. And thus blind was Belisarius himself, concerning the intrigues of Antonina.

Witness that noble dame's affair with the youth Theodosius; when her deluded lord charged upon the scandal-mongers with the very horns she had bestowed upon him.

Upon one occasion, seized with a sudden desire to palliate Annatoo's thievings, Samoa proudly intimated, that the lady was the most virtuous of her sex.

But alas, poor Annatoo, why say more? And bethinking me of the hard fate that so soon overtook thee, I almost repent what has already and too faithfully been portrayed.

Chapter XXXVI

The Parki Gives Up The Ghost

A long calm in the boat, and now, God help us, another in the brigantine. It was airless and profound.

In that hot calm, we lay fixed and frozen in like Parry at the Pole. The sun played upon the glassy sea like the sun upon the glaciers.

At the end of two days we lifted up our eyes and beheld a low, creeping, hungry cloud expanding like an army, wing and wing, along the eastern horizon. Instantly Jarl bode me take heed.

Here be it said, that though for weeks and weeks reign over the equatorial latitudes of the Pacific, the mildest and sunniest of days; that nevertheless, when storms do come, they come in their strength: spending in a few, brief blasts their concentrated rage. They come like the Mamelukes: they charge, and away.

It wanted full an hour to sunset; but the sun was well nigh obscured. It seemed toiling among bleak Scythian steeps in the hazy background. Above the storm-cloud flitted ominous patches of scud, rapidly advancing and receding: Attila's skirmishers, thrown forward in the van of his Huns. Beneath, a fitful shadow slid along the surface. As we gazed, the cloud came nearer; accelerating its approach.

With all haste we proceeded to furl the sails, which, owing to the calm, had been hanging loose in the brails. And by help of a spare boom, used on the forecastle-deck sit a sweep or great oar, we endeavored to cast the brigantine's head toward the foe.

The storm seemed about to overtake us; but we felt no breeze. The noiseless cloud stole on; its advancing shadow lowering over a distinct and prominent milk-white crest upon the surface of the ocean. But now this line of surging foam came rolling down upon us like a white charge of cavalry: mad Hotspur and plumed Murat at its head; pouring right forward in a continuous frothy cascade, which curled over, and fell upon the glassy sea before it.

Still, no breath of air. But of a sudden, like a blow from a man's hand, and before our canvas could be secured, the stunned craft, giving one lurch to port, was stricken down on her beam-ends; the roaring tide dashed high up against her windward side, and drops of brine fell upon the deck, heavy as drops of gore.

It was all a din and a mist; a crashing of spars and of ropes; a horrible blending of sights and of sounds; as for an instant we seemed in the hot heart of the gale; our cordage, like harp-strings, shrieking above the fury of the blast. The masts rose, and swayed, and dipped their trucks in the sea. And like unto some stricken buffalo brought low to the plain, the brigantine's black hull, shaggy with sea-weed, lay panting on its flank in the foam.

Frantically we clung to the uppermost bulwarks. And now, loud above the roar of the sea, was suddenly heard a sharp, splintering sound, as of a Norway woodman felling a pine in the forest. It was brave Jarl, who foremost of all had snatched from its rack against the mainmast, the ax, always there kept.

"Cut the lanyards to windward!" he cried; and again buried his ax into the mast. He was quickly obeyed. And upon cutting the third lanyard of the five, he shouted for us to pause. Dropping his ax, he climbed up to windward. As he clutched the rail, the wounded mast snapped in twain with a report like a cannon. A slight smoke was perceptible where it broke. The remaining lanyards parted. From the violent strain upon them, the two shrouds flew madly into the air, and one of the great blocks at their ends, striking Annatoo upon the forehead, she let go her hold upon a stanchion, and sliding across the aslant deck, was swallowed up in the whirlpool under our lea. Samoa shrieked. But there was no time to mourn; no hand could reach to save.

By the connecting stays, the mainmast carried over with it the foremast; when we instantly righted, and for the time were saved; my own royal Viking our saviour.

The first fury of the gale was gone. But far to leeward was seen the even, white line of its onset, pawing the ocean into foam. All round us, the sea boiled like ten thousand caldrons; and through eddy, wave, and surge, our almost water-logged craft waded heavily; every dead clash ringing hollow against her hull, like blows upon a coffin.

We floated a wreck. With every pitch we lifted our dangling jib-boom into the air; and beating against the side, were the shattered fragments of the masts. From these we made all haste to be free, by cutting the rigging that held them.

Soon, the worst of the gale was blown over. But the sea ran high. Yet the rack and scud of the tempest, its mad, tearing foam, was subdued into immense, long-extended, and long-rolling billows; the white cream on their crests like snow on the Andes. Ever and anon we hung poised on their brows; when the furrowed ocean all round looked like a panorama from Chimborazo.

A few hours more, and the surges went down. There was a moderate sea, a steady breeze, and a clear, starry sky. Such was the storm that came after our calm.

Chapter XXXVII

Once More They Take To The Chamois

Try the pumps. We dropped the sinker, and found the Parki bleeding at every pore. Up from her well, the water, spring-like, came bubbling, pure and limpid as the water of Saratoga. Her time had come. But by keeping two hands at the pumps, we had no doubt she would float till daylight; previous to which we liked not to abandon her.

The interval was employed in clanging at the pump-breaks, and preparing the Chamois for our reception. So soon as the sea permitted, we lowered it over the side; and letting it float under the stern, stowed it with water and provisions, together with various other things, including muskets and cutlasses.

Shortly after daylight, a violent jostling and thumping under foot showed that the water, gaining rapidly in the, hold, spite of all pumping, had floated the lighter casks up-ward to the deck, against which they were striking.

Now, owing to the number of empty butts in the hold, there would have been, perhaps, but small danger of the vessel's sinking outright—all awash as her decks would soon be—were it not, that many of her timbers were of a native wood, which, like the Teak of India, is specifically heavier than water. This, with the pearl shells on board, counteracted the buoyancy of the casks.

At last, the sun—long waited for—arose; the Parki meantime sinking lower and lower.

All things being in readiness, we proceeded to embark from the wreck, as from a wharf.

But not without some show of love for our poor brigantine.

To a seaman, a ship is no piece of mechanism merely; but a creature of thoughts and fancies, instinct with life. Standing at her vibrating helm, you feel her beating pulse. I have loved ships, as I have loved men.

To abandon the poor Parki was like leaving to its fate something that could feel. It was meet that she should die decently and bravely.

All this thought the Skyeman. Samoa and I were in the boat, calling upon him to enter quickly, lest the vessel should sink, and carry us down in the eddies; for already she had gone round twice. But cutting adrift the last fragments of her broken shrouds, and putting her decks in order, Jarl buried his ax in the splintered stump of the mainmast, and not till then did he join us.

We slowly cheered, and sailed away.

Not ten minutes after, the hull rolled convulsively in the sea; went round once more; lifted its sharp prow as a man with arms pointed for a dive; gave a long seething plunge; and went down.

Many of her old planks were twice wrecked; once strown upon ocean's beach; now dropped into its lowermost vaults, with the bones of drowned ships and drowned men.

Once more afloat in our shell! But not with the intrepid spirit that shoved off with us from the deck of the Arcturion. A bold deed done from impulse, for the time carries few or no misgivings along with it. But forced upon you, its terrors stare you in the face. So now. I had pushed from the Arcturion with a stout heart; but quitting the sinking Parki, my heart sunk with her.

With a fair wind, we held on our way westward, hoping to see land before many days.

Chapter XXXVIII

The Sea On Fire

The night following our abandonment of the Parki, was made memorable by a remarkable spectacle.

Slumbering in the bottom of the boat, Jarl and I were suddenly awakened by Samoa. Starting, we beheld the ocean of a pallid white color, corruscating all over with tiny golden sparkles. But the pervading hue of the water cast a cadaverous gleam upon the boat, so that we looked to each other like ghosts. For many rods astern our wake was revealed in a line of rushing illuminated foam; while here and there beneath the surface, the tracks of sharks were denoted by vivid, greenish trails, crossing and recrossing each other in every direction. Farther away, and distributed in clusters, floated on the sea, like constellations in the heavens, innumerable Medusae, a species of small, round, refulgent fish, only to be met with in the South Seas and the Indian Ocean.

Suddenly, as we gazed, there shot high into the air a bushy jet of flashes, accompanied by the unmistakable deep breathing sound of a sperm whale. Soon, the sea all round us spouted in fountains of fire; and vast forms, emitting a glare from their flanks, and ever and anon raising their heads above water, and shaking off the sparkles, showed where an immense shoal of Cachalots had risen from below to sport in these phosphorescent billows.

The vapor jetted forth was far more radiant than any portion of the sea; ascribable perhaps to the originally luminous fluid contracting still more brilliancy from its passage through the spouting canal of the whales.

We were in great fear, lest without any vicious intention the Leviathans might destroy us, by coming into close contact with our boat. We would have shunned them; but they were all round and round us. Nevertheless we were safe; for as we parted the pallid brine, the peculiar irradiation which shot from about our keel seemed to deter them. Apparently discovering us of a sudden, many of them plunged headlong down into the water, tossing their fiery tails high into the air, and leaving the sea still more sparkling from the violent surging of their descent.

Their general course seemed the same as our own; to the westward. To remove from them, we at last out oars, and pulled toward the north. So doing, we were steadily pursued by a solitary whale, that must have taken our Chamois for a kindred fish. Spite of all our efforts, he drew nearer and nearer; at length rubbing his fiery flank against the Chamois' gunwale, here and there leaving long strips of the glossy transparent substance which thin as gossamer invests the body of the Cachalot.

In terror at a sight so new, Samoa shrank. But Jarl and I, more used to the intimate companionship of the whales, pushed the boat away from it with our oars: a thing often done in the fishery.

The close vicinity of the whale revived in the so long astute Skyeman all the enthusiasm of his daring vocation. However quiet by nature, a thorough-bred whaleman betrays no little excitement in sight of his game. And it required some persuasion to prevent Jarl from darting his harpoon: insanity under present circumstances; and of course without object. But "Oh! for a dart," cried my Viking. And "Where's now our old ship?" he added reminiscently.

But to my great joy the monster at last departed; rejoining the shoal, whose lofty spoutings of flame were still visible upon the distant line of the horizon; showing there, like the fitful starts of the Aurora Borealis.

The sea retained its luminosity for about three hours; at the expiration of half that period beginning to fade; and excepting occasional faint illuminations consequent upon the rapid darting of fish under water, the phenomenon at last wholly disappeared.

Heretofore, I had beheld several exhibitions of marine phosphorescence, both in the Atlantic and Pacific. But nothing in comparison with what was seen that night. In the Atlantic, there is very seldom any portion of the ocean luminous, except the crests of the waves; and these mostly appear so during wet, murky weather. Whereas, in the Pacific, all instances of the sort, previously corning under my notice, had been marked by patches of greenish light, unattended with any pallidness of sea. Save twice on the coast of Peru, where I was summoned from my hammock to the alarming midnight cry of "All hands ahoy! tack ship!" And rushing on deck, beheld the sea white as a shroud; for which reason it was feared we were on soundings.

Now, sailors love marvels, and love to repeat them. And from many an old shipmate I have heard various sage opinings, concerning the phenomenon in question. Dismissing, as destitute of sound philosophic probability, the extravagant notion of one of my nautical friends—no less a philosopher than my Viking himself—namely: that the phosphoresence of the sea is caused by a commotion among the mermaids, whose golden locks, all torn and disheveled, do irradiate the waters at such times; I proceed to record more reliable theories.

Faraday might, perhaps, impute the phenomenon to a peculiarly electrical condition of the atmosphere; and to that solely. But herein, my scientific friend would be stoutly contradicted by many intelligent seamen, who, in part, impute it to the presence of large quantities of putrescent animal matter; with which the sea is well known to abound.

And it would seem not unreasonable to suppose, that it is by this means that the fluid itself becomes charged with the luminous principle. Draw a bucket of water from the phosphorescent ocean, and it still retains traces of fire; but, standing awhile, this soon subsides. Now pour it along the deck, and it is a stream of flame; caused by its renewed agitation. Empty the bucket, and for a space sparkles cling to it tenaciously; and every stave seems ignited.

But after all, this seeming ignition of the sea can not be wholly produced by dead matter therein. There are many living fish, phosphorescent; and, under certain conditions, by a rapid throwing off of luminous particles must largely contribute to the result. Not to particularize this circumstance as true of divers species of sharks, cuttle-fish, and many others of the larger varieties of the finny tribes; the myriads of microscopic mollusca, well known to swarm off soundings, might alone be deemed almost sufficient to kindle a fire in the brine.

But these are only surmises; likely, but uncertain.

After science comes sentiment.

A French naturalist maintains, that the nocturnal radiance of the fire-fly is purposely intended as an attraction to the opposite sex; that the artful insect illuminates its body for a beacon to love. Thus: perched upon the edge of a leaf, and waiting the approach of her Leander, who comes buffeting with his wings the aroma of the flowers, some insect Hero may show a torch to her gossamer gallant.

But alas, thrice alas, for the poor little fire-fish of the sea, whose radiance but reveals them to their foes, and lights the way to their destruction.

Chapter XXXIX

They Fall In With Strangers

After quitting the Parki, we had much calm weather, varied by light breezes. And sailing smoothly over a sea, so recently one sheet of foam, I could not avoid bethinking me, how fortunate it was, that the gale had overtaken us in the brigantine, and not in the Chamois. For deservedly high as the whale-shallop ranks as a sea boat; still, in a severe storm, the larger your craft the greater your sense of security. Wherefore, the thousand reckless souls tenanting a line-of- battle ship scoff at the most awful hurricanes; though, in reality, they may be less safe in their wooden-walled Troy, than those who contend with the gale in a clipper.

But not only did I congratulate myself upon salvation from the past, but upon the prospect for the future. For storms happening so seldom in these seas, one just blown over is almost a sure guarantee of very many weeks' calm weather to come.

Now sun followed sun; and no land. And at length it almost seemed as if we must have sailed past the remotest presumable westerly limit of the chain of islands we sought; a lurking suspicion which I sedulously kept to myself However, I could not but nourish a latent faith that all would yet be well.

On the ninth day my forebodings were over. In the gray of the dawn, perched upon the peak of our sail, a noddy was seen fast asleep. This freak was true to the nature of that curious fowl, whose name is significant of its drowsiness. Its plumage was snow-white, its bill and legs blood-red; the latter looking like little pantalettes. In a sly attempt at catching the bird, Samoa captured three tail- feathers; the alarmed creature flying away with a scream, and leaving its quills in his hand.

Sailing on, we gradually broke in upon immense low-sailing flights of other aquatic fowls, mostly of those species which are seldom found far from land: terns, frigate-birds, mollymeaux, reef-pigeons, boobies, gulls, and the like. They darkened the air; their wings making overhead an incessant rustling like the simultaneous turning over of ten thousand leaves. The smaller sort skimmed the sea like pebbles sent skipping from the shore. Over these, flew myriads of birds of broader wing. While high above all, soared in air the daring "Diver," or sea-kite, the power of whose vision is truly wonderful. It perceives the little flying-fish in the water, at a height which can not be less than four hundred feet. Spirally wheeling and screaming as it goes, the sea-kite, bill foremost, darts downward, swoops into the water, and for a moment altogether disappearing, emerges at last; its prey firmly trussed in its claws. But bearing it aloft, the bold bandit is quickly assailed by other birds of prey, that strive to wrest from him his booty. And snatched from his talons, you see the fish falling through the air, till again caught up in the very act of descent, by the fleetest of its pursuers.

Leaving these sights astern, we presently picked up the slimy husk of a cocoanut, all over green barnacles. And shortly after, passed two or three limbs of trees, and the solitary trunk of a palm; which, upon sailing nearer, seemed but very recently started on its endless voyage. As noon came on; the dark purple land-haze, which had been dimly descried resting upon the western horizon, was very nearly obscured. Nevertheless, behind that dim drapery we doubted not bright boughs were waving.

We were now in high spirits. Samoa between times humming to himself some heathenish ditty, and Jarl ten times more intent on his silence than ever; yet his eye full of expectation and gazing broad off from our bow. Of a sudden, shading his face with his hand, he gazed fixedly for an instant, and then springing to his feet, uttered the long-drawn sound—"Sail ho!"

Just tipping the furthest edge of the sky was a little speck, dancing into view every time we rose upon the swells. It looked like one of many birds; for half intercepting our view, fell showers of plumage: a flight of milk-white noddies flying downward to the sea.

But soon the birds are seen no more. Yet there remains the speck; plainly a sail; but too small for a ship. Was it a boat after a whale? The vessel to which it belonged far astern, and shrouded by the haze? So it seemed.

Quietly, however, we waited the stranger's nearer approach; confident, that for some time he would not be able to perceive us, owing to our being in what mariners denominate the "sun-glade," or that part of the ocean upon which the sun's rays flash with peculiar intensity.

As the sail drew nigh, its failing to glisten white led us to doubt whether it was indeed a whale-boat. Presently, it showed yellow; and Samoa declared, that it must be the sail of some island craft. True. The stranger proving a large double-canoe, like those used by the Polynesians in making passages between distant islands.

The Upoluan was now clamorous for a meeting, to which Jarl was averse. Deliberating a moment, I directed the muskets to be loaded; then setting the sail the wind on our quarter—we headed away for the canoe, now sailing at right angles with our previous course.

Here it must be mentioned, that from the various gay cloths and other things provided for barter by the captain of the Parki, I had very strikingly improved my costume; making it free, flowing, and eastern. I looked like an Emir. Nor had my Viking neglected to follow my example; though with some few modifications of his own. With his long tangled hair and harpoon, he looked like the sea-god, that boards ships, for the first time crossing the Equator. For tatooed Samoa, he yet sported both kilt and turban, reminding one of a tawny leopard, though his spots were all in one place. Besides this raiment of ours, against emergencies we had provided our boat with divers nankeens and silks.

But now into full view comes a yoke of huge clumsy prows, shaggy with carving, and driving through the water with considerable velocity; the immense sprawling sail holding the wind like a bag. She seemed full of men; and from the dissonant cries borne over to us, and the canoe's widely yawing, it was plain that we had occasioned no small sensation. They seemed undetermined what course to pursue: whether to court a meeting, or avoid it; whether to regard us as friends or foes.

As we came still nearer, distinctly beholding their faces, we loudly hailed them, inviting them to furl their sails, and allow us to board them. But no answer was returned; their confusion increasing. And now, within less than two ships'-lengths, they swept right across our bow, gazing at us with blended curiosity and fear.

Their craft was about thirty feet long, consisting of a pair of parallel canoes, very narrow, and at the distance of a yard or so, lengthwise, united by stout cross-timbers, lashed across the four gunwales. Upon these timbers was a raised platform or dais, quite dry; and astern an arched cabin or tent; behind which, were two broad-bladed paddles terminating in rude shark-tails, by which the craft was steered.

The yard, spreading a yellow sail, was a crooked bough, supported obliquely in the crotch of a mast, to which the green bark was still clinging. Here and there were little tufts of moss. The high, beaked prow of that canoe in which the mast was placed, resembled a rude altar; and all round it was suspended a great variety of fruits, including scores of cocoanuts, unhusked. This prow was railed off, forming a sort of chancel within.

The foremost beam, crossing the gunwales, extended some twelve feet beyond the side of the dais; and at regular intervals hereupon, stout cords were fastened, which, leading up to the head of the mast, answered the purpose of shrouds. The breeze was now streaming fresh; and, as if to force down into the water the windward side of the craft, five men stood upon this long beam, grasping five shrouds. Yet they failed to counterbalance the pressure of the sail; and owing to the opposite inclination of the twin canoes, these living statues were elevated high above the water; their appearance rendered still more striking by their eager attitudes, and the apparent peril of their position, as the mad spray from the bow dashed over them. Suddenly, the Islanders threw their craft into the wind; while, for ourselves, we lay on our oars, fearful of alarming them by now coming nearer. But hailing them again, we said we were friends; and had friendly gifts for them, if they would peaceably permit us to approach. This understood, there ensued a mighty clamor; insomuch, that I bade Jarl and Samoa out oars, and row very gently toward the strangers. Whereupon, amid a storm of vociferations, some of them hurried to the furthest side of their dais; standing with arms arched over their heads, as if for a dive; others menacing us with clubs and spears; and one, an old man with a bamboo trellis on his head forming a sort of arbor for his hair, planted himself full before the tent, stretching behind him a wide plaited sling.

Upon this hostile display, Samoa dropped his oar, and brought his piece to bear upon the old man, who, by his attitude, seemed to menace us with the fate of the great braggart of Gath. But I quickly knocked down the muzzle of his musket, and forbade the slightest token of hostility; enjoining it upon my companions, nevertheless, to keep well on their guard.

We now ceased rowing, and after a few minutes' uproar in the canoe, they ran to the steering-paddles, and forcing round their craft before the wind, rapidly ran away from us. With all haste we set our sail, and pulling also at our oars, soon overtook them, determined upon coming into closer communion.

Chapter XL

Sire And Sons

Seeing flight was useless, the Islanders again stopped their canoe, and once more we cautiously drew nearer; myself crying out to them not to be fearful; and Samoa, with the odd humor of his race, averring that he had known every soul of them from his infancy.

We approached within two or three yards; when we paused, which somewhat allayed their alarm. Fastening a red China handkerchief to the blade of our long mid-ship oar, I waved it in the air. A lively clapping of hands, and many wild exclamations.

While yet waving the flag, I whispered to Jarl to give the boat a sheer toward the canoe, which being adroitly done, brought the bow, where I stood, still nearer to the Islanders. I then dropped the silk among them; and the Islander, who caught it, at once handed it to the warlike old man with the sling; who, on seating himself, spread it before him; while the rest crowding round, glanced rapidly from the wonderful gift, to the more wonderful donors.

This old man was the superior of the party. And Samoa asserted, that he must be a priest of the country to which the Islanders belonged; that the craft could be no other than one of their sacred canoes, bound on some priestly voyage. All this he inferred from the altar- like prow, and there being no women on board.

Bent upon conciliating the old priest, I dropped into the canoe another silk handkerchief; while Samoa loudly exclaimed, that we were only three men, and were peaceably inclined. Meantime, old Aaron, fastening the two silks crosswise over his shoulders, like a brace of Highland plaids, crosslegged sat, and eyed us.

It was a curious sight. The old priest, like a scroll of old parchment, covered all over with hieroglyphical devices, harder to interpret, I'll warrant, than any old Sanscrit manuscript. And upon his broad brow, deep-graven in wrinkles, were characters still more mysterious, which no Champollion nor gipsy could have deciphered. He looked old as the elderly hills; eyes sunken, though bright; and head white as the summit of Mont Blanc.

The rest were a youthful and comely set: their complexion that of Gold Sherry, and all tattooed after this pattern: two broad cross- stripes on the chest and back; reaching down to the waist, like a foot-soldier's harness. Their faces were full of expression; and their mouths were full of fine teeth; so that the parting of their lips, was as the opening of pearl oysters. Marked, here and there, after the style of Tahiti, with little round figures in blue, dotted in the middle with a spot of vermilion, their brawny brown thighs looked not unlike the gallant hams of Westphalia, spotted with the red dust of Cayenne.

But what a marvelous resemblance in the features of all. Were they born at one birth? This resemblance was heightened by their uniform marks. But it was subsequently ascertained, that they were the children of one sire; and that sire, old Aaron; who, no doubt, reposed upon his sons, as an old general upon the trophies of his youth.

They were the children of as many mothers; and he was training them up for the priesthood.

Chapter XLI

A Fray

So bent were the strangers upon concealing who they were, and the object of their voyage, that it was some time ere we could obtain the information we desired.

They pointed toward the tent, as if it contained their Eleusinian mysteries. And the old priest gave us to know, that it would be profanation to enter it.

But all this only roused my curiosity to unravel the wonder.

At last I succeeded.

In that mysterious tent was concealed a beautiful maiden. And, in pursuance of a barbarous custom, by Aleema, the priest, she was being borne an offering from the island of Amma to the gods of Tedaidee.

Now, hearing of the maiden, I waited for no more. Need I add, how stirred was my soul toward this invisible victim; and how hotly I swore, that precious blood of hers should never smoke upon an altar. If we drowned for it, I was bent upon rescuing the captive. But as yet, no gentle signal of distress had been waved to us from the tent. Thence, no sound could be heard, but an occasional rustle of the matting. Was it possible, that one about to be immolated could proceed thus tranquilly to her fate?

But desperately as I resolved to accomplish the deliverance of the maiden, it was best to set heedfully about it. I desired no shedding of blood; though the odds were against us.

The old priest seemed determined to prevent us from boarding his craft. But being equally determined the other way, I cautiously laid the bow of the Chamois against the canoe's quarter, so as to present the smallest possible chance for a hostile entrance into our boat. Then, Samoa, knife in ear, and myself with a cutlass, stepped upon the dais, leaving Jarl in the boat's head, equipped with his harpoon; three loaded muskets lying by his side. He was strictly enjoined to resist the slightest demonstration toward our craft.

As we boarded the canoe, the Islanders slowly retreated; meantime earnestly conferring in whispers; all but the old priest, who, still seated, presented an undaunted though troubled front. To our surprise, he motioned us to sit down by him; which we did; taking care, however, not to cut off our communication with Jarl.

With the hope of inspiring good will, I now unfolded a roll of printed cotton, and spreading it before the priest, directed his attention to the pictorial embellishments thereon, representing some hundreds of sailor boys simultaneously ascending some hundreds of uniform sections of a ship's rigging. Glancing at them a moment, by a significant sign, he gave me to know, that long previous he himself had ascended the shrouds of a ship. Making this allusion, his countenance was overcast with a ferocious expression, as if something terrific was connected with the reminiscence. But it soon passed away, and somewhat abruptly he assumed an air of much merriment.

While we were thus sitting together, and my whole soul full of the thoughts of the captive, and how best to accomplish my purpose, and often gazing toward the tent; I all at once noticed a movement among the strangers. Almost in the same instant, Samoa, right across the face of Aleema, and in his ordinary tones, bade me take heed to myself, for mischief was brewing. Hardly was this warning uttered, when, with carved clubs in their hands, the Islanders completely surrounded us. Then up rose the old priest, and gave us to know, that we were wholly in his power, and if we did not swear to depart in our boat forthwith, and molest him no more, the peril be ours.

"Depart and you live; stay and you die."

Fifteen to three. Madness to gainsay his mandate. Yet a beautiful maiden was at stake.

The knife before dangling in Samoa's ear was now in his hand. Jarl cried out for us to regain the boat, several of the Islanders making a rush for it. No time to think. All passed quicker than it can be said. They closed in upon us, to push us from the canoe: Rudely the old priest flung me from his side, menacing me with his dagger, the sharp spine of a fish. A thrust and a threat! Ere I knew it, my cutlass made a quick lunge. A curse from the priest's mouth; red blood from his side; he tottered, stared about him, and fell over like a brown hemlock into the sea. A yell of maledictions rose on the air. A wild cry was heard from the tent. Making a dead breach among the crowd, we now dashed side by side for the boat. Springing into it, we found Jarl battling with two Islanders; while the rest were still howling upon the dais. Rage and grief had almost disabled them.

With one stroke of my cutlass, I now parted the line that held us to the canoe, and with Samoa falling upon the two Islanders, by Jarl's help, we quickly mastered them; forcing them down into the bottom of the boat.

The Skyeman and Samoa holding passive the captives, I quickly set our sail, and snatching the sheet at the cavil, we rapidly shot from the canoe. The strangers defying us with their spears; several couching them as if to dart; while others held back their hands, as if to prevent them from jeopardizing the lives of their countrymen in the Chamois.

Seemingly untoward events oftentimes lead to successful results: Far from destroying all chance of rescuing the captive, our temporary flight, indispensable for the safety of Jarl, only made the success of our enterprise more probable. For having made prisoners two of the strangers, I determined to retain them as hostages, through whom to effect my plans without further bloodshed.

And here it must needs be related, that some of the natives were wounded in the fray: while all three of their assailants had received several bruises.

Chapter XLII

Remorse

During the skirmish not a single musket had been discharged. The first snatched by Jarl had missed fire, and ere he could seize another, it was close quarters with him, and no gestures to spare. His harpoon was his all. And truly, there is nothing like steel in a fray. It comes and it goes with a will, and is never a-weary. Your sword is your life, and that of your foe; to keep or to take as it happens. Closer home does it go than a rammer; and fighting with steel is a play without ever an interlude. There are points more deadly than bullets; and stocks packed full of subtle tubes, whence comes an impulse more reliable than powder.

Binding our prisoners lengthwise across the boat's seats, we rowed for the canoe, making signs of amity.

Now, if there be any thing fitted to make a high tide ebb in the veins, it is the sight of a vanquished foe, inferior to yourself in powers of destruction; but whom some necessity has forced you to subdue. All victories are not triumphs, nor all who conquer, heroes.

As we drew near the canoe, it was plain, that the loss of their sire had again for the instant overcome the survivors. Raising hands, they cursed us; and at intervals sent forth a low, piercing wail, peculiar to their race. As before, faint cries were heard from the tent. And all the while rose and fell on the sea, the ill-fated canoe.

As I gazed at this sight, what iron mace fell on my soul; what curse rang sharp in my ear! It was I, who was the author of the deed that caused the shrill wails that I heard. By this hand, the dead man had died. Remorse smote me hard; and like lightning I asked myself, whether the death-deed I had done was sprung of a virtuous motive, the rescuing a captive from thrall; or whether beneath that pretense, I had engaged in this fatal affray for some other, and selfish purpose; the companionship of a beautiful maid. But throttling the thought, I swore to be gay. Am I not rescuing the maiden? Let them go down who withstand me.

At the dismal spectacle before him, Jarl, hitherto menacing our prisoners with his weapon, in order to intimidate their countrymen, honest Jarl dropped his harpoon. But shaking his knife in the air, Samoa yet defied the strangers; nor could we prevent him. His heathenish blood was up.

Standing foremost in the boat, I now assured the strangers, that all we sought at their hands was the maiden in the tent. That captive surrendered, our own, unharmed, should be restored. If not, they must die. With a cry, they started to their feet, and brandished their clubs; but, seeing Jarl's harpoon quivering over the hearts of our prisoners, they quickly retreated; at last signifying their acquiescence in my demand. Upon this, I sprang to the dais, and across it indicating a line near the bow, signed the Islanders to retire beyond it. Then, calling upon them one by one to deliver their weapons, they were passed into the boat.

The Chamois was now brought round to the canoe's stern; and leaving Jarl to defend it as before, the Upoluan rejoined me on the dais. By these precautions—the hostages still remaining bound hand and foot in the boat—we deemed ourselves entirely secure.

Attended by Samoa, I stood before the tent, now still as the grave.

Chapter XLIII

The Tent Entered

By means of thin spaces between the braids of matting, the place was open to the air, but not to view. There was also a round opening on one side, only large enough, however, to admit the arm; but this aperture was partially closed from within. In front, a deep-dyed rug of osiers, covering the entrance way, was intricately laced to the standing part of the tent. As I divided this lacing with my cutlass, there arose an outburst of voices from the Islanders. And they covered their faces, as the interior was revealed to my gaze.

Before me crouched a beautiful girl. Her hands were drooping. And, like a saint from a shrine, she looked sadly out from her long, fair hair. A low wail issued from her lips, and she trembled like a sound. There were tears on her cheek, and a rose-colored pearl on her bosom.

Did I dream?—A snow-white skin: blue, firmament eyes: Golconda locks. For an instant spell-bound I stood; while with a slow, apprehensive movement, and still gazing fixedly, the captive gathered more closely about her a gauze-like robe. Taking one step within, and partially dropping the curtain of the tent, I so stood, as to have both sight and speech of Samoa, who tarried without; while the maiden, crouching in the farther corner of the retreat, was wholly screened from all eyes but mine.

Crossing my hands before me, I now stood without speaking. For the soul of me, I could not link this mysterious creature with the tawny strangers. She seemed of another race. So powerful was this impression, that unconsciously, I addressed her in my own tongue. She started, and bending over, listened intently, as if to the first faint echo of something dimly remembered. Again I spoke, when throwing back her hair, the maiden looked up with a piercing, bewildered gaze. But her eyes soon fell, and bending over once more, she resumed her former attitude. At length she slowly chanted to herself several musical words, unlike those of the Islanders; but though I knew not what they meant, they vaguely seemed familiar.

Impatient to learn her story, I now questioned her in Polynesian. But with much earnestness, she signed me to address her as before. Soon perceiving, however, that without comprehending the meaning of the words I employed, she seemed merely touched by something pleasing in their sound, I once more addressed her in Polynesian; saying that I was all eagerness to hear her history.

After much hesitation she complied; starting with alarm at every sound from without; yet all the while deeply regarding me.

Broken as these disclosures were at the time, they are here presented in the form in which they were afterward more fully narrated.

So unearthly was the story, that at first I little comprehended it; and was almost persuaded that the luckless maiden was some beautiful maniac.

She declared herself more than mortal, a maiden from Oroolia, the Island of Delights, somewhere in the paradisiacal archipelago of the Polynesians. To this isle, while yet an infant, by some mystical power, she had been spirited from Amma, the place of her nativity. Her name was Yillah. And hardly had the waters of Oroolia washed white her olive skin, and tinged her hair with gold, when one day strolling in the woodlands, she was snared in the tendrils of a vine. Drawing her into its bowers, it gently transformed her into one of its blossoms, leaving her conscious soul folded up in the transparent petals.

Here hung Yillah in a trance, the world without all tinged with the rosy hue of her prison. At length when her spirit was about to burst forth in the opening flower, the blossom was snapped from its stem; and borne by a soft wind to the sea; where it fell into the opening valve of a shell; which in good time was cast upon the beach of the Island of Amma.

In a dream, these events were revealed to Aleema the priest; who by a spell unlocking its pearly casket, took forth the bud, which now showed signs of opening in the reviving air, and bore faint shadowy revealings, as of the dawn behind crimson clouds. Suddenly expanding, the blossom exhaled away in perfumes; floating a rosy mist in the air. Condensing at last, there emerged from this mist the same radiant young Yillah as before; her locks all moist, and a rose- colored pearl on her bosom. Enshrined as a goddess, the wonderful child now tarried in the sacred temple of Apo, buried in a dell; never beheld of mortal eyes save Aleema's.

Moon after moon passed away, and at last, only four days gone by, Aleema came to her with a dream; that the spirits in Oroolia had recalled her home by the way of Tedaidee, on whose coast gurgled up in the sea an enchanted spring; which streaming over upon the brine, flowed on between blue watery banks; and, plunging into a vortex, went round and round, descending into depths unknown. Into this whirlpool Yillah was to descend in a canoe, at last to well up in an inland fountain of Oroolia.

Chapter XLIV

Away

Though clothed in language of my own, the maiden's story is in substance the same as she related. Yet were not these things narrated as past events; she merely recounted them as impressions of her childhood, and of her destiny yet unaccomplished. And mystical as the tale most assuredly was, my knowledge of the strange arts of the island priesthood, and the rapt fancies indulged in by many of their victims, deprived it in good part of the effect it otherwise would have produced.

For ulterior purposes connected with their sacerdotal supremacy, the priests of these climes oftentimes secrete mere infants in their temples; and jealously secluding them from all intercourse with the world, craftily delude them, as they grow up, into the wildest conceits.

Thus wrought upon, their pupils almost lose their humanity in the constant indulgence of seraphic imaginings. In many cases becoming inspired as oracles; and as such, they are sometimes resorted to by devotees; always screened from view, however, in the recesses of the temples. But in every instance, their end is certain. Beguiled with some fairy tale about revisiting the islands of Paradise, they are led to the secret sacrifice, and perish unknown to their kindred.

But, would that all this had been hidden from me at the time. For Yillah was lovely enough to be really divine; and so I might have been tranced into a belief of her mystical legends.

But with what passionate exultation did I find myself the deliverer of this beautiful maiden; who, thinking no harm, and rapt in a dream, was being borne to her fate on the coast of Tedaidee. Nor now, for a moment, did the death of Aleema her guardian seem to hang heavy upon my heart. I rejoiced that I had sent him to his gods; that in place of the sea moss growing over sweet Yillah drowned in the sea, the vile priest himself had sunk to the bottom.

But though he had sunk in the deep, his ghost sunk not in the deep waters of my soul. However in exultations its surface foamed up, at bottom guilt brooded. Sifted out, my motives to this enterprise justified not the mad deed, which, in a moment of rage, I had done: though, those motives had been covered with a gracious pretense; concealing myself from myself. But I beat down the thought.

In relating her story, the maiden frequently interrupted it with questions concerning myself:—Whence I came: being white, from Oroolia? Whither I was going: to Amma? And what had happened to Aleema? For she had been dismayed at the fray, though knowing not what it could mean; and she had heard the priest's name called upon in lamentations. These questions for the time I endeavored to evade; only inducing her to fancy me some gentle demigod, that had come over the sea from her own fabulous Oroolia. And all this she must verily have believed. For whom, like me, ere this could she have beheld? Still fixed she her eyes upon me strangely, and hung upon the accents of my voice.

While this scene was passing, the strangers began to show signs of impatience, and a voice from the Chamois repeatedly hailed us to accelerate our movements.

My course was quickly decided. The only obstacle to be encountered was the possibility of Yillah's alarm at being suddenly borne into my prow. For this event I now sought to prepare her. I informed the damsel that Aleema had been dispatched on a long errand to Oroolia; leaving to my care, for the present, the guardianship of the lovely Yillah; and that therefore, it was necessary to carry her tent into my own canoe, then waiting to receive it.

This intelligence she received with the utmost concern; and not knowing to what her perplexity might lead, I thought fit to transport her into the Chamois, while yet overwhelmed by the announcement of my intention.

Quitting her retreat, I apprised Jarl of my design; and then, no more delay!

At bottom, the tent was attached to a light framework of bamboos; and from its upper corners, four cords, like those of a marquee, confined it to the dais. These, Samoa's knife soon parted; when lifting the light tent, we speedily transferred it to the Chamois; a wild yell going up from the Islanders, which drowned the faint cries of the maiden. But we heeded not the din. Toss in the fruit, hanging from the altar-prow! It was done; and then running up our sail, we glided away;—Chamois, tent, hostages, and all. Rushing to the now vacant stern of their canoe, the Islanders once more lifted up their hands and their voices in curses.

A suitable distance gained, we paused to fling overboard the arms we had taken; and Jarl proceeded to liberate the hostages.

Meanwhile, I entered the tent, and by many tokens, sought to allay the maiden's alarm. Thus engaged, violent plunges were heard: our prisoners taking to the sea to regain their canoe. All dripping, they were received by their brethren with wild caresses.

From something now said by the captives, the rest seemed suddenly inspirited with hopes of revenge; again wildly shaking their spears, just before picked up from the sea. With great clamor and confusion they soon set their mat-sail; and instead of sailing southward for Tedaidee, or northward for Amma their home, they steered straight after us, in our wake.

Foremost in the prow stood three; javelins poised for a dart; at intervals, raising a yell.

Did they mean to pursue me? Full in my rear they came on, baying like hounds on their game. Yillah trembled at their cries. My own heart beat hard with undefinable dread. The corpse of Aleema seemed floating before: its avengers were raging behind.

But soon these phantoms departed. For very soon it appeared that in vain the pagans pursued. Their craft, our fleet Chamois outleaped. And farther and farther astern dropped the evil-boding canoe, till at last but a speck; when a great swell of the sea surged up before it, and it was seen no more. Samoa swore that it must have swamped, and gone down. But however it was, my heart lightened apace. I saw none but ourselves on the sea: I remembered that our keel left no track as it sailed.

Let the Oregon Indian through brush, bramble, and brier, hunt his enemy's trail, far over the mountains and down in the vales; comes he to the water, he snuffs idly in air.

Chapter XLV

Reminiscences

In resecuing the gentle Yillah from the hands of the Islanders, a design seemed accomplished. But what was now to be done? Here, in our adventurous Chamois, was a damsel more lovely than the flushes of morning; and for companions, whom had she but me and my comrades? Besides, her bosom still throbbed with alarms, her fancies all roving through mazes.

How subdue these dangerous imaginings? How gently dispel them?

But one way there was: to lead her thoughts toward me, as her friend and preserver; and a better and wiser than Aleema the priest. Yet could not this be effected but by still maintaining my assumption of a divine origin in the blessed isle of Oroolia; and thus fostering in her heart the mysterious interest, with which from the first she had regarded me. But if punctilious reserve on the part of her deliverer should teach her to regard him as some frigid stranger from the Arctic Zone, what sympathy could she have for him? and hence, what peace of mind, having no one else to cling to?

Now re-entering the tent, she again inquired where tarried Aleema.

"Think not of him, sweet Yillah," I cried. "Look on me. Am I not white like yourself? Behold, though since quitting Oroolia the sun has dyed my cheek, am I not even as you? Am I brown like the dusky Aleema? They snatched you away from your isle in the sea, too early for you to remember me there. But you have not been forgotten by me, sweetest Yillah. Ha! ha! shook we not the palm-trees together, and chased we not the rolling nuts down the glen? Did we not dive into the grotto on the sea-shore, and come up together in the cool cavern in the hill? In my home in Oroolia, dear Yillah, I have a lock of your hair, ere yet it was golden: a little dark tress like a ring. How your cheeks were then changing from olive to white. And when shall I forget the hour, that I came upon you sleeping among the flowers, with roses and lilies for cheeks. Still forgetful? Know you not my voice? Those little spirits in your eyes have seen me before. They mimic me now as they sport in their lakes. All the past a dim blank? Think of the time when we ran up and down in our arbor, where the green vines grew over the great ribs of the stranded whale. Oh Yillah, little Yillah, has it all come to this? am I forever forgotten? Yet over the wide watery world have I sought thee: from isle to isle, from sea to sea. And now we part not. Aleema is gone. My prow shall keep kissing the waves, till it kisses the beach at Oroolia. Yillah, look up."

Sunk the ghost of Aleema: Sweet Yillah was mine!

Chapter XLVI

The Chamois With A Roving Commission

Through the assiduity of my Viking, ere nightfall our Chamois was again in good order. And with many subtle and seamanlike splices the light tent was lashed in its place; the sail taken up by a reef.

My comrades now questioned me, as to my purposes; whether they had been modified by the events of the day. I replied that our destination was still the islands to the westward.

But from these we had steadily been drifting all the morning long; so that now no loom of the land was visible. But our prow was kept pointing as before.

As evening came on, my comrades fell fast asleep, leaving me at the helm.

How soft and how dreamy the light of the hour. The rays of the sun, setting behind golden-barred clouds, came to me like the gleaming of a shaded light behind a lattice. And the low breeze, pervaded with the peculiar balm of the mid-Pacific near land, was fragrant as the breath of a bride.

Such was the scene; so still and witching that the hand of Yillah in mine seemed no hand, but a touch. Visions flitted before me and in me; something hummed in my ear; all the air was a lay.

And now entered a thought into my heart. I reflected how serenely we might thus glide along, far removed from all care and anxiety. And then, what different scenes might await us upon any of the shores roundabout. But there seemed no danger in the balmy sea; the assured vicinity of land imparting a sense of security. We had ample supplies for several days more, and thanks to the Pagan canoe, an abundance of fruit.

Besides, what cared I now for the green groves and bright shore? Was not Yillah my shore and my grove? my meadow, my mead, my soft shady vine, and my arbor? Of all things desirable and delightful, the full- plumed sheaf, and my own right arm the band? Enough: no shore for me yet. One sweep of the helm, and our light prow headed round toward the vague land of song, sun, and vine: the fabled South.

As we glided along, strange Yillah gazed down in the sea, and would fain have had me plunge into it with her, to rove through its depths. But I started dismayed; in fancy, I saw the stark body of the priest drifting by. Again that phantom obtruded; again guilt laid his red hand on my soul. But I laughed. Was not Yillah my own? by my arm rescued from ill? To do her a good, I had periled myself. So down, down, Aleema.

When next morning, starting from slumber, my comrades beheld the sun on our beam, instead of astern as before at that hour, they eagerly inquired, "Whither now?" But very briefly I gave them to know, that after devoting the night to the due consideration of a matter so important, I had determined upon voyaging for the island Tedaidee, in place of the land to the westward.

At this, they were not displeased. But to tell the plain truth, I harbored some shadowy purpose of merely hovering about for a while, till I felt more landwardly inclined.

But had I not declared to Yillah, that our destination was the fairy isle she spoke of, even Oroolia? Yet that shore was so exceedingly remote, and the folly of endeavoring to reach it in a craft built with hands, so very apparent, that what wonder I really nourished no thought of it?

So away floated the Chamois, like a vagrant cloud in the heavens: bound, no one knew whither.

Chapter XLVII

Yillah, Jarl, And Samoa

But time to tell, how Samoa and Jarl regarded this mystical Yillah; and how Yillah regarded them.

As Beauty from the Beast, so at first shrank the damsel from my one- armed companion. But seeing my confidence in the savage, a reaction soon followed. And in accordance with that curious law, by which, under certain conditions, the ugliest mortals become only amiably hideous, Yillah at length came to look upon Samoa as a sort of harmless and good-natured goblin. Whence came he, she cared not; or what was his history; or in what manner his fortunes were united to mine.

May be, she held him a being of spontaneous origin.

Now, as every where women are the tamers of the menageries of men; so Yillah in good time tamed down Samoa to the relinquishment of that horrible thing in his ear, and persuaded him to substitute a vacancy for the bauble in his nose. On his part, however, all this was conditional. He stipulated for the privilege of restoring both trinkets upon suitable occasions.

But if thus gayly the damsel sported with Samoa; how different his emotions toward her? The fate to which she had been destined, and every nameless thing about her, appealed to all his native superstitions, which ascribed to beings of her complexion a more than terrestrial origin. When permitted to approach her, he looked timid and awkwardly strange; suggesting the likeness of some clumsy satyr, drawing in his horns; slowly wagging his tail; crouching abashed before some radiant spirit.

And this reverence of his was most pleasing to me, Bravo! thought I; be a pagan forever. No more than myself; for, after a different fashion, Yillah was an idol to both.

But what of my Viking? Why, of good Jarl I grieve to say, that the old-fashioned interest he took in my affairs led him to look upon Yillah as a sort of intruder, an Ammonite syren, who might lead me astray. This would now and then provoke a phillipic; but he would only turn toward my resentment his devotion; and then I was silent.

Unsophisticated as a wild flower in the germ, Yillah seemed incapable of perceiving the contrasted lights in which she was regarded by our companions. And like a true beauty seemed to cherish the presumption, that it was quite impossible for such a person as hers to prove otherwise than irresistible to all.

She betrayed much surprise at my Vikings appearance. But most of all was she struck by a characteristic device upon the arm of the wonderful mariner—our Saviour on the cross, in blue; with the crown of thorns, and three drops of blood in vermilion, falling one by one from each hand and foot.

Now, honest Jarl did vastly pride himself upon this ornament. It was the only piece of vanity about him. And like a lady keeping gloveless her hand to show off a fine Turquoise ring, he invariably wore that sleeve of his frock rolled up, the better to display the embellishment.

And round and round would Yillah turn Jarl's arm, till Jarl was fain to stand firm, for fear of revolving all over. How such untutored homage would have thrilled the heart of the ingenious artist!

Eventually, through the Upoluan, she made overtures to the Skyeman, concerning the possession of his picture in her own proper right. In her very simplicity, little heeding, that like a landscape in fresco, it could not be removed.

Chapter XLVIII

Something Under The Surface

Not to omit an occurrence of considerable interest, we must needs here present some account of a curious retinue of fish which overtook our Chamois, a day or two after parting with the canoe.

A violent creaming and frothing in our rear announced their approach. Soon we found ourselves the nucleus of an incredible multitude of finny creatures, mostly anonymous.

First, far in advance of our prow, swam the helmeted Silver-heads; side by side, in uniform ranks, like an army. Then came the Boneetas, with their flashing blue flanks. Then, like a third distinct regiment, wormed and twisted through the water like Archimedean screws, the quivering Wriggle-tails; followed in turn by the rank and file of the Trigger-fish—so called from their quaint dorsal fins being set in their backs with a comical curve, as if at half-cock. Far astern the rear was brought up by endless battalions of Yellow- backs, right martially vested in buff.

And slow sailing overhead were flights of birds; a wing in the air for every fin in the sea.

But let the sea-fowls fly on: turn we to the fish.

Their numbers were amazing; countless as the tears shed for perfidious lovers. Far abroad on both flanks, they swam in long lines, tier above tier; the water alive with their hosts. Locusts of the sea, peradventure, going to fall with a blight upon some green, mossy province of Neptune. And tame and fearless they were, as the first fish that swam in Euphrates; hardly evading the hand; insomuch that Samoa caught many without lure or line.

They formed a decorous escort; paddling along by our barnacled sides, as if they had been with us from the very beginning; neither scared by our craft's surging in the water; nor in the least sympathetic at losing a comrade by the hand of Samoa. They closed in their ranks and swam on.

How innocent, yet heartless they looked! Had a plank dropped out of our boat, we had sunk to the bottom; and belike, our cheerful retinue would have paid the last rites to our remains.

But still we kept company; as sociably as you please; Samoa helping himself when he listed, and Yillah clapping her hands as the radiant creatures, by a simultaneous turning round on their silvery bellies, caused the whole sea to glow like a burnished shield.

But what has befallen this poor little Boneeta astern, that he swims so toilingly on, with gills showing purple? What has he there, towing behind? It is tangled sea-kelp clinging to its fins. But the clogged thing strains to keep up with its fellows. Yet little they heed. Away they go; every fish for itself, and any fish for Samoa.

At last the poor Boneeta is seen no more. The myriad fins swim on; a lonely waste, where the lost one drops behind.

Strange fish! All the live-long day, they were there by our side; and at night still tarried and shone; more crystal and scaly in the pale moonbeams, than in the golden glare of the sun.

How prettily they swim; all silver life; darting hither and thither between their long ranks, and touching their noses, and scraping acquaintance. No mourning they wear for the Boneeta left far astern; nor for those so cruelly killed by Samoa. No, no; all is glee, fishy glee, and frolicking fun; light hearts and light fins; gay backs and gay spirits.—Swim away, swim away! my merry fins all. Let us roam the flood; let us follow this monster fish with the barnacled sides; this strange-looking fish, so high out of water; that goes without fins. What fish can it be? What rippling is that? Dost hear the great monster breathe? Why, 'tis sharp at both ends; a tail either way; nor eyes has it any, nor mouth. What a curious fish! what a comical fish! But more comical far, those creatures above, on its hollow back, clinging thereto like the snaky eels, that cling and slide on the back of the Sword fish, our terrible foe. But what curious eels these are! Do they deem themselves pretty as we? No, no; for sure, they behold our limber fins, our speckled and beautiful scales. Poor, powerless things! How they must wish they were we, that roam the flood, and scour the seas with a wish. Swim away; merry fins, swim away! Let him drop, that fellow that halts; make a lane; close in, and fill up. Let him drown, if he can not keep pace. No laggards for us:—

We fish, we fish, we merrily swim,
We care not for friend nor for foe:
Our fins are stout,
Our tails are out,
As through the seas we go.

Fish, Fish, we are fish with red gills;
Naught disturbs us, our blood is at zero:
We are buoyant because of our bags,
Being many, each fish is a hero.
We care not what is it, this life
That we follow, this phantom unknown:
To swim, it's exceedingly pleasant,—
So swim away, making a foam.
This strange looking thing by our side,
Not for safety, around it we flee:—
Its shadow's so shady, that's all,—
We only swim under its lee.
And as for the eels there above,
And as for the fowls in the air,
We care not for them nor their ways,
As we cheerily glide afar!

We fish, we fish, we merrily swim,
We care not for friend nor for foe:
Our fins are stout,
Our tails are out,
As through the seas we go.

But how now, my fine fish! what alarms your long ranks, and tosses them all into a hubbub of scales and of foam? Never mind that long knave with the spear there, astern. Pipe away, merry fish, and give us a stave or two more, keeping time with your doggerel tails. But no, no! their singing was over. Grim death, in the shape of a Chevalier, was after them.

How they changed their boastful tune! How they hugged the vilified boat! How they wished they were in it, the braggarts! And how they all tingled with fear!

For, now here, now there, is heard a terrific rushing sound under water, betokening the onslaught of the dread fish of prey, that with spear ever in rest, charges in upon the out-skirts of the shoal, transfixing the fish on his weapon. Re-treating and shaking them off, the Chevalier devours them; then returns to the charge.

Hugging the boat to desperation, the poor fish fairly crowded themselves up to the surface, and floundered upon each other, as men are lifted off their feet in a mob. They clung to us thus, out of a fancied security in our presence. Knowing this, we felt no little alarm for ourselves, dreading lest the Chevalier might despise our boat, full as much as his prey; and in pursuing the fish, run through the poor Chamois with a lunge. A jacket, rolled up, was kept in readiness to be thrust into the first opening made; while as the thousand fins audibly patted against our slender planks, we felt nervously enough; as if treading upon thin, crackling ice.

At length, to our no small delight, the enemy swam away; and again by our side merrily paddled our escort; ten times merrier than ever.

Chapter XLIX

Yillah

While for a few days, now this way, now that, as our craft glides along, surrounded by these locusts of the deep, let the story of Yillah flow on.

Of her beauty say I nothing. It was that of a crystal lake in a fathomless wood: all light and shade; full of fleeting revealings; now shadowed in depths; now sunny in dimples; but all sparkling and shifting, and blending together.

But her wild beauty was a vail to things still more strange. As often she gazed so earnestly into my eyes, like some pure spirit looking far down into my soul, and seeing therein some upturned faces, I started in amaze, and asked what spell was on me, that thus she gazed.

Often she entreated me to repeat over and over again certain syllables of my language. These she would chant to herself, pausing now and then, as if striving to discover wherein lay their charm.

In her accent, there was something very different from that of the people of the canoe. Wherein lay the difference. I knew not; but it enabled her to pronounce with readiness all the words which I taught her; even as if recalling sounds long forgotten.

If all this filled me with wonder, how much was that wonder increased, and yet baffled again, by considering her complexion, and the cast of her features.

After endeavoring in various ways to account for these things, I was led to imagine, that the damsel must be an Albino (Tulla) occasionally to be met with among the people of the Pacific. These persons are of an exceedingly delicate white skin, tinted with a faint rose hue, like the lips of a shell. Their hair is golden. But, unlike the Albinos of other climes, their eyes are invariably blue, and no way intolerant of light.

As a race, the Tullas die early. And hence the belief, that they pertain to some distant sphere, and only through irregularities in the providence of the gods, come to make their appearance upon earth: whence, the oversight discovered, they are hastily snatched. And it is chiefly on this account, that in those islands where human sacrifices are offered, the Tullas are deemed the most suitable oblations for the altar, to which from their birth many are prospectively devoted. It was these considerations, united to others, which at times induced me to fancy, that by the priest, Yillah was regarded as one of these beings. So mystical, however, her revelations concerning her past history, that often I knew not what to divine. But plainly they showed that she had not the remotest conception of her real origin.

But these conceits of a state of being anterior to an earthly existence may have originated in one of those celestial visions seen transparently stealing over the face of a slumbering child. And craftily drawn forth and re-echoed by another, and at times repeated over to her with many additions, these imaginings must at length have assumed in her mind a hue of reality, heightened into conviction by the dreamy seclusion of her life.

But now, let her subsequent and more credible history be related, as from time to time she rehearsed it.

Chapter L

Yillah In Ardair

In the verdant glen of Ardair, far in the silent interior of Amma, shut in by hoar old cliffs, Yillah the maiden abode.

So small and so deep was this glen, so surrounded on all sides by steep acclivities, and so vividly green its verdure, and deceptive the shadows that played there; that, from above, it seemed more like a lake of cool, balmy air, than a glen: its woodlands and grasses gleaming shadowy all, like sea groves and mosses beneath the calm sea.

Here, none came but Aleema the priest, who at times was absent for days together. But at certain seasons, an unseen multitude with loud chants stood upon the verge of the neighboring precipices, and traversing those shaded wilds, slowly retreated; their voices lessening and lessening, as they wended their way through the more distant groves.

At other times, Yillah being immured in the temple of Apo, a band of men entering the vale, surrounded her retreat, dancing there till evening came. Meanwhile, heaps of fruit, garlands of flowers, and baskets of fish, were laid upon an altar without, where stood Aleema, arrayed in white tappa, and muttering to himself, as the offerings were laid at his feet.

When Aleema was gone, Yillah went forth into the glen, and wandered among the trees, and reposed by the banks of the stream. And ever as she strolled, looked down upon her the grim old cliffs, bearded with trailing moss.

Toward the lower end of the vale, its lofty walls advancing and overhanging their base, almost met in mid air. And a great rock, hurled from an adjacent height, and falling into the space intercepted, there remained fixed. Aerial trees shot up from its surface; birds nested in its clefts; and strange vines roved abroad, overrunning the tops of the trees, lying thereon in coils and undulations, like anacondas basking in the light. Beneath this rock, was a lofty wall of ponderous stones. Between its crevices, peeps were had of a long and leafy arcade, quivering far away to where the sea rolled in the sun. Lower down, these crevices gave an outlet to the waters of the brook, which, in a long cascade, poured over sloping green ledges near the foot of the wall, into a deep shady pool; whose rocky sides, by the perpetual eddying of the water, had been worn into a grotesque resemblance to a group of giants, with heads submerged, indolently reclining about the basin.

In this pool, Yillah would bathe. And once, emerging, she heard the echoes of a voice, and called aloud. But the only reply, was the rustling of branches, as some one, invisible, fled down the valley beyond. Soon after, a stone rolled inward, and Aleema the priest stood before her; saying that the voice she had heard was his. But it was not.

At last the weary days grew, longer and longer, and the maiden pined for companionship. When the breeze blew not, but slept in the caves of the mountains, and all the leaves of the trees stood motionless as tears in the eye, Yillah would sadden, and call upon the spirits in her soul to awaken. She sang low airs, she thought she had heard in Oroolia; but started affrighted, as from dingles and dells, came back to her strains more wild than hers. And ever, when sad, Aleema would seek to cheer her soul, by calling to mind the bright scenes of Oroolia the Blest, to which place, he averred, she was shortly to return, never more to depart.

Now, at the head of the vale of Ardair, rose a tall, dark peak, presenting at the top the grim profile of a human face; whose shadow, every afternoon, crept down the verdant side of the mountain: a silent phantom, stealing all over the bosom of the glen.

At times, when the phantom drew near, Aleema would take Yillah forth, and waiting its approach, lay her down by the shadow, disposing her arms in a caress; saying, "Oh, Apo! dost accept thy bride?" And at last, when it crept beyond the place where he stood, and buried the whole valley in gloom; Aleema would say, "Arise Yillah; Apo hath stretched himself to sleep in Ardair. Go, slumber where thou wilt; for thou wilt slumber in his arms."

And so, every night, slept the maiden in the arms of grim Apo.

One day when Yillah had come to love the wild shadow, as something that every day moved before her eyes, where all was so deathfully still; she went forth alone to watch it, as softly it slid down from the peak. Of a sudden, when its face was just edging a chasm, that made it to look as if parting its lips, she heard a loud voice, and thought it was Apo calling "Yillah! Yillah!" But now it seemed like the voice she had heard while bathing in the pool. Glancing upward, she beheld a beautiful open-armed youth, gazing down upon her from an inaccessible crag. But presently, there was a rustling in the groves behind, and swift as thought, something darted through the air. The youth bounded forward. Yillah opened her arms to receive him; but he fell upon the cliff, and was seen no more. As alarmed, and in tears, she fled from the scene, some one out of sight ran before her through the wood.

Upon recounting this adventure to Aleema, he said, that the being she had seen, must have been a bad spirit come to molest her; and that Apo had slain him.

The sight of this youth, filled Yillah with wild yearnings to escape from her lonely retreat; for a glimpse of some one beside the priest and the phantom, suggested vague thoughts of worlds of fair beings, in regions beyond Ardair. But Aleema sought to put away these conceits; saying, that ere long she would be journeying to Oroolia, there to rejoin the spirits she dimly remembered.

Soon after, he came to her with a shell—one of those ever moaning of ocean—and placing it to her ear, bade her list to the being within, which in that little shell had voyaged from Oroolia to bear her company in Amma.

Now, the maiden oft held it to her ear, and closing her eyes, listened and listened to its soft inner breathings, till visions were born of the sound, and her soul lay for hours in a trance of delight.

And again the priest came, and brought her a milk-white bird, with a bill jet-black, and eyes like stars. "In this, lurks the soul of a maiden; it hath flown from Oroolia to greet you." The soft stranger willingly nestled in her bosom; turning its bright eyes upon hers, and softly warbling.

Many days passed; and Yillah, the bird, and the shell were inseparable. The bird grew familiar; pecked seeds from her mouth; perched upon her shoulder, and sang in her ear; and at night, folded its wings in her bosom, and, like a sea-fowl, went softly to sleep: rising and falling upon the maiden's heart. And every morning it flew from its nest, and fluttered and chirped; and sailed to and fro; and blithely sang; and brushed Yillah's cheek till she woke. Then came to her hand: and Yillah, looking earnestly in its eyes, saw strange faces there; and said to herself as she gazed—"These are two souls, not one."

But at last, going forth into the groves with the bird, it suddenly flew from her side, and perched in a bough; and throwing back its white downy throat, there gushed from its bill a clear warbling jet, like a little fountain in air. Now the song ceased; when up and away toward the head of the vale, flew the bird. "Lil! Lil! come back, leave me not, blest souls of the maidens." But on flew the bird, far up a defile, winging its way till a speck.

It was shortly after this, and upon the evening of a day which had been tumultuous with sounds of warfare beyond the lower wall of the glen; that Aleema came to Yillah in alarm; saying—"Yillah, the time has come to follow thy bird; come, return to thy home in Oroolia." And he told her the way she would voyage there: by the vortex on the coast of Tedaidee. That night, being veiled and placed in the tent, the maiden was borne to the sea-side, where the canoe was in waiting. And setting sail quickly, by next morning the island of Amma was no longer in sight.

And this was the voyage, whose sequel has already been recounted.

Chapter LI

The Dream Begins To Fade

Stripped of the strange associations, with which a mind like Yillah's must have invested every incident of her life, the story of her abode in Ardair seemed not incredible.

But so etherealized had she become from the wild conceits she nourished, that she verily believed herself a being of the lands of dreams. Her fabulous past was her present.

Yet as our intimacy grew closer and closer, these fancies seemed to be losing their hold. And often she questioned me concerning my own reminiscences of her shadowy isle. And cautiously I sought to produce the impression, that whatever I had said of that clime, had been revealed to me in dreams; but that in these dreams, her own lineaments had smiled upon me; and hence the impulse which had sent me roving after the substance of this spiritual image.

And true it was to say so; and right it was to swear it, upon her white arms crossed. For oh, Yillah; were you not the earthly semblance of that sweet vision, that haunted my earliest thoughts?

At first she had wildly believed, that the nameless affinities between us, were owing to our having in times gone by dwelt together in the same ethereal region. But thoughts like these were fast dying out. Yet not without many strange scrutinies. More intently than ever she gazed into my eyes; rested her ear against my heart, and listened to its beatings. And love, which in the eye of its object ever seeks to invest itself with some rare superiority, love, sometimes induced me to prop my failing divinity; though it was I myself who had undermined it.

But if it was with many regrets, that in the sight of Yillah, I perceived myself thus dwarfing down to a mortal; it was with quite contrary emotions, that I contemplated the extinguishment in her heart of the notion of her own spirituality. For as such thoughts were chased away, she clung the more closely to me, as unto one without whom she would be desolate indeed.

And now, at intervals, she was sad, and often gazed long and fixedly into the sea. Nor would she say why it was, that she did so; until at length she yielded; and replied, that whatever false things Aleema might have instilled into her mind; of this much she was certain: that the whirlpool on the coast of Tedaidee prefigured her fate; that in the waters she saw lustrous eyes, and beckoning phantoms, and strange shapes smoothing her a couch among the mosses.

Her dreams seemed mine. Many visions I had of the green corse of the priest, outstretching its arms in the water, to receive pale Yillah, as she sunk in the sea.

But these forebodings departed, no happiness in the universe like ours. We lived and we loved; life and love were united; in gladness glided our days.

Chapter LII

World Ho!

Five suns rose and set. And Yillah pining for the shore, we turned our prow due west, and next morning came in sight of land.

It was innumerable islands; lifting themselves bluely through the azure air, and looking upon the distant sea, like haycocks in a hazy field. Towering above all, and mid-most, rose a mighty peak; one fleecy cloud sloping against its summit; a column wreathed. Beyond, like purple steeps in heaven at set of sun, stretched far away, what seemed lands on lands, in infinite perspective.

Gliding on, the islands grew more distinct; rising up from the billows to greet us; revealing hills, vales, and peaks, grouped within a milk-white zone of reef, so vast, that in the distance all was dim. The jeweled vapors, ere-while hovering over these violet shores, now seemed to be shedding their gems; and as the almost level rays of the sun, shooting through the air like a variegated prism, touched the verdant land, it trembled all over with dewy sparkles.

Still nearer we came: our sail faintly distended as the breeze died away from our vicinity to the isles. The billows rolled listlessly by, as if conscious that their long task was nigh done; while gleamed the white reef, like the trail of a great fish in a calm. But as yet, no sign of paddle or canoe; no distant smoke; no shining thatch. Bravo! good comrades, we've discovered some new constellation in the sea.

Sweet Yillah, no more of Oroolia; see you not this flowery land? Nevermore shall we desire to roam.

Voyaging along the zone, we came to an opening; and quitting the firmament blue of the open sea, we glided in upon the still, green waters of the wide lagoon. Mapped out in the broad shadows of the isles, and tinted here and there with the reflected hues of the sun clouds, the mild waters stretched all around us like another sky. Near by the break in the reef, was a little island, with palm trees harping in the breeze; an aviary of alluring sounds, that seemed calling upon us to land. And here, Yillah, whom the sight of the verdure had made glad, threw out a merry suggestion. Nothing less, than to plant our mast, sail-set, upon the highest hill; and fly away, island and all; trees rocking, birds caroling, flowers springing; away, away, across the wide waters, to Oroolia! But alas! how weigh the isle's coral anchor, leagues down in the fathomless sea?

We glanced around; but all the islands seemed slumbering in the flooding light.

"A canoe! a canoe!" cried Samoa, as three proas showed themselves rounding a neighboring shore. Instantly we sailed for them; but after shooting to and fro for a time, and standing up and gazing at us, the Islanders retreated behind the headland. Hardly were they out of sight, when from many a shore roundabout, other proas pushed off. Soon the water all round us was enlivened by fleets of canoes, darting hither and thither like frighted water-fowls. Presently they all made for one island.

From their actions we argued that these people could have had but little or no intercourse with whites; and most probably knew not how to account for our appearance among them. Desirous, therefore, of a friendly meeting, ere any hostile suspicions might arise, we pointed our craft for the island, whither all the canoes were now hastening. Whereupon, those which had not yet reached their destination, turned and fled; while the occupants of the proas that had landed, ran into the groves, and were lost to view.

Crossing the distinct outer line of the isle's shadow on the water, we gained the shore; and gliding along its margin, passing canoe after canoe, hauled up on the silent beach, which otherwise seemed entirely innocent of man.

A dilemma. But I decided at last upon disembarking Jarl and Samoa, to seek out and conciliate the natives. So, landing them upon a jutting buttress of coral, whence they waded to the shore; I pushed off with Yillah into the water beyond, to await the event.

Full an hour must have elapsed; when, to our great joy, loud shouts were heard; and there burst into view a tumultuous crowd, in the midst of which my Viking was descried, mounted upon the shoulders of two brawny natives; while the Upoluan, striding on in advance, seemed resisting a similar attempt to elevate him in the world.

Good omens both.

"Come ashore!" cried Jarl. "Aramai!" cried Samoa; while storms of interjections went up from the Islanders who with extravagant gestures danced about the beach.

Further caution seemed needless: I pointed our prow for the shore. No sooner was this perceived, than, raising an applauding shout, the Islanders ran up to their waists in the sea. And skimming like a gull over the smooth lagoon, the light shallop darted in among them. Quick as thought, fifty hands were on the gunwale: and, with all its contents, lifted bodily into the air, the little Chamois, upon many a dripping shoulder, was borne deep into the groves. Yillah shrieked at the rocking motion, and when the boughs of the trees brushed against the tent.

With his staff, an old man now pointed to a couple of twin-like trees, some four paces apart; and a little way from the ground conveniently crotched.

And here, eftsoons, they deposited their burden; lowering the Chamois gently between the forks of the trees, whose willow-like foliage fringed the tent and its inmate.

Chapter LIII

The Chamois Ashore

Until now, enveloped in her robe, and crouching like a fawn, Yillah had been well nigh hidden from view. But presently she withdrew her hood.

What saw the Islanders, that they so gazed and adored in silence: some retreating, some creeping nearer, and the women all in a flutter? Long they gazed; and following Samoa's example, stretched forth their arms in reverence.

The adoration of the maiden was extended to myself. Indeed, from the singular gestures employed, I had all along suspected, that we were being received with unwonted honors.

I now sought to get speech of my comrades. But so obstreperous was the crowd, that it was next to impossible. Jarl was still in his perch in the air; his enthusiastic bearers not yet suffering him to alight. Samoa, however, who had managed to keep out of the saddle, by-and-by contrived to draw nearer to the Chamois.

He advised me, by no means to descend for the present; since in any event we were sure of remaining unmolested therein; the Islanders regarding it as sacred.

The Upoluan attracted a great deal of attention; chiefly from his style of tattooing, which, together with other peculiarities, so interested the natives, that they were perpetually hanging about him, putting eager questions, and all the time keeping up a violent clamor.

But despite the large demand upon his lungs, Samoa made out to inform me, that notwithstanding the multitude assembled, there was no high chief, or person of consequence present; the king of the place, also those of the islands adjacent, being absent at a festival in another quarter of the Archipelago. But upon the first distant glimpse of the Chamois, fleet canoes had been dispatched to announce the surprising event that had happened.

In good time, the crowd becoming less tumultuous, and abandoning the siege of Samoa, I availed myself of this welcome lull, and called upon him and my Viking to enter the Chamois; desirous of condensing our forces against all emergencies.

Samoa now gave me to understand, that from all he could learn, the Islanders regarded me as a superior being. They had inquired of him, whether I was not white Taji, a sort of half-and-half deity, now and then an Avatar among them, and ranking among their inferior ex- officio demi-gods. To this, Samoa had said ay; adding, moreover, all he could to encourage the idea.

He now entreated me, at the first opportunity, to announce myself as Taji: declaring that if once received under that title, the unbounded hospitality of our final reception would be certain; and our persons fenced about from all harm.

Encouraging this. But it was best to be wary. For although among some barbarians the first strangers landing upon their shores, are frequently hailed as divine; and in more than one wild land have been actually styled gods, as a familiar designation; yet this has not exempted the celestial visitants from peril, when too much presuming upon the reception extended to them. In sudden tumults they have been slain outright, and while full faith in their divinity had in no wise abated. The sad fate of an eminent navigator is a well-known illustration of this unaccountable waywardness.

With no small anxiety, therefore, we awaited the approach of some of the dignitaries of Mardi; for by this collective appellation, the people informed us, their islands were known.

We waited not long. Of a sudden, from the sea-side, a single shrill cry was heard. A moment more, and the blast of numerous conch shells startled the air; a confused clamor drew nearer and nearer; and flying our eyes in the direction of these sounds, we impatiently awaited what was to follow.

Chapter LIV

A Gentleman From The Sun

Never before had I seen the deep foliage of woodlands navigated by canoes. But on they came sailing through the leaves; two abreast; borne on men's shoulders; in each a chief, carried along to the measured march of his bearers; paddle blades reversed under arms. As they emerged, the multitude made gestures of homage. At the distance of some eight or ten paces the procession halted; when the kings alighted to the ground.

They were fine-looking men, arrayed in various garbs. Rare the show of stained feathers, and jewels, and other adornments. Brave the floating of dyed mantles.

The regal bearing of these personages, the deference paid them, and their entire self-possession, not a little surprised me. And it seemed preposterous, to assume a divine dignity in the presence of these undoubted potentates of terra firma. Taji seemed oozing from my fingers' ends. But courage! and erecting my crest, I strove to look every inch the character I had determined to assume.

For a time, it was almost impossible to tell with what emotions precisely the chiefs were regarding me. They said not a word.

But plucking up heart of grace, I crossed my cutlass on my chest, and reposing my hand on the hilt, addressed their High Mightinesses thus. "Men of Mardi, I come from the sun. When this morning it rose and touched the wave, I pushed my shallop from its golden beach, and hither sailed before its level rays. I am Taji."

More would have been added, but I paused for the effect of my exordium.

Stepping back a pace or two, the chiefs eagerly conversed.

Emboldened, I returned to the charge, and labored hard to impress them with just such impressions of me and mine, as I deemed desirable. The gentle Yillah was a seraph from the sun; Samoa I had picked off a reef in my route from that orb; and as for the Skyeman, why, as his name imported, he came from above. In a word, we were all strolling divinities.

Advancing toward the Chamois, one of the kings, a calm old man, now addressed me as follows:—"Is this indeed Taji? he, who according to a tradition, was to return to us after five thousand moons? But that period is yet unexpired. What bring'st thou hither then, Taji, before thy time? Thou wast but a quarrelsome demi-god, say the legends, when thou dwelt among our sires. But wherefore comest thou, Taji? Truly, thou wilt interfere with the worship of thy images, and we have plenty of gods besides thee. But comest thou to fight?—We have plenty of spears, and desire not thine. Comest thou to dwell?— Small are the houses of Mardi. Or comest thou to fish in the sea? Tell us, Taji."

Now, all this was a series of posers hard to be answered; furnishing a curious example, moreover, of the reception given to strange demi- gods when they travel without their portmanteaus; and also of the familiar manner in which these kings address the immortals. Much I mourned that I had not previously studied better my part, and learned the precise nature of my previous existence in the land.

But nothing like carrying it bravely.

"Attend. Taji comes, old man, because it pleases him to come. And Taji will depart when it suits him. Ask the shades of your sires whether Taji thus scurvily greeted them, when they came stalking into his presence in the land of spirits. No. Taji spread the banquet. He removed their mantles. He kindled a fire to drive away the damp. He said not, 'Come you to fight, you fogs and vapors? come you to dwell? or come you to fish in the sea?' Go to, then, kings of Mardi!"

Upon this, the old king fell back; and his place was supplied by a noble chief, of a free, frank bearing. Advancing quickly toward the boat, he exclaimed—"I am Media, the son of Media. Thrice welcome, Taji. On my island of Odo hast thou an altar. I claim thee for my guest." He then reminded the rest, that the strangers had voyaged far, and needed repose. And, furthermore, that he proposed escorting them forthwith to his own dominions; where, next day, he would be happy to welcome all visitants.

And good as his word, he commanded his followers to range themselves under the Chamois. Springing out of our prow, the Upoluan was followed by Jarl; leaving Yillah and Taji to be borne therein toward the sea.

Soon, we were once more afloat; by our side, Media sociably seated; six of his paddlers, perched upon the gunwale, swiftly urging us over the lagoon.

The transition from the grove to the sea was instantaneous. All seemed a dream.

The place to which we were hastening, being some distance away, as we rounded isle after isle, the extent of the Archipelago grew upon us greatly.

Chapter LV

Tiffin In A Temple

Upon at last drawing nigh to Odo, its appearance somewhat disappointed me. A small island, of moderate elevation.

But plumb not the height of the house that feasts you. The beach was lined with expectant natives, who, lifting the Chamois, carried us up the beach.

Alighting, as they were bearing us along, King Media, designating a canoe-house hard by, ordered our craft to be deposited therein. This being done, we stepped upon the soil. It was the first we had pressed in very many days. It sent a sympathetic thrill through our frames.

Turning his steps inland, Media signed us to follow.

Soon we came to a rude sort of inclosure, fenced in by an imposing wall. Here a halt was sounded, and in great haste the natives proceeded to throw down a portion of the stones. This accomplished, we were signed to enter the fortress thus carried by storm. Upon an artificial mound, opposite the breach, stood a small structure of bamboo, open in front. Within, was a long pedestal, like a settee, supporting three images, also of wood, and about the size of men; bearing, likewise, a remote resemblance to that species of animated nature. Before these idols was an altar, and at its base many fine mats.

Entering the temple, as if he felt very much at home, Media disposed these mats so as to form a very pleasant lounge; where he deferentially entreated Yillah to recline. Then deliberately removing the first idol, he motioned me to seat myself in its place. Setting aside the middle one, he quietly established himself in its stead. The displaced ciphers, meanwhile, standing upright before us, and their blank faces looking upon this occasion unusually expressive. As yet, not a syllable as to the meaning of this cavalier treatment of their wooden godships.

We now tranquilly awaited what next might happen, and I earnestly prayed, that if sacrilege was being committed, the vengeance of the gods might be averted from an ignoramus like me; notwithstanding the petitioner himself hailed from the other world. Perfect silence was preserved: Jarl and Samoa standing a little without the temple; the first looking quite composed, but his comrade casting wondering glances at my sociable apotheosis with Media.

Now happening to glance upon the image last removed, I was not long in detecting a certain resemblance between it and our host. Both were decorated in the same manner; the carving on the idol exactly corresponding with the tattooing of the king.

Presently, the silence was relieved by a commotion without: and a butler approached, staggering under an immense wooden trencher; which, with profound genuflexions, he deposited upon the altar before us. The tray was loaded like any harvest wain; heaped up with good things sundry and divers: Bread-fruit, and cocoanuts, and plantains, and guavas; all pleasant to the eye, and furnishing good earnest of something equally pleasant to the palate.

Transported at the sight of these viands, after so long an estrangement from full indulgence in things green, I was forthwith proceeding to help Yillah and myself, when, like lightning, a most unwelcome query obtruded. Did deities dine? Then also recurred what Media had declared about my shrine in Odo. Was this it? Self- sacrilegious demigod that I was, was I going to gluttonize on the very offerings, laid before me in my own sacred fane? Give heed to thy ways, oh Taji, lest thou stumble and be lost.

But hereupon, what saw we, but his cool majesty of Odo tranquilly proceeding to lunch in the temple?

How now? Was Media too a god? Egad, it must be so. Else, why his image here in the fane, and the original so entirely at his ease, with legs full cosily tucked away under the very altar itself. This put to flight all appalling apprehensions of the necessity of starving to keep up the assumption of my divinity. So without more ado I helped myself right and left; taking the best care of Yillah; who over fed her flushed beauty with juicy fruits, thereby transferring to her cheek the sweet glow of the guava.

Our hunger appeased, and Media in token thereof celestially laying his hand upon the appropriate region, we proceeded to quit the inclosure. But coming to the wall where the breach had been made, lo, and behold, no breach was to be seen. But down it came tumbling again, and forth we issued.

This overthrowing of walls, be it known, is an incidental compliment paid distinguished personages in this part of Mardi. It would seem to signify, that such gentry can go nowhere without creating an impression; even upon the most obdurate substances.

But to return to our ambrosial lunch.

Sublimate, as you will, the idea of our ethereality as intellectual beings; no sensible man can harbor a doubt, but that there is a vast deal of satisfaction in dining. More: there is a savor of life and immortality in substantial fare. Like balloons, we are nothing till filled.

And well knowing this, nature has provided this jolly round board, our globe, which in an endless sequence of courses and crops, spreads a perpetual feast. Though, as with most public banquets, there is no small crowding, and many go away famished from plenty.

Chapter LVI

King Media A Host

Striking into a grove, about sunset we emerged upon a fine, clear space, and spied a city in the woods.

In the middle of all, like a generalissimo's marquee among tents, was a structure more imposing than the rest. Here, abode King Media.

Disposed round a space some fifty yards square, were many palm posts staked firmly in the earth. A man's height from the ground, these supported numerous horizontal trunks, upon which lay a flooring of habiscus. High over this dais, but resting upon independent supports beyond, a gable-ended roof sloped away to within a short distance of the ground.

Such was the palace.

We entered it by an arched, arbored entrance, at one of its palmetto- thatched ends. But not through this exclusive portal entered the Islanders. Humbly stooping, they found ingress under the drooping eaves. A custom immemorial, and well calculated to remind all contumacious subjects of the dignity of the habitation thus entered.

Three steps led to the summit of the dais, where piles of soft mats, and light pillows of woven grass, stuffed with the golden down of a wild thistle, invited all loiterers to lounge.

How pleasant the twilight that welled up from under the low eaves, above which we were seated. And how obvious now the design of the roof. No shade more grateful and complete; the garish sun lingering without like some lackey in waiting.

But who is this in the corner, gaping at us like a butler in a quandary? Media's household deity, in the guise of a plethoric monster, his enormous head lolling back, and wide, gaping mouth stuffed full of fresh fruits and green leaves. Truly, had the idol possessed a soul under his knotty ribs, how tantalizing to hold so glorious a mouthful without the power of deglutition. Far worse than the inexorable lock-jaw, which will not admit of the step preliminary to a swallow.

This jolly Josh image was that of an inferior deity, the god of Good Cheer, and often after, we met with his merry round mouth in many other abodes in Mardi. Daily, his jaws are replenished, as a flower vase in summer.

But did the demi-divine Media thus brook the perpetual presence of a subaltern divinity? Still more; did he render it homage? But ere long the Mardian mythology will be discussed, thereby making plain what may now seem anomalous.

Politely escorting us into his palace, Media did the honors by inviting his guests to recline. He then seemed very anxious to impress us with the fact, that, by bringing us to his home, and thereby charging the royal larder with our maintenance, he had taken no hasty or imprudent step. His merry butlers kept piling round us viands, till we were well nigh walled in. At every fresh deposit, Media directing our attention to the same, as yet additional evidence of his ample resources as a host. The evidence was finally closed by dragging under the eaves a felled plantain tree, the spike of red ripe fruit, sprouting therefrom, blushing all over, at so rude an introduction to the notice of strangers.

During this scene, Jarl was privily nudging Samoa, in wonderment, to know what upon earth it all meant. But Samoa, scarcely deigning to notice interrogatories propounded through the elbow, only let drop a vague hint or two.

It was quite amusing, what airs Samoa now gave himself, at least toward my Viking. Among the Mardians he was at home. And who, when there, stretches not out his legs, and says unto himself, "Who is greater than I?"

To be plain: concerning himself and the Skyeman, the tables were turned. At sea, Jarl had been the oracle: an old sea-sage, learned in hemp and helm. But our craft high and dry, the Upoluan lifted his crest as the erudite pagan; master of Gog and Magog, expounder of all things heathenish and obscure.

An hour or two was now laughed away in very charming conversation with Media; when I hinted, that a couch and solitude would be acceptable. Whereupon, seizing a taper, our host escorted us without the palace. And ushering us into a handsome unoccupied mansion, gave me to understand that the same was mine. Mounting to the dais, he then instituted a vigorous investigation, to discern whether every thing was in order. Not fancying something about the mats, he rolled them up into bundles, and one by one sent them flying at the heads of his servitors; who, upon that gentle hint made off with them, soon after returning with fresh ones. These, with mathematical precision, Media in person now spread on the dais; looking carefully to the fringes or ruffles with which they were bordered, as if striving to impart to them a sentimental expression.

This done, he withdrew.

Chapter LVII

Taji Takes Counsel With Himself

My brief intercourse with our host, had by this time enabled me to form a pretty good notion of the light, in which I was held by him and his more intelligent subjects.

His free and easy carriage evinced, that though acknowledging my assumptions, he was no way overawed by them; treating me as familiarly, indeed, as if I were a mere mortal, one of the abject generation of mushrooms.

The scene in the temple, however, had done much toward explaining this demeanor of his. A demi-god in his own proper person, my claims to a similar dignity neither struck him with wonder, nor lessened his good opinion of himself.

As for any thing foreign in my aspect, and my ignorance of Mardian customs—-all this, instead of begetting a doubt unfavorable to my pretensions, but strengthened the conviction of them as verities. Thus has it been in similar instances; but to a much greater extent. The celebrated navigator referred to in a preceding chapter, was hailed by the Hawaiians as one of their demi-gods, returned to earth, after a wide tour of the universe. And they worshiped him as such, though incessantly he was interrogating them, as to who under the sun his worshipers were; how their ancestors came on the island; and whether they would have the kindness to provide his followers with plenty of pork during his stay.

But a word or two concerning the idols in the shrine at Odo. Superadded to the homage rendered him as a temporal prince, Media was there worshiped as a spiritual being. In his corporeal absence, his effigy receiving all oblations intended for him. And in the days of his boyhood, listening to the old legends of the Mardian mythology, Media had conceived a strong liking for the fabulous Taji; a deity whom he had often declared was worthy a niche in any temple extant. Hence he had honored my image with a place in his own special shrine; placing it side by side with his worshipful likeness.

I appreciated the compliment. But of the close companionship of the other image there, I was heartily ashamed. And with reason. The nuisance in question being the image of a deified maker of plantain-pudding, lately deceased; who had been famed far and wide as the most notable fellow of his profession in the whole Archipelago. During his sublunary career, having been attached to the household of Media, his grateful master had afterward seen fit to crown his celebrity by this posthumous distinction: a circumstance sadly subtracting from the dignity of an apotheosis. Nor must it here be omitted, that in this part of Mardi culinary artists are accounted worthy of high consideration. For among these people of Odo, the matter of eating and drinking is held a matter of life and of death. "Drag away my queen from my arms," said old Tyty when overcome of Adommo, "but leave me my cook."

Now, among the Mardians there were plenty of incarnated deities to keep me in countenance. Most of the kings of the Archipelago, besides Media, claiming homage as demi-gods; and that, too, by virtue of hereditary descent, the divine spark being transmissable from father to son. In illustration of this, was the fact, that in several instances the people of the land addressed the supreme god Oro, in the very same terms employed in the political adoration of their sublunary rulers.

Ay: there were deities in Mardi far greater and taller than I: right royal monarchs to boot, living in jolly round tabernacles of jolly brown clay; and feasting, and roystering, and lording it in yellow tabernacles of bamboo. These demi-gods had wherewithal to sustain their lofty pretensions. If need were, could crush out of him the infidelity of a non-conformist. And by this immaculate union of church and state, god and king, in their own proper persons reigned supreme Caesars over the souls and bodies of their subjects.

Beside these mighty magnates, I and my divinity shrank into nothing. In their woodland ante-chambers plebeian deities were kept lingering. For be it known, that in due time we met with several decayed, broken down demi-gods: magnificos of no mark in Mardi; having no temples wherein to feast personal admirers, or spiritual devotees. They wandered about forlorn and friendless. And oftentimes in their dinnerless despair hugely gluttonized, and would fain have grown fat, by reflecting upon the magnificence of their genealogies. But poor fellows! like shabby Scotch lords in London in King James's time, the very multitude of them confounded distinction. And since they could show no rent-roll, they were permitted to fume unheeded.

Upon the whole, so numerous were living and breathing gods in Mardi, that I held my divinity but cheaply. And seeing such a host of immortals, and hearing of multitudes more, purely spiritual in their nature, haunting woodlands and streams; my views of theology grew strangely confused; I began to bethink me of the Jew that rejected the Talmud, and his all-permeating principle, to which Goethe and others have subscribed.

Instead, then, of being struck with the audacity of endeavoring to palm myself off as a god—the way in which the thing first impressed me—I now perceived that I might be a god as much as I pleased, and yet not whisk a lion's tail after all at least on that special account.

As for Media's reception, its graciousness was not wholly owing to the divine character imputed to me. His, he believed to be the same. But to a whim, a freakishness in his soul, which led him to fancy me as one among many, not as one with no peer.

But the apparent unconcern of King Media with respect to my godship, by no means so much surprised me, as his unaffected indifference to my amazing voyage from the sun; his indifference to the sun itself; and all the wonderful circumstances that must have attended my departure. Whether he had ever been there himself, that he regarded a solar trip with so much unconcern, almost became a question in my mind. Certain it is, that as a mere traveler he must have deemed me no very great prodigy.

My surprise at these things was enhanced by reflecting, that to the people of the Archipelago the map of Mardi was the map of the world. With the exception of certain islands out of sight and at an indefinite distance, they had no certain knowledge of any isles but their own.

And, no long time elapsed ere I had still additional reasons to cease wondering at the easy faith accorded to the story which I had given of myself. For these Mardians were familiar with still greater marvels than mine; verily believing in prodigies of all sorts. Any one of them put my exploits to the blush.

Look to thy ways then, Taji, thought I, and carry not thy crest too high. Of a surety, thou hast more peers than inferiors. Thou art overtopped all round. Bear thyself discreetly and not haughtily, Taji. It will not answer to give thyself airs. Abstain from all consequential allusions to the other world, and the genteel deities among whom thou hast circled. Sport not too jauntily thy raiment, because it is novel in Mardi; nor boast of the fleetness of thy Chamois, because it is unlike a canoe. Vaunt not of thy pedigree, Taji; for Media himself will measure it with thee there by the furlong. Be not a "snob," Taji.

So then, weighing all things well, and myself severely, I resolved to follow my Mentor's wise counsel; neither arrogating aught, nor abating of just dues; but circulating freely, sociably, and frankly, among the gods, heroes, high priests, kings, and gentlemen, that made up the principalities of Mardi.

Chapter LVIII

Mardi By Night And Yillah By Day

During the night following our arrival, many dreams were no doubt dreamt in Odo. But my thoughts were wakeful. And while all others slept, obeying a restless impulse, I stole without into the magical starlight. There are those who in a strange land ever love to view it by night.

It has been said, that the opening in the groves where was situated Media's city, was elevated above the surrounding plains. Hence was commanded a broad reach of prospect.

Far and wide was deep low-sobbing repose of man and nature. The groves were motionless; and in the meadows, like goblins, the shadows advanced and retreated. Full before me, lay the Mardian fleet of isles, profoundly at anchor within their coral harbor. Near by was one belted round by a frothy luminous reef, wherein it lay, like Saturn in its ring.

From all their summits, went up a milk-white smoke, as from Indian wigwams in the hazy harvest-moon. And floating away, these vapors blended with the faint mist, as of a cataract, hovering over the circumvallating reef. Far beyond all, and far into the infinite night, surged the jet-black ocean.

But how tranquil the wide lagoon, which mirrored the burning spots in heaven! Deep down into its innermost heart penetrated the slanting rays of Hesperus like a shaft of light, sunk far into mysterious Golcondas, where myriad gnomes seemed toiling. Soon a light breeze rippled the water, and the shaft was seen no more. But the moon's bright wake was still revealed: a silver track, tipping every wave-crest in its course, till each seemed a pearly, scroll-prowed nautilus, buoyant with some elfin crew.

From earth to heaven! High above me was Night's shadowy bower, traversed, vine-like, by the Milky Way, and heavy with golden clusterings. Oh stars! oh eyes, that see me, wheresoe'er I roam: serene, intent, inscrutable for aye, tell me Sybils, what I am.— Wondrous worlds on worlds! Lo, round and round me, shining, awful spells: all glorious, vivid constellations, God's diadem ye are! To you, ye stars, man owes his subtlest raptures, thoughts unspeakable, yet full of faith.

But how your mild effulgence stings the boding heart. Am I a murderer, stars?

Hours pass. The starry trance is departed. Long waited for, the dawn now comes.

First, breaking along the waking face; peeping from out the languid lids; then shining forth in longer glances; till, like the sun, up comes the soul, and sheds its rays abroad.

When thus my Yillah did daily dawn, how she lit up my world; tinging more rosily the roseate clouds, that in her summer cheek played to and fro, like clouds in Italian air.

Chapter LIX

Their Morning Meal

Not wholly is our world made up of bright stars and bright eyes: so now to our story.

A conscientious host should ever be up betimes, to look after the welfare of his guests, and see to it that their day begin auspiciously. King Media announced the advent of the sun, by rustling at my bower's eaves in person.

A repast was spread in an adjoining arbor, which Media's pages had smoothed for our reception, and where his subordinate chiefs were in attendance. Here we reclined upon mats. Balmy and fresh blew the breath of the morning; golden vapors were upon the mountains, silver sheen upon the grass; and the birds were at matins in the groves; their bright plumage flashing into view, here and there, as if some rainbow were crouching in the foliage.

Spread before us were viands, served in quaint-shaped, curiously-dyed gourds, not Sevres, but almost as tasteful; and like true porcelain, fire had tempered them. Green and yielding, they are plucked from the tree; and emptied of their pulp, are scratched over with minute marks, like those of a line engraving. The ground prepared, the various figures are carefully etched. And the outlines filled up with delicate punctures, certain vegetable oils are poured over them, for coloring. Filled with a peculiar species of earth, the gourd is now placed in an oven in the ground. And in due time exhumed, emptied of its contents, and washed in the stream, it presents a deep-dyed exterior; every figure distinctly traced and opaque, but the ground semi-transparent. In some cases, owing to the variety of dyes employed, each figure is of a different hue.

More glorious goblets than these for the drinking of wine, went never from hand to mouth. Capacious as pitchers, they almost superseded decanters.

Now, in a tropical climate, fruit, with light wines, forms the only fit meal of a morning. And with orchards and vineyards forever in sight, who but the Hetman of the Cossacs would desire more? We had plenty of the juice of the grape. But of this hereafter; there are some fine old cellars, and plenty of good cheer in store.

During the repast, Media, for a time, was much taken up with our raiment. He begged me to examine for a moment the texture of his right royal robe, and observe how much superior it was to my own. It put my mantle to the blush; being tastefully stained with rare devices in red and black; and bordered with dyed fringes of feathers, and tassels of red birds' claws.

Next came under observation the Skyeman's Guayaquil hat; at whose preposterous shape, our host laughed in derision; clapping a great conical calabash upon the head of an attendant, and saying that now he was Jarl. At this, and all similar sallies, Samoa was sure to roar louder than any; though mirth was no constitutional thing with him. But he seemed rejoiced at the opportunity of turning upon us the ridicule, which as a barbarian among whites, he himself had so often experienced.

These pleasantries over, King Media very slightly drew himself up, as if to make amends for his previous unbending. He discoursed imperially with his chiefs; nodded his sovereign will to his pages; called for another gourd of wine; in all respects carrying his royalty bravely.

The repast concluded, we journeyed to the canoe-house, where we found the little Chamois stabled like a steed. One solitary depredation had been committed. Its sides and bottom had been completely denuded of the minute green barnacles, and short sea-grass, which, like so many leeches, had fastened to our planks during our long, lazy voyage.

By the people they had been devoured as dainties.

Chapter LX

Belshazzar On The Bench

Now, Media was king of Odo. And from the simplicity of his manners hitherto, and his easy, frank demeanor toward ourselves, had we foolishly doubted that fact, no skepticism could have survived an illustration of it, which this very day we witnessed at noon.

For at high noon, Media was wont to don his dignity with his symbols of state; and sit on his judgment divan or throne, to hear and try all causes brought before him, and fulminate his royal decrees.

This divan was elevated at one end of a spacious arbor, formed by an avenue of regal palms, which in brave state, held aloft their majestical canopy.

The crown of the island prince was of the primitive old Eastern style; in shape, similar, perhaps, to that jauntily sported as a foraging cap by his sacred majesty King Nimrod, who so lustily followed the hounds. It was a plaited turban of red tappa, radiated by the pointed and polished white bones of the Ray-fish. These diverged from a bandeau or fillet of the most precious pearls; brought up from the sea by the deepest diving mermen of Mardi. From the middle of the crown rose a tri-foiled spear-head. And a spear- headed scepter graced the right hand of the king.

Now, for all the rant of your democrats, a fine king on a throne is a very fine sight to behold. He looks very much like a god. No wonder that his more dutiful subjects so swore, that their good lord and master King Media was demi-divine.

A king on his throne! Ah, believe me, ye Gracchi, ye Acephali, ye Levelers, it is something worth seeing, be sure; whether beheld at Babylon the Tremendous, when Nebuchadnezzar was crowned; at old Scone in the days of Macbeth; at Rheims, among Oriflammes, at the coronation of Louis le Grand; at Westminster Abbey, when the gentlemanly George doffed his beaver for a diadem; or under the soft shade of palm trees on an isle in the sea.

Man lording it over man, man kneeling to man, is a spectacle that Gabriel might well travel hitherward to behold; for never did he behold it in heaven. But Darius giving laws to the Medes and the Persians, or the conqueror of Bactria with king-cattle yoked to his car, was not a whit more sublime, than Beau Brummel magnificently ringing for his valet.

A king on his throne! It is Jupiter nodding in the councils of Olympus; Satan, seen among the coronets in Hell.

A king on his throne! It is the sun over a mountain; the sun over law-giving Sinai; the sun in our system: planets, duke-like, dancing attendance, and baronial satellites in waiting.

A king on his throne! After all, but a gentleman seated. And thus sat the good lord, King Media.

Time passed. And after trying and dismissing several minor affairs, Media called for certain witnesses to testify concerning one Jiromo, a foolhardy wight, who had been silly enough to plot against the majesty now sitting judge and jury upon him.

His guilt was clear. And the witnesses being heard, from a bunch of palm plumes Media taking a leaf, placed it in the hand of a runner or pursuivant, saying, "This to Jiromo, where he is prisoned; with his king's compliments; say we here wait for his head."

It was doffed like a turban before a Dey, and brought back on the instant.

Now came certain lean-visaged, poverty-stricken, and hence suspicious-looking varlets, grumbling and growling, and amiable as Bruin. They came muttering some wild jargon about "bulwarks," "bulkheads," "cofferdams," "safeguards," "noble charters," "shields," and "paladiums," "great and glorious birthrights," and other unintelligible gibberish.

Of the pursuivants, these worthies asked audience of Media.

"Go, kneel at the throne," was the answer.

"Our knee-pans are stiff with sciatics," was the rheumatic reply.

"An artifice to keep on your legs," said the pursuivants.

And advancing they salamed, and told Media the excuse of those sour- looking varlets. Whereupon my lord commanded them to down on their marrow-bones instanter, either before him or the headsman, whichsoever they pleased.

They preferred the former. And as they there kneeled, in vain did men with sharp ears (who abound in all courts) prick their auriculars, to list to that strange crackling and firing off of bone balls and sockets, ever incident to the genuflections of rheumatic courtiers.

In a row, then, these selfsame knee-pans did kneel before the king; who eyed them as eagles in air do goslings on dunghills; or hunters, hounds crouching round their calves.

"Your prayer?" said Media.

It was a petition, that thereafter all differences between man and man in Ode, together with all alleged offenses against the state, might be tried by twelve good men and true. These twelve to be unobnoxious to the party or parties concerned; their peers; and previously unbiased touching the matter at issue. Furthermore, that unanimity in these twelve should be indispensable to a verdict; and no dinner be vouchsafed till unanimity came.

Loud and long laughed King Media in scorn.

"This be your judge," he cried, swaying his scepter. "What! are twelve wise men more wise than one? or will twelve fools, put together, make one sage? Are twelve honest men more honest than one? or twelve knaves less knavish than one? And if, of twelve men, three be fools, and three wise, three knaves, and three upright, how obtain real unanimity from such?

"But if twelve judges be better than one, then are twelve hundred better than twelve. But take the whole populace for a judge, and you will long wait for a unanimous verdict.

"If upon a thing dubious, there be little unanimity in the conflicting opinions of one man's mind, how expect it in the uproar of twelve puzzled brains? though much unanimity be found in twelve hungry stomachs.

"Judges unobnoxious to the accused! Apply it to a criminal case. Ha! ha! if peradventure a Cacti be rejected, because he had seen the accused commit the crime for which he is arraigned. Then, his mind would be biased: no impartiality from him! Or your testy accused might object to another, because of his tomahawk nose, or a cruel squint of the eye.

"Of all follies the most foolish! Know ye from me, that true peers render not true verdicts. Jiromo was a rebel. Had I tried him by his peers, I had tried him by rebels; and the rebel had rebelled to some purpose.

"Away! As unerring justice dwells in a unity, and as one judge will at last judge the world beyond all appeal; so—though often here below justice be hard to attain—does man come nearest the mark, when he imitates that model divine. Hence, one judge is better than twelve."

"And as Justice, in ideal, is ever painted high lifted above the crowd; so, from the exaltation of his rank, an honest king is the best of those unical judges, which individually are better than twelve. And therefore am I, King Media, the best judge in this land."

"Subjects! so long as I live, I will rule you and judge you alone. And though you here kneeled before me till you grew into the ground, and there took root, no yea to your petition will you get from this throne. I am king: ye are slaves. Mine to command: yours to obey. And this hour I decree, that henceforth no gibberish of bulwarks and bulkheads be heard in this land. For a dead bulwark and a bulkhead, to dam off sedition, will I make of that man, who again but breathes those bulky words. Ho! spears! see that these knee-pans here kneel till set of sun."

High noon was now passed; and removing his crown, and placing it on the dais for the kneelers to look at during their devotions, King Media departed from that place, and once more played the agreeable host.

Chapter LXI

An Incognito

For the rest of that day, and several that followed, we were continually receiving visits from the neighboring islands; whose inhabitants in fleets and flotillas flocked round Odo to behold the guests of its lord. Among them came many messengers from the neighboring kings with soft speeches and gifts.

But it were needless to detail our various interviews, or relate in what manifold ways, the royal strangers gave token of their interest concerning us.

Upon the third day, however, there was noticed a mysterious figure, like the inscrutable incognitos sometimes encountered, crossing the tower-shadowed Plaza of Assignations at Lima. It was enveloped in a dark robe of tappa, so drawn and plaited about the limbs; and with one hand, so wimpled about the face, as only to expose a solitary eye. But that eye was a world. Now it was fixed upon Yillah with a sinister glance, and now upon me, but with a different expression. However great the crowd, however tumultuous, that fathomless eye gazed on; till at last it seemed no eye, but a spirit, forever prying into my soul. Often I strove to approach it, but it would evade me, soon reappearing.

Pointing out the apparition to Media, I intreated him to take means to fix it, that my suspicions might be dispelled, as to its being incorporeal. He replied that, by courtesy, incognitos were sacred. Insomuch that the close-plaited robe and the wimple were secure as a castle. At last, to my relief, the phantom disappeared, and was seen no more.

Numerous and fervent the invitations received to return the calls wherewith we were honored. But for the present we declined them; preferring to establish ourselves firmly in the heart of Media, ere encountering the vicissitudes of roaming. In a multitude of acquaintances is less security, than in one faithful friend.

Now, while these civilities were being received, and on the fourth morning after our arrival, there landed on the beach three black-eyed damsels, deep brunettes, habited in long variegated robes, and with gay blossoms on their heads.

With many salams, the strangers were ushered into my presence by an old white-haired servitor of Media's, who with a parting conge murmured, "From Queen Hautia," then departed. Surprised, I stood mute, and welcomed them.

The first, with many smiles and blandishments, waved before me a many-tinted Iris: the flag-flower streaming with pennons. Advancing, the second then presented three rose-hued purple-veined Circea flowers, the dew still clinging to them. The third placed in my hand a moss-rose bud; then, a Venus-car.

"Thanks for your favors! now your message."

Starting at this reception, graciously intended, they conferred a moment; when the Iris-bearer said in winning phrase, "We come from Hautia, whose moss-rose you hold."

"All thanks to Hautia then; the bud is very fragrant."

Then she pointed to the Venus-car.

"This too is sweet; thanks to Hautia for her flowers. Pray, bring me more."

"He mocks our mistress," and gliding from me, they waved witch- hazels, leaving me alone and wondering.

Informing Media of this scene, he smiled; threw out queer hints of Hautia; but knew not what her message meant.

At first this affair occasioned me no little uneasiness, with much matter for marveling; but in the novel pleasure of our sojourn in Odo, it soon slipped from my mind; nor for some time, did I again hear aught of Queen Hautia.

Chapter LXII

Taji Retires From The World

After a while, when the strangers came not in shoals as before, I proposed to our host, a stroll over his dominions; desirous of beholding the same, and secretly induced by the hope of selecting an abode, more agreeable to my fastidious taste, than the one already assigned me.

The ramble over—a pleasant one it was—it resulted in a determination on my part to quit Odo. Yet not to go very far; only ten or twelve yards, to a little green tuft of an islet; one of many, which here and there, all round the island, nestled like birds' nests in the branching boughs of the coral grove, whose roots laid hold of the foundations of the deep. Between these islets and the shore, extended shelving ledges, with shallows above, just sufficient to float a canoe. One of these islets was wooded and wined; an arbor in the sea. And here, Media permitting, I decided to dwell.

Not long was Media in complying; nor long, ere my retreat was in readiness. Laced together, the twisting boughs were closely thatched. And thatched were the sides also, with deep crimson pandannus leaves; whose long, forked spears, lifted by the breeze, caused the whole place to blaze, as with flames. Canes, laid on palm trunks, formed the floor. How elastic! In vogue all over Odo, among the chiefs, it imparted such a buoyancy to the person, that to this special cause may be imputed in good part the famous fine spirits of the nobles.

Hypochondriac! essay the elastic flooring! It shall so pleasantly and gently jolt thee, as to shake up, and pack off the stagnant humors mantling thy pool-like soul.

Such was my dwelling. But I make no mention of sundry little appurtenances of tropical housekeeping: calabashes, cocoanut shells, and rolls of fine tappa; till with Yillah seated at last in my arbor, I looked round, and wanted for naught.

But what of Jarl and Samoa? Why Jarl must needs be fanciful, as well as myself. Like a bachelor in chambers, he settled down right opposite to me, on the main land, in a little wigwam in the grove.

But Samoa, following not his comrade's example, still tarried in the camp of the Hittites and Jebusites of Odo. Beguiling men of their leisure by his marvelous stories: and maidens of their hearts by his marvelous wiles.

When I chose, I was completely undisturbed in my arbor; an ukase of Media's forbidding indiscriminate intrusion. But thrice in the day came a garrulous old man with my viands.

Thus sequestered, however, I could not entirely elude the pryings of the people of the neighboring islands; who often passed by, slowly paddling, and earnestly regarding my retreat. But gliding along at a distance, and never essaying a landing, their occasional vicinity troubled me but little. But now and then of an evening, when thick and fleet the shadows were falling, dim glimpses of a canoe would be spied; hovering about the place like a ghost. And once, in the stillness of the night, hearing the near ripple of a prow, I sallied forth, but the phantom quickly departed.

That night, Yillah shuddered as she slept. "The whirl-pool," she murmured, "sweet mosses." Next day she was lost in reveries, plucking pensive hyacinths, or gazing intently into the lagoon.

Chapter LXIII

Odo And Its Lord

Time now to enter upon some further description of the island and its lord.

And first for Media: a gallant gentleman and king. From a goodly stock he came. In his endless pedigree, reckoning deities by decimals, innumerable kings, and scores of great heroes, chiefs, and priests. Nor in person, did he belie his origin. No far-descended dwarf was he, the least of a receding race. He stood like a palm tree; about whose acanthus capital droops not more gracefully the silken fringes, than Media's locks upon his noble brow. Strong was his arm to wield the club, or hurl the javelin; and potent, I ween, round a maiden's waist.

Thus much here for Media. Now comes his isle.

Our pleasant ramble found it a little round world by itself; full of beauties as a garden; chequered by charming groves; watered by roving brooks; and fringed all round by a border of palm trees, whose roots drew nourishment from the water. But though abounding in other quarters of the Archipelago, not a solitary bread-fruit grew in Odo. A noteworthy circumstance, observable in these regions, where islands close adjoining, so differ in their soil, that certain fruits growing genially in one, are foreign to another. But Odo was famed for its guavas, whose flavor was likened to the flavor of new-blown lips; and for its grapes, whose juices prompted many a laugh and many a groan.

Beside the city where Media dwelt, there were few other clusters of habitations in Odo. The higher classes living, here and there, in separate households; but not as eremites. Some buried themselves in the cool, quivering bosoms of the groves. Others, fancying a marine vicinity, dwelt hard by the beach in little cages of bamboo; whence of mornings they sallied out with jocund cries, and went plunging into the refreshing bath, whose frothy margin was the threshold of their dwellings. Others still, like birds, built their nests among the sylvan nooks of the elevated interior; whence all below, and hazy green, lay steeped in languor the island's throbbing heart.

Thus dwelt the chiefs and merry men of mark. The common sort, including serfs, and Helots, war-captives held in bondage, lived in secret places, hard to find. Whence it came, that, to a stranger, the whole isle looked care-free and beautiful. Deep among the ravines and the rocks, these beings lived in noisome caves, lairs for beasts, not human homes; or built them coops of rotten boughs—living trees were banned them—whose mouldy hearts hatched vermin. Fearing infection of some plague, born of this filth, the chiefs of Odo seldom passed that way and looking round within their green retreats, and pouring out their wine, and plucking from orchards of the best, marveled how these swine could grovel in the mire, and wear such sallow cheeks. But they offered no sweet homes; from that mire they never sought to drag them out; they open threw no orchard; and intermitted not the mandates that condemned their drudges to a life of deaths. Sad sight! to see those round-shouldered Helots, stooping in their trenches: artificial, three in number, and concentric: the isle well nigh surrounding. And herein, fed by oozy loam, and kindly dew from heaven, and bitter sweat from men, grew as in hot-beds the nutritious Taro.

Toil is man's allotment; toil of brain, or toil of hands, or a grief that's more than either, the grief and sin of idleness. But when man toils and slays himself for masters who withhold the life he gives to them— then, then, the soul screams out, and every sinew cracks. So with these poor serfs. And few of them could choose but be the brutes they seemed.

Now needs it to be said, that Odo was no land of pleasure unalloyed, and plenty without a pause?— Odo, in whose lurking-places infants turned from breasts, whence flowed no nourishment.—Odo, in whose inmost haunts, dark groves were brooding, passing which you heard most dismal cries, and voices cursing Media. There, men were scourged; their crime, a heresy; the heresy, that Media was no demigod. For this they shrieked. Their fathers shrieked before; their fathers, who, tormented, said, "Happy we to groan, that our children's children may be glad." But their children's children howled. Yet these, too, echoed previous generations, and loudly swore, "The pit that's dug for us may prove another's grave."

But let all pass. To look at, and to roam about of holidays, Odo seemed a happy land. The palm-trees waved—though here and there you marked one sear and palsy-smitten; the flowers bloomed—though dead ones moldered in decay; the waves ran up the strand in glee—though, receding, they sometimes left behind bones mixed with shells.

But else than these, no sign of death was seen throughout the isle. Did men in Odo live for aye? Was Ponce de Leon's fountain there? For near and far, you saw no ranks and files of graves, no generations harvested in winrows. In Odo, no hard-hearted nabob slept beneath a gentle epitaph; no requiescat-in-pace mocked a sinner damned; no memento-mori admonished men to live while yet they might. Here Death hid his skull; and hid it in the sea, the common sepulcher of Odo. Not dust to dust, but dust to brine; not hearses but canoes. For all who died upon that isle were carried out beyond the outer reef, and there were buried with their sires' sires. Hence came the thought, that of gusty nights, when round the isles, and high toward heaven, flew the white reef's rack and foam, that then and there, kept chattering watch and ward, the myriads that were ocean- tombed.

But why these watery obsequies?

Odo was but a little isle, and must the living make way for the dead, and Life's small colony be dislodged by Death's grim hosts; as the gaunt tribes of Tamerlane o'erspread the tented pastures of the Khan?

And now, what follows, said these Islanders: "Why sow corruption in the soil which yields us life? We would not pluck our grapes from over graves. This earth's an urn for flowers, not for ashes."

They said that Oro, the supreme, had made a cemetery of the sea.

And what more glorious grave? Was Mausolus more sublimely urned? Or do the minster-lamps that burn before the tomb of Charlemagne, show more of pomp, than all the stars, that blaze above the shipwrecked mariner?

But no more of the dead; men shrug their shoulders, and love not their company; though full soon we shall all have them for fellows.

Chapter LXIV

Yillah A Phantom

For a time we were happy in Odo: Yillah and I in our islet. Nor did the pearl on her bosom glow more rosily than the roses in her cheeks; though at intervals they waned and departed; and deadly pale was her glance, when she murmured of the whirlpool and mosses. As pale my soul, bethinking me of Aleema the priest.

But day by day, did her spell weave round me its magic, and all the hidden things of her being grew more lovely and strange. Did I commune with a spirit? Often I thought that Paradise had overtaken me on earth, and that Yillah was verily an angel, and hence the mysteries that hallowed her.

But how fleeting our joys. Storms follow bright dawnings.—Long memories of short-lived scenes, sad thoughts of joyous hours—how common are ye to all mankind. When happy, do we pause and say—"Lo, thy felicity, my soul?" No: happiness seldom seems happiness, except when looked back upon from woes. A flowery landscape, you must come out of, to behold.

Sped the hours, the days, the one brief moment of our joys. Fairy bower in the fair lagoon, scene of sylvan ease and heart's repose,— Oh, Yillah, Yillah! All the woods repeat the sound, the wild, wild woods of my wild soul. Yillah! Yillah! cry the small strange voices in me, and evermore, and far and deep, they echo on.

Days passed. When one morning I found the arbor vacant. Gone! A dream. I closed my eyes, and would have dreamed her back. In vain. Starting, I called upon her name; but none replied. Fleeing from the islet, I gained the neighboring shore, and searched among the woods; and my comrades meeting, besought their aid. But idle all. No glimpse of aught, save trees and flowers. Then Media was sought out; the event made known; and quickly, bands were summoned to range the isle.

Noon came; but no Yillah. When Media averred she was no longer in Odo. Whither she was gone, or how, he knew not; nor could any imagine.

At this juncture, there chanced to arrive certain messengers from abroad; who, presuming that all was well with Taji, came with renewed invitations to visit various pleasant places round about. Among these, came Queen Hautia's heralds, with their Iris flag, once more bringing flowers. But they came and went unheeded.

Setting out to return, these envoys were accompanied by numerous followers of Media, dispatched to the neighboring islands, to seek out the missing Yillah. But three days passed; and, one by one, they all returned; and stood before me silently.

For a time I raved. Then, falling into outer repose, lived for a space in moods and reveries, with eyes that knew no closing, one glance forever fixed.

They strove to rouse me. Girls danced and sang; and tales of fairy times were told; of monstrous imps, and youths enchanted; of groves and gardens in the sea. Yet still I moved not, hearing all, yet noting naught. Media cried, "For shame, oh Taji; thou, a god?" and placed a spear in my nerveless hand. And Jarl loud called upon me to awake. Samoa marveled.

Still sped the days. And at length, my memory was restored. The thoughts of things broke over me like returning billows on a beach long bared. A rush, a foam of recollections!—Sweet Yillah gone, and I bereaved.

Another interval, and that mood was past. Misery became a memory. The keen pang a deep vibration. The remembrance seemed the thing remembered; though bowed with sadness. There are thoughts that lie and glitter deep: tearful pearls beneath life's sea, that surges still, and rolls sunlit, whatever it may hide. Common woes, like fluids, mix all round. Not so with that other grief. Some mourners load the air with lamentations; but the loudest notes are struck from hollows. Their tears flow fast: but the deep spring only wells.

At last I turned to Media, saying I must hie from Odo, and rove throughout all Mardi; for Yillah might yet be found.

But hereafter, in words, little more of the maiden, till perchance her fate be learned.

Chapter LXV

Taji Makes Three Acquaintances

Down to this period, I had restrained Samoa from wandering to the neighboring islands, though he had much desired it, in compliance with the invitations continually received. But now I informed both him, and his comrade, of the tour I purposed; desiring their company.

Upon the announcement of my intention to depart, to my no small surprise Media also proposed to accompany me: a proposition gladly embraced. It seems, that for some reason, he had not as yet extended his travels to the more distant islands. Hence the voyage in prospect was particularly agreeable to him. Nor did he forbear any pains to insure its prosperity; assuring me, furthermore, that its object must eventually be crowned with success. "I myself am interested in this pursuit," said he; "and trust me, Yillah will be found."

For the tour of the lagoon, the docile Chamois was proposed; but Media dissented; saying, that it befitted not the lord of Odo to voyage in the equipage of his guest. Therefore, three canoes were selected from his own royal fleet.

One for ourselves, and a trio of companions whom he purposed introducing to my notice; the rest were reserved for attendants.

Thanks to Media's taste and heedfulness, the strangers above mentioned proved truly acceptable.

The first was Mohi, or Braid-Beard, so called from the manner in which he wore that appendage, exceedingly long and gray. He was a venerable teller of stories and legends, one of the Keepers of the Chronicles of the Kings of Mardi.

The second was Babbalanja, a man of a mystical aspect, habited in a voluminous robe. He was learned in Mardian lore; much given to quotations from ancient and obsolete authorities: the Ponderings of Old Bardianna: the Pandects of Alla-Malolla.

Third and last, was Yoomy, or the Warbler. A youthful, long-haired, blue-eyed minstrel; all fits and starts; at times, absent of mind, and wan of cheek; but always very neat and pretty in his apparel; wearing the most becoming of turbans, a Bird of Paradise feather its plume, and sporting the gayest of sashes. Most given was Yoomy to amorous melodies, and rondos, and roundelays, very witching to hear. But at times disdaining the oaten reed, like a clarion he burst forth with lusty lays of arms and battle; or, in mournful strains, sounded elegies for departed bards and heroes.

Thus much for Yoomy as a minstrel. In other respects, it would be hard to depict him. He was so capricious a mortal; so swayed by contrary moods; so lofty, so humble, so sad, so merry; so made up of a thousand contradictions, that we must e'en let him depict himself as our story progresses. And herein it is hoped he will succeed; since no one in Mardi comprehended him.

Now the trio, thus destined for companions on our voyage, had for some time been anxious to take the tour of the Archipelago. In particular, Babbalanja had often expressed the most ardent desire to visit every one of the isles, in quest of some object, mysteriously hinted. He murmured deep concern for my loss, the sincerest sympathy; and pressing my hand more than once, said lowly, "Your pursuit is mine, noble Taji. Where'er you search, I follow."

So, too, Yoomy addressed me; but with still more feeling. And something like this, also, Braid-Beard repeated.

But to my sorrow, I marked that both Mohi and Babbalanja, especially the last, seemed not so buoyant of hope, concerning lost Yillah, as the youthful Yoomy, and his high-spirited lord, King Media.

As our voyage would embrace no small period of time, it behoved King Media to appoint some trustworthy regent, to rule during his absence. This regent was found in Almanni, a stem-eyed, resolute warrior, a kinsman of the king.

All things at last in readiness, and the ensuing morning appointed for a start, Media, on the beach, at eventide, when both light and water waned, drew a rude map of the lagoon, to compensate for the obstructions in the way of a comprehensive glance at it from Odo.

And thus was sketched the plan of our voyage; which islands first to visit; and which to touch at, when we should be homeward bound.

Chapter LXVI

True each to his word, up came the sun, and round to my isle came Media.

How glorious a morning! The new-born clouds all dappled with gold, and streaked with violet; the sun in high spirits; and the pleasant air cooled overnight by the blending circumambient fountains, forever playing all round the reef; the lagoon within, the coral-rimmed basin, into which they poured, subsiding, hereabouts, into green tranquillity.

But what monsters of canoes! Would they devour an innocent voyager? their great black prows curling aloft, and thrown back like trunks of elephants; a dark, snaky length behind, like the sea-serpent's train.

The prow of the foremost terminated in a large, open, shark's mouth, garnished with ten rows of pearly human teeth, curiously inserted into the sculptured wood. The gunwale was ornamented with rows of rich spotted Leopard and Tiger-shells; here and there, varied by others, flat and round, and spirally traced; gay serpents petrified in coils. These were imbedded in a grooved margin, by means of a resinous compound, exhaling such spices, that the canoes were odoriferous as the Indian chests of the Maldives.

The likeness of the foremost canoe to an elephant, was helped by a sort of canopied Howdah in its stern, of heavy, russet-dyed tappa, tasselled at the corners with long bunches of cocoanut fibres, stained red. These swayed to and fro, like the fox-tails on a Tuscarora robe.

But what is this, in the head of the canoe, just under the shark's mouth? A grinning little imp of an image; a ring in its nose; cowrie shells jingling at its ears; with an abominable leer, like that of Silenus reeling on his ass. It was taking its ease; cosily smoking a pipe; its bowl, a duodecimo edition of the face of the smoker. This image looked sternward; everlastingly mocking us.

Of these canoes, it may be well to state, that although during our stay in Odo, so many barges and shallops had touched there, nothing similar to Media's had been seen. But inquiring whence his sea-equipage came, we were thereupon taught to reverence the same as antiquities and heir-looms; claw-keeled, dragon-prowed crafts of a bygone generation; at present, superseded in general use by the more swan-like canoes, significant of the advanced stage of marine architecture in Mardi. No sooner was this known, than what had seemed almost hideous in my eyes, became merely grotesque. Nor could I help being greatly delighted with the good old family pride of our host.

The upper corners of our sails displayed the family crest of Media; three upright boars' tusks, in an heraldic field argent. A fierce device: Whom rends he?

All things in readiness, we glided away: the multitude waving adieu; and our flotilla disposed in the following order.

First went the royal Elephant, carrying Media, myself, Jarl, and Samoa; Mohi the Teller of Legends, Babbalanja, and Yoomy, and six vivacious paddlers; their broad paddle-blades carved with the royal boars' tusks, the same tattooed on their chests for a livery.

And thus, as Media had promised, we voyaged in state. To crown all, seated sideways in the high, open shark's-mouth of our prow was a little dwarf of a boy, one of Media's pages, a red conch-shell, bugle-wise suspended at his side. Among various other offices, it was the duty of little Vee-Vee to announce the advent of his master, upon drawing near to the islands in our route. Two short bars, projecting from one side of the prow, furnished him the means of ascent to his perch.

As we gained the open lagoon with bellied sails, and paddles playing, a sheaf of foam borne upright at our prow; Yoomy, standing where the spicy spray flew over him, stretched forth his hand and cried— "The dawn of day is passed, and Mardi lies all before us: all her isles, and all her lakes; all her stores of good and evil. Storms may come, our barks may drown. But blow before us, all ye winds; give us a lively blast, good clarion; rally round us all our wits; and be this voyage full gayly sailed, for Yillah will yet be found."

Chapter LXVII

Little King Peepi

Valapee, or the Isle of Yams, being within plain sight of Media's dominions, we were not very long in drawing nigh to its shores.

Two long parallel elevations, rising some three arrow-flights into the air, double-ridge the island's entire length, lapping between, a widening vale, so level withal, that at either extremity, the green of its groves blends with the green of the lagoon; and the isle seems divided by a strait.

Within several paces of the beach, our canoes keeled the bottom, and camel-like mutely hinted that we voyagers must dismount.

Hereupon, the assembled islanders ran into the water, and with bent shoulders obsequiously desired the honor of transporting us to land. The beach gained, all present wearing robes instantly stripped them to the waist; a naked chest being their salute to kings. Very convenient for the common people, this; their half-clad forms presenting a perpetual and profound salutation.

Presently, Peepi, the ruler of Valapee drew near: a boy, hardly ten years old, striding the neck of a burly mute, bearing a long spear erect before him, to which was attached a canopy of five broad banana leaves, new plucked. Thus shaded, little Peepi advanced, steadying himself by the forelock of his bearer.

Besides his bright red robe, the young prince wore nothing but the symbol of Valapeean royalty; a string of small, close-fitting, concave shells, coiled and ambushed in his profuse, curly hair; one end falling over his ear, revealing a serpent's head, curiously carved from a nutmeg.

Quite proverbial, the unembarrassed air of young slips of royalty. But there was something so surprisingly precocious in this young Peepi, that at first one hardly knew what to conclude.

The first compliments over, the company were invited inland to a shady retreat.

As we pursued the path, walking between old Mohi the keeper of chronicles and Samoa the Upoluan, Babbalanja besought the former to enlighten a stranger concerning the history of this curious Peepi. Whereupon the chronicler gave us the following account; for all of which he alone is responsible.

Peepi, it seems, had been proclaimed king before he was born; his sire dying some few weeks previous to that event; and vacating his divan, declared that he left a monarch behind.

Marvels were told of Peepi. Along with the royal dignity, and superadded to the soul possessed in his own proper person, the infant monarch was supposed to have inherited the valiant spirits of some twenty heroes, sages, simpletons, and demi-gods, previously lodged in his sire.

Most opulent in spiritual gifts was this lord of Valapee; the legatee, moreover, of numerous anonymous souls, bequeathed to him by their late loyal proprietors. By a slavish act of his convocation of chiefs, he also possessed the reversion of all and singular the immortal spirits, whose first grantees might die intestate in Valapee. Servile, yet audacious senators! thus prospectively to administrate away the inalienable rights of posterity. But while yet unborn, the people of Valapee had been deprived of more than they now sought to wrest from their descendants. And former Peepies, infant and adult, had received homage more profound, than Peepi the Present. Witness the demeanor of the chieftains of old, upon every new investiture of the royal serpent. In a fever of loyalty, they were wont to present themselves before the heir to the isle, to go through with the court ceremony of the Pupera; a curious proceeding, so called: inverted endeavors to assume an erect posture: the nasal organ the base.

It was to the frequent practice of this ceremony, that most intelligent observers imputed the flattened noses of the elderly chiefs of the island; who, nevertheless, much gloried therein.

It was these chiefs, also, who still observed the old-fashioned custom of retiring from the presence of royalty with their heads between their thighs; so that while advancing in the contrary direction, their faces might be still deferentially turned toward their lord and master. A fine view of him did they obtain. All objects look well through an arch.

But to return to Peepi, the inheritor of souls and subjects. It was an article of faith with the people of Valapee, that Peepi not only actually possessed the souls bequeathed to him; but that his own was enriched by their peculiar qualities: The headlong valor of the late Tongatona; the pusillanimous discretion of Blandoo; the cunning of Voyo; the simplicity of Raymonda; the prodigality of Zonoree; the thrift of Titonti.

But had all these, and similar opposite qualities, simultaneously acted as motives upon Peepi, certes, he would have been a most pitiable mortal, in a ceaseless eddy of resolves, incapable of a solitary act.

But blessed be the gods, it was otherwise. Though it fared little better for his subjects as it was. His assorted souls were uppermost and active in him, one by one. Today, valiant Tongatona ruled the isle, meditating wars and invasions; tomorrow, thrice discreet Blandoo, who, disbanding the levies, turned his attention to the terraces of yams. And so on in rotation to the end.

Whence, though capable of action, Peepi, by reason of these revolving souls in him, was one of the most unreliable of beings. What the open-handed Zonoree promised freely to-day, the parsimonious Titonti withheld to-morrow; and forever Raymonda was annulling the doings of Voyo; and Voyo the doings of Raymonda.

What marvel then, that in Valapee all was legislative uproar and confusion; advance and retreat; abrogations and revivals; foundations without superstructures; nothing permanent but the island itself.

Nor were there those in the neighboring countries, who failed to reap profit from this everlasting transition state of the affairs of the kingdom. All boons from Peepi were entreated when the prodigal Zonoree was lord of the ascendant. And audacious claims were urged upon the state when the pusillanimous Blandoo shrank from the thought of resisting them.

Thus subject to contrary impulses, over which he had not the faintest control, Peepi was plainly denuded of all moral obligation to virtue. He was no more a free agent, than the heart which beat in his bosom. Wherefore, his complaisant parliament had passed a law, recognizing that curious, but alarming fact; solemnly proclaiming, that King Peepi was minus a conscience. Agreeable to truth. But when they went further, and vowed by statute, that Peepi could do no wrong, they assuredly did violence to the truth; besides, making a sad blunder in their logic. For far from possessing an absolute aversion to evil, by his very nature it was the hardest thing in the world for Peepi to do right.

Taking all these things into consideration, then, no wonder that this wholly irresponsible young prince should be a lad of considerable assurance, and the easiest manners imaginable.

Chapter LXVIII

How Teeth Were Regarded In Valapee

Coiling through the thickets, like the track of a serpent, wound along the path we pursued. And ere long we came to a spacious grove, embowering an oval arbor. Here, we reclined at our ease, and refreshments were served.

Little worthy of mention occurred, save this. Happening to catch a glimpse of the white even teeth of Hohora one of our attendants, King Peepi coolly begged of Media the favor, to have those same dentals drawn on the spot, and presented to him.

Now human teeth, extracted, are reckoned among the most valuable ornaments in Mardi. So open wide thy strong box, Hohora, and show thy treasures. What a gallant array! standing shoulder to shoulder, without a hiatus between. A complete set of jewelry, indeed, thought Peepi. But, it seems, not destined for him; Media leaving it to the present proprietor, whether his dentals should change owners or not.

And here, to prepare the way for certain things hereafter to be narrated, something farther needs be said concerning the light in which men's molars are regarded in Mardi.

Strung together, they are sported for necklaces, or hung in drops from the ear; they are wrought into dice; in lieu of silken locks, are exchanged for love tokens.

As in all lands, men smite their breasts, and tear their hair, when transported with grief; so, in some countries, teeth are stricken out under the sway of similar emotions. To a very great extent, this was once practiced in the Hawaiian Islands, ere idol and altar went down. Still living in Oahu, are many old chiefs, who were present at the famous obsequies of their royal old generalissimo, Tammahammaha, when there is no telling how many pounds of ivory were cast upon his grave.

Ah! had the regal white elephants of Siam been there, doubtless they had offered up their long, hooked tusks, whereon they impale the leopards, their foes; and the unicorn had surrendered that fixed bayonet in his forehead; and the imperial Cachalot-whale, the long chain of white towers in his jaw; yea, over that grim warrior's grave, the mooses, and elks, and stags, and fallow-deer had stacked their antlers, as soldiers their arms on the field.

Terrific shade of tattooed Tammahammaha! if, from a vile dragon's molars, rose mailed men, what heroes shall spring from the cannibal canines once pertaining to warriors themselves!—Am I the witch of Endor, that I conjure up this ghost? Or, King Saul, that I so quake at the sight? For, lo! roundabout me Tammahammaha's tattooing expands, till all the sky seems a tiger's skin. But now, the spotted phantom sweeps by; as a man-of-war's main-sail, cloud-like, blown far to leeward in a gale.

Banquo down, we return.

In Valapee, prevails not the barbarous Hindoo custom of offering up widows to the shades of their lords; for, bereaved, the widows there marry again. Nor yet prevails the savage Hawaiian custom of offering up teeth to the manes of the dead; for, at the decease of a friend, the people rob not their own mouths to testify their woe. On the contrary, they extract the teeth from the departed, distributing them among the mourners for memorial legacies; as elsewhere, silver spoons are bestowed.

From the high value ascribed to dentals throughout the archipelago of Mardi, and also from their convenient size, they are circulated as money; strings of teeth being regarded by these people very much as belts of wampum among the Winnebagoes of the North; or cowries, among the Bengalese. So, that in Valapee the very beggars are born with a snug investment in their mouths; too soon, however, to be appropriated by their lords; leaving them toothless for the rest of their days, and forcing them to diet on poee-pudding and banana blanc-mange.

As a currency, teeth are far less clumsy than cocoanuts; which, among certain remote barbarians, circulate for coin; one nut being equivalent, perhaps, to a penny. The voyager who records the fact, chuckles over it hugely; as evincing the simplicity of those heathens; not knowing that he himself was the simpleton; since that currency of theirs was purposely devised by the men, to check the extravagance of their women; cocoanuts, for spending money, being such a burden to carry.

It only remains to be added, that the most solemn oath of a native of Valapee is that sworn by his tooth. "By this tooth," said Bondo to Noojoomo, "by this tooth I swear to be avenged upon thee, oh Noojoomo!"

Chapter LXIX

The Company Discourse, And Braid-Beard Rehearses A Legend

Finding in Valapee no trace of her whom we sought, and but little pleased with the cringing demeanor of the people, and the wayward follies of Peepi their lord, we early withdrew from the isle.

As we glided away, King Media issued a sociable decree. He declared it his royal pleasure, that throughout the voyage, all stiffness and state etiquette should be suspended: nothing must occur to mar the freedom of the party. To further this charming plan, he doffed his symbols of royalty, put off his crown, laid aside his scepter, and assured us that he would not wear them again, except when we landed; and not invariably, then.

"Are we not all now friends and companions?" he said. "So companions and friends let us be. I unbend my bow; do ye likewise."

"But are we not to be dignified?" asked Babbalanja.

"If dignity be free and natural, be as dignified as you please; but away with rigidities."

"Away they go," said Babbalanja; "and, my lord, now that you mind me of it, I have often thought, that it is all folly and vanity for any man to attempt a dignified carriage. Why, my lord,"—frankly crossing his legs where he lay—"the king, who receives his ambassadors with a majestic toss of the head, may have just recovered from the tooth- ache. That thought should cant over the spine he bears so bravely."

"Have a care, sir! there is a king within hearing."

"Pardon, my lord; I was merely availing myself of the immunity bestowed upon the company. Hereafter, permit a subject to rebel against your sociable decrees. I will not be so frank any more."

"Well put, Babbalanja; come nearer; here, cross your legs by mine; you have risen a cubit in my regard. Vee-Vee, bring us that gourd of wine; so, pass it round with the cups. Now, Yoomy, a song!"

And a song was sung.

And thus did we sail; pleasantly reclining on the mats stretched out beneath the canopied howdah.

At length, we drew nigh to a rock, called Pella, or The Theft. A high, green crag, toppling over its base, and flinging a cavernous shadow upon the lagoon beneath, bubbling with the moisture that dropped.

Passing under this cliff was like finding yourself, as some sea- hunters unexpectedly have, beneath the open, upper jaw of a whale; which, descending, infallibly entombs you. But familiar with the rock, our paddlers only threw back their heads, to catch the cool, pleasant tricklings from the mosses above.

Wiping away several glittering beads from his beard, old Mohi turning round where he sat, just outside the canopy, solemnly affirmed, that the drinking of that water had cured many a man of ambition.

"How so, old man?" demanded Media.

"Because of its passing through the ashes of ten kings, of yore buried in a sepulcher, hewn in the heart of the rock."

"Mighty kings, and famous, doubtless," said Babbalanja, "whose bones were thought worthy of so noble and enduring as urn. Pray, Mohi, their names and terrible deeds."

"Alas! their sepulcher only remains."

"And, no doubt, like many others, they made that sepul for themselves. They sleep sound, my word for it, old man. But I very much question, if, were the rock rent, any ashes would be found. Mohi, I deny that those kings ever had any bones to bury."

"Why, Babbalanja," said Media, "since you intimate that they never had ghosts to give up, you ignore them in toto; denying the very fact of their being even defunct."

"Ten thousand pardons, my lord, no such discourtesy would I do the anonymous memory of the illustrious dead. But whether they ever lived or not, it is all the same with them now. Yet, grant that they lived; then, if death be a deaf-and-dumb death, a triumphal procession over their graves would concern them not. If a birth into brightness, then Mardi must seem to them the most trivial of reminiscences. Or, perhaps, theirs may be an utter lapse of memory concerning sublunary things; and they themselves be not themselves, as the butterfly is not the larva."

Said Yoomy, "Then, Babbalanja, you account that a fit illustration of the miraculous change to be wrought in man after death?"

"No; for the analogy has an unsatisfactory end. From its chrysalis state, the silkworm but becomes a moth, that very quickly expires. Its longest existence is as a worm. All vanity, vanity, Yoomy, to seek in nature for positive warranty to these aspirations of ours. Through all her provinces, nature seems to promise immortality to life, but destruction to beings. Or, as old Bardianna has it, if not against us, nature is not for us."

Said Media, rising, "Babbalanja, you have indeed put aside the courtier; talking of worms and caterpillars to me, a king and a demi- god! To renown, for your theme: a more agreeable topic."

"Pardon, once again, my lord. And since you will, let us discourse of that subject. First, I lay it down for an indubitable maxim, that in itself all posthumous renown, which is the only renown, is valueless. Be not offended, my lord. To the nobly ambitious, renown hereafter may be something to anticipate. But analyzed, that feverish typhoid feeling of theirs may be nothing more than a flickering fancy, that now, while living, they are recognized as those who will be as famous in their shrouds, as in their girdles."

Said Yoomy, "But those great and good deeds, Babbalanja, of which the philosophers so often discourse: must it not be sweet to believe that their memory will long survive us; and we ourselves in them?"

"I speak now," said Babbalanja, "of the ravening for fame which even appeased, like thirst slaked in the desert, yields no felicity, but only relief; and which discriminates not in aught that will satisfy its cravings. But let me resume. Not an hour ago, Braid-Beard was telling us that story of prince Ottimo, who inodorous while living, expressed much delight at the prospect of being perfumed and embalmed, when dead. But was not Ottimo the most eccentric of mortals? For few men issue orders for their shrouds, to inspect their quality beforehand. Far more anxious are they about the texture of the sheets in which their living limbs lie. And, my lord, with some rare exceptions, does not all Mardi, by its actions, declare, that it is far better to be notorious now, than famous hereafter?"

"A base sentiment, my lord," said Yoomy. "Did not poor Bonja, the unappreciated poet, console himself for the neglect of his contemporaries, by inspiriting thoughts of the future?"

"In plain words by bethinking him of the glorious harvest of bravos his ghost would reap for him," said Babbalanja; "but Banjo,—Bonjo,— Binjo,—I never heard of him."

"Nor I," said Mohi.

"Nor I," said Media.

"Poor fellow!" cried Babbalanja; "I fear me his harvest is not yet ripe."

"Alas!" cried Yoomy; "he died more than a century ago."

"But now that you speak of unappreciated poets, Yoomy," said Babbalanja, "Shall I give you a piece of my mind?" "Do," said Mohi, stroking his beard.

"He, who on all hands passes for a cypher to-day, if at all remembered hereafter, will be sure to pass for the same. For there is more likelihood of being overrated while living, than of being underrated when dead. And to insure your fame, you must die."

"A rather discouraging thought for your race. But answer: I assume that King Media is but a mortal like you; now, how may I best perpetuate my name?"

Long pondered Babbalanja; then said, "Carve it, my lord, deep into a ponderous stone, and sink it, face downward, into the sea; for the unseen foundations of the deep are more enduring than the palpable tops of the mountains."

Sailing past Pella, we gained a view of its farther side; and seated in a lofty cleft, beheld a lonely fisherman; solitary as a seal on an iceberg; his motionless line in the water.

"What recks he of the ten kings," said Babbalanja.

"Mohi," said Media, "methinks there is another tradition concerning that rock: let us have it."

"In old times of genii and giants, there dwelt in barren lands, not very remote from our outer reef, but since submerged, a band of evil- minded, envious goblins, furlongs in stature, and with immeasurable arms; who from time to time cast covetous glances upon our blooming isles. Long they lusted; till at last, they waded through the sea, strode over the reef, and seizing the nearest islet, rolled it over and over, toward an adjoining outlet.

"But the task was hard; and day-break surprised them in the midst of their audacious thieving; while in the very act of giving the devoted land another doughty surge and Somerset. Leaving it bottom upward and midway poised, gardens under water, its foundations in air, they precipitately fled; in their great haste, deserting a comrade, vainly struggling to liberate his foot caught beneath the overturned land."

"This poor fellow now raised such an outcry, as to awaken the god Upi, or the Archer, stretched out on a long cloud in the East; who forthwith resolved to make an example of the unwilling lingerer. Snatching his bow, he let fly an arrow. But overshooting its mark, it pierced through and through, the lofty promontory of a neighboring island; making an arch in it, which remaineth even unto this day. A second arrow, however, accomplished its errand: the slain giant sinking prone to the bottom."

"And now," added Mohi, "glance over the gunwale, and you will see his remains petrified into white ribs of coral."

"Ay, there they are," said Yoomy, looking down into the water where they gleamed. "A fanciful legend, Braid-beard."

"Very entertaining," said Media.

"Even so," said Babbalanja. "But perhaps we lost time in listening to it; for though we know it, we are none the wiser."

"Be not a cynic," said Media. "No pastime is lost time."

Musing a moment, Babbalanja replied, "My lord, that maxim may be good as it stands; but had you made six words of it, instead of six syllables, you had uttered a better and a deeper."

Chapter LXX

The Minstrel Leads Off With A Paddle-Song; And A Message Is Received From Abroad

From seaward now came a breeze so blithesome and fresh, that it made us impatient of Babbalanja's philosophy, and Mohi's incredible legends. One and all, we called upon the minstrel Yoomy to give us something in unison with the spirited waves wide-foaming around us.

"If my lord will permit, we will give Taji the Paddle-Chant of the warriors of King Bello."

"By all means," said Media.

So the three canoes were brought side to side; their sails rolled up; and paddles in hand, our paddlers seated themselves sideways on the gunwales; Yoomy, as leader, occupying the place of the foremast, or Bow-Paddler of the royal barge.

Whereupon the six rows of paddle-blades being uplifted, and every eye on the minstrel, this song was sung, with actions corresponding; the canoes at last shooting through the water, with a violent roll.

(All.)
Thrice waved on high,
Our paddles fly:
Thrice round the head, thrice dropt to feet:
And then well timed,
Of one stout mind,
All fall, and back the waters heap!

(Bow-Paddler.)
Who lifts this chant?
Who sounds this vaunt?

(All.)
The wild sea song, to the billows' throng,
Rising, falling,
Hoarsely calling,
Now high, now low, as fast we go,
Fast on our flying foe!

(Bow-Paddler.)
Who lifts this chant?
Who sounds this vaunt?

(All.)
Dip, dip, in the brine our paddles dip,
Dip, dip, the fins of our swimming ship!
How the waters part,
As on we dart;
Our sharp prows fly,
And curl on high,
As the upright fin of the rushing shark,
Rushing fast and far on his flying mark!
Like him we prey;
Like him we slay;
Swim on the fog,
Our prow a blow!

(Bow-Paddler.)
Who lifts this chant?
Who sounds this vaunt?

(All.)
Heap back; heap back; the waters back!
Pile them high astern, in billows black;
Till we leave our wake,
In the slope we make;
And rush and ride,
On the torrent's tide!

Here we were overtaken by a swift gliding canoe, which, bearing down upon us before the wind, lowered its sail when close by: its occupants signing our paddlers to desist.

I started.

The strangers were three hooded damsels the enigmatical Queen Hautia's heralds.

Their pursuit surprised and perplexed me. Nor was there wanting a vague feeling of alarm to heighten these emotions. But perhaps I was mistaken, and this time they meant not me.

Seated in the prow, the foremost waved her Iris flag. Cried Yoomy, "Some message! Taji, that Iris points to you."

It was then, I first divined, that some meaning must have lurked in those flowers they had twice brought me before.

The second damsel now flung over to me Circe flowers; then, a faded jonquil, buried in a tuft of wormwood leaves.

The third sat in the shallop's stern, and as it glided from us, thrice waved oleanders.

"What dumb show is this?" cried Media. "But it looks like poetry: minstrel, you should know."

"Interpret then," said I.

"Shall I, then, be your Flora's flute, and Hautia's dragoman? Held aloft, the Iris signified a message. These purple-woven Circe flowers mean that some spell is weaving. That golden, pining jonquil, which you hold, buried in those wormwood leaves, says plainly to you— Bitter love in absence."

Said Media, "Well done, Taji, you have killed a queen." "Yet no Queen Hautia have these eyes beheld."

Said Babbalanja, "The thrice waved oleanders, Yoomy; what meant they?"

"Beware—beware—beware."

"Then that, at least, seems kindly meant," said Babbalanja; "Taji, beware of Hautia."

Chapter LXXI

They Land Upon The Island Of Juam

Crossing the lagoon, our course now lay along the reef to Juam; a name bestowed upon one of the largest islands hereabout; and also, collectively, upon several wooded isles engulfing it, which together were known as the dominions of one monarch. That monarch was Donjalolo. Just turned of twenty-five, he was accounted not only the handsomest man in his dominions, but throughout the lagoon. His comeliness, however, was so feminine, that he was sometimes called "Fonoo," or the Girl.

Our first view of Juam was imposing. A dark green pile of cliffs, towering some one hundred toises; at top, presenting a range of steep, gable-pointed projections; as if some Titanic hammer and chisel had shaped the mass.

Sailing nearer, we perceived an extraordinary rolling of the sea; which bursting into the lagoon through an adjoining breach in the reef, surged toward Juam in enormous billows. At last, dashing against the wall of the cliff; they played there in unceasing fountains. But under the brow of a beetling crag, the spray came and went unequally. There, the blue billows seemed swallowed up, and lost.

Right regally was Juam guarded. For, at this point, the rock was pierced by a cave, into which the great waves chased each other like lions; after a hollow, subterraneous roaring issuing forth with manes disheveled.

Cautiously evading the dangerous currents here ruffling the lagoon, we rounded the wall of cliff; and shot upon a smooth expanse; on one side, hemmed in by the long, verdent, northern shore of Juam; and across the water, sentineled by its tributary islets.

With sonorous Vee-Vee in the shark's mouth, we swept toward the beach, tumultuous with a throng.

Our canoes were secured. And surrounded by eager glances, we passed the lower ends of several populous valleys; and crossing a wide, open meadow, gradually ascending, came to a range of light-green bluffs. Here, we wended our way down a narrow defile, almost cleaving this quarter of the island to its base. Black crags frowned overhead: among them the shouts of the Islanders reverberated. Yet steeper grew the defile, and more overhanging the crags till at last, the keystone of the arch seemed dropped into its place. We found ourselves in a subterranean tunnel, dimly lighted by a span of white day at the end.

Emerging, what a scene was revealed! All round, embracing a circuit of some three leagues, stood heights inaccessible, here and there, forming buttresses, sheltering deep recesses between. The bosom of the place was vivid with verdure.

Shining aslant into this wild hollow, the afternoon sun lighted up its eastern side with tints of gold. But opposite, brooded a somber shadow, double-shading the secret places between the salient spurs of the mountains. Thus cut in twain by masses of day and night, it seemed as if some Last Judgment had been enacted in the glen.

No sooner did we emerge from the defile, than we became sensible of a dull, jarring sound; and Yoomy was almost tempted to turn and flee, when informed that the sea-cavern, whose mouth we had passed, was believed to penetrate deep into the opposite hills; and that the surface of the amphitheater was depressed beneath that of the lagoon. But all over the lowermost hillsides, and sloping into the glen, stood grand old groves; still and stately, as if no insolent waves were throbbing in the mountain's heart.

Such was Willamilla, the hereditary abode of the young monarch of Juam.

Was Yillah immured in this strange retreat? But from those around us naught could we learn.

Our attention was now directed to the habitations of the glen; comprised in two handsome villages; one to the west, the other to the east; both stretching along the base of the cliffs.

Said Media, "Had we arrived at Willamilla in the morning, we had found Donjalolo and his court in the eastern village; but being afternoon, we must travel farther, and seek him in his western retreat; for that is now in the shade."

Wending our way, Media added, that aside from his elevated station as a monarch, Donjalolo was famed for many uncommon traits; but more especially for certain peculiar deprivations, under which he labored.

Whereupon Braid-Beard unrolled his old chronicles; and regaled us with the history, which will be found in the following chapter.

Chapter LXXII

A Book From The Chronicles Of Mohi

Many ages ago, there reigned in Juam a king called Teei. This Teei's succession to the sovereignty was long disputed by his brother Marjora; who at last rallying round him an army, after many vicissitudes, defeated the unfortunate monarch in a stout fight of clubs on the beach.

In those days, Willamilla during a certain period of the year was a place set apart for royal games and diversions; and was furnished with suitable accommodations for king and court. From its peculiar position, moreover, it was regarded as the last stronghold of the Juam monarchy: in remote times having twice withstood the most desperate assaults from without. And when Roonoonoo, a famous upstart, sought to subdue all the isles in this part of the Archipelago, it was to Willamilla that the banded kings had repaired to take counsel together; and while there conferring, were surprised at the sudden onslaught of Roonoonoo in person. But in the end, the rebel was captured, he and all his army, and impaled on the tops of the hills.

Now, defeated and fleeing for his life, Teei with his surviving followers was driven across the plain toward the mountains. But to cut him off from all escape to inland Willamilla, Marjora dispatched a fleet band of warriors to occupy the entrance of the defile. Nevertheless, Teei the pursued ran faster than his pursuers; first gained the spot; and with his chiefs, fled swiftly down the gorge, closely hunted by Marjora's men. But arriving at the further end, they in vain sought to defend it. And after much desperate fighting, the main body of the foe corning up with great slaughter the fugitives were driven into the glen.

They ran to the opposite wall of cliff; where turning, they fought at bay, blood for blood, and life for life, till at last, overwhelmed by numbers, they were all put to the point of the spear.

With fratricidal hate, singled out by the ferocious Marjora, Teei fell by that brother's hand. When stripping from the body the regal girdle, the victor wound it round his own loins; thus proclaiming himself king over Juam.

Long torn by this intestine war, the island acquiesced in the new sovereignty. But at length a sacred oracle declared, that since the conqueror had slain his brother in deep Willamilla, so that Teei never more issued from that refuge of death; therefore, the same fate should be Marjora's; for never, thenceforth, from that glen, should he go forth; neither Marjora; nor any son of his girdled loins; nor his son's sons; nor the uttermost scion of his race.

But except this denunciation, naught was denounced against the usurper; who, mindful of the tenure by which he reigned, ruled over the island for many moons; at his death bequeathing the girdle to his son.

In those days, the wildest superstitions concerning the interference of the gods in things temporal, prevailed to a much greater extent than at present. Hence Marjora himself, called sometimes in the traditions of the island, The-Heart-of-Black-Coral, even unscrupulous Marjora had quailed before the oracle. "He bowed his head," say the legends. Nor was it then questioned, by his most devoted adherents, that had he dared to act counter to that edict, he had dropped dead, the very instant he went under the shadow of the defile. This persuasion also guided the conduct of the son of Marjora, and that of his grandson.

But there at last came to pass a change in the popular fancies concerning this ancient anathema. The penalty denounced against the posterity of the usurper should they issue from the glen, came to be regarded as only applicable to an invested monarch, not to his relatives, or heirs.

A most favorable construction of the ban; for all those related to the king, freely passed in and out of Willamilla.

From the time of the usurpation, there had always been observed a certain ceremony upon investing the heir to the sovereignty with the girdle of Teei. Upon these occasions, the chief priests of the island were present, acting an important part. For the space of as many days, as there had reigned kings of Marjora's dynasty, the inner mouth of the defile remained sealed; the new monarch placing the last stone in the gap. This symbolized his relinquishment forever of all purpose of passing out of the glen. And without this observance, was no king girdled in Juam.

It was likewise an invariable custom, for the heir to receive the regal investiture immediately upon the decease of his sire. No delay was permitted. And instantly upon being girdled, he proceeded to take part in the ceremony of closing the cave; his predecessor yet remaining uninterred on the purple mat where he died.

In the history of the island, three instances were recorded; wherein, upon the vacation of the sovereignty, the immediate heir had voluntarily renounced all claim to the succession, rather than surrender the privilege of roving, to which he had been entitled, as a prince of the blood.

Said Rani, one of these young princes, in reply to the remonstrances of his friends, "What! shall I be a king, only to be a slave? Teei's girdle would clasp my waist less tightly, than my soul would be banded by the mountains of Willamilla. A subject, I am free. No slave in Juam but its king; for all the tassels round his loins."

To guard against a similar resolution in the mind of his only son, the wise sire of Donjalolo, ardently desirous of perpetuating his dignities in a child so well beloved, had from his earliest infancy, restrained the boy from passing out of the glen, to contract in the free air of the Archipelago, tastes and predilections fatal to the inheritance of the girdle.

But as he grew in years, so impatient became young Donjalolo of the king his father's watchfulness over him, though hitherto a most dutiful son, that at last he was prevailed upon by his youthful companions to appoint a day, on which to go abroad, and visit Mardi. Hearing this determination, the old king sought to vanquish it. But in vain. And early on the morning of the day, that Donjalolo was to set out, he swallowed poison, and died; in order to force his son into the instant assumption of the honors thus suddenly inherited.

The event, but not its dreadful circumstances, was communicated to the prince; as with a gay party of young chiefs, he was about to enter the mouth of the defile.

"My sire dead!" cried Donjalolo. "So sudden, it seems a bolt from Heaven." And bursting into exclamations of grief, he wept upon the bosom of Talara his friend.

But starting from his side:—"My fate converges to a point. If I but cross that shadow, my kingdom is lost. One lifting of my foot, and the girdle goes to my proud uncle Darfi, who would so joy to be my master. Haughty Dwarf! Oh Oro! would that I had ere this passed thee, fatal cavern; and seen for myself, what outer Mardi is. Say ye true, comrades, that Willamilla is less lovely than the valleys without? that there is bright light in the eyes of the maidens of Mina? and wisdom in the hearts of the old priests of Maramma; that it is pleasant to tread the green earth where you will; and breathe the free ocean air? Would, oh would, that I were but the least of yonder sun-clouds, that look down alike on Willamilla and all places besides, that I might determine aright. Yet why do I pause? did not Rani, and Atama, and Mardonna, my ancestors, each see for himself, free Mardi; and did they not fly the proffered girdle; choosing rather to be free to come and go, than bury themselves forever in this fatal glen? Oh Mardi! Mardi! art thou then so fair to see? Is liberty a thing so glorious? Yet can I be no king, and behold thee! Too late, too late, to view thy charms and then return. My sire! my sire! thou hast wrung my heart with this agony of doubt. Tell me, comrades,—for ye have seen it,—is Mardi sweeter to behold, than it is royal to reign over Juam? Silent, are ye? Knowing what ye do, were ye me, would ye be kings? Tell me, Talara.—No king: no king:—that were to obey, and not command. And none hath Donjalolo ere obeyed but the king his father. A king, and my voice may be heard in farthest Mardi, though I abide in narrow Willamilla. My sire! my sire! Ye flying clouds, what look ye down upon? Tell me, what ye see abroad? Methinks sweet spices breathe from out the cave."

"Hail, Donjalolo, King of Juam," now sounded with acclamations from the groves.

Starting, the young prince beheld a multitude approaching: warriors with spears, and maidens with flowers; and Kubla, a priest, lifting on high the tasseled girdle of Teei, and waving it toward him.

The young chiefs fell back. Kubla, advancing, came close to the prince, and unclasping the badge of royalty, exclaimed, "Donjalolo, this instant it is king or subject with thee: wilt thou be girdled monarch?"

Gazing one moment up the dark defile, then staring vacantly, Donjalolo turned and met the eager gaze of Darfi. Stripping off his mantle, the next instant he was a king.

Loud shouted the multitude, and exulted; but after mutely assisting at the closing of the cavern, the new-girdled monarch retired sadly to his dwelling, and was not seen again for many days.

Chapter LXXIII

Something More Of The Prince

Previous to recording our stay in his dominions, it only remains to be related of Donjalolo, that after assuming the girdle, a change came over him.

During the lifetime of his father, he had been famed for his temperance and discretion. But when Mardi was forever shut out; and he remembered the law of his isle, interdicting abdication to its kings; he gradually fell into desperate courses, to drown the emotions at times distracting him.

His generous spirit thirsting after some energetic career, found itself narrowed down within the little glen of Willamilla, where ardent impulses seemed idle. But these are hard to die; and repulsed all round, recoil upon themselves.

So with Donjalolo; who, in many a riotous scene, wasted the powers which might have compassed the noblest designs.

Not many years had elapsed since the death of the king, his father. But the still youthful prince was no longer the bright-eyed and elastic boy who at the dawn of day had sallied out to behold the landscapes of the neighboring isles.

Not more effeminate Sardanapalus, than he. And, at intervals, he was the victim of unaccountable vagaries; haunted by specters, and beckoned to by the ghosts of his sires.

At times, loathing his vicious pursuits, which brought him no solid satisfaction, but ever filled him with final disgust, he would resolve to amend his ways; solacing himself for his bitter captivity, by the society of the wise and discreet.

But brief the interval of repentance. Anew, he burst into excesses, a hundred fold more insane than ever.

Thus vacillating between virtue and vice; to neither constant, and upbraided by both; his mind, like his person in the glen, was continually passing and repassing between opposite extremes.

Chapter LXXIV

Advancing Deeper Into The Vale, They Encounter Donjalolo

From the mouth of the cavern, a broad shaded way over-arched by fraternal trees embracing in mid-air, conducted us to a cross-path, on either hand leading to the opposite cliffs, shading the twin villages before mentioned.

Level as a meadow, was the bosom of the glen. Here, nodding with green orchards of the Bread-fruit and the Palm; there, flashing with golden plantations of the Banana. Emerging from these, we came out upon a grassy mead, skirting a projection of the mountain. And soon we crossed a bridge of boughs, spanning a trench, thickly planted with roots of the Tara, like alligators, or Hollanders, reveling in the soft alluvial. Strolling on, the wild beauty of the mountains excited our attention. The topmost crags poured over with vines; which, undulating in the air, seemed leafy cascades; their sources the upland groves.

Midway up the precipice, along a shelf of rock, sprouted the multitudinous roots of an apparently trunkless tree. Shooting from under the shallow soil, they spread all over the rocks below, covering them with an intricate net-work. While far aloft, great boughs—each a copse—clambered to the very summit of the mountain; then bending over, struck anew into the soil; forming along the verge an interminable colonnade; all manner of antic architecture standing against the sky.

According to Mohi, this tree was truly wonderful; its seed having been dropped from the moon; where were plenty more similar forests, causing the dark spots on its surface.

Here and there, the cool fluid in the veins of the mountains gushed forth in living springs; their waters received in green mossy tanks, half buried in grasses.

In one place, a considerable stream, bounding far out from a wooded height, ere reaching the ground was dispersed in a wide misty shower, falling so far from the base of the cliff; that walking close underneath, you felt little moisture. Passing this fall of vapors, we spied many Islanders taking a bath.

But what is yonder swaying of the foliage? And what now issues forth, like a habitation astir? Donjalolo drawing nigh to his guests.

He came in a fair sedan; a bower, resting upon three long, parallel poles, borne by thirty men, gayly attired; five at each pole-end. Decked with dyed tappas, and looped with garlands of newly-plucked flowers, from which, at every step, the fragrant petals were blown; with a sumptuous, elastic motion the gay sedan came on; leaving behind it a long, rosy wake of fluttering leaves and odors.

Drawing near, it revealed a slender, enervate youth, of pallid beauty, reclining upon a crimson mat, near the festooned arch of the bower. His anointed head was resting against the bosom of a girl; another stirred the air, with a fan of Pintado plumes. The pupils of his eyes were as floating isles in the sea. In a soft low tone he murmured "Media!"

The bearers paused; and Media advancing; the Island Kings bowed their foreheads together.

Through tubes ignited at the end, Donjaloln's reclining attendants now blew an aromatic incense around him. These were composed of the stimulating leaves of the "Aina," mixed with the long yellow blades of a sweet-scented upland grass; forming a hollow stem. In general, the agreeable fumes of the "Aina" were created by one's own inhalations; but Donjalolo deeming the solace too dearly purchased by any exertion of the royal lungs, regaled himself through those of his attendants, whose lips were as moss-rose buds after a shower.

In silence the young prince now eyed us attentively; meanwhile gently waving his hand, to obtain a better view through the wreaths of vapor. He was about to address us, when chancing to catch a glimpse of Samoa, he suddenly started; averted his glance; and wildly commanded the warrior out of sight. Upon this, his attendants would have soothed him; and Media desired the Upoluan to withdraw.

While we were yet lost in wonder at this scene, Donjalolo, with eyes closed, fell back into the arms of his damsels. Recovering, he fetched a deep sigh, and gazed vacantly around.

It seems, that he had fancied Samoa the noon-day specter of his ancestor Marjora; the usurper having been deprived of an arm in the battle which gained him the girdle. Poor prince: this was one of those crazy conceits, so puzzling to his subjects.

Media now hastened to assure Donjalolo, that Samoa, though no cherub to behold, was good flesh and blood, nevertheless. And soon the king unconcernedly gazed; his monomania having departed as a dream.

But still suffering from the effects of an overnight feast, he presently murmured forth a desire to be left to his women; adding that his people would not fail to provide for the entertainment of his guests.

The curtains of the sedan were now drawn; and soon it disappeared in the groves. Journeying on, ere long we arrived at the western side of the glen; where one of the many little arbors scattered among the trees, was assigned for our abode. Here, we reclined to an agreeable repast. After which, we strolled forth to view the valley at large; more especially the far-famed palaces of the prince.

Chapter LXXV

Time And Temples

In the oriental Pilgrimage of the pious old Purchas, and in the fine old folio Voyages of Hakluyt, Thevenot, Ramusio, and De Bry, we read of many glorious old Asiatic temples, very long in erecting. And veracious Gaudentia di Lucca hath a wondrous narration of the time consumed in rearing that mighty three-hundred-and-seventy-five- pillared Temple of the Year, somewhere beyond Libya; whereof, the columns did signify days, and all round fronted upon concentric zones of palaces, cross-cut by twelve grand avenues symbolizing the signs of the zodiac, all radiating from the sun-dome in their midst. And in that wild eastern tale of his, Marco Polo tells us, how the Great Mogul began him a pleasure-palace on so imperial a scale, that his grandson had much ado to complete it.

But no matter for marveling all this: great towers take time to construct.

And so of all else.

And that which long endures full-fledged, must have long lain in the germ. And duration is not of the future, but of the past; and eternity is eternal, because it has been, and though a strong new monument be builded to-day, it only is lasting because its blocks are old as the sun. It is not the Pyramids that are ancient, but the eternal granite whereof they are made; which had been equally ancient though yet in the quarry. For to make an eternity, we must build with eternities; whence, the vanity of the cry for any thing alike durable and new; and the folly of the reproach—Your granite hath come from the old-fashioned hills. For we are not gods and creators; and the controversialists have debated, whether indeed the All-Plastic Power itself can do more than mold. In all the universe is but one original; and the very suns must to their source for their fire; and we Prometheuses must to them for ours; which, when had, only perpetual Vestal tending will keep alive.

But let us back from fire to store. No fine firm fabric ever yet grew like a gourd. Nero's House of Gold was not raised in a day; nor the Mexican House of the Sun; nor the Alhambra; nor the Escurial; nor

Titus's Amphitheater; nor the Illinois Mounds; nor Diana's great columns at Ephesus; nor Pompey's proud Pillar; nor the Parthenon; nor the Altar of Belus; nor Stonehenge; nor Solomon's Temple; nor Tadmor's towers; nor Susa's bastions; nor Persepolis' pediments. Round and round, the Moorish turret at Seville was not wound heavenward in the revolution of a day; and from its first founding, five hundred years did circle, ere Strasbourg's great spire lifted its five hundred feet into the air. No: nor were the great grottos of Elephanta hewn out in an hour; nor did the Troglodytes dig Kentucky's Mammoth Cave in a sun; nor that of Trophonius, nor Antiparos; nor the Giant's Causeway. Nor were the subterranean arched sewers of Etruria channeled in a trice; nor the airy arched aqueducts of Nerva thrown over their values in the ides of a month. Nor was Virginia's Natural Bridge worn under in a year; nor, in geology, were the eternal Grampians upheaved in an age. And who shall count the cycles that revolved ere earth's interior sedimentary strata were crystalized into stone. Nor Peak of Piko, nor Teneriffe, were chiseled into obelisks in a decade; nor had Mount Athos been turned into Alexander's statue so soon. And the bower of Artaxerxes took a whole Persian summer to grow; and the Czar's Ice Palace a long Muscovite winter to congeal. No, no: nor was the Pyramid of Cheops masoned in a month; though, once built, the sands left by the deluge might not have submerged such a pile. Nor were the broad boughs of Charles' Oak grown in a spring; though they outlived the royal dynasties of Tudor and Stuart. Nor were the parts of the great Iliad put together in haste; though old Homer's temple shall lift up its dome, when St. Peter's is a legend. Even man himself lives months ere his Maker deems him fit to be born; and ere his proud shaft gains its full stature, twenty-one long Julian years must elapse. And his whole mortal life brings not his immortal soul to maturity; nor will all eternity perfect him. Yea, with uttermost reverence, as to human understanding, increase of dominion seems increase of power; and day by day new planets are being added to elder-born Saturn, even as six thousand years ago our own Earth made one more in this system; so, in incident, not in essence, may the Infinite himself be not less than more infinite now, than when old Aldebaran rolled forth from his hand. And if time was, when this round Earth, which to innumerable mortals has seemed an empire never to be wholly explored; which, in its seas, concealed all the Indies over four thousand five hundred years; if time was, when this great quarry of Assyrias and Romes was not extant; then, time may have been, when the whole material universe lived its Dark Ages; yea, when the Ineffable Silence, proceeding from its unimaginable remoteness, espied it as an isle in the sea. And herein is no derogation. For the Immeasurable's altitude is not heightened by the arches of Mahomet's heavens; and were all space a vacuum, yet would it be a fullness; for to Himself His own universe is He.

Thus deeper and deeper into Time's endless tunnel, does the winged soul, like a night-hawk, wend her wild way; and finds eternities before and behind; and her last limit is her everlasting beginning.

But sent over the broad flooded sphere, even Noah's dove came back, and perched on his hand. So comes back my spirit to me, and folds up her wings.

Thus, then, though Time be the mightiest of Alarics, yet is he the mightiest mason of all. And a tutor, and a counselor, and a physician, and a scribe, and a poet, and a sage, and a king.

Yea, and a gardener, as ere long will be shown.

But first must we return to the glen.

Chapter LXXVI

Whether the hard condition of their kingly state, very naturally demanding some luxurious requital, prevailed upon the monarchs of Juam to house themselves so delightfully as they did; whether buried alive in their glen, they sought to center therein a secret world of enjoyment; however it may have been, throughout the Archipelago this saying was a proverb—"You are lodged like the king in Willamilla." Hereby was expressed the utmost sumptuousness of a palace.

A well warranted saying; for of all the bright places, where my soul loves to linger, the haunts of Donjalolo are most delicious.

In the eastern quarter of the glen was the House of the Morning. This fanciful palace was raised upon a natural mound, many rods square, almost completely filling up a deep recess between deep-green and projecting cliffs, overlooking many abodes distributed in the shadows of the groves beyond.

Now, if it indeed be, that from the time employed in its construction, any just notion may be formed of the stateliness of an edifice, it must needs be determined, that this retreat of Donjalolo could not be otherwise than imposing.

Full five hundred moons was the palace in completing; for by some architectural arborist, its quadrangular foundations had been laid in seed-cocoanuts, requiring that period to sprout up into pillars. In front, these were horizontally connected, by elaborately carved beams, of a scarlet hue, inserted into the vital wood; which, swelling out, and over lapping, firmly secured them. The beams supported the rafters, inclining from the rear; while over the aromatic grasses covering the roof, waved the tufted tops of the Palms, green capitals to their dusky shafts.

Through and through this vibrating verdure, bright birds flitted and sang; the scented and variegated thatch seemed a hanging-garden; and between it and the Palm tops, was leaf-hung an arbor in the air.

Without these columns, stood a second and third colonnade, forming the most beautiful bowers; advancing through which, you fancied that the palace beyond must be chambered in a fountain, or frozen in a crystal. Three sparkling rivulets flowing from the heights were led across its summit, through great trunks half buried in the thatch; and emptying into a sculptured channel, running along the eaves, poured over in one wide sheet, plaited and transparent. Received into a basin beneath, they were thence conducted down the vale.

The sides of the palace were hedged by Diomi bushes bearing a flower, from its perfume, called Lenora, or Sweet Breath; and within these odorous hedges, were heavy piles of mats, richly dyed and embroidered.

Here lounging of a glowing noon, the plaited cascade playing, the verdure waving, and the birds melodious, it was hard to say, whether you were an inmate of a garden in the glen, or a grotto in the sea.

But enough for the nonce, of the House of the Morning. Cross we the hollow, to the House of the Afternoon.

Chapter LXXVII

The House Of The Afternoon

For the most part, the House of the Afternoon was but a wing built against a mansion wrought by the hand of Nature herself; a grotto running into the side of the mountain. From high over the mouth of this grotto, sloped a long arbor, supported by great blocks of stone, rudely chiseled into the likeness of idols, each bearing a carved lizard on its chest: a sergeant's guard of the gods condescendingly doing duty as posts.

From the grotto thus vestibuled, issued hilariously forth the most considerable stream of the glen; which, seemingly overjoyed to find daylight in Willamilla, sprang into the arbor with a cheery, white bound. But its youthful enthusiasm was soon repressed; its waters being caught in a large stone basin, scooped out of the natural rock; whence, staid and decorous, they traversed sundry moats; at last meandering away, to join floods with the streams trained to do service at the other end of the vale.

Truant streams: the livelong day wending their loitering path to the subterraneous outlet, flowing into which, they disappeared. But no wonder they loitered; passing such ravishing landscapes. Thus with life: man bounds out of night; runs and babbles in the sun; then returns to his darkness again; though, peradventure, once more to emerge.

But the grotto was not a mere outlet to the stream. Flowing through a dark flume in the rock, on both sides it left a dry, elevated shelf, to which you ascend from the arbor by three artificially-wrought steps, sideways disposed, to avoid the spray of the rejoicing cataract. Mounting these, and pursuing the edge of the flume, the grotto gradually expands and heightens; your way lighted by rays in the inner distance. At last you come to a lofty subterraneous dome, lit from above by a cleft in the mountain; while full before you, in the opposite wall, from a low, black arch, midway up, and inaccessible, the stream, with a hollow ring and a dash, falls in a long, snowy column into a bottomless pool, whence, after many an eddy and whirl, it entered the flume, and away with a rush. Half hidden from view by an overhanging brow of the rock, the white fall looked like the sheeted ghost of the grotto.

Yet gallantly bedecked was the cave, as any old armorial hall hung round with banners and arras. Streaming from the cleft, vines swung in the air; or crawled along the rocks, wherever a tendril could be fixed. High up, their leaves were green; but lower down, they were shriveled; and dyed of many colors; and tattered and torn with much rustling; as old banners again; sore raveled with much triumphing.

In the middle of this hall in the hill was incarcerated the stone image of one Demi, the tutelar deity of Willamina. All green and oozy like a stone under water, poor Demi looked as if sore harassed with sciatics and lumbagos.

But he was cheered from aloft, by the promise of receiving a garland all blooming on his crown; the Dryads sporting in the woodlands above, forever peeping down the cleft, and essaying to drop him a coronal.

Now, the still, panting glen of Willamilla, nested so close by the mountains, and a goodly green mark for the archer in the sun, would have been almost untenable were it not for the grotto. Hereby, it breathed the blessed breezes of Omi; a mountain promontory buttressing the island to the east, receiving the cool stream of the upland Trades; much pleasanter than the currents beneath.

At all times, even in the brooding noon-day, a gush of cool air came hand-in-hand with the cool waters, that burst with a shout into the palace of Donjalolo. And as, after first refreshing the king, as in loyalty bound, the stream flowed at large through the glen, and bathed its verdure; so, the blessed breezes of Omi, not only made pleasant the House of the Afternoon; but finding ample outlet in its wide, open front, blew forth upon the bosom of all Willamilla.

"Come let us take the air of Omi," was a very common saying in the glen. And the speaker would hie with his comrade toward the grotto; and flinging himself on the turf, pass his hand through his locks, and recline; making a joy and a business of breathing; for truly the breezes of Omi were as air-wine to the lungs.

Yet was not this breeze over-cool; though at times the zephyrs grew boisterous. Especially at the season of high sea, when the strong Trades drawn down the cleft in the mountain, rushed forth from the grotto with wonderful force. Crossing it then, you had much ado to keep your robe on your back.

Thus much for the House of the Afternoon. Whither—after spending the shady morning under the eastern cliffs of the glen—daily, at a certain hour, Donjalolo in his palanquin was borne; there, finding new shades; and there tarrying till evening; when again he was transported whence he came: thereby anticipating the revolution of the sun. Thus dodging day's luminary through life, the prince hied to and fro in his dominions; on his smooth, spotless brow Sol's rays never shining.

Chapter LXXVIII

Babbalanja Solus

Of the House of the Afternoon something yet remains to be said.

It was chiefly distinguished by its pavement, where, according to the strange customs of the isle, were inlaid the reputed skeletons of Donjalolo's sires; each surrounded by a mosaic of corals,—red, white, and black, intermixed with vitreous stones fallen from the skies in a meteoric shower. These delineated the tattooing of the departed. Near by, were imbedded their arms: mace, bow, and spear, in similar marquetry; and over each skull was the likeness of a scepter.

First and conspicuous lay the half-decayed remains of Marjora, the father of these Coral Kings; by his side, the storied, sickle-shaped weapon, wherewith he slew his brother Teei.

"Line of kings and row of scepters," said Babbalanja as he gazed. "Donjalolo, come forth and ponder on thy sires. Here they lie, from dread Marjora down to him who fathered thee. Here are their bones, their spears, and their javelins; their scepters, and the very fashion of their tattooing: all that can be got together of what they were. Tell me, oh king, what are thy thoughts? Dotest thou on these thy sires? Art thou more truly royal, that they were kings? Or more a man, that they were men? Is it a fable, or a verity about Marjora and the murdered Teei? But here is the mighty conqueror,—ask him. Speak to him: son to sire: king to king. Prick him; beg; buffet; entreat; spurn; split the globe, he will not budge. Walk over and over thy whole ancestral line, and they will not start. They are not here. Ay, the dead are not to be found, even in their graves. Nor have they simply departed; for they willed not to go; they died not by choice; whithersoever they have gone, thither have they been dragged; and if so be, they are extinct, their nihilities went not more against their grain, than their forced quitting of Mardi. Either way, something has become of them that they sought not. Truly, had stout-hearted Marjora sworn to live here in Willamilla for ay, and kept the vow, that would have been royalty indeed; but here he lies. Marjora! rise! Juam revolteth! Lo, I stamp upon thy scepter; base menials tread upon thee where thou liest! Up, king, up! What? no reply? Are not these bones thine? Oh, how the living triumph over the dead! Marjora! answer. Art thou? or art thou not? I see thee not; I hear thee not; I feel thee not; eyes, ears, hands, are worthless to test thy being; and if thou art, thou art something beyond all human thought to compass. We must have other faculties to know thee by. Why, thou art not even a sightless sound; not the echo of an echo; here are thy bones. Donjalolo, methinks I see thee fallen upon by assassins:—which of thy fathers riseth to the rescue? I see thee dying:—which of them telleth thee what cheer beyond the grave? But they have gone to the land unknown. Meet phrase. Where is it? Not one of Oro's priests telleth a straight story concerning it; 'twill be hard finding their paradises. Touching the life of Alma, in Mohi's chronicles, 'tis related, that a man was once raised from the tomb. But rubbed he not his eyes, and stared he not most vacantly? Not one revelation did he make. Ye gods! to have been a bystander there!

"At best, 'tis but a hope. But will a longing bring the thing desired? Doth dread avert its object? An instinct is no preservative. The fire I shrink from, may consume me.—But dead, and yet alive; alive, yet dead;—thus say the sages of Maramma. But die we then living? Yet if our dead fathers somewhere and somehow live, why not our unborn sons? For backward or forward, eternity is the same; already have we been the nothing we dread to be. Icy thought! But bring it home,—it will not stay. What ho, hot heart of mine: to beat thus lustily awhile, to feel in the red rushing blood, and then be ashes,—can this be so? But peace, peace, thou liar in me, telling me I am immortal—shall I not be as these bones? To come to this! But the balsam-dropping palms, whose boles run milk, whose plumes wave boastful in the air, they perish in their prime, and bow their blasted trunks. Nothing abideth; the river of yesterday floweth not to-day; the sun's rising is a setting; living is dying; the very mountains melt; and all revolve:—systems and asteroids; the sun wheels through the zodiac, and the zodiac is a revolution. Ah gods! in all this universal stir, am I to prove one stable thing?

"Grim chiefs in skeletons, avaunt! Ye are but dust; belike the dust of beggars; for on this bed, paupers may lie down with kings, and filch their skulls. This, great Marjora's arm? No, some old paralytic's. Ye, kings? ye, men? Where are your vouchers? I do reject your brother-hood, ye libelous remains. But no, no; despise them not, oh Babbalanja! Thy own skeleton, thou thyself dost carry with thee, through this mortal life; and aye would view it, but for kind nature's screen; thou art death alive; and e'en to what's before thee wilt thou come. Ay, thy children's children will walk over thee: thou, voiceless as a calm."

And over the Coral Kings, Babbalanja paced in profound meditation.

Chapter LXXIX

The Center Of Many Circumferences

Like Donjalolo himself, we hie to and fro; for back now must we pace to the House of the Morning.

In its rear, there diverged three separate arbors, leading to less public apartments.

Traversing the central arbor, and fancying it will soon lead you to open ground, you suddenly come upon the most private retreat of the prince: a square structure; plain as a pyramid; and without, as inscrutable. Down to the very ground, its walls are thatched; but on the farther side a passage-way opens, which you enter. But not yet are you within. Scarce a yard distant, stands an inner thatched wall, blank as the first. Passing along the intervening corridor, lighted by narrow apertures, you reach the opposite side, and a second opening is revealed. This entering, another corridor; lighted as the first, but more dim, and a third blank wall. And thus, three times three, you worm round and round, the twilight lessening as you proceed; until at last, you enter the citadel itself: the innermost arbor of a nest; whereof, each has its roof, distinct from the rest.

The heart of the place is but small; illuminated by a range of open sky-lights, downward contracting.

Innumerable as the leaves of an endless folio, multitudinous mats cover the floor; whereon reclining by night, like Pharaoh on the top of his patrimonial pile, the inmate looks heavenward, and heavenward only; gazing at the torchlight processions in the skies, when, in state, the suns march to be crowned.

And here, in this impenetrable retreat, centrally slumbered the universe-rounded, zodiac-belted, horizon-zoned, sea-girt, reef- sashed, mountain-locked, arbor-nested, royalty-girdled, arm-clasped, self-hugged, indivisible Donjalolo, absolute monarch of Juam:—the husk-inhusked meat in a nut; the innermost spark in a ruby; the juice-nested seed in a goldenrinded orange; the red royal stone in an effeminate peach; the insphered sphere of spheres.

Chapter LXXX

Donjalolo In The Bosom Of His Family

To pretend to relate the manner in which Juam's ruler passed his captive days, without making suitable mention of his harem, would be to paint one's full-length likeness and omit the face. For it was his harem that did much to stamp the character of Donjalolo.

And had he possessed but a single spouse, most discourteous, surely, to have overlooked the princess; much more, then, as it is; and by how-much the more, a plurality exceeds a unit.

Exclusive of the female attendants, by day waiting upon the person of the king, he had wives thirty in number, corresponding in name to the nights of the moon. For, in Juam, time is not reckoned by days, but by nights; each night of the lunar month having its own designation; which, relatively only, is extended to the day.

In uniform succession, the thirty wives ruled queen of the king's heart. An arrangement most wise and judicious; precluding much of that jealousy and confusion prevalent in ill-regulated seraglios. For as thirty spouses must be either more desirable, or less desirable than one; so is a harem thirty times more difficult to manage than an establishment with one solitary mistress. But Donjalolo's wives were so nicely drilled, that for the most part, things went on very smoothly. Nor were his brows much furrowed with wrinkles referable to domestic cares and tribulations. Although, as in due time will be seen, from these he was not altogether exempt.

Now, according to Braid-Beard, who, among other abstruse political researches, had accurately informed himself concerning the internal administration of Donjalolo's harem, the following was the method pursued therein.

On the Aquella, or First Night of the month, the queen of that name assumes her diadem, and reigns. So too with Azzolino the Second, and Velluvi the Third Night of the Moon; and so on, even unto the utter eclipse thereof; through Calends, Nones, and Ides.

For convenience, the king is furnished with a card, whereon are copied the various ciphers upon the arms of his queens; and parallel thereto, the hieroglyphics significant of the corresponding Nights of the month. Glancing over this, Donjalolo predicts the true time of the rising and setting of all his stars.

This Moon of wives was lodged in two spacious seraglios, which few mortals beheld. For, so deeply were they buried in a grove; so overpowered with verdure; so overrun with vines; and so hazy with the incense of flowers; that they were almost invisible, unless closely approached. Certain it was, that it demanded no small enterprise, diligence, and sagacity, to explore the mysterious wood in search of them. Though a strange, sweet, humming sound, as of the clustering and swarming of warm bees among roses, at last hinted the royal honey at hand. High in air, toward the summit of the cliff, overlooking this side of the glen, a narrow ledge of rocks might have been seen, from which, rumor whispered, was to be caught an angular peep at the tip of the apex of the roof of the nearest seraglio. But this wild report had never been established. Nor, indeed, was it susceptible of a test. For was not that rock inaccessible as the eyrie of young eagles? But to guard against the possibility of any visual profanation, Donjalolo had authorized an edict, forever tabooing that rock to foot of man or pinion of fowl. Birds and bipeds both trembled and obeyed; taking a wide circuit to avoid the spot.

Access to the seraglios was had by corresponding arbors leading from the palace. The seraglio to the right was denominated "Ravi" (Before), that to the left "Zono" (After). The meaning of which was, that upon the termination of her reign the queen wended her way to the Zono; there tarrying with her predecessors till the Ravi was emptied; when the entire Moon of wives, swallow-like, migrated back whence they came; and the procession was gone over again.

In due order, the queens reposed upon mats inwoven with their respective ciphers. In the Ravi, the mat of the queen-apparent, or next in succession, was spread by the portal. In the Zono, the newly- widowed queen reposed furthest from it.

But alas for all method where thirty wives are concerned. Notwithstanding these excellent arrangements, the mature result of ages of progressive improvement in the economy of the royal seraglios in Willamilla, it must needs be related, that at times the order of precedence became confused, and was very hard to restore.

At intervals, some one of the wives was weeded out, to the no small delight of the remainder; but to their equal vexation her place would soon after be supplied by some beautiful stranger; who assuming the denomination of the vacated Night of the Moon, thenceforth commenced her monthly revolutions in the king's infallible calendar.

In constant attendance, was a band of old men; woe-begone, thin of leg, and puny of frame; whose grateful task it was, to tarry in the garden of Donjalolo's delights, without ever touching the roses. Along with innumerable other duties, they were perpetually kept coming and going upon ten thousand errands; for they had it in strict charge to obey the slightest behests of the damsels; and with all imaginable expedition to run, fly, swim, or dissolve into impalpable air, at the shortest possible notice.

So laborious their avocations, that none could discharge them for more than a twelvemonth, at the end of that period giving up the ghost out of pure exhaustion of the locomotive apparatus. It was this constant drain upon the stock of masculine old age in the glen, that so bethinned its small population of gray-beards and hoary-heads. And any old man hitherto exempted, who happened to receive a summons to repair to the palace, and there wait the pleasure of the king: this unfortunate, at once suspecting his doom, put his arbor in order; oiled and suppled his joints; took a long farewell of his friends; selected his burial-place; and going resigned to his fate, in due time expired like the rest.

Had any one of them cast about for some alleviating circumstance, he might possibly have derived some little consolation from the thought, that though a slave to the whims of thirty princesses, he was nevertheless one of their guardians, and as such, he might ingeniously have concluded, their superior. But small consolation this. For the damsels were as blithe as larks, more playful than kittens; never looking sad and sentimental, projecting clandestine escapes. But supplied with the thirtieth part of all that Aspasia could desire; glorying in being the spouses of a king; nor in the remotest degree anxious about eventual dowers; they were care-free, content, and rejoicing, as the rays of the morning.

Poor old men, then; it would be hard to distill out of your fate, one drop of the balm of consolation. For, commissioned to watch over those who forever kept you on the trot, affording you no time to hunt up peccadilloes; was not this circumstance an aggravation of hard times? a sharpening and edge-giving to the steel in your souls?

But much yet remains unsaid.

To dwell no more upon the eternal wear-and-tear incident to these attenuated old warders, they were intensely hated by the damsels. Inasmuch, as it was archly opined, for what ulterior purposes they were retained.

Nightly couching, on guard, round the seraglio, like fangless old bronze dragons round a fountain enchanted, the old men ever and anon cried out mightily, by reason of sore pinches and scratches received in the dark: And tri-trebly-tri-triply girt about as he was, Donjalolo himself started from his slumbers, raced round and round through his ten thousand corridors; at last bursting all dizzy among his twenty-nine queens, to see what under the seventh-heavens was the matter. When, lo and behold! there lay the innocents all sound asleep; the dragons moaning over their mysterious bruises.

Ah me! his harem, like all large families, was the delight and the torment of the days and nights of Donjalolo.

And in one special matter was he either eminently miserable, or otherwise: for all his multiplicity of wives, he had never an heir. Not his, the proud paternal glance of the Grand Turk Solyman, looking round upon a hundred sons, all bone of his bone, and squinting with his squint.

Chapter LXXXI

Wherein Babbalanja Relates The Adventure Of One Karkeke In The Land Of Shades

At our morning repast on the second day of our stay in the hollow, our party indulged in much lively discourse.

"Samoa," said I, "those isles of yours, of whose beauty you so often make vauntful mention, can those isles, good Samoa, furnish a valley in all respects equal to Willamilla?"

Disdainful answer was made, that Willamilla might be endurable enough for a sojourn, but as a permanent abode, any glen of his own natal isle was unspeakably superior.

"In the great valley of Savaii," cried Samoa, "for every leaf grown here in Willamilla, grows a stately tree; and for every tree here waving, in Savaii flourishes a goodly warrior."

Immeasurable was the disgust of the Upoluan for the enervated subjects of Donjalolo; and for Donjalolo himself; though it was shrewdly divined, that his annoying reception at the hands of the royalty of Juam, had something to do with his disdain.

To Jarl, no similar question was put; for he was sadly deficient in a taste for the picturesque. But he cursorily observed, that in his blue-water opinion, Willamilla was next to uninhabitable, all view of the sea being intercepted.

And here it may be well to relate a comical blunder on the part of honest Jarl; concerning which, Samoa, the savage, often afterward twitted him; as indicating a rusticity, and want of polish in his breeding. It rather originated, however, in his not heeding the conventionalities of the strange people among whom he was thrown.

The anecdote is not an epic; but here it is.

Reclining in our arbor, we breakfasted upon a marble slab; so frost- white, and flowingly traced with blue veins, that it seemed a little lake sheeted over with ice: Diana's virgin bosom congealed.

Before each guest was a richly carved bowl and gourd, fruit and wine freighted also the empty hemisphere of a small nut, the purpose of which was a problem. Now, King Jarl scorned to admit the slightest degree of under-breeding in the matter of polite feeding. So nothing was a problem to him. At once reminded of the morsel of Arvaroot in his mouth, a substitute for another sort of sedative then unattainable, he was instantly illuminated concerning the purpose of the nut; and very complacently introduced each to the other; in the innocence of his ignorance making no doubt that he had acquitted himself with discretion; the little hemisphere plainly being intended as a place of temporary deposit for the Arva of the guests.

The company were astounded: Samoa more than all. King Jarl, meanwhile, looking at all present with the utmost serenity. At length, one of the horrified attendants, using two sticks for a forceps, disappeared with the obnoxious nut, Upon which, the meal proceeded.

This attendant was not seen again for many days; which gave rise to the supposition, that journeying to the sea-side, he had embarked for some distant strand; there, to bury out of sight the abomination with which he was freighted.

Upon this, his egregious misadventure, calculated to do discredit to our party, and bring Media himself into contempt, Babbalanja had no scruples in taking Jarl roundly to task. He assured him, that it argued but little brains to evince a desire to be thought familiar with all things; that however desirable as incidental attainments, conventionalities, in themselves, were the very least of arbitrary trifles; the knowledge of them, innate with no man. "Moreover Jarl," he added, "in essence, conventionalities are but mimickings, at which monkeys succeed best. Hence, when you find yourself at a loss in these matters, wait patiently, and mark what the other monkeys do: and then follow suit. And by so doing, you will gain a vast reputation as an accomplished ape. Above all things, follow not the silly example of the young spark Karkeke, of whom Mohi was telling me. Dying, and entering the other world with a mincing gait, and there finding certain customs quite strange and new; such as friendly shades passing through each other by way of a salutation;— Karkeke, nevertheless, resolved to show no sign of embarrassment. Accosted by a phantom, with wings folded pensively, plumes interlocked across its chest, he off head; and stood obsequiously before it. Staring at him for an instant, the spirit cut him dead; murmuring to itself, 'Ah, some terrestrial bumpkin, I fancy,' and passed on with its celestial nose in the highly rarified air. But silly Karkeke undertaking to replace his head, found that it would no more stay on; but forever tumbled off; even in the act of nodding a salute; which calamity kept putting him out of countenance. And thus through all eternity is he punished for his folly, in having pretended to be wise, wherein he was ignorant. Head under arm, he wanders about, the scorn and ridicule of the other world."

Our repast concluded, messengers arrived from the prince, courteously inviting our presence at the House of the Morning. Thither we went; journeying in sedans, sent across the hollow, for that purpose, by Donjalolo.

Chapter LXXXII

How Donjalolo, Sent Agents To The Surrounding Isles; With The Result

Ere recounting what was beheld on entering the House of the Morning, some previous information is needful. Though so many of Donjalolo's days were consumed by sloth and luxury, there came to him certain intervals of thoughtfulness, when all his curiosity concerning the things of outer Mardi revived with augmented intensity. In these moods, he would send abroad deputations, inviting to Willamilla the kings of the neighboring islands; together with the most celebrated priests, bards, story-tellers, magicians, and wise men; that he might hear them converse of those things, which he could not behold for himself.

But at last, he bethought him, that the various narrations he had heard, could not have been otherwise than unavoidably faulty; by reason that they had been principally obtained from the inhabitants of the countries described; who, very naturally, must have been inclined to partiality or uncandidness in their statements. Wherefore he had very lately dispatched to the isles special agents of his own; honest of heart, keen of eye, and shrewd of understanding; to seek out every thing that promised to illuminate him concerning the places they visited, and also to collect various specimens of interesting objects; so that at last he might avail himself of the researches of others, and see with their eyes.

But though two observers were sent to every one of the neighboring lands; yet each was to act independently; make his own inquiries; form his own conclusions; and return with his own specimens; wholly regardless of the proceedings of the other.

It so came to pass, that on the very day of our arrival in the glen, these pilgrims returned from their travels. And Donjalolo had set apart the following morning to giving them a grand public reception. And it was to this, that our party had been invited, as related in the chapter preceding.

In the great Palm-hall of the House of the Morning, we were assigned distinguished mats, to the right of the prince; his chiefs, attendants, and subjects assembled in the open colonnades without.

When all was in readiness, in marched the company of savans and travelers; and humbly standing in a semi-circle before the king, their numerous hampers were deposited at their feet.

Donjalolo was now in high spirits, thinking of the rich store of reliable information about to be furnished.

"Zuma," said he, addressing the foremost of the company, "you and Varnopi were directed to explore the island of Rafona. Proceed now, and relate all you know of that place. Your narration heard, we will list to Varnopi."

With a profound inclination the traveler obeyed.

But soon Donjalolo interrupted him. "What say you, Zuma, about the secret cavern, and the treasures therein? A very different account, this, from all I have heard hitherto; but perhaps yours is the true version. Go on."

But very soon, poor Zuma was again interrupted by exclamations of surprise. Nay, even to the very end of his mountings.

But when he had done, Donjalolo observed, that if from any cause Zuma was in error or obscure, Varnopi would not fail to set him right.

So Varnopi was called upon.

But not long had Varnopi proceeded, when Donjalolo changed color.

"What!" he exclaimed, "will ye contradict each other before our very face. Oh Oro! how hard is truth to be come at by proxy! Fifty accounts have I had of Rafona; none of which wholly agreed; and here, these two varlets, sent expressly to behold and report, these two lying knaves, speak crookedly both. How is it? Are the lenses in their eyes diverse-hued, that objects seem different to both; for undeniable is it, that the things they thus clashingly speak of are to be known for the same; though represented with unlike colors and qualities. But dumb things can not lie nor err. Unpack thy hampers, Zuma. Here, bring them close: now: what is this?"

"That," tremblingly replied Zuma, "is a specimen of the famous reef- bar on the west side of the island of Rafona; your highness perceives its deep red dyes."

Said Donjalolo, "Varnopi, hast thou a piece of this coral, also?"

"I have, your highness," said Varnopi; "here it is."

Taking it from his hand, Donjalolo gazed at its bleached, white hue; then dashing it to the pavement, "Oh mighty Oro! Truth dwells in her fountains; where every one must drink for himself. For me, vain all hope of ever knowing Mardi! Away! Better know nothing, than be deceived. Break up!"

And Donjalolo rose, and retired.

All present now broke out in a storm of vociferation; some siding with Zuma; others with Varnopi; each of whom, in turn, was declared the man to be relied upon.

Marking all this, Babbalanja, who had been silently looking on, leaning against one of the palm pillars, quietly observed to Media:— "My lord, I have seen this same reef at Rafona. In various places, it is of various hues. As for Zuma and Varnopi, both are wrong, and both are right."

Chapter LXXXIII

They Visit The Tributary Islets

In Willamilla, no Yillah being found, on the third day we took leave of Donjalolo; who lavished upon us many caresses and, somewhat reluctantly on Media's part, we quitted the vale.

One by one, we now visited the outer villages of Juam; and crossing the waters, wandered several days among its tributary isles. There we saw the viceroys of him who reigned in the hollow: chieftains of whom Donjalolo was proud; so honest, humble, and faithful; so bent upon ameliorating the condition of those under their rule. For, be it said, Donjalolo was a charitable prince; in his serious intervals, ever seeking the welfare of his subjects, though after an imperial view of his own. But alas, in that sunny donjon among the mountains, where he dwelt, how could Donjalolo be sure, that the things he decreed were executed in regions forever remote from his view. Ah! very bland, very innocent, very pious, the faces his viceroys presented during their monthly visits to Willamilla. But as cruel their visage, when, returned to their islets, they abandoned themselves to all the license of tyrants; like Verres reveling down the rights of the Sicilians.

Like Carmelites, they came to Donjalolo, barefooted; but in their homes, their proud latchets were tied by their slaves. Before their king-belted prince, they stood rope-girdled like self-abased monks of St. Francis; but with those ropes, before their palaces, they hung Innocence and Truth.

As still seeking Yillah, and still disappointed, we roved through the lands which these chieftains ruled, Babbalanja exclaimed—"Let us depart; idle our search, in isles that have viceroys for kings."

At early dawn, about embarking for a distant land, there came to us certain messengers of Donjalolo, saying that their lord the king, repenting of so soon parting company with Media and Taji, besought them to return with all haste; for that very morning, in Willamilla, a regal banquet was preparing; to which many neighboring kings had been invited, most of whom had already arrived.

Declaring that there was no alternative but compliance, Media acceded; and with the king's messengers we returned to the glen.

Chapter LXXXIV

Taji Sits Down To Dinner With Five-And-Twenty Kings, And A Royal Time They Have

It was afternoon when we emerged from the defile. And informed that our host was receiving his guests in the House of the Afternoon, thither we directed our steps.

Soft in our face, blew the blessed breezes of Omi, stirring the leaves overhead; while, here and there, through the trees, showed the idol-bearers of the royal retreat, hand in hand, linked with festoons of flowers. Still beyond, on a level, sparkled the nodding crowns of the kings, like the constellation Corona-Borealis, the horizon just gained.

Close by his noon-tide friend, the cascade at the mouth of the grotto, reposed on his crimson mat, Donjalolo:—arrayed in a vestment of the finest white tappa of Mardi, figured all over with bright yellow lizards, so curiously stained in the gauze, that he seemed overrun, as with golden mice.

Marjora's girdle girdled his loins, tasseled with the congregated teeth of his sires. A jeweled turban-tiara, milk-white, surmounted his brow, over which waved a copse of Pintado plumes.

But what sways in his hand? A scepter, similar to those likenesses of scepters, imbedded among the corals at his feet. A polished thigh- bone; by Braid-Beard declared once Teei's the Murdered. For to emphasize his intention utterly to rule, Marjora himself had selected this emblem of dominion over mankind.

But even this last despite done to dead Teei had once been transcended. In the usurper's time, prevailed the belief, that the saliva of kings must never touch ground; and Mohi's Chronicles made mention, that during the life time of Marjora, Teei's skull had been devoted to the basest of purposes: Marjora's, the hate no turf could bury.

Yet, traditions like these ever seem dubious. There be many who deny the hump, moral and physical, of Gloster Richard.

Still advancing unperceived, in social hilarity we descried their Highnesses, chatting together like the most plebeian of mortals; full as merry as the monks of old. But marking our approach, all changed. A pair of potentates, who had been playfully trifling, hurriedly adjusted their diadems, threw themselves into attitudes, looking stately as statues. Phidias turned not out his Jupiter so soon.

In various-dyed robes the five-and-twenty kings were arrayed; and various their features, as the rows of lips, eyes and ears in John Caspar Lavater's physiognomical charts. Nevertheless, to a king, all their noses were aquiline.

There were long fox-tail beards of silver gray, and enameled chins, like those of girls; bald pates and Merovingian locks; smooth brows and wrinkles: forms erect and stooping; an eye that squinted; one king was deaf; by his side, another that was halt; and not far off, a dotard. They were old and young, tall and short, handsome and ugly, fat and lean, cunning and simple.

With animated courtesy our host received us; assigning a neighboring bower for Babbalanja and the rest; and among so many right-royal, demi-divine guests, how could the demi-gods Media and Taji be otherwise than at home?

The unwonted sprightliness of Donjalolo surprised us. But he was in one of those relapses of desperate gayety in-variably following his failures in efforts to amend his life. And the bootless issue of his late mission to outer Mardi had thrown him into a mood for revelry. Nor had he lately shunned a wild wine, called Morando.

A slave now appearing with a bowl of this beverage, it circulated freely.

Not to gainsay the truth, we fancied the Morando much. A nutty, pungent flavor it had; like some kinds of arrack distilled in the Philippine isles. And a marvelous effect did it have, in dissolving the crystalization of the brain; leaving nothing but precious little drops of good humor, beading round the bowl of the cranium.

Meanwhile, garlanded boys, climbing the limbs of the idol-pillars, and stirruping their feet in their most holy mouths, suspended hangings of crimson tappa all round the hall; so that sweeping the pavement they rustled in the breeze from the grot.

Presently, stalwart slaves advanced; bearing a mighty basin of a porphyry hue, deep-hollowed out of a tree. Outside, were innumerable grotesque conceits; conspicuous among which, for a border, was an endless string of the royal lizards circumnavigating the basin in inverted chase of their tails.

Peculiar to the groves of Willamilla, the yellow lizard formed part of the arms of Juam. And when Donjalolo's messenger went abroad, they carried its effigy, as the emblem of their royal master; themselves being known, as the Gentlemen of the Golden Lizard.

The porphyry-hued basin planted full in our midst, the attendants forthwith filled the same with the living waters from the cascade; a proceeding, for which some of the company were at a loss to account, unless his highness, our host, with all the coolness of royalty, purposed cooling himself still further, by taking a bath in presence of his guests. A conjecture, most premature; for directly, the basin being filled to within a few inches of the lizards, the attendants fell to launching therein divers goodly sized trenchers, all laden with choice viands:—wild boar meat; humps of grampuses; embrowned bread-fruit, roasted in odoriferous fires of sandal wood, but suffered to cool; gold fish, dressed with the fragrant juices of berries; citron sauce; rolls of the baked paste of yams; juicy bananas, steeped in a saccharine oil; marmalade of plantains; jellies of guava; confections of the treacle of palm sap; and many other dainties; besides numerous stained calabashes of Morando, and other beverages, fixed in carved floats to make them buoyant.

The guests assigned seats, by the woven handles attached to his purple mat, the prince, our host, was now gently moved by his servitors to the head of the porphyry-hued basin. Where, flanked by lofty crowned-heads, white-tiaraed, and radiant with royalty, he sat; like snow-turbaned Mont Blanc, at sunrise presiding over the head waters of the Rhone; to right and left, looming the gilded summits of the Simplon, the Gothard, the Jungfrau, the Great St. Bernard, and the Grand Glockner.

Yet turbid from the launching of its freight, Lake Como tossed to and fro its navies of good cheer, the shadows of the king-peaks wildly flitting thereupon.

But no frigid wine and fruit cooler, Lake Como; as at first it did seem; but a tropical dining table, its surface a slab of light blue St. Pons marble in a state of fluidity.

Now, many a crown was doffed; scepters laid aside; girdles slackened; and among those verdant viands the bearded kings like goats did browse; or tusking their wild boar's meat, like mastiffs ate.

And like unto some well-fought fight, beginning calmly, but pressing forward to a fiery rush, this well-fought feast did now wax warm.

A few royal epicures, however, there were: epicures intent upon concoctions, admixtures, and masterly compoundings; who comported themselves with all due deliberation and dignity; hurrying themselves into no reckless deglutition of the dainties. Ah! admirable conceit, Lake Como: superseding attendants. For, from hand to hand the trenchers sailed; no sooner gaining one port, than dispatched over sea to another.

Well suited they were for the occasion; sailing high out of water, to resist the convivial swell at times ruffling the sociable sea; and sharp at both ends, still better adapting them to easy navigation.

But soon, the Morando, in triumphant decanters, went round, reeling like barks before a breeze. But their voyages were brief; and ere long, in certain havens, the accumulation of empty vessels threatened to bridge the lake with pontoons. In those directions, Trade winds were setting. But full soon, cut out were all unladen and unprofitable gourds; and replaced by jolly-bellied calabashes, for a time sailing deep, yawing heavily to the push.

At last, the whole flotilla of trenchers—wrecks and all—were sent swimming to the further end of Lake Como; and thence removed, gave place to ruddy hillocks of fruit, and floating islands of flowers. Chief among the former, a quince-like, golden sphere, that filled the air with such fragrance, you thought you were tasting its flavor.

Nor did the wine cease flowing. That day the Juam grape did bleed; that day the tendril ringlets of the vines, did all uncurl and grape by grape, in sheer dismay, the sun ripe clusters dropped. Grape-glad were five-and-twenty kings: five-and-twenty kings were merry.

Morando's vintage had no end; nor other liquids, in the royal cellar stored, somewhere secret in the grot. Oh! where's the endless Niger's source? Search ye here, or search ye there; on, on, through ravine, vega, vale—no head waters will ye find. But why need gain the hidden spring, when its lavish stream flows by? At three-fold mouths that Delta-grot discharged; rivers golden, white, and red.

But who may sing for aye? Down I come, and light upon the old and prosy plain.

Among other decanters set afloat, was a pompous, lordly-looking demijohn, but old and reverend withal, that sailed about, consequential as an autocrat going to be crowned, or a treasure- freighted argosie bound home before the wind. It looked solemn, however, though it reeled; peradventure, far gone with its own potent contents.

Oh! russet shores of Rhine and Rhone! oh, mellow memories of ripe old vintages! oh, cobwebs in the Pyramids! oh, dust on Pharaoh's tomb!— all, all recur, as I bethink me of that glorious gourd, its contents cogent as Tokay, itself as old as Mohi's legends; more venerable to look at than his beard. Whence came it? Buried in vases, so saith the label, with the heart of old Marjora, now dead one hundred thousand moons. Exhumed at last, it looked no wine, but was shrunk into a subtile syrup.

This special calabash was distinguished by numerous trappings, caparisoned like the sacred bay steed led before the Great Khan of Tartary. A most curious and betasseled network encased it; and the royal lizard was jealously twisted about its neck, like a hand on a throat containing some invaluable secret.

All Hail, Marzilla! King's Own Royal Particular! A vinous Percy! Dating back to the Conquest! Distilled of yore from purple berries growing in the purple valley of Ardair! Thrice hail.

But the imperial Marzilla was not for all; gods only could partake; the Kings and demigods of the isles; excluding left-handed descendants of sad rakes of immortals, in old times breaking heads and hearts in Mardi, bequeathing bars-sinister to many mortals, who now in vain might urge a claim to a cup-full of right regal Marzilla.

The Royal Particular was pressed upon me, by the now jovial Donjalolo. With his own sceptered hand charging my flagon to the brim, he declared his despotic pleasure, that I should quaff it off to the last lingering globule. No hard calamity, truly; for the drinking of this wine was as the singing of a mighty ode, or frenzied lyric to the soul.

"Drink, Taji," cried Donjalolo, "drink deep. In this wine a king's heart is dissolved. Drink long; in this wine lurk the seeds of the life everlasting. Drink deep; drink long: thou drinkest wisdom and valor at every draught. Drink forever, oh Taji, for thou drinkest that which will enable thee to stand up and speak out before mighty Oro himself."

"Borabolla," he added, turning round upon a domed old king at his left, "Was it not the god Xipho, who begged of my great-great- grandsire a draught of this same wine, saying he was about to beget a hero?"

"Even so. And thy glorious Marzilla produced thrice valiant Ononna, who slew the giants of the reef."

"Ha, ha, hear'st that, oh Taji?" And Donjalolo drained another cup.

Amazing! the flexibility of the royal elbow, and the rigidity of the royal spine! More especially as we had been impressed with a notion of their debility. But, sometimes these seemingly enervated young blades approve themselves steadier of limb, than veteran revelers of very long standing.

"Discharge the basin, and refill it with wine," cried Donjalolo. "Break all empty gourds! Drink, kings, and dash your cups at every draught."

So saying, he started from his purple mat; and with one foot planted unknowingly upon the skull of Marjora; while all the skeletons grinned at him from the pavement; Donjalolo, holding on high his blood-red goblet, burst forth with the following invocation:—

Ha, ha, gods and kings; fill high, one and all;
Drink, drink! shout and drink! mad respond to the call!
Fill fast, and fill frill; 'gainst the goblet ne'er sin;
Quaff there, at high tide, to the uttermost rim:—
Flood-tide, and soul-tide to the brim!

Who with wine in him fears? who thinks of his cares?
Who sighs to be wise, when wine in him flares?
Water sinks down below, in currents full slow;
But wine mounts on high with its genial glow:—
Welling up, till the brain overflow!

As the spheres, with a roll, some fiery of soul,
Others golden, with music, revolve round the pole;

So let our cups, radiant with many hued wines,
Round and round in groups circle, our Zodiac's Signs:—
Round reeling, and ringing their chimes!

Then drink, gods and kings; wine merriment brings;
It bounds through the veins; there, jubilant sings.
Let it ebb, then, and flow; wine never grows dim;
Drain down that bright tide at the foam beaded rim:—
Fill up, every cup, to the brim!

Caught by all present, the chorus resounded again and again. The beaded wine danced on many a beard; the cataract lifted higher its voice; the grotto sent back a shout; the ghosts of the Coral Monarchs seemed starting from their insulted bones. But ha, ha, ha, roared forth the five-and-twenty kings—alive, not dead—holding both hands to their girdles, and baying out their laughter from abysses; like Nimrod's hounds over some fallen elk.

Mad and crazy revelers, how ye drank and roared! but kings no more: vestures loosed; and scepters rolling on the ground.

Glorious agrarian, thou wine! bringing all hearts on a level, and at last all legs to the earth; even those of kings, who, to do them justice, have been much maligned for imputed qualities not theirs. For whoso has touched flagons with monarchs, bear they their back bones never so stiffly on the throne, well know the rascals, to be at bottom royal good fellows; capable of a vinous frankness exceeding that of base-born men. Was not Alexander a boon companion? And daft Cambyses? and what of old Rowley, as good a judge of wine and other matters, as ever sipped claret or kisses.

If ever Taji joins a club, be it a Beef-Steak Club of Kings!

Donjalolo emptied yet another cup.

The mirth now blew a gale; like a ship's shrouds in a Typhoon, every tendon vibrated; the breezes of Omi came forth with a rush; the hangings shook; the goblets danced fandangos; and Donjalolo, clapping his hands, called before him his dancing women.

Forth came from the grotto a reed-like burst of song, making all start, and look that way to behold such enchanting strains. Sounds heralding sights! Swimming in the air, emerged the nymphs, lustrous arms interlocked like Indian jugglers' glittering snakes. Round the cascade they thronged; then paused in its spray. Of a sudden, seemed to spring from its midst, a young form of foam, that danced into the soul like a thought. At last, sideways floating off, it subsided into the grotto, a wave. Evening drawing on apace, the crimson draperies were lifted, and festooned to the arms of the idol-pillars, admitting the rosy light of the even.

Yielding to the re-action of the banquet, the kings now reclined; and two mute damsels entered: one with a gourd of scented waters; the other with napkins. Bending over Donjalolo's steaming head, the first let fall a shower of aromatic drops, slowly aborbed by her companion. Thus, in turn, all were served; nothing heard but deep breathing.

In a marble vase they now kindled some incense: a handful of spices.

Shortly after, came three of the king's beautiful smokers; who, lighting their tubes at this odorous fire, blew over the company the sedative fumes of the Aina.

Steeped in languor, I strove against it long; essayed to struggle out of the enchanted mist. But a syren hand seemed ever upon me, pressing me back.

Half-revealed, as in a dream, and the last sight that I saw, was Donjalolo:—eyes closed, face pale, locks moist, borne slowly to his sedan, to cross the hollow, and wake in the seclusion of his harem.

Chapter LXXXV

After Dinner

As in dreams I behold thee again, Willamila! as in dreams, once again I stroll through thy cool shady groves, oh fairest of the vallies of Mardi! the thought of that mad merry feasting steals over my soul till I faint.

Prostrate here and there over the bones of Donjalolo's sires, the royal bacchanals lay slumbering till noon.

"Which are the deadest?" said Babbalanja, peeping in, "the live kings, or the dead ones?"

But the former were drooping flowers sought to be revived by watering. At intervals the sedulous attendants went to and fro, besprinkling their heads with the scented contents of their vases.

At length, one by one, the five-and-twenty kings lifted their ambrosial curls; and shaking the dew therefrom, like eagles opened their right royal eyes, and dilated their aquiline nostrils, full upon the golden rays of the sun.

But why absented himself, Donjalolo? Had he cavalierly left them to survive the banquet by themselves? But this apparent incivility was soon explained by heralds, announcing to their prone majesties, that through the over solicitude of his slaves, their lord the king had been borne to his harem, without being a party to the act. But to make amends, in his sedan, Donjalolo was even now drawing nigh. Not, however, again to make merry; but socially to sleep in company with his guests; for, together they had all got high, and together they must all lie low.

So at it they went: each king to his bones, and slumbered like heroes till evening; when, availing themselves of the cool moonlight approaching, the royal guests bade adieu to their host; and summoning their followers, quitted the glen.

Early next day, having determined to depart for our canoes, we proceeded to the House of the Morning, to take leave of Donjalolo.

An amazing change, one night of solitude had wrought! Pale and languid, we found him reclining: one hand on his throbbing temples.

Near an overturned vessel of wine, the royal girdle lay tossed at his feet. He had waved off his frightened attendants, who crouched out of sight.

We advanced.

"Do ye too leave me? Ready enough are ye to partake of my banquetings, which, to such as ye, are but mad incidents in one round of more tranquil diversions. But heed me not, Media;—I am mad. Oh, ye gods! am I forever a captive?—Ay, free king of Odo, when you list, condescend to visit the poor slave in Willamilla. I account them but charity, your visits; would fain allure ye by sumptuous fare. Go, leave me; go, and be rovers again throughout blooming Mardi. For, me, I am here for aye.—Bring me wine, slaves! quick! that I may pledge my guests fitly. Alas, Media, at the bottom of this cup are no sparkles as at top. Oh, treacherous, treacherous friend! full of smiles and daggers. Yet for such as me, oh wine, thou art e'en a prop, though it pierce the side; for man must lean. Thou wine art the friend of the friendless, though a foe to all. King Media, let us drink. More cups!—And now, farewell."

Falling back, he averted his face; and silently we quitted the palace.

Chapter LXXXVI

Of Those Scamps The Plujii

The beach gained, we embarked.

In good time our party recovered from the seriousness into which we had been thrown; and a rather long passage being now before us, we whiled away the hours as best we might.

Among many entertaining, narrations, old Braid-Beard, crossing his calves, and peaking his beard, regaled us with some account of certain invisible spirits, ycleped the Plujii, arrant little knaves as ever gulped moonshine.

They were spoken of as inhabiting the island of Quelquo, in a remote corner of the lagoon; the innocent people of which island were sadly fretted and put out by their diabolical proceedings. Not to be wondered at; since, dwelling as they did in the air, and completely inaccessible, these spirits were peculiarly provocative of ire.

Detestable Plujii! With malice aforethought, they brought about high winds that destroyed the banana plantations, and tumbled over the heads of its occupants many a bamboo dwelling. They cracked the calabashes; soured the "poee;" induced the colic; begat the spleen; and almost rent people in twain with stitches in the side. In short, from whatever evil, the cause of which the Islanders could not directly impute to their gods, or in their own opinion was not referable to themselves,—of that very thing must the invisible Plujii be guilty. With horrible dreams, and blood-thirsty gnats, they invaded the most innocent slumbers.

All things they bedeviled. A man with a wry neck ascribed it to the Plujii; he with a bad memory railed against the Plujii; and the boy, bruising his finger, also cursed those abominable spirits.

Nor, to some minds, at least, was there wanting strong presumptive evidence, that at times, with invisible fingers, the above mentioned Plujii did leave direct and tangible traces of their presence; pinching and pounding the unfortunate Islanders; pulling their hair; plucking their ears, and tweaking their beards and their noses. And thus perpetually vexing, incensing, tormenting, and exasperating their helpless victims, the atrocious Plujii reveled in their malicious dominion over the souls and bodies of the people of Quelquo.

What it was, that induced them to enact such a part, Oro only knew; and never but once, it seems, did old Mohi endeavor to find out.

Once upon a time, visiting Quelquo, he chanced to encounter an old woman almost doubled together, both hands upon her abdomen; in that manner running about distracted.

"My good woman," said he, "what under the firmament is the matter?"

"The Plujii! the Plujii!" affectionately caressing the field of their operations.

"But why do they torment you?" he soothingly inquired. "How should I know? and what good would it do me if I did?"

And on she ran.

At this part of his narration, Mohi was interrupted by Media; who, much to the surprise of all present, observed, that, unbeknown to him (Braid-Beard), he happened to have been on that very island, at that very time, and saw that identical old lady in the very midst of those abdominal tribulations.

"That she was really in great distress," he went on to say, "was plainly to be seen; but that in that particular instance, your Plujii had any hand in tormenting her, I had some boisterous doubts. For, hearing that an hour or two previous she had been partaking of some twenty unripe bananas, I rather fancied that that circumstance might have had something to do with her sufferings. But however it was, all the herb-leeches on the island would not have altered her own opinions on the subject."

"No," said Braid-Beard; "a post-mortem examination would not have satisfied her ghost."

"Curious to relate," he continued, "the people of that island never abuse the Plujii, notwithstanding all they suffer at their hands, unless under direct provocation; and a settled matter of faith is it, that at such times all bitter words and hasty objurgations are entirely overlooked, nay, pardoned on the spot, by the unseen genii against whom they are directed."

"Magnanimous Plujii!" cried Media. "But, Babbalanja, do you, who run a tilt at all things, suffer this silly conceit to be uttered with impunity in your presence? Why so silent?"

"I have been thinking, my lord," said Babbalanja, "that though the people of that island may at times err, in imputing their calamities to the Plujii, that, nevertheless, upon the whole, they indulge in a reasonable belief. For, Plujii or no Plujii, it is undeniable, that in ten thousand ways, as if by a malicious agency, we mortals are woefully put out and tormented; and that, too, by things in themselves so exceedingly trivial, that it would seem almost impiety to ascribe them to the august gods. No; there must exist some greatly inferior spirits; so insignificant, comparatively, as to be overlooked by the supernal powers; and through them it must be, that we are thus grievously annoyed. At any rate; such a theory would supply a hiatus in my system of meta-physics."

"Well, peace to the Plujii," said Media; "they trouble not me."

Chapter LXXXVII

Nora-Bamma

Still onward gliding, the lagoon a calm.

Hours pass; and full before us, round and green, a Moslem turban by us floats—Nora-Bamma, Isle of Nods.

Noon-tide rolls its flood. Vibrates the air, and trembles. And by illusion optical, thin-draped in azure haze, drift here and there the brilliant lands: swans, peacock-plumaged, sailing through the sky. Down to earth hath heaven come; hard telling sun-clouds from the isles.

And high in air nods Nora-Bamma. Nid-nods its tufted summit like three ostrich plumes; its beetling crags, bent poppies, shadows, willowy shores, all nod; its streams are murmuring down the hills; its wavelets hush the shore.

Who dwells in Nora-Bamma? Dreamers, hypochondriacs, somnambulists; who, from the cark and care of outer Mardi fleeing, in the poppy's jaded odors, seek oblivion for the past, and ecstasies to come.

Open-eyed, they sleep and dream; on their roof-trees, grapes unheeded drop. In Nora-Bamma, whispers are as shouts; and at a zephyr's breath, from the woodlands shake the leaves, as of humming-birds, a flight.

All this spake Braid-Beard, of the isle. How that none ere touched its strand, without rendering instant tribute of a nap; how that those who thither voyaged, in golden quest of golden gourds, fast dropped asleep, ere one was plucked; waking not till night; how that you must needs rub hard your eyes, would you wander through the isle; and how that silent specters would be met, haunting twilight groves, and dreamy meads; hither gliding, thither fading, end or purpose none.

True or false, so much for Mohi's Nora Bamma.

But as we floated on, it looked the place described. We yawned, and yawned, as crews of vessels may; as in warm Indian seas, their winnowing sails all swoon, when by them glides some opium argosie.

Chapter LXXXVIII

In A Calm, Hautia's Heralds Approach

"How still!" cried Babbalanja. "This calm is like unto Oro's everlasting serenity, and like unto man's last despair."

But now the silence was broken by a strange, distant, intermitted melody in the water.

Gazing over the side, we saw naught but a far-darting ray in its depths.

Then Yoomy, before buried in a reverie, burst forth with a verse, sudden as a jet from a Geyser.

Like the fish of the bright and twittering fin,
Bright fish! diving deep as high soars the lark,
So, far, far, far, doth the maiden swim,
Wild song, wild light, in still ocean's dark.

"What maiden, minstrel?" cried Media.

"None of these," answered Yoomy, pointing out a shallop gliding near.

"The damsels three:—Taji, they pursue you yet." That still canoe drew nigh, the Iris in its prow.

Gliding slowly by, one damsel flung a Venus-car, the leaves yet fresh.

Said Yoomy—"Fly to love."

The second maiden flung a pallid blossom, buried in hemlock leaves.

Said Yoomy, starting—"I have wrought a death."

Then came showering Venus-cars, and glorious moss-roses numberless, and odorous handfuls of Verbena.

Said Yoomy—"Yet fly, oh fly to me: all rosy joys and sweets are mine."

Then the damsels floated on.

"Was ever queen more enigmatical?" cried Media—"Love,—death,—joy, —fly to me? But what says Taji?"

"That I turn not back for Hautia; whoe'er she be, that wild witch I contemn."

"Then spread our pinions wide! a breeze! up sails! ply paddles all! Come, Flora's flute, float forth a song."

To pieces picking the thorny roses culled from Hautia's gifts, and holding up their blighted cores, thus plumed and turbaned Yoomy sang, leaning against the mast:—

Oh! royal is the rose,
But barbed with many a dart;
Beware, beware the rose,
'Tis cankered at the heart.

Sweet, sweet the sunny down,
Oh! lily, lily, lily down!
Sweet, sweet, Verbena's bloom!
 Oh! pleasant, gentle, musky bloom!

Dread, dread the sunny down;
Lo! lily-hooded asp;
Blooms, blooms no more Verbena;
White-withered in your clasp.

Chapter LXXXIX

Braid-Beard Rehearses The Origin Of The Isle Of Rogues

Judge not things by their names. This, the maxim illustrated respecting the isle toward which we were sailing.

Ohonoo was its designation, in other words the Land of Rogues. So what but a nest of villains and pirates could one fancy it to be: a downright Tortuga, swarming with "Brethren of the coast,"—such as Montbars, L'Ollonais, Bartolomeo, Peter of Dieppe, and desperadoes of that kidney. But not so. The men of Ohonoo were as honest as any in Mardi. They had a suspicious appellative for their island, true; but not thus seemed it to them. For, upon nothing did they so much plume themselves as upon this very name. Why? Its origin went back to old times; and being venerable they gloried therein; though they disclaimed its present applicability to any of their race; showing, that words are but algebraic signs, conveying no meaning except what you please. And to be called one thing, is oftentimes to be another.

But how came the Ohonoose by their name?

Listen, and Braid-Beard, our Herodotus, will tell.

Long and long ago, there were banished to Ohonoo all the bucaniers, flibustiers, thieves, and malefactors of the neighboring islands; who, becoming at last quite a numerous community, resolved to make a stand for their dignity, and number one among the nations of Mardi. And even as before they had been weeded out of the surrounding countries; so now, they went to weeding out themselves; banishing all objectionable persons to still another island.

These events happened at a period so remote, that at present it was uncertain whether those twice banished, were thrust into their second exile by reason of their superlative knavery, or because of their comparative honesty. If the latter, then must the residue have been a precious enough set of scoundrels.

However it was, the commonwealth of knaves now mustered together their gray-beards, and wise-pates, and knowing-ones, of which last there was a plenty, chose a king to rule over them, and went to political housekeeping for themselves.

And in the fullness of time, this people became numerous and mighty. And the more numerous and mighty they waxed, by so much the more did they take pride and glory in their origin, frequently reverting to it with manifold boastings. The proud device of their monarch was a hand with the forefinger crooked, emblematic of the peculatory propensities of his ancestors.

And all this, at greater length, said Mohi.

"It would seem, then, my lord," said Babbalanja, reclining, "as if these men of Ohonoo had canonized the derelictions of their progenitors, though the same traits are deemed scandalous among themselves. But it is time that makes the difference. The knave of a thousand years ago seems a fine old fellow full of spirit and fun, little malice in his soul; whereas, the knave of to-day seems a sour- visaged wight, with nothing to redeem him. Many great scoundrels of our Chronicler's chronicles are heroes to us:—witness, Marjora the usurper. Ay, time truly works wonders. It sublimates wine; it sublimates fame; nay, is the creator thereof; it enriches and darkens our spears of the Palm; enriches and enlightens the mind; it ripens cherries and young lips; festoons old ruins, and ivies old heads; imparts a relish to old yams, and a pungency to the Ponderings of old Bardianna; of fables distills truths; and finally, smooths, levels, glosses, softens, melts, and meliorates all things. Why, my lord, round Mardi itself is all the better for its antiquity, and the more to be revered; to the cozy-minded, more comfortable to dwell in. Ah! if ever it lay in embryo like a green seed in the pod, what a damp, shapeless thing it must have been, and how unpleasant from the traces of its recent creation. The first man, quoth old Bardianna, must have felt like one going into a new habitation, where the bamboos are green. Is there not a legend in Maramma, that his family were long troubled with influenzas and catarrhs?"

"Oh Time, Time, Time!" cried Yoomy—"it is Time, old midsummer Time, that has made the old world what it is. Time hoared the old mountains, and balded their old summits, and spread the old prairies, and built the old forests, and molded the old vales. It is Time that has worn glorious old channels for the glorious old rivers, and rounded the old lakes, and deepened the old sea! It is Time—"

"Ay, full time to cease," cried Media. "What have you to do with cogitations not in verse, minstrel? Leave prose to Babbalanja, who is prosy enough."

"Even so," said Babbalanja, "Yoomy, you have overstepped your province. My lord Media well knows, that your business is to make the metal in you jingle in tags, not ring in the ingot."

Chapter XC

Rare Sport At Ohonoo

Approached from the northward, Ohonoo, midway cloven down to the sea, one half a level plain; the other, three mountain terraces—Ohonoo looks like the first steps of a gigantic way to the sun. And such, if Braid-Beard spoke truth, it had formerly been.

"Ere Mardi was made," said that true old chronicler, "Vivo, one of the genii, built a ladder of mountains whereby to go up and go down. And of this ladder, the island of Ohonoo was the base. But wandering here and there, incognito in a vapor, so much wickedness did Vivo spy out, that in high dudgeon he hurried up his ladder, knocking the mountains from under him as he went. These here and there fell into the lagoon, forming many isles, now green and luxuriant; which, with those sprouting from seeds dropped by a bird from the moon, comprise all the groups in the reef."

Surely, oh, surely, if I live till Mardi be forgotten by Mardi, I shall not forget the sight that greeted us, as we drew nigh the shores of this same island of Ohonoo; for was not all Ohonoo bathing in the surf of the sea?

But let the picture be painted.

Where eastward the ocean rolls surging against the outer reef of Mardi, there, facing a flood-gate in the barrier, stands cloven Ohonoo; her plains sloping outward to the sea, her mountains a bulwark behind. As at Juam, where the wild billows from seaward roll in upon its cliffs; much more at Ohonoo, in billowy battalions charge they hotly into the lagoon, and fall on the isle like an army from the deep. But charge they never so boldly, and charge they forever, old Ohonoo gallantly throws them back till all before her is one scud and rack. So charged the bright billows of cuirassiers at Waterloo: so hurled them off the long line of living walls, whose base was as the sea-beach, wreck-strown, in a gale.

Without the break in the reef wide banks of coral shelve off, creating the bar, where the waves muster for the onset, thundering in water-bolts, that shake the whole reef, till its very spray trembles. And then is it, that the swimmers of Ohonoo most delight to gambol in the surf.

For this sport, a surf-board is indispensable: some five feet in length; the width of a man's body; convex on both sides; highly polished; and rounded at the ends. It is held in high estimation; invariably oiled after use; and hung up conspicuously in the dwelling of the owner.

Ranged on the beach, the bathers, by hundreds dash in; and diving under the swells, make straight for the outer sea, pausing not till the comparatively smooth expanse beyond has been gained. Here, throwing themselves upon their boards, tranquilly they wait for a billow that suits. Snatching them up, it hurries them landward, volume and speed both increasing, till it races along a watery wall, like the smooth, awful verge of Niagara. Hanging over this scroll, looking down from it as from a precipice, the bathers halloo; every limb in motion to preserve their place on the very crest of the wave. Should they fall behind, the squadrons that follow would whelm them; dismounted, and thrown forward, as certainly would they be run over by the steed they ride. 'Tis like charging at the head of cavalry: you must on.

An expert swimmer shifts his position on his plank; now half striding it; and anon, like a rider in the ring, poising himself upright in the scud, coming on like a man in the air.

At last all is lost in scud and vapor, as the overgrown billow bursts like a bomb. Adroitly emerging, the swimmers thread their way out; and like seals at the Orkneys, stand dripping upon the shore.

Landing in smooth water, some distance from the scene, we strolled forward; and meeting a group resting, inquired for Uhia, their king. He was pointed out in the foam. But presently drawing nigh, he embraced Media, bidding all welcome.

The bathing over, and evening at hand, Uhia and his subjects repaired to their canoes; and we to ours.

Landing at another quarter of the island, we journeyed up a valley called Monlova, and were soon housed in a very pleasant retreat of our host.

Soon supper was spread. But though the viands were rare, and the red wine went round and round like a foaming bay horse in the ring; yet we marked, that despite the stimulus of his day's good sport, and the stimulus of his brave good cheer, Uhia our host was moody and still.

Said Babbalanja "My lord, he fills wine cups for others to quaff."

But whispered King Media, "Though Uhia be sad, be we merry, merry men."

And merry some were, and merrily went to their mats.

Chapter XCI

Of King Uhia And His Subjects

As beseemed him, Uhia was royally lodged. Ample his roof. Beneath it a hundred attendants nightly laying their heads. But long since, he had disbanded his damsels.

Springing from syren embrace—"They shall sap and mine me no more" he cried "my destiny commands me. I will don my manhood. By Keevi! no more will I clasp a waist."

"From that time forth," said Braid-Beard, "young Uhia spread like the tufted top of the Palm; his thigh grew brawny as the limb of the Banian; his arm waxed strong as the back bone of the shark; yea, his voice grew sonorous as a conch."

"And now he bent his whole soul to the accomplishment of the destiny believed to be his. Nothing less than bodily to remove Ohonoo to the center of the lagoon, in fulfillment of an old prophecy running thus— When a certain island shall stir from its foundations and stand in the middle of the still water, then shall the ruler of that island be ruler of all Mardi."

The task was hard, but how glorious the reward! So at it he went, and all Ohonoo helped him. Not by hands, but by calling in the magicians. Thus far, nevertheless, in vain. But Uhia had hopes.

Now, informed of all this, said Babbalanja to Media, "My lord, if the continual looking-forward to something greater, be better than an acquiescence in things present; then, wild as it is, this belief of Uhia's he should hug to his heart, as erewhile his wives. But my lord, this faith it is, that robs his days of peace; his nights of sweet unconsciousness. For holding himself foreordained to the dominion of the entire Archipelago, he upbraids the gods for laggards, and curses himself as deprived of his rights; nay, as having had wrested from him, what he never possessed. Discontent dwarfs his horizon till he spans it with his hand. 'Most miserable of demi-gods,' he cries, 'here am I cooped up in this insignificant islet, only one hundred leagues by fifty, when scores of broad empires own me not for their lord.' Yet Uhia himself is envied. 'Ah!' cries Karrolono, one of his chieftains, master of a snug little glen, 'Here am I cabined in this paltry cell among the mountains, when that great King Uhia is lord of the whole island, and every cubic mile of matter therein.' But this same Karrolono is envied. 'Hard, oh beggarly lot is mine,' cries Donno, one of his retainers. 'Here am I fixed and screwed down to this paltry plantation, when my lord Karrolono owns the whole glen, ten long parasangs from cliff to sea.' But Donno too is envied. 'Alas, cursed fate!' cries his servitor Flavona. 'Here am I made to trudge, sweat, and labor all day, when Donno my master does nothing but command.' But others envy Flavona; and those who envy him are envied in turn; even down to poor bed- ridden Manta, who dying of want, groans forth, 'Abandoned wretch that I am! here I miserably perish, while so many beggars gad about and live!' But surely; none envy Manta! Yes; great Uhia himself. 'Ah!' cries the king. 'Here am I vexed and tormented by ambition; no peace night nor day; my temples chafed sore by this cursed crown that I wear; while that ignoble wight Manta, gives up the ghost with none to molest him.'"

In vain we wandered up and down in this isle, and peered into its innermost recesses: no Yillah was there.

Chapter XCII

The God Keevi And The Precipice Op Mondo

One object of interest in Ohonoo was the original image of Keevi the god of Thieves; hence, from time immemorial, the tutelar deity of the isle.

His shrine was a natural niche in a cliff, walling in the valley of Monlova And here stood Keevi, with his five eyes, ten hands, and three pair of legs, equipped at all points for the vocation over which he presided. Of mighty girth, his arms terminated in hands, every finger a limb, spreading in multiplied digits: palms twice five, and fifty fingers.

According to the legend, Keevi fell from a golden cloud, burying himself to the thighs in the earth, tearing up the soil all round. Three meditative mortals, strolling by at the time, had a narrow escape.

A wonderful recital; but none of us voyagers durst flout it. Did they not show us the identical spot where the idol fell? We descended into the hollow, now verdant. Questionless, Keevi himself would have vouched for the truth of the miracle, had he not been unfortunately dumb. But by far the most cogent, and pointed argument advanced in support of this story, is a spear which the priests of Keevi brought forth, for Babbalanja to view.

"Let me look at it closer," said Babbalanja.

And turning it over and over and curiously inspecting it, "Wonderful spear," he cried. "Doubtless, my reverends, this self-same spear must have persuaded many recusants!"

"Nay, the most stubborn," they answered.

"And all afterward quoted as additional authority for the truth of the legend?"

"Assuredly."

From the sea to the shrine of this god, the fine valley of Monlova ascends with a gentle gradation, hardly perceptible; but upon turning round toward the water, one is surprised to find himself high elevated above its surface. Pass on, and the same silent ascent deceives you; and the valley contracts; and on both sides the cliffs advance; till at last you come to a narrow space, shouldered by buttresses of rock. Beyond, through this cleft, all is blue sky. If the Trades blow high, and you came unawares upon the spot, you would think Keevi himself pushing you forward with all his hands; so powerful is the current of air rushing through this elevated defile. But expostulate not with the tornado that blows you along; sail on; but soft; look down; the land breaks off in one sheer descent of a thousand feet, right down to the wide plain below. So sudden and profound this precipice, that you seem to look off from one world to another. In a dreamy, sunny day, the spangled plain beneath assumes an uncertain fleeting aspect. Had you a deep-sea-lead you would almost be tempted to sound the ocean-haze at your feet.

This, mortal! is the precipice of Mondo.

From this brink, spear in hand, sprang fifty rebel warriors, driven back into the vale by a superior force. Finding no spot to stand at bay, with a fierce shout they took the fatal leap.

Said Mohi, "Their souls ascended, ere their bodies touched."

This tragical event took place many generations gone by, and now a dizzy, devious way conducts one, firm of foot, from the verge to the plain. But none ever ascended. So perilous, indeed, is the descent itself, that the islanders venture not the feat, without invoking supernatural aid. Flanking the precipice beneath beetling rocks, stand the guardian deities of Mondo; and on altars before them, are placed the propitiatory offerings of the traveler.

To the right of the brink of the precipice, and far over it, projects a narrow ledge. The test of legitimacy in the Ohonoo monarchs is to stand hereon, arms folded, and javelins darting by.

And there in his youth Uhia stood.

"How felt you, cousin?" asked Media.

"Like the King of Ohonoo," he replied. "As I shall again feel; when King of all Mardi."

Chapter XCIII

Babbalanja Steps In Between Mohi And Yoomy; And Yoomy Relates A Legend

Embarking from Ohonoo, we at length found ourselves gliding by the pleasant shores of Tupia, an islet which according to Braid-Beard had for ages remained uninhabited by man. Much curiosity being expressed to know more of the isle, Mohi was about to turn over his chronicles, when, with modesty, the minstrel Yoomy interposed; saying, that if my Lord Media permitted, he himself would relate the legend. From its nature, deeming the same pertaining to his province as poet; though, as yet, it had not been versified. But he added, that true pearl shells rang musically, though not strung upon a cord.

Upon this presumptuous interference, Mohi looked highly offended; and nervously twitching his beard, uttered something invidious about frippery young poetasters being too full of silly imaginings to tell a plain tale.

Said Yoomy, in reply, adjusting his turban, "Old Mohi, let us not clash. I honor your calling; but, with submission, your chronicles are more wild than my cantos. I deal in pure conceits of my own; which have a shapeliness and a unity, however unsubstantial; but you, Braid-Beard, deal in mangled realities. In all your chapters, you yourself grope in the dark. Much truth is not in thee, historian. Besides, Mohi: my songs perpetuate many things which you sage scribes entirely overlook. Have you not oftentimes come to me, and my ever dewy ballads for information, in which you and your musty old chronicles were deficient?"

"In much that is precious, Mohi, we poets are the true historians; we embalm; you corrode."

To this Mohi, with some ire, was about to make answer, when, flinging over his shoulder a new fold of his mantle, Babbalanja spoke thus: "Peace, rivals. As Bardianna has it, like all who dispute upon pretensions of their own, you are each nearest the right, when you speak of the other; and furthest therefrom, when you speak of yourselves."

Said Mohi and Yoomy in a breath, "Who sought your opinion, philosopher? you filcher from old Bardianna, and monger of maxims!"

"You, who have so long marked the vices of Mardi, that you flatter yourself you have none of your own," added Braid-Beard.

"You, who only seem wise, because of the contrasting follies of others, and not of any great wisdom in yourself," continued the minstrel, with unwonted asperity."

"Now here," said Babballanja, "am I charged upon by a bearded old ram, and a lamb. One butting with his carious and brittle old frontlet; the other pushing with its silly head before its horns are sprouted. But this comes of being impartial. Had I espoused the cause of Yoomy versus Mohi, or that of Mohi versus Yoomy, I had been sure to have had at least one voice in my favor. The impartialist insulteth all sides, saith old Bardianna; but smite with but one hand, and the other shall be kissed.—Oh incomparable Bardianna!"

"Will no one lay that troubled old ghost," exclaimed Media, devoutly. "Proceed with thy legend, Yoomy; and see to it, that it be brief; for I mistrust me, these legends do but test the patience of the hearers. But draw a long breath, and begin."

"A long bow," muttered Mohi.

And Yoomy began.

"It is now about ten hundred thousand moons—"

"Great Oro! How long since, say you?" cried Mohi, making Gothic arches of his brows.

Looking at him disdainfully, but vouchsafing no reply, Yoomy began over again.

"It is now above ten hundred thousand moons, since there died the last of a marvelous race, once inhabiting the very shores by which we are sailing. They were a very diminutive people, only a few inches high—"

"Stop, minstrel," cried Mohi; "how many pennyweights did they weigh?"

Continued Yoomy, unheedingly, "They were covered all over with a soft, silky down, like that on the rind of the Avee; and there grew upon their heads a green, lance-leaved vine, of a most delicate texture. For convenience, the manikins reduced their tendrils, sporting, nothing but coronals. Whereas, priding themselves upon the redundancy of their tresses, the little maidens assiduously watered them with the early dew of the morning; so that all wreathed and festooned with verdure, they moved about in arbors, trailing after them trains."

"I can hear no more," exclaimed Mohi, stopping his ears.

Continued Yoomy, "The damsels lured to their bowers, certain red- plumaged insect-birds, and taught them to nestle therein, and warble; which, with the pleasant vibrating of the leaves, when the little maidens moved, produced a strange blending of sweet, singing sounds. The little maidens embraced not with their arms, but with their viny locks; whose tendrils instinctively twined about their lovers, till both were lost in the bower."

"And what then?" asked Mohi, who, notwithstanding the fingers in his ears, somehow contrived to listen; "What then?"

Vouchsafing no reply, Yoomy went on.

"At a certain age, but while yet the maidens were very young, their vines bore blossoms. Ah! fatal symptoms. For soon as they burst, the maidens died in their arbors; and were buried in the valleys; and their vines spread forth; and the flowers bloomed; but the maidens themselves were no more. And now disdaining the earth, the vines shot upward: climbing to the topmost boughs of the trees; and flowering in the sunshine forever and aye."

Yoomy here paused for a space; but presently continued:

"The little eyes of the people of Tupia were very strange to behold: full of stars, that shone from within, like the Pleiades, deep- bosomed in blue. And like the stars, they were intolerant of sunlight; and slumbering through the day, the people of Tupia only went abroad by night. But it was chiefly when the moon was at full, that they were mostly in spirits.

"Then the little manikins would dive down into the sea, and rove about in the coral groves, making love to the mermaids. Or, racing round, make a mad merry night of it with the sea-urchins:—plucking the reverend mullets by the beard; serenading the turtles in their cells; worrying the sea-nettles; or tormenting with their antics the touchy torpedos. Sometimes they went prying about with the starfish, that have an eye at the end of each ray; and often with coral files in their hands stole upon slumbering swordfish, slyly blunting their weapons. In short, these stout little manikins were passionately fond of the sea, and swore by wave and billow, that sooner or later they would embark thereon in nautilus shells, and spend the rest of their roving days thousands of inches from Tupia. Too true, they were shameless little rakes. Oft would they return to their sweethearts, sporting musky girdles of sea-kelp, tasseled with green little pouches of grass, brimful of seed-pearls; and jingling their coin in the ears of the damsels, throw out inuendoes about the beautiful and bountiful mermaids: how wealthy and amorous they were, and how they delighted in the company of the brave gallants of Tupia. Ah! at such heartless bravadoes, how mourned the poor little nymphs. Deep into their arbors they went; and their little hearts burst like rose-buds, and filled the whole air with an odorous grief. But when their lovers were gentle and true, no happier maidens haunted the lilies than they. By some mystical process they wrought minute balls of light: touchy, mercurial globules, very hard to handle; and with these, at pitch and toss, they played in the groves. Or mischievously inclined, they toiled all night long at braiding the moon-beams together, and entangling the plaited end to a bough; so that at night, the poor planet had much ado to set."

Here Yoomy once more was mute.

"Pause you to invent as you go on?" said old Mohi, elevating his chin, till his beard was horizontal.

Yoomy resumed.

"Little or nothing more, my masters, is extant of the legend; only it must be mentioned, that these little people were very tasteful in their personal adornings; the manikins wearing girdles of fragrant leaves, and necklaces of aromatic seeds; and the little damsels, not content with their vines, and their verdure, sporting pearls in their ears; bracelets of wee little porpoise teeth; and oftentimes dancing with their mates in the moonlit glades, coquettishly fanned themselves with the transparent wings of the flying fish."

"Now, I appeal to you, royal Media; to you, noble Taji; to you, Babbalanja;" said the chronicler, with an impressive gesture, "whether this seems a credible history: Yoomy has invented."

"But perhaps he has entertained, old Mohi," said Babbalanja.

"He has not spoken the truth," persisted the chronicler.

"Mohi," said Babbalanja, "truth is in things, and not in words: truth is voiceless; so at least saith old Bardianna. And I, Babbalanja, assert, that what are vulgarly called fictions are as much realities as the gross mattock of Dididi, the digger of trenches; for things visible are but conceits of the eye: things imaginative, conceits of the fancy. If duped by one, we are equally duped by the other."

"Clear as this water," said Yoomy.

"Opaque as this paddle," said Mohi, "But, come now, thou oracle, if all things are deceptive, tell us what is truth?"

"The old interrogatory; did they not ask it when the world began? But ask it no more. As old Bardianna hath it, that question is more final than any answer."

Chapter XCIV

Of That Jolly Old Lord, Borabolla; And That Jolly Island Of His, Mondoldo; And Of The Fish-Ponds, And The Hereafters Of Fish

Drawing near Mondoldo, our next place of destination, we were greeted by six fine canoes, gayly tricked out with streamers, and all alive with the gestures of their occupants. King Borabolla and court were hastening to welcome our approach; Media, unbeknown to all, having notified him at the Banquet of the Five-and-Twenty Kings, of our intention to visit his dominions.

Soon, side by side, these canoes floated with ours; each barge of Odo courteously flanked by those of Mondoldo.

Not long were we in identifying Borabolla: the portly, pleasant old monarch, seated cross-legged upon a dais, projecting over the bow of the largest canoe of the six, close-grappling to the side of the Sea Elephant.

Was he not a goodly round sight to behold? Round all over; round of eye and of head; and like the jolly round Earth, roundest and biggest about the Equator. A girdle of red was his Equinoctial Line, giving a compactness to his plumpness.

This old Borabolla permitted naught to come between his head and the sun; not even gray hairs. Bald as a gourd, right down on his brazen skull, the rays of the luminary converged.

He was all hilarity; full of allusions to the feast at Willamilla, where he had done royal execution. Rare old Borabolla! thou wert made for dining out; thy ample mouth an inlet for good cheer, and a sally-port for good humor.

Bustling about on his dais, he now gave orders for the occupants of our canoes to be summarily emptied into his own; saying, that in that manner only did he allow guests to touch the beach of Mondoldo.

So, with no little trouble—for the waves were grown somewhat riotous—we proceeded to comply; bethinking ourselves all the while, how annoying is sometimes an over-strained act of hospitality.

We were now but little less than a mile from the shore. But what of that? There was plenty of time, thought Borabolla, for a hasty lunch, and the getting of a subsequent appetite ere we effected a landing. So viands were produced; to which the guests were invited to pay heedful attention; or take the consequences, and famish till the long voyage in prospect was ended.

Soon the water shoaled (approaching land is like nearing truth in metaphysics), and ere we yet touched the beach, Borabolla declared, that we were already landed. Which paradoxical assertion implied, that the hospitality of Mondoldo was such, that in all directions it radiated far out upon the lagoon, embracing a great circle; so that no canoe could sail by the island, without its occupants being so long its guests.

In most hospitable vicinity to the water, was a fine large structure, inclosed by a stockade; both rather dilapidated; as if the cost of entertaining its guests, prevented outlays for repairing the place. But it was one of Borabolla's maxims, that generally your tumble-down old homesteads yield the most entertainment; their very dilapidation betokening their having seen good service in hospitality; whereas, spruce-looking, finical portals, have a phiz full of meaning; for niggards are oftentimes neat.

Now, after what has been said, who so silly as to fancy, that because Borabolla's mansion was inclosed by a stockade, that the same was intended as a defense against guests? By no means. In the palisade was a mighty breach, not an entrance-way, wide enough to admit six Daniel Lamberts abreast.

"Look," cried Borabolla, as landing we stepped toward the place. "Look Media! look all. These gates, you here see, lashed back with osiers, have been so lashed during my life-time; and just where they stand, shall they rot; ay, they shall perish wide open."

"But why have them at all?" inquired Media.

"Ah! there you have old Borabolla," cried the other.

"No," said Babbalanja, "a fence whose gate is ever kept open, seems unnecessary, I grant; nevertheless, it gives a notable hint, otherwise not so aptly conveyed; for is not the open gate the sign of the open heart?"

"Right, right," cried Borabolla; "so enter both, cousin Media;" and with one hand smiting his chest, with the other he waved us on.

But if the stockade seemed all open gate, the structure within seemed only a roof; for nothing but a slender pillar here and there, supported it.

"This is my mode of building," said Borabolla; "I will have no outside to my palaces. Walls are superfluous. And to a high-minded guest, the entering a narrow doorway is like passing under a yoke; every time he goes in, or comes out, it reminds him, that he is being entertained at the cost of another. So storm in all round."

Within, was one wide field-bed; where reclining, we looked up to endless rows of brown calabashes, and trenchers suspended along the rafters; promissory of ample cheer as regiments of old hams in a baronial refectory.

They were replenished with both meat and drink; the trenchers readily accessible by means of cords; but the gourds containing arrack, suspended neck downward, were within easy reach where they swung.

Seeing all these indications of hard roystering; like a cautious young bridegroom at his own marriage merry-making, Taji stood on his guard. And when Borabolla urged him to empty a gourd or two, by way of making room in him for the incidental repast about to be served, Taji civilly declined; not wishing to cumber the floor, before the cloth was laid.

Jarl, however, yielding to importunity, and unmindful of the unities of time and place, went freely about, from gourd to gourd, concocting in him a punch. At which, Samoa expressed much surprise, that he should be so unobservant as not to know, that in Mardi, guests might be pressed to demean themselves, without its being expected that so they would do. A true toss-pot himself, he bode his time.

The second lunch over, Borabolla placed both hands to the ground, and giving the sigh of the fat man, after three vigorous efforts, succeeded in gaining his pins; which pins of his, were but small for his body; insomuch that they hugely staggered about, under the fine old load they carried.

The specific object of his thus striving after an erect posture, was to put himself in motion, and conduct us to his fish-ponds, famous throughout the Archipelago as the hobby of the king of Mondoldo. Furthermore, as the great repast of the day, yet to take place, was to be a grand piscatory one, our host was all anxiety, that we should have a glimpse of our fish, while yet alive and hearty.

We were alarmed at perceiving, that certain servitors were preparing to accompany us with trenchers of edibles. It begat the notion, that our trip to the fish-ponds was to prove a long journey. But they were not three hundred yards distant; though Borabolla being a veteran traveler, never stirred from his abode without his battalion of butlers.

The ponds were four in number, close bordering the water, embracing about an acre each, and situated in a low fen, draining several valleys. The excavated soil was thrown up in dykes, made tight by being beaten all over, while in a soft state, with the heavy, flat ends of Palm stalks. Lving side by side, by three connecting trenches, these ponds could be made to communicate at pleasure; while two additional canals afforded means of letting in upon them the salt waters of the lagoon on one hand, or those of an inland stream on the other. And by a third canal with four branches, together or separately, they could be partially drained. Thus, the waters could be mixed to suit any gills; and the young fish taken from the sea, passed through a stated process of freshening; so that by the time they graduated, the salt was well out of them, like the brains out of some diplomaed collegians.

Fresh-water fish are only to be obtained in Mondoldo by the artificial process above mentioned; as the streams and brooks abound not in trout or other Waltonian prey.

Taken all floundering from the sea, Borabolla's fish, passing through their regular training for the table, and daily tended by their keepers, in course of time became quite tame and communicative. To prove which, calling his Head Ranger, the king bade him administer the customary supply of edibles.

Accordingly, mouthfuls were thrown into the ponds. Whereupon, the fish darted in a shoal toward the margin; some leaping out of the water in their eagerness. Crouching on the bank, the Ranger now called several by name, patted their scales, carrying on some heathenish nursery-talk, like St. Anthony, in ancient Coptic, instilling virtuous principles into his finny flock on the sea shore.

But alas, for the hair-shirted old dominie's backsliding disciples. For, of all nature's animated kingdoms, fish are the most unchristian, inhospitable, heartless, and cold-blooded of creatures. At least, so seem they to strangers; though at bottom, somehow, they must be all right. And truly it is not to be wondered at, that the very reverend Anthony strove after the conversion of fish. For, whoso shall Christianize, and by so doing, humanize the sharks, will do a greater good, by the saving of human life in all time to come, than though he made catechumens of the head-hunting Dyaks of Borneo, or the blood-bibbing Battas of Sumatra. And are these Dyaks and Battas one whit better than tiger-sharks? Nay, are they so good? Were a Batta your intimate friend, you would often mistake an orang-outang for him; and have orang-outangs immortal souls? True, the Battas believe in a hereafter; but of what sort? Full of Blue-Beards and bloody bones. So, also, the sharks; who hold that Paradise is one vast Pacific, ploughed by navies of mortals, whom an endless gale forever drops into their maws.

Not wholly a surmise. For, does it not appear a little unreasonable to imagine, that there is any creature, fish, flesh, or fowl, so little in love with life, as not to cherish hopes of a future state? Why does man believe in it? One reason, reckoned cogent, is, that he desires it. Who shall say, then, that the leviathan this day harpooned on the coast of Japan, goes not straight to his ancestor, who rolled all Jonah, as a sweet morsel, under his tongue?

Though herein, some sailors are slow believers, or at best hold themselves in a state of philosophical suspense. Say they—"That catastrophe took place in the Mediterranean; and the only whales frequenting the Mediterranean, are of a sort having not a swallow large enough to pass a man entire; for those Mediterranean whales feed upon small things, as horses upon oats." But hence, the sailors draw a rash inference. Are not the Straits of Gibralter wide enough to admit a sperm-whale, even though none have sailed through, since Nineveh and the gourd in its suburbs dried up?

As for the possible hereafter of the whales; a creature eighty feet long without stockings, and thirty feet round the waist before dinner, is not inconsiderately to be consigned to annihilation.

Chapter XCV

That Jolly Old Lord Borabolla Laughs On Both Sides Of His Face

"A very good palace, this, coz, for you and me," said waddling old Borabolla to Media, as, returned from our excursion, he slowly lowered himself down to his mat, sighing like a grampus.

By this, he again made known the vastness of his hospitality, which led him for the nonce to parcel out his kingdom with his guests.

But apart from these extravagant expressions of good feeling, Borabolla was the prince of good fellows. His great tun of a person was indispensable to the housing of his bullock-heart; under which, any lean wight would have sunk. But alas! unlike Media and Taji, Borabolla, though a crowned king, was accounted no demi-god; his obesity excluding him from that honor. Indeed, in some quarters of Mardi, certain pagans maintain, that no fat man can be even immortal. A dogma! truly, which should be thrown to the dogs. For fat men are the salt and savor of the earth; full of good humor, high spirits, fun, and all manner of jollity. Their breath clears the atmosphere: their exhalations air the world. Of men, they are the good measures; brimmed, heaped, pressed down, piled up, and running over. They are as ships from Teneriffe; swimming deep, full of old wine, and twenty steps down into their holds. Soft and susceptible, all round they are easy of entreaty. Wherefore, for all their rotundity, they are too often circumnavigated by hatchet-faced knaves. Ah! a fat uncle, with a fat paunch, and a fat purse, is a joy and a delight to all nephews; to philosophers, a subject of endless speculation, as to how many droves of oxen and Lake Eries of wine might have run through his great mill during the full term of his mortal career. Fat men not immortal! This very instant, old Lambert is rubbing his jolly abdomen in Paradise.

Now, to the fact of his not being rated a demi-god, was perhaps ascribable the circumstance, that Borabolla comported himself with less dignity, than was the wont of their Mardian majesties. And truth to say, to have seen him regaling himself with one of his favorite cuttle-fish, its long snaky arms and feelers instinctively twining round his head as he ate; few intelligent observers would have opined that the individual before them was the sovereign lord of Mondoldo.

But what of the banquet of fish? Shall we tell how the old king ungirdled himself thereto; how as the feast waxed toward its close, with one sad exception, he still remained sunny-sided all round; his disc of a face joyous as the South Side of Madeira in the hilarious season of grapes? Shall we tell how we all grew glad and frank; and how the din of the dinner was heard far into night?

We will.

When Media ate slowly, Borabolla took him to task, bidding him dispatch his viands more speedily.

Whereupon said Media "But Borabolla, my round fellow, that would abridge the pleasure."

"Not at all, my dear demi-god; do like me: eat fast and eat long."

In the middle of the feast, a huge skin of wine was brought in. The portly peltry of a goat; its horns embattling its effigy head; its mouth the nozzle; and its long beard flowed to its jet-black hoofs. With many ceremonial salams, the attendants bore it along, placing it at one end of the convivial mats, full in front of Borabolla; where seated upon its haunches it made one of the party.

Brimming a ram's horn, the mellowest of bugles, Borabolla bowed to his silent guest, and thus spoke— "In this wine, which yet smells of the grape, I pledge you my reverend old toper, my lord Capricornus; you alone have enough; and here's full skins to the rest!"

"How jolly he is," whispered Media to Babbalanja.

"Ay, his lungs laugh loud; but is laughing, rejoicing?"

"Help! help!" cried Borabolla "lay me down! lay me down! good gods, what a twinge!"

The goblet fell from his hand; the purple flew from his wine to his face; and Borabolla fell back into the arms of his servitors. "That gout! that gout!" he groaned. "Lord! lord! no more cursed wine will I drink!"

Then at ten paces distant, a clumsy attendant let fall a trencher— "Take it off my foot, you knave!"

Afar off another entered gallanting a calabash—"Look out for my toe, you hound!"

During all this, the attendants tenderly nursed him. And in good time, with its thousand fangs, the gout-fiend departed for a while.

Reprieved, the old king brightened up; by degrees becoming jolly as ever.

"Come! let us be merry again," he cried, "what shall we eat? and what shall we drink? that infernal gout is gone; come, what will your worships have?"

So at it once more we went.

But of our feast, little more remains to be related than this;—that out of it, grew a wondrous kindness between Borabolla and Jarl. Strange to tell, from the first our fat host had regarded my Viking with a most friendly eye. Still stranger to add, this feeling was returned. But though they thus fancied each other, they were very unlike; Borabolla and Jarl. Nevertheless, thus is it ever. And as the convex fits not into the convex, but into the concave; so do men fit into their opposites; and so fitted Borabolla's arched paunch into Jarl's, hollowed out to receive it.

But how now? Borabolla was jolly and loud: Jarl demure and silent; Borabolla a king: Jarl only a Viking;— how came they together? Very plain, to repeat:—because they were heterogeneous; and hence the affinity. But as the affinity between those chemical opposites chlorine and hydrogen, is promoted by caloric; so the affinity between Borabolla and Jarl was promoted by the warmth of the wine that they drank at this feast. For of all blessed fluids, the juice of the grape is the greatest foe to cohesion. True, it tightens the girdle; but then it loosens the tongue, and opens the heart.

In sum, Borabolla loved Jarl; and Jarl, pleased with this sociable monarch, for all his garrulity, esteemed him the most sensible old gentleman and king he had as yet seen in Mardi. For this reason, perhaps; that his talkativeness favored that silence in listeners, which was my Viking's delight in himself.

Repeatedly during the banquet, our host besought Taji to allow his henchman to remain on the island, after the rest of our party should depart; and he faithfully promised to surrender Jarl, whenever we should return to claim him.

But though I harbored no distrust of Borabolla's friendly intentions, I could not so readily consent to his request; for with Jarl for my one only companion, had I not both famished and feasted? was he not my only link to things past?

Things past!—Ah Yillah! for all its mirth, and though we hunted wide, we found thee not in Mondoldo.

Chapter XCVI

Samoa A Surgeon

The second day of our stay in Mondoldo was signalized by a noteworthy exhibition of the surgical skill of Samoa; who had often boasted, that though well versed in the science of breaking men's heads, he was equally an adept in mending their crockery.

Overnight, Borabolla had directed his corps of sea-divers to repair early on the morrow, to a noted section of the great Mardian reef, for the purpose of procuring for our regalement some of the fine Hawk's-bill turtle, whose secret retreats were among the cells and galleries of that submerged wall of coral, from whose foamy coping no plummet dropped ever yet touched bottom.

These turtles were only to be obtained by diving far down under the surface; and then swimming along horizontally, and peering into the coral honeycomb; snatching at a flipper when seen, as at a pinion in a range of billing dove-cotes.

As the king's divers were thus employed, one of them, Karhownoo by name, perceived a Devil-shark, so called, swimming wistfully toward him from out his summer grotto in the reef. No way petrified by the sight, and pursuing the usual method adopted by these divers in such emergencies, Karhownoo, splashing the water, instantly swam toward the stranger. But the shark, undaunted, advanced: a thing so unusual, and fearful, that, in an agony of fright, the diver shot up for the surface. Heedless, he looked not up as he went; and when within a few inches of the open air, dashed his head against a projection of the reef. He would have sank into the live tomb beneath, were it not that three of his companions, standing on the brink, perceived his peril, and dragged him into safety.

Seeing the poor fellow was insensible, they endeavored, ineffectually, to revive him; and at last, placing him in their canoe, made all haste for the shore. Here a crowd soon gathered, and the diver was borne to a habitation, close adjoining Borabolla's; whence, hearing of the disaster, we sallied out to render assistance.

Upon entering the hut, the benevolent old king commanded it to be cleared; and then proceeded to examine the sufferer.

The skull proved to be very badly fractured; in one place, splintered.

"Let me mend it," said Samoa, with ardor.

And being told of his experience in such matters, Borabolla surrendered the patient.

With a gourd of water, and a tappa cloth, the one-armed Upoluan carefully washed the wound; and then calling for a sharp splinter of bamboo, and a thin, semi-transparent cup of cocoa-nut shell, he went about the operation: nothing less than the "Tomoti" (head-mending), in other words the trepan.

The patient still continuing insensible, the fragments were disengaged by help of a bamboo scalpel; when a piece of the drinking cup—previously dipped in the milk of a cocoanut—was nicely fitted into the vacancy, the skin as nicely adjusted over it, and the operation was complete.

And now, while all present were crying out in admiration of Samoa's artistic skill, and Samoa himself stood complacently regarding his workmanship, Babbalanja suggested, that it might be well to ascertain whether the patient survived. When, upon sounding his heart, the diver was found to be dead.

The bystanders loudly lamented; but declared the surgeon a man of marvelous science.

Returning to Borabolla's, much conversation ensued, concerning the sad scene we had witnessed, which presently branched into a learned discussion upon matters of surgery at large.

At length, Samoa regaled the company with a story; for the truth of which no one but him can vouch, for no one but him was by, at the time; though there is testimony to show that it involves nothing at variance with the customs of certain barbarous tribes.

Read on.

Chapter XCVII

Faith And Knowledge

A thing incredible is about to be related; but a thing may be incredible and still be true; sometimes it is incredible because it is true. And many infidels but disbelieve the least incredible things; and many bigots reject the most obvious. But let us hold fast to all we have; and stop all leaks in our faith; lest an opening, but of a hand's breadth, should sink our seventy-fours. The wide Atlantic can rush in at one port-hole; and if we surrender a plank, we surrender the fleet. Panoplied in all the armor of St. Paul, morion, hauberk, and greaves, let us fight the Turks inch by inch, and yield them naught but our corpse.

But let us not turn round upon friends, confounding them with foes. For dissenters only assent to more than we. Though Milton was a heretic to the creed of Athanasius, his faith exceeded that of Athanasius himself; and the faith of Athanasius that of Thomas, the disciple, who with his own eyes beheld the mark of the nails. Whence it comes that though we be all Christians now, the best of us had perhaps been otherwise in the days of Thomas.

The higher the intelligence, the more faith, and the less credulity: Gabriel rejects more than we, but out-believes us all. The greatest marvels are first truths; and first truths the last unto which we attain. Things nearest are furthest off. Though your ear be next-door to your brain, it is forever removed from your sight. Man has a more comprehensive view of the moon, than the man in the moon himself. We know the moon is round; he only infers it. It is because we ourselves are in ourselves, that we know ourselves not. And it is only of our easy faith, that we are not infidels throughout; and only of our lack of faith, that we believe what we do.

In some universe-old truths, all mankind are disbelievers. Do you believe that you lived three thousand years ago? That you were at the taking of Tyre, were overwhelmed in Gomorrah? No. But for me, I was at the subsiding of the Deluge, and helped swab the ground, and build the first house. With the Israelites, I fainted in the wilderness; was in court, when Solomon outdid all the judges before him. I, it was, who suppressed the lost work of Manetho, on the Egyptian theology, as containing mysteries not to be revealed to posterity, and things at war with the canonical scriptures; I, who originated the conspiracy against that purple murderer, Domitian; I, who in the senate moved, that great and good Aurelian be emperor. I instigated the abdication of Diocletian, and Charles the Fifth; I touched Isabella's heart, that she hearkened to Columbus. I am he, that from the king's minions hid the Charter in the old oak at Hartford; I harbored Goffe and Whalley: I am the leader of the Mohawk masks, who in the Old Commonwealth's harbor, overboard threw the East India Company's Souchong; I am the Vailed Persian Prophet; I, the man in the iron mask; I, Junius.

Chapter XCVIII

The Tale Of A Traveler

It was Samoa, who told the incredible tale; and he told it as a traveler. But stay-at-homes say travelers lie. Yet a voyage to Ethiopia would cure them of that; for few skeptics are travelers; fewer travelers liars, though the proverb respecting them lies. It is false, as some say, that Bruce was cousin-german to Baron Munchausen; but true, as Bruce said, that the Abysinnians cut live steaks from their cattle. It was, in good part, his villainous transcribers, who made monstrosities of Mandeville's travels. And though all liars go to Gehenna; yet, assuming that Mandeville died before Dante; still, though Dante took the census of Hell, we find not Sir John, under the likeness of a roasted neat's tongue, in that infernalest of infernos, The Inferno.

But let not the truth be postponed. To the stand, Samoa, and through your interpreter, speak.

Once upon a time, during his endless sea-rovings, the Upoluan was called upon to cobble the head of a friend, grievously hurt in a desperate fight of slings.

Upon examination, that part of the brain proving as much injured as the cranium itself, a young pig was obtained; and preliminaries being over, part of its live brain was placed in the cavity, the trepan accomplished with cocoanut shell, and the scalp drawn over and secured.

This man died not, but lived. But from being a warrior of great sense and spirit, he became a perverse-minded and piggish fellow, showing many of the characteristics of his swinish grafting. He survived the operation more than a year; at the end of that period, however, going mad, and dying in his delirium.

Stoutly backed by the narrator, this anecdote was credited by some present. But Babbalanja held out to the last.

"Yet, if this story be true," said he, "and since it is well settled, that our brains are somehow the organs of sense; then, I see not why human reason could not be put into a pig, by letting into its cranium the contents of a man's. I have long thought, that men, pigs, and plants, are but curious physiological experiments; and that science would at last enable philosophers to produce new species of beings, by somehow mixing, and concocting the essential ingredients of various creatures; and so forming new combinations. My friend Atahalpa, the astrologer and alchymist, has long had a jar, in which he has been endeavoring to hatch a fairy, the ingredients being compounded according to a receipt of his own."

But little they heeded Babbalanja. It was the traveler's tale that most arrested attention.

Tough the thews, and tough the tales of Samoa.

Chapter XCIX

"Marnee Ora, Ora Marnee"

During the afternoon of the day of the diver's decease, preparations were making for paying the last rites to his remains, and carrying them by torch-light to their sepulcher, the sea; for, as in Odo, so was the custom here.

Meanwhile, all over the isle, to and fro went heralds, dismally arrayed, beating shark-skin drums; and, at intervals, crying—"A man is dead; let no fires be kindled; have mercy, oh Oro!—Let no canoes put to sea till the burial. This night, oh Oro!—Let no food be cooked."

And ever and anon, passed and repassed these, others in brave attire; with castanets of pearl shells, making gay music; and these sang—

Be merry, oh men of Mondoldo,
A maiden this night is to wed:
Be merry, oh damsels of Mardi,—
Flowers, flowers for the bridal bed.

Informed that the preliminary rites were about being rendered, we repaired to the arbor, whither the body had been removed.

Arrayed in white, it was laid out on a mat; its arms mutely crossed, between its lips an asphodel; at the feet, a withered hawthorn bough.

The relatives were wailing, and cutting themselves with shells, so that blood flowed, and spotted their vesture.

Upon remonstrating with the most abandoned of these mourners, the wife of the diver, she exclaimed, "Yes; great is the pain, but greater my affliction."

Another, the deaf sire of the dead, went staggering about, and groping; saying, that he was now quite blind; for some months previous he had lost one eye in the death of his eldest son and now the other was gone.

"I am childless," he cried; "henceforth call me Roi Mori," that is, Twice-Blind.

While the relatives were thus violently lamenting, the rest of the company occasionally scratched themselves with their shells; but very slightly, and mostly on the soles of their feet; from long exposure, quite callous. This was interrupted, however, when the real mourners averted their eyes; though at no time was there any deviation in the length of their faces.

But on all sides, lamentations afresh broke forth, upon the appearance of a person who had been called in to assist in solemnizing the obsequies, and also to console the afflicted.

In rotundity, he was another Borabolla. He puffed and panted.

As he approached the corpse, a sobbing silence ensued; when holding the hand of the dead, between his, the stranger thus spoke:—

"Mourn not, oh friends of Karhownoo, that this your brother lives not. His wounded head pains him no more; he would not feel it, did a javelin pierce him. Yea; Karhownoo is exempt from all the ills and evils of this miserable Mardi!"

Hereupon, the Twice-Blind, who being deaf, heard not what was said, tore his gray hair, and cried, "Alas! alas! my boy; thou wert the merriest man in Mardi, and now thy pranks are over!"

But the other proceeded—"Mourn not, I say, oh friends of Karhownoo; the dead whom ye deplore is happier than the living; is not his spirit in the aerial isles?"

"True! true!" responded the raving wife, mingling her blood with her tears, "my own poor hapless Karhownoo is thrice happy in Paradise!" And anew she wailed, and lacerated her cheeks.

"Rave not, I say."

But she only raved the more.

And now the good stranger departed; saying, he must hie to a wedding, waiting his presence in an arbor adjoining.

Understanding that the removal of the body would not take place till midnight, we thought to behold the mode of marrying in Mondoldo.

Drawing near the place, we were greeted by merry voices, and much singing, which greatly increased when the good stranger was perceived.

Gayly arrayed in fine robes, with plumes on their heads, the bride and groom stood in the middle of a joyous throng, in readiness for the nuptial bond to be tied.

Standing before them, the stranger was given a cord, so bedecked with flowers, as to disguise its stout fibers; and taking: the bride's hands, he bound them together to a ritual chant; about her neck, in festoons, disposing the flowery ends of the cord. Then turning to the groom, he was given another, also beflowered; but attached thereto was a great stone, very much carved, and stained; indeed, so every way disguised, that a person not knowing what it was, and lifting it, would be greatly amazed at its weight. This cord being attached to the waist of the groom, he leaned over toward the bride, by reason of the burden of the drop.

All present now united in a chant, and danced about the happy pair, who meanwhile looked ill at ease; the one being so bound by the hands, and the other solely weighed down by his stone.

A pause ensuing, the good stranger, turning them back to back, thus spoke:—

"By thy flowery gyves, oh bride, I make thee a wife; and by thy burdensome stone, oh groom, I make thee a husband. Live and be happy, both; for the wise and good Oro hath placed us in Mardi to be glad. Doth not all nature rejoice in her green groves and her flowers? and woo and wed not the fowls of the air, trilling their bliss in their bowers? Live then, and be happy, oh bride and groom; for Oro is offended with the unhappy, since he meant them to be gay."

And the ceremony ended with a joyful feast.

But not all nuptials in Mardi were like these. Others were wedded with different rites; without the stone and flowery gyves. These were they who plighted their troth with tears not smiles, and made responses in the heart.

Returning from the house of the merry to the house of the mournful, we lingered till midnight to witness the issuing forth of the body.

By torch light, numerous canoes, with paddlers standing by, were drawn up on the beach, to accommodate those who purposed following the poor diver to his home.

The remains embarked, some confusion ensued concerning the occupancy of the rest of the shallops. At last the procession glided off, our party included. Two by two, forming a long line of torches trailing round the isle, the canoes all headed toward the opening in the reef.

For a time, a decorous silence was preserved; but presently, some whispering was heard; perhaps melancholy discoursing touching the close of the diver's career. But we were shocked to discover, that poor Karhownoo was not much in their thoughts; they were conversing about the next bread-fruit harvest, and the recent arrival of King Media and party at Mondoldo. From far in advance, however, were heard the lamentations of the true mourners, the relatives of the diver.

Passing the reef, and sailing a little distance therefrom, the canoes were disposed in a circle; the one bearing the corpse in the center. Certain ceremonies over, the body was committed to the waves; the white foam lighting up the last, long plunge of the diver, to see sights more strange than ever he saw in the brooding cells of the Turtle Reef.

And now, while in the still midnight, all present were gazing down into the ocean, watching the white wake of the corpse, ever and anon illuminated by sparkles, an unknown voice was heard, and all started and vacantly stared, as this wild song was sung:—

We drop our dead in the sea,
The bottomless, bottomless sea;
Each bubble a hollow sigh,
As it sinks forever and aye.

We drop our dead in the sea,—
The dead reek not of aught;
We drop our dead in the sea,—
The sea ne'er gives it a thought.

Sink, sink, oh corpse, still sink,
Far down in the bottomless sea,
Where the unknown forms do prowl,
Down, down in the bottomless sea.

'Tis night above, and night all round,
And night will it be with thee;
As thou sinkest, and sinkest for aye,
Deeper down in the bottomless sea.

The mysterious voice died away; no sign of the corpse was now seen; and mute with amaze, the company long listed to the low moan of the billows and the sad sough of the breeze.

At last, without speaking, the obsequies were concluded by sliding into the ocean a carved tablet of Palmetto, to mark the place of the burial. But a wave-crest received it, and fast it floated away.

Returning to the isle, long silence prevailed. But at length, as if the scene in which they had just taken part, afresh reminded them of the mournful event which had called them together, the company again recurred to it; some present, sadly and incidentally alluding to Borabolla's banquet of turtle, thereby postponed.

Chapter C

The Pursuer Himself Is Pursued

Next morning, when much to the chagrin of Borabolla we were preparing to quit his isle, came tidings to the palace, of a wonderful event, occurring in one of the "Motoos," or little islets of the great reef; which "Motoo" was included in the dominions of the king.

The men who brought these tidings were highly excited; and no sooner did they make known what they knew, than all Mondoldo was in a tumult of marveling.

Their story was this.

Going at day break to the Motoo to fish, they perceived a strange proa beached on its seaward shore; and presently were hailed by voices; and saw among the palm trees, three specter-like men, who were not of Mardi.

The first amazement of the fishermen over, in reply to their eager questions, the strangers related, that they were the survivors of a company of men, natives of some unknown island to the northeast; whence they had embarked for another country, distant three days' sail to the southward of theirs. But falling in with a terrible adventure, in which their sire had been slain, they altered their course to pursue the fugitive who murdered him; one and all vowing, never more to see home, until their father's fate was avenged. The murderer's proa outsailing theirs, soon ran out of sight; yet after him they blindly steered by day and by night: steering by the blood- red star in Bootes. Soon, a violent gale overtook them; driving them to and fro; leaving them they knew not where. But still struggling against strange currents, at times counteracting their sailing, they drifted on their way; nigh to famishing for water; and no shore in sight. In long calms, in vain they held up their dry gourds to heaven, and cried "send us a breeze, sweet gods!" The calm still brooded; and ere it was gone, all but three gasped; and dead from thirst, were plunged into the sea. The breeze which followed the calm, soon brought them in sight of a low, uninhabited isle; where tarrying many days, they laid in good store of cocoanuts and water, and again embarked.

The next land they saw was Mardi; and they landed on the Motoo, still intent on revenge.

This recital filled Taji with horror.

Who could these avengers be, but the sons of him I had slain. I had thought them far hence, and myself forgotten; and now, like adders, they started up in my path, as I hunted for Yillah.

But I dissembled my thoughts.

Without waiting to hear more, Borabolla, all curiosity to behold the strangers, instantly dispatched to the Motoo one of his fleetest canoes, with orders to return with the voyagers.

Ere long they came in sight; and perceiving that strange pros in tow of the king's, Samoa cried out: "Lo! Taji, the canoe that was going to Tedaidee!"

Too true; the same double-keeled craft, now sorely broken, the fatal dais in wild disarray: the canoe, the canoe of Aleema! And with it came the spearmen three, who, when the Chamois was fleeing from their bow, had poised their javelins. But so wan their aspect now, their faces looked like skulls.

Then came over me the wild dream of Yillah; and, for a space, like a madman, I raved. It seemed as if the mysterious damsel must still be there; the rescue yet to be achieved. In my delirium I rushed upon the skeletons, as they landed—"Hide not the maiden!" But interposing, Media led me aside; when my transports abated.

Now, instantly, the strangers knew who I was; and, brandishing their javelins, they rushed upon me, as I had on them, with a yell. But deeming us all mad, the crowd held us apart; when, writhing in the arms that restrained them, the pale specters foamed out their curses again and again: "Oh murderer! white curses upon thee! Bleached be thy soul with our hate! Living, our brethren cursed thee; and dying, dry-lipped, they cursed thee again. They died not through famishing for water, but for revenge upon thee! Thy blood, their thirst would have slaked!"

I lay fainting against the hard-throbbing heart of Samoa, while they showered their yells through the air. Once more, in my thoughts, the green corpse of the priest drifted by.

Among the people of Mondoldo, a violent commotion now raged. They were amazed at Taji's recognition by the strangers, and at the deadly ferocity they betrayed.

Rallying upon this, and perceiving that by divulging all they knew, these sons of Aleema might stir up the Islanders against me, I resolved to anticipate their story; and, turning to Borabolla, said— "In these strangers, oh, king! you behold the survivors of a band we encountered on our voyage. From them I rescued a maiden, called Yillah, whom they were carrying captive. Little more of their history do I know."

"Their maledictions?" exclaimed Borabolla.

"Are they not delirious with suffering?" I cried. "They know not what they say."

So, moved by all this, he commanded them to be guarded, and conducted within his palisade; and having supplied them with cheer, entered into earnest discourse. Yet all the while, the pale strangers on me fixed their eyes; deep, dry, crater-like hollows, lurid with flames, reflected from the fear-frozen glacier, my soul.

But though their hatred appalled, spite of that spell, again the sweet dream of Yillah stole over me, with all the mysterious things by her narrated, but left unexplained. And now, before me were those who might reveal the lost maiden's whole history, previous to the fatal affray.

Thus impelled, I besought them to disclose what they knew.

But, "Where now is your Yillah?" they cried. "Is the murderer wedded and merry? Bring forth the maiden!"

Yet, though they tore out my heart's core, I told them not of my loss.

Then, anxious, to learn the history of Yillah, all present commanded them to divulge it; and breathlessly I heard what follows.

"Of Yillah, we know only this:—that many moons ago, a mighty canoe, full of beings, white, like this murderer Taji, touched at our island of Amma. Received with wonder, they were worshiped as gods; were feasted all over the land. Their chief was a tower to behold; and with him, was a being, whose cheeks were of the color of the red coral; her eye, tender as the blue of the sky. Every day our people brought her offerings of fruit and flowers; which last she would not retain for herself; but hung them round the neck of her child, Yillah; then only an infant in her mother's arms; a bud, nestling close to a flower, full-blown. All went well between our people and the gods, till at last they slew three of our countrymen, charged with stealing from their great canoe. Our warriors retired to the hills, brooding over revenge. Three days went by; when by night, descending to the plain, in silence they embarked; gained the great vessel, and slaughtered every soul but Yillah. The bud was torn from the flower; and, by our father Aleema, was carried to the Valley of Ardair; there set apart as a sacred offering for Apo, our deity. Many moons passed; and there arose a tumult, hostile to our sire's longer holding custody of Yillah; when, foreseeing that the holy glen would ere long be burst open, he embarked the maiden in yonder canoe, to accelerate her sacrifice at the great shrine of Apo, in Tedaidee.—The rest thou knowest, murderer!"

"Yillah! Yillah!" now hunted again that sound through my soul. "Oh, Yillah! too late, too late have I learned what thou art!"

Apprised of the disappearance of their former captive, the meager strangers exulted; declaring that Apo had taken her to himself. For me, ere long, my blood they would quaff from my skull.

But though I shrunk from their horrible threats, I dissembled anew; and turning, again swore that they raved.

"Ay!" they retorted, "we rave and raven for you; and your white heart will we have!"

Perceiving the violence of their rage, and persuaded from what I said, that much suffering at sea must have maddened them; Borabolla thought fit to confine them for the present; so that they could not molest me.

Chapter CI

The Iris

That evening, in the groves, came to me three gliding forms:—Hautia's heralds: the Iris mixed with nettles. Said Yoomy, "A cruel message!"

With the right hand, the second syren presented glossy, green wax- myrtle berries, those that burn like tapers; the third, a lily of the valley, crushed in its own broad leaf.

This done, they earnestly eyed Yoomy; who, after much pondering, said—"I speak for Hautia; who by these berries says, I will enlighten you."

"Oh, give me then that light! say, where is Yillah?" and I rushed upon the heralds.

But eluding me, they looked reproachfully at Yoomy; and seemed offended.

"Then, I am wrong," said Yoomy. "It is thus:—Taji, you have been enlightened, but the lily you seek is crushed."

Then fell my heart, and the phantoms nodded; flinging upon me bilberries, like rose pearls, which bruised against my skin, left stains.

Waving oleanders, they retreated.

"Harm! treachery! beware!" cried Yoomy.

Then they glided through the wood: one showering dead leaves along the path I trod, the others gayly waving bunches of spring-crocuses, yellow, white, and purple; and thus they vanished.

Said Yoomy, "Sad your path, but merry Hautia's."

"Then merry may she be, whoe'er she is; and though woe be mine, I turn not from that to Hautia; nor ever will I woo her, though she woo me till I die;—though Yillah never bless my eyes."

Chapter CII

They Depart From Mondoldo

Night passed; and next morning we made preparations for leaving Mondoldo that day.

But fearing anew, lest after our departure, the men of Amma might stir up against me the people of the isle, I determined to yield to the earnest solicitations of Borabolla, and leave Jarl behind, for a remembrance of Taji; if necessary, to vindicate his name. Apprised hereof, my follower was loth to acquiesce. His guiltless spirit feared not the strangers: less selfish considerations prevailed. He was willing to remain on the island for a time, but not without me. Yet, setting forth my reasons; and assuring him, that our tour would not be long in completing, when we would not fail to return, previous to sailing for Odo, he at last, but reluctantly, assented.

At Mondoldo, we also parted with Samoa. Whether it was, that he feared the avengers, whom he may have thought would follow on my track; or whether the islands of Mardi answered not in attractiveness to the picture his fancy had painted; or whether the restraint put upon him by the domineering presence of King Media, was too irksome withal; or whether, indeed, he relished not those disquisitions with which Babbalanja regaled us: however it may have been, certain it was, that Samoa was impatient of the voyage. He besought permission to return to Odo, there to await my return; and a canoe of Mondoldo being about to proceed in that direction, permission was granted; and departing for the other side of the island, from thence he embarked.

Long after, dark tidings came, that at early dawn he had been found dead in the canoe: three arrows in his side.

Yoomy was at a loss to account for the departure of Samoa; who, while ashore, had expressed much desire to roam.

Media, however, declared that he must be returning to some inamorata.

But Babbalanja averred, that the Upoluan was not the first man, who had turned back, after beginning a voyage like our own.

To this, after musing, Yoomy assented. Indeed, I had noticed, that already the Warbler had abated those sanguine assurances of success, with which he had departed from Odo. The futility of our search thus far, seemed ominous to him, of the end.

On the eve of embarking, we were accompanied to the beach by Borabolla; who, with his own hand, suspended from the shark's mouth of Media's canoe, three red-ripe bunches of plantains, a farewell gift to his guests.

Though he spoke not a word, Jarl was long in taking leave. His eyes seemed to say, I will see you no more.

At length we pushed from the strand; Borabolla waving his adieus with a green leaf of banana; our comrade ruefully eyeing the receding canoes; and the multitude loudly invoking for us a prosperous voyage.

But to my horror, there suddenly dashed through the crowd, the three specter sons of Aleema, escaped from their prison. With clenched hands, they stood in the water, and cursed me anew. And with that curse in our sails, we swept off.

Chapter CIII

As They Sail

As the canoes now glided across the lagoon, I gave myself up to reverie; and revolving over all that the men of Amma had rehearsed of the history of Yillah, I one by one unriddled the mysteries, before so baffling. Now, all was made plain: no secret remaining, but the subsequent event of her disappearance. Yes, Hautia! enlightened I had been but where was Yillah?

Then I recalled that last interview with Hautia's messengers, so full of enigmas; and wondered, whether Yoomy had interpreted aright. Unseen, and unsolicited; still pursuing me with omens, with taunts, and with wooings, mysterious Hautia appalled me. Vaguely I began to fear her. And the thought, that perhaps again and again, her heralds would haunt me, filled me with a nameless dread, which I almost shrank from acknowledging. Inwardly I prayed, that never more they might appear.

While full of these thoughts, Media interrupted them by saying, that the minstrel was about to begin one of his chants, a thing of his own composing; and therefore, as he himself said, all critics must be lenient; for Yoomy, at times, not always, was a timid youth, distrustful of his own sweet genius for poesy.

The words were about a curious hereafter, believed in by some people in Mardi: a sort of nocturnal Paradise, where the sun and its heat are excluded: one long, lunar day, with twinkling stars to keep company.

THE SONG
Far off in the sea is Marlena,
A land of shades and streams,

A land of many delights.
Dark and bold, thy shores,
Marlena; But green, and timorous, thy soft knolls,
Crouching behind the woodlands.
All shady thy hills; all gleaming thy springs,
Like eyes in the earth looking at you.
How charming thy haunts Marlena!—
Oh, the waters that flow through Onimoo:
Oh, the leaves that rustle through Ponoo:
Oh, the roses that blossom in Tarma:
Come, and see the valley of Vina:
How sweet, how sweet, the Isles from Hind:
'Tis aye afternoon of the full, full moon,
And ever the season of fruit,
And ever the hour of flowers,
And never the time of rains and gales,
All in and about Marlena.
Soft sigh the boughs in the stilly air,
Soft lap the beach the billows there;
And in the woods or by the streams,
You needs must nod in the Land of Dreams.

"Yoomy," said old Mohi with a yawn, "you composed that song, then, did you?"

"I did," said Yoomy, placing his turban a little to one side.

"Then, minstrel, you shall sing me to sleep every night, especially with that song of Marlena; it is soporific as the airs of Nora-Bamma."

"Mean you, old man, that my lines, setting forth the luxurious repose to be enjoyed hereafter, are composed with such skill, that the description begets the reality; or would you ironically suggest, that the song is a sleepy thing itself?"

"An important discrimination," said Media; "which mean you, Mohi?"

"Now, are you not a silly boy," said Babbalanja, "when from the ambiguity of his speech, you could so easily have derived something flattering, thus to seek to extract unpleasantness from it? Be wise, Yoomy; and hereafter, whenever a remark like that seems equivocal, be sure to wrest commendation from it, though you torture it to the quick."

"And most sure am I, that I would ever do so; but often I so incline to a distrust of my powers, that I am far more keenly alive to censure, than to praise; and always deem it the more sincere of the two; and no praise so much elates me, as censure depresses."

Chapter CIV

Wherein Babbalanja Broaches A Diabolical Theory, And, In His Own Person, Proves It

"A truce!" cried Media, "here comes a gallant before the wind.— Look, Taji!"

Turning, we descried a sharp-prowed canoe, dashing on, under the pressure of an immense triangular sail, whose outer edges were streaming with long, crimson pennons. Flying before it, were several small craft, belonging to the poorer sort of Islanders.

"Out of his way there, ye laggards," cried Media, "or that mad prince, Tribonnora, will ride over ye with a rush!"

"And who is Tribonnora," said Babbalanja, "that he thus bravely diverts himself, running down innocent paddlers?"

"A harum-scarum young chief," replied Media, "heir to three islands; he likes nothing better than the sport you now see see him at."

"He must be possessed by a devil," said Mohi.

Said Babbalanja, "Then he is only like all of us." "What say you?" cried Media.

"I say, as old Bardianna in the Nine hundred and ninety ninth book of his immortal Ponderings saith, that all men—"

"As I live, my lord, he has swamped three canoes," cried Mohi, pointing off the beam.

But just then a fiery fin-back whale, having broken into the paddock of the lagoon, threw up a high fountain of foam, almost under Tribonnora's nose; who, quickly turning about his canoe, cur-like slunk off; his steering-paddle between his legs.

Comments over; "Babbalanja, you were going to quote," said Media. "Proceed."

"Thank you, my lord. Says old Bardianna, 'All men are possessed by devils; but as these devils are sent into men, and kept in them, for an additional punishment; not garrisoning a fortress, but limboed in a bridewell; so, it may be more just to say, that the devils themselves are possessed by men, not men by them.'"

"Faith!" cried Media, "though sometimes a bore, your old Bardianna is a trump."

"I have long been of that mind, my lord. But let me go on. Says Bardianna, 'Devils are divers;—strong devils, and weak devils; knowing devils, and silly devils; mad devils, and mild devils; devils, merely devils; devils, themselves bedeviled; devils, doubly bedeviled."

"And in the devil's name, what sort of a devil is yours?" cried Mohi.

"Of him anon; interrupt me not, old man. Thus, then, my lord, as devils are divers, divers are the devils in men. Whence, the wide difference we see. But after all, the main difference is this:—that one man's devil is only more of a devil than another's; and be bedeviled as much as you will; yet, may you perform the most bedeviled of actions with impunity, so long as you only bedevil yourself. For it is only when your deviltry injures another, that the other devils conspire to confine yours for a mad one. That is to say, if you be easily handled. For there are many bedeviled Bedlamites in Mardi, doing an infinity of mischief, who are too brawny in the arms to be tied."

"A very devilish doctrine that," cried Mohi. "I don't believe it."

"My lord," said Babbalanja, "here's collateral proof;—the sage lawgiver Yamjamma, who flourished long before Bardianna, roundly asserts, that all men who knowingly do evil are bedeviled; for good is happiness; happiness the object of living; and evil is not good."

"If the sage Yamjamma said that," said old Mohi, "the sage Yamjamma might have bettered the saying; it's not quite so plain as it might be."

"Yamjamma disdained to be plain; he scorned to be fully comprehended by mortals. Like all oracles, he dealt in dark sayings. But old Bardianna was of another sort; he spoke right out, going straight to the point like a javelin; especially when he laid it down for a universal maxim, that minus exceptions, all men are bedeviled."

"Of course, then," said Media, "you include yourself among the number."

"Most assuredly; and so did old Bardianna; who somewhere says, that being thoroughly bedeviled himself, he was so much the better qualified to discourse upon the deviltries of his neighbors. But in another place he seems to contradict himself, by asserting, that he is not so sensible of his own deviltry as of other people's."

"Hold!" cried Media, "who have we here?" and he pointed ahead of our prow to three men in the water, urging themselves along, each with a paddle.

We made haste to overtake them.

"Who are you?" said Media, "where from, and where bound?"

"From Variora," they answered, "and bound to Mondoldo." "And did that devil Tribonnora swamp your canoe?" asked Media, offering to help them into ours.

"We had no such useless incumbrance to lose," they replied, resting on their backs, and panting with their exertions. "If we had had a canoe, we would have had to paddle it along with us; whereas we have only our bodies to paddle."

"You are a parcel of loons," exclaimed Media. "But go your ways, if you are satisfied with your locomotion, well and good."

"Now, it is an extreme case, I grant," said Babbalanja, "but those poor devils there, help to establish old Bardianna's position. They belong to that species of our bedeviled race, called simpletons; but their devils harming none but themselves, are permitted to be at large with the fish. Whereas, Tribonnora's devil, who daily runs down canoes, drowning their occupants, belongs to the species of out and out devils; but being high in station, and strongly backed by kith and kin, Tribonnora can not be mastered, and put in a strait jacket. For myself, I think my devil is some where between these two extremes; at any rate, he belongs to that class of devils who harm not other devils."

"I am not so sure of that," retorted Media. "Methinks this doctrine of yours, about all mankind being bedeviled, will work a deal of mischief; seeing that by implication it absolves you mortals from moral accountability. Further-more; as your doctrine is exceedingly evil, by Yamjamma's theory it follows, that you must be proportionably bedeviled; and since it harms others, your devil is of the number of those whom it is best to limbo; and since he is one of those that can be limboed, limboed he shall be in you."

And so saying, he humorously commanded his attendants to lay hands upon the bedeviled philosopher, and place a bandage upon his mouth, that he might no more disseminate his devilish doctrine.

Against this, Babbalanja demurred, protesting that he was no orang- outang, to be so rudely handled.

"Better and better," said Media, "you but illustrate Bardianna's theory; that men are not sensible of their being bedeviled."

Thus tantalized, Babbalanja displayed few signs of philosophy.

Whereupon, said Media, "Assuredly his devil is foaming; behold his mouth!" And he commanded him to be bound hand and foot.

At length, seeing all resistance ineffectual, Babbalanja submitted; but not without many objurgations.

Presently, however, they released him; when Media inquired, how he relished the application of his theory; and whether he was still' of old Bardianna's mind?

To which, haughtily adjusting his robe, Babbalanja replied, "The strong arm, my lord, is no argument, though it overcomes all logic."

END OF VOLUME I.

Herman Melville – A Short Biography

Herman Melville was born in New York City on August 1st, 1819, the third of eight children.

At the age of 7 Melville contracted scarlet fever which was to permanently diminish his eyesight. At this time Melville was described as being "very backwards in speech and somewhat slow in comprehension."

Melville attended the Albany Academy from October 1830 to October 1831, where he took the standard preparatory course; reading and spelling; penmanship; arithmetic; English grammar; geography; natural history; universal, Greek, Roman and English history; classical biography; and Jewish antiquities.

The reasons for Melville leaving the Academy after a year are unknown although his brothers continued their education there for a few more months.

In December, Melville's father returned from New York City by steamboat, but difficult weather forced him to travel the last 70 miles in an open carriage in freezing temperatures. A cold developed into delirium and by January 28th, not yet fifty, his father was dead. Melville, at home by now, most probably witnessed much of this event and two decades later he described scenes that must have been very similar in the death of Pierre's father in Pierre.

The family were now in very straitened times. Just 14 Melville took a job in a bank paying $150 a year that he obtained via his uncle, Peter Gansevoort, who was one of the directors of the New York State Bank.

Melville was briefly able to attend again the Albany Academy from October 1836 to March 1837, where he studied the classics.

After a failed stint as a surveyor he signed on to go to sea and travelled across the Atlantic to Liverpool and then on further voyages to the Pacific on adventures which would soon become the architecture of his novels. Whilst travelling he joined a mutiny, was jailed, fell in love with a South Pacific beauty and became known as a figure of opposition to the coercion of native Hawaiians to the Christian religion.

He drew from these experiences in his books Typee, Omoo, and White-Jacket. These were published as novels, the first initially in London in 1846.

They sold very well and enabled him to write full time although royalties were not vast. (During his career it is estimated his writing brought him no more than $10,000)

After a three-month courtship of Elizabeth Shaw, daughter of a prominent Boston family, her father was the Chief Justice of the Massachusetts Supreme Judicial Court, they decided to marry. Her father initially turned down Melville's request but on August 14th, 1847 they married. After initially settling in New York they moved to Massachusetts.

In September of 1850, Melville borrowed $3,000 from his father-in-law Lemuel Shaw to buy a 160-acre farm in Pittsfield. Melville christened the new home 'Arrowhead', due to the quantity of arrowheads dug up around the property during planting season.

That winter, Melville on an impulse paid a visit to the writer Nathaniel Hawthorne. At the time Hawthorne was finishing The House of the Seven Gables and "not in the mood for company". Hawthorne's wife Sophia entertained him while he waited for Hawthorne to come down for supper, and gave him copies of Twice-Told Tales and, The Grandfather's Chair. Melville, sensing a friendship developing, invited them to Arrowhead during the coming weeks. When Sophia agreed, he looked forward to "discussing the Universe with a bottle of brandy & cigars" with Hawthorne.

By 1851 his masterpiece, Moby Dick, was ready to be published. It is perhaps, and certainly at the time, one of the most ambitious novels ever written. However, it never sold out its initial print run of 3,000 and Melville's earnings on this masterpiece were a mere $556.37.

In succeeding years his reputation waned and he found life increasingly difficult. His family was growing, now four children, and a stable income was essential.

From 1853 to 1856, Melville began to publish his short stories in the growing magazine market, most notably "Bartleby, the Scrivener" (1853), "The Encantadas" (1854), and "Benito Cereno" (1855). These and others were later collected together and published in 1856 as the Plazza Tales.

In 1857, he travelled to England where, for the first time since 1852, he reunited with Hawthorne. He then went on to tour the Near East. The Confidence-Man was the last prose work that he published that same year. It received little attention.

With his finances in a disappointing state Melville took the advice of friends that a change in career was called for. For many others public lecturing had proved very rewarding. From late 1857 to 1860, Melville embarked upon three lecture tours, where he spoke mainly on Roman statuary and sightseeing in Rome. These lectures mocked the pseudo-intellectualism of lyceum culture. His words though were ignored by contemporary audiences.

In the 1860's he wrote many poems, many based on the Civil War. But there was no publisher for him and no audience.

In 1866, Melville's wife and her relatives used their influence to obtain a position for him as customs inspector for the City of New York, With his writings almost ignored they moved to New York where Melville joined the New York Customs house and worked there for the next 19 years.

For Melville his early promise and great talents seemed to be getting him nowhere in literary terms. Despite periods of drinking, depression and other ails Elizabeth stood by her husband despite calls from other family members and the marriage held together.

In 1876 he was at last able to publish privately his 16,000 line epic poem Clarel, in which a young American student of divinity travels to Jerusalem to renew his faith. It was to no avail. The book had an initial printing of 350 copies, but sales failed miserably, and the unsold copies were burned when Melville was unable to afford to buy them at cost.

On December 31st, 1885 Melville was at last able to retire. His wife had inherited several small legacies and with her astute ways it was enough to provide them with a reasonable income and Melville had enough to buy further precious books and supplies.

In these last few years Melville finished two poetry collections which were printed privately, although only 25 copies of each; John Marr and Other Sailors (1888) and Timoleon (1891).

Herman Melville, novelist, poet, short story writer and essayist, died at his home on September 28rh 1891 from cardiovascular disease.

He was interred in the Woodlawn Cemetery in The Bronx, New York City.

He was the first writer to have his works collected and published by the Library of America.

Novels, Short Stories & Poetry

Typee: A Peep at Polynesian Life (1846)
Omoo: A Narrative of Adventures in the South Seas (1847)
Mardi: And a Voyage Thither (1849)
Redburn: His First Voyage (1849)
White-Jacket; or, The World in a Man-of-War (1850)
Moby-Dick; or, The Whale (1851)
Pierre: or, The Ambiguities (1852)
Isle of the Cross (1853 unpublished, and now lost)
Cock-A-doodle-Doo (Short story) (1852)
Bartleby, the Scrivener (Short story) (1853)
The Encantadas, or Enchanted Isles (Short story) (1854)
Poor Man's Pudding and Rich Man's Crumbs (Short story) (1854)
The Happy Failure (Short story) (1854)
The Lightning-Rod Man (Short story) (1854)
The Fiddler (Short story) (1854)
Benito Cereno (1855)
Israel Potter: His Fifty Years of Exile (1855)
The Paradise of Batchelors and the Tartarus of Maids (Short story) (1855)
The Bell-Tower (Short story) (1855)
Jimmy Rose (Short story) (1855)
The Gees (Short story) (1856)
I and My Chimney (Short story) (1856)
The Apple-Tree Story (Short story) (1856)
The Confidence-Man: His Masquerade (1857)
The Piazza (Short story) (1856)
Battle-Pieces and Aspects of the War (Poetry) (1866)
Clarel: A Poem and Pilgrimage in the Holy Land (Epic poem) (1876)
John Marr and Other Sailors (Poetry) (1888)
Timoleon (Poetry) (1891)
Billy Budd, Sailor (An Inside Narrative) (1891 unfinished, published posthumously in 1924)

Essays

Fragments from a Writing Desk, No. 1 (May 4, 1839)
Fragments from a Writing Desk, No. 2 (May 18, 1839)
Etchings of a Whaling Cruise (1847)
Authentic Anecdotes of 'Old Zack" (July 24 to September 11, 1847)
Mr Parkman's Tour (March 31, 1849)
Cooper's New Novel (April 28, 1849)
A Thought on Book-Binding (March 16, 1850)
Hawthorne and His Mosses (August 17 and August 24, 1850)

www.ingramcontent.com/pod-product-compliance
Lightning Source LLC
Chambersburg PA
CBHW072140170626
46813CB00004BA/1626